fARLEY dUNN

aLL
fALL dOwn

THREE SKILLET

ALL FALL DOWN, Dunn, Farley L

First Edition

THE SE'YAN'T CHRONICLES, Book 1

 THREE SKILLET

www.ThreeSkilletPublishing.com

ISBN 978-1-943189-06-9

For Auntie Em . . .

Inspiration flows two ways.

"Sing to me, oh stars. Sing my way to you . . ."

—Excerpt from *The Last JumpShip and the Story of Cmdr. Bethany D'Arc*
Comm Offic'r Carlos Rodriguez Calderón
(3295 A.D.)

—Preface—

Book of Ran'gun, *Readings from Ch. 2, Vs. 16-18. ALL CHANT:*

2:16-a. And in that day God arose from his slumber, speaking to all his host. 16-b. I have heard the anguish of my people. No longer will I leave them in their sufferings. I will cast myself from the heavens, and the waters shall be my sky. I shall divide myself throughout all the lands under the sea, and they shall be my home. 17. When my people gather to me, I will make them whole again. 18. Selah.

—Excerpt from *Holy Writ of Poi'ntr'in*

Section 1

ALL SE'YAN'T BURNED, and death ravaged the cities and fields.

In the skies above Se'Yan't, Rjorck burned also, his native homeworld decimated, all his people wiped from its face.

A whimper escaped his throat as he reached one hand and gently touched the bloody trenches in his flesh, the swollen bands where the restraining straps had bound his wrists and feet. The tender skin, caressed with battered fingertips, roiled as he closed his eyes to the memories of the pain. It was too many years since he last entered the seas of Se'Yan't, and now he faced a lifetime of deaths for his people. Ah, the torture he endured to deflect attention from those who remained in Se'Yan't's protecting seas, hoping some could return to a world left in peace, once again walking underneath the brilliance of its twin suns.

However, even those who had entered the seas for their year-of-months, their c'habor-reneis't, were taken as they returned from the waters, only to be tortured when they could not tell the answers the minions of MegaCorp had insisted his people share. Despite all his centuries on Earth, he had only thought he knew humans and their greed, their capacity for cruelty. How could he have been so wrong?

He wanted to weep, but tears would not come.

Waves of sorrow knifed through him, cutting his soul—his hyr'yan't—in two, and he accepted that he had lost all options except one. That option, though, might be worse than all the suffering he had endured at the hands of the humans, and certainly it would mean his final death, the dry-death from which none could return.

He had only one thing, his poi'ntr'in, to give.

There, in the darkest moment of his many lives, he turned his eyes inward. For a man to look inside himself and glimpse his wellspring of power, his poi'ntr'in, to see himself as the gods see him, to admit he has nothing, is nothing, can be nothing . . . to have reached the end of his days, willing to share his innermost being, his joys, his poi'ntr'in . . . to claim its raw power for his own designs—would it be enough?

Looking inside himself with his true eyes, really seeing his reservoir of inner strength for the first time, he knew his poi'ntr'in would perform whatever he asked of it. Whatever the cost, the time had come.

"Do it," he commanded aloud, his hoarse voice filled with emotion, and in that moment, his poi'ntr'in burst from him, filling the room with brilliance.

CAPTGEN'L WILLANE BOFSKY tapped the panel once, wakening the glassine filling the wall before him. The substrate of the molecules shifted, and with a drawn breath of anticipation, he watched it change to transparency. Without warning, piercing light seared his eyes. Screaming klaxons started drumming, and the sizzle of melting glassine began to permeate the room.

In the background, a melodious, feminine voice echoed, "Emergency escape pods now cycling online."

Covering his face against the brilliance, CaptGen'l Bofsky slapped a panel on the wall and yelled, "All crew, battle stations! Updates! Have the shields been breached? First Offic'r Chero'nen, report—" Then his words were torn from him as a brilliant light stabbed into the room, pulling screams of anguish from those alongside him.

The radiance—Rjorck, his poi'ntr'in cast free from his body—reached out, thrusting, its fingers probing dark corners and dark-hearted men. His intent guided it, although not consciously. He simply wished to return to Se'Yan't, and his poi'ntr'in took the steps necessary to provide him with that end.

When the light found those who had decimated his world, it reached inside and demanded payment from them, requiring of them that which they had taken from the dead: the very soul-essence of his people. Then it dropped the hyr'yan't-stealers on the floor, letting them writhe in the pain of coming death until all life was gone.

Rjorck stepped through the empty glassine frame, a shining god, the power of his poi'ntr'in filling the room ahead of him. He moved into the corridor, the brilliance of his poi'ntr'in preceding him, fingers of light stabbing ahead, reaching, feeling the way, leading him to a place he dimly remembered: a landing bay, a transportation pod, a way home. If only he could reach passage to return to his planet, to feel the waters of his warm, blue seas, to bask one last time underneath his world's treasured lemon skies, then to have given up his soul, his hyr'yan't, would be worth all the cost.

Leaving a trail of soulless, lifeless shapes in his wake, his poi'ntr'in continued to grow stronger, releasing its power, helping him in his most desperate time of need.

"Return to Se'Yan't. C'habor-reneis't. Must go-and-return.

Must . . . get . . . there . . . ah, this release of power is strong."
He groaned as he stumbled, one lined, parchment hand pressing against the corridor's bare metal wall. "I can barely control it."

As he walked unsteadily ahead, his inner power continually reached into distant parts of the ship, only marginally under his control, taking out souls, twisting equipment, burning bioware, probing the ship, searching for his way home.

THE LANDING POD FLEW from the fearsome MegaCorp starstrike class battleship. Rjorck stood inside, his arms spread wide, his feet akimbo, as the last of his inner wellspring flooded from him. The brilliance of his poi'ntr'in filled the small pod and burst forth, reaching lightning fingers out towards the mighty battleship, stabbing through the melting glassine windows, deep into the ship's weapons systems. Before more than just a few of the warship's emergency escape pods managed to fling themselves from the mighty vessel, his poi'ntr'in worked its vengeful deeds. With a stab on this circuit, a twist of that dial, an overload surge added just so, the light withdrew.

As his lifeboat dropped him gently through the atmosphere, a spectacular devastation even greater than he could have intended graced his beloved planet with a third sun for the briefest of moments.

But Rjorck never knew. His own sun, his poi'ntr'in, had gone out as well.

One Day Earlier

"A FULL YEAR we've been here! A wasted year! You do nothing in the sea except *disappear!* Where do you go? Why do only the old enter the sea to die, but we have plucked only the young as they emerge? I will know!" UnderGen'l Ma'jene Holcum thumbed the NeuroShok, holding it toward Rjorck as the tip began to sizzle. "Or have you begun to *enjoy* the pain?"

"Ahhhh!" Rjorck contorted away from the NeuroShok stick, its jolts of electric lightning quivering through his body. His back slowly dropped to the surface of the table as if expecting the pain to still be there to greet it. Ragged gasps of air tore his parched throat as the anguish forced his lungs to expand.

"This interrogation chamber is your world now. Can you even remember any other? Do you think this pain will give you release? You are a fool, if you think so." Holcum laughed, and the sound was cruel.

Her answer was already there for her to see, in the many days he had spent tied to this table, wallowing in his own filth, with only enough water being trickled down his throat to enable him to speak, and for the many handfuls of days before that. It had been a full year he had endured her torture, left in darkness . . . or light, unable to remember. His sweat-soaked head rolled to one side as his blood-shot eyes pleaded with her.

"I beg of you—" He sucked air over his cracked tongue as he marshaled yet another appeal. "UnderGen'l Holcum, there is no other secret. We swim in the seas; that is all. You have it on your VidPlay. You've shown me the clips again and again. What my people do is nothing else other than what you see."

"You lie!" She reached forward with the NeuroShok one more time.

NOT EVERYONE ONBOARD the great MegaCorp battleship approved of CaptGen'l Bofsky's and UnderGen'l Holcum's cruelty.

Not all deserved to die.

"You should hear Bofsky and Holcum warring over who makes the next victim scream." UnderPriv't Rom'n Rezalton, Academy trained, although now devoid of rank, surviving with the lowest of inductees, stripped his overjacket off.

Disgust pasted contempt on his face.

"It's a rarified world up there. Thank the stars we're both down here." Redzik Ajadijon, also an underpriv't, although due to inexperience rather than deceit and lies, laughed. "I'm sorry, Rom'n. It's that sour face you wear. It must be really bad up there. Who would want to be up on top? I hear one of the overoffic'rs sent his sweetie away, afraid something big was going down." He made a heart symbol with his fingers. "They only care about their own, never us down here. Sissies, to the man." He laughed again.

"Who was sent away?" Despite no longer being part of the "offic'r's" club, Rom'n still maintained connections with many of those on the upper decks.

"D'Arc. You know her?"

"Bethany, jumpship commander?" Did he know her? She'd had a thing for him when they were together at the academy. "She's sweet on Rob't, um, Thangorsen. They were a couple the last time I heard."

"That's the guy, in logistics now, someone important in the rat race upstairs. But hey, who cares, anyway? The best of the ranks are here with us, in the belly of the beast and forgotten. I like it that way." He reached and clapped the other man on the shoulder, squeezing quickly before shoving him away.

Rom'n forced a smile on his face. "You know how to put things in perspective, my friend. Thank you."

"Now, I have a treat for you. First, I have this report to deliver. But I just received a performance bonus. The credits are burning a hole in my pay account. How about you and me head out for some refreshment and good company, some soul renewing?" He held up a glass, the images inside flickering with the movement. "As soon as I drop this off. Corridor D, okay?"

"I'll be waiting on you, be sure of that." Rom'n reached a hand out, and they clasped for a moment before Redzik disappeared out the door.

The smile fell from his face. He had been there, an offic'r, part of that elite, before Holcum's trickery had forced his fall from grace. He had been swept up in her reign of terror, an integral player, right up to the end.

"You believe in me, Redzik. I couldn't have a better friend than you."

Shaking off his dismal mood, he grabbed his ID cards from the top shelf of his stor'lok and headed out the door. His eyes were damp, but he would never admit to that. It was only the air currents, and they would dry when he got to a better part of the ship.

"SHE IS QUITE GOOD, that Holcum. I trained her myself, you know. Many people on many worlds have enjoyed the caress of that touch." CaptGen'l Willane Bofsky stepped away, allowing the glassine to opaque. He reached down and straightened the cuff on his overuniform's sleeve. "Although few of those ever will again," he said to himself.

"But, Ser," First Offic'r Chero'nen ventured. "No more have come from the sea for many days. This Rjorck is the last native alive. And we still don't know their secret."

"It wasn't about getting answers to which I referred," growled Bofsky.

Opening the weapons cabinet, the captgen'l wrapped his hand around a NeuroShok stick and headed out the door, a red flush of anticipation rising above his finely starched collar.

Section 2

Date: March 17, 2810 A.D. (O.E. Standard)
To: Chair, University of NAS
From: Alb't deFralin, SSM.rl.
RE: Preliminary Report

No man is an island.

Someone nearly ten centuries ago made that statement, and it is as true today as it was then.

Only by peeling away the layers of the present can we truly understand the events that have brought us to this point. A world—Rejuvenant for some of you, and Se'Yan't for others—has been decimated. We can look at the damage that has been done and hope that it never happens again, or we can dig into the motivations that have caused this precipitous disaster, and find ways to ensure it never happens again.

I would like to suggest we ask ourselves a question: What would bring a person or persons to such a base level, to wipe genocide across the face of an entire world?

We know the history of MegaCorp, the documented abuses of power that tipped the scales of justice the wrong direction. However, we must dig deeper, revealing those whose hands wielded the knives. Who cut the throats of the innocents, and what drove them to such horrid abuses of human rights? Only by knowing the individuals' stories can calamities such as we are facing now hope to be averted in the future.

In my esteemed position upon Se'Yan't, having been given the authority and privilege to come to this world and ensure its redemption, I would like to propose that the University of New American States extend a team to pursue the histories of the individuals involved in this travesty against humankind and the universe.

If the University should be so kind as to consider my proposal, may I also suggest a novel approach to understanding the motivating forces that have visited this travesty upon Rejuvenant. We know the culminating events. Begin there and slowly work backwards until the foundations of MegaCorp's depravations are laid bare.

I leave the matter in your kind hands, although I fear I have opened a door to a fetid cesspool that may surely choke any who step through.

Respectfully,
Alb't deFralin, SSM.rl.

Section 3

The Decimation of Rejuvenant: A Regressive Study of the Motivations that Precipitated the Misuse of Power by Mega-Corp Minions

El'Tirest'n Ragusin, SSM.rl.adjunct
Historical Studies 2250-Present
University of New American States in Conjunction with New Boston College and Ganymede Fellowship of Higher Learning

Summary:

It is an established fact that unchecked military abuse of civilian populations can precipitate inbred hatred that can and will erupt at inopportune times. (*Military Might Does Not Make Right,* Farsi Largo, SSM.dr.edu, 2767) Care should be taken when admitting civilian populations into a military environment to ensure background stability. (*Childhood Monsters Made Real,* Sister Marta Spin'ter, DRL.rl, 2591)

Deleted for brevity: Contents, Discussion, and Annotations. Please message Adjunct Ragusin Heirs and Assigns, care of UNAS/UT for additional information.

All information in this report is the sole property of UNAS/UT and may be referenced in any educational document with permission from UNAS/UT. Due to the unusual nature of these studies, several of the compilations rely heavily on inference and such should be taken into account.

Original Draft, 2815 A.D. (O.E. Standard)

Approved: Natal La'Sterene, Senior Chancellor, University of Terra (formerly UNAS), by the Hand of the Terran Supreme Father on 3301 A.D.

Study 1

Compiled by: Alb't deFralin, SSM.rl, UNAS
Subject: Rjorck
Location: Rejuvenant/Se'Yan't
Earth-Reference Date: 2800 A.D. (O.E. Standard)

"LEAVE EVERYTHING! Come aboard now!"

Desperation—as well as determination—had Rjorck's weary body moving as a much younger man. He slammed his fist down on the autopilot trigger, starting the warm-up procedure that would ensure the safety of these five hundred of his kin, all those who had been able to reach his ship in time.

His aged face leaped at him from a reflective panel, and his haggard expression caught him by surprise. It was only the adrenalin rush of his desperation that kept him going. At least the transport's ignition sequence and liftoff were now on automatic. It would take them away from beautiful Se'Yan't to a distant world, a place where his people could find shelter from these humans.

He turned to his sister. She had done well. Her poi'ntr'in had not let her down.

"Adhor'k, remain here. I must help the others inside." He brushed her arm in gratitude as he turned from the control center, glad his old muscles still responded at his command. His strength would not last long, he knew, for his body screamed in protest. This must be done, though, and there was no one else. He also knew he had only minutes left to hurry the rest of the refugees on board before the doors closed. He could only trust it was enough time. MegaCorp's deathship was even now raining down firepower on those who scrambled for the safety of the transport.

He peered at the sky, taking a moment to scan the heavens, the pause bringing home the weight of the heaviness he carried in his heart.

"Will you simply kill those you cannot torture for your answers?" His muttered words filled with bitterness, he turned again to his people, determined to do what he could.

Rushing down the loading ramp, knowing the transport *must* leave now, he called out, encouraging as many aboard as possible. Even as the last Autowarn light blinked a glowing red and the mighty door began to swing closed, he lifted a final re'anlt to clamber through the shrinking opening. He ignored the hands reaching for him as the plasteel metal doors clanged shut with finality, the flat sheet of the loading ramp withdrawing into the belly of the ship.

Stepping back, his energy now drained, he felt lighter in his heart. He would not be leaving Se'Yan't. His time for c'habor-reneis't was too near. Leaving, for him, meant he would meet his dry-death while in hiding with his people. Some would find safety in this escape, those who had answered Adhor'k's call, those who had come. He was of no importance. Let the humans wipe all remaining people from this planet. When they tired of this place, his people would again live under its yellow, no, *lemon* sky, swim in its blue waters, and enjoy the warmth of its twin suns.

24

He held up a hand to shade his eyes as the transport, his people's seedship, picked up speed to arch across the heavens out of the reach of MegaCorp. He felt the first wave of hope swell inside his breast.

Then, even that was flayed from him. His eyes welled with tears as he watched the air ripped apart, the lemon sky shredding into flaming contrails heading straight for the transport. A searing hiss of unimaginable power brought the burning smell of ozone-laced energy to his nostrils. He knew both that sound and that smell. No longer was the fleeing vessel a seedship. It had become a deathship, the dry-death coming for all five hundred aboard.

Falling to his knees in anguish, he watched the flaming air as it reached out to decimate his hopes and his people, enveloping their ship, shredding it into a hundred exploding parts, and casting the blazing contents from the tortured sky.

Ahhh! Adhor'k! His re'anlts, his family. All was lost. All were gone. He had failed them again. His head fell to his chest, his body cowed with despair.

He didn't even turn at the hiss of air escaping the airtight seals of the MegaCorp landing pod coming to rest at his back.

"Take that man! I know this one from Earth. He will certainly have the information I require. Place him aboard my pod for transport to the ship."

"Yes, CaptGen'l, Ser." UnderGen'l Ma'jene Holcum whipped a pair of ziptites from her belt.

CaptGen'l Willane Bofsky turned to board as Holcum snapped the restraints around Rjorck's wrists. Pausing, the captgen'l glared at him. "You will tell me what I require, or your people's secrets die with you. You are the last. We have cleansed this world of your vermin."

With a click of his heels, CaptGen'l Willane Bofsky strode purposefully up the ramp and through the door.

Study 2

Compiled by: Adel' Eriks'n, SSM.rl.sub.adjunct, UNAS
Subject: Adhor'k
Location: Rejuvenant/Se'Yan't
Earth-Reference Date: 2800 A.D. (O.E. Standard)

Hours Earlier

ADHOR'K KNELT BY HER sister's torn and bleeding body. Shadow fingers caressed them, the leaves of the plants holding the suns' light at bay. She placed a palm against her re'anlt's cooling face, feeling her own grow wet with tears.

"My beloved. You have been denied the most precious of our planet's gifts. C'habor-reneis't will never be yours. You shall return to become one with the soil of Se'Yan't. I would cry the ocean for you, sister. Ahhh!" Her heart wrenched as she stood and shook her fist at the sky. "The dry-death is all you allowed her! Do you know what you've done? What you've taken? Do you care?"

Looking out over the beautiful yellow sky blanketing the green fields of the rift valley spread out below her, she felt the incredible splendor of her world softening her pain. She was grateful for this one small favor—her sister had died the dry-death here on her home world, *not in that death-delivering ship in the skies overhead!*

The lengthening shadows meant the "little night," the last eclipse of Se'Yan't's minor sun for many handfuls of days, would soon hide her grief. Tomorrow, this world's twin suns would again flood the land with the harshness of eternal day, the dueling shadows they cast across the landscape given as teasing respite from the probing tongues of warmth. Then she could think again.

26

I would cry the ocean for you, my sister.

As she knelt to pick up her sister's lifeless form, tears fell from her face to the limp form in her arms as if to wash the dry-death away. Only the death remained. Even a sea of tears could not undo what was already done.

ADHOR'K CAUGHT SIGHT of Rjorck by a large outcropping, the sun glinting on his hair. He stood tall, but age cast a pall over his face. Leaping from the rise on which she stood, and landing heavily beside him on the sea-washed stones lining the beach, she felt her remaining resolve drain from her

He gazed at her, and she felt his compassion. Glancing the way she had come, she saw smoke rising in the distance. It was death following her every move.

"I am sorry, brother, Bringer of News. Violence has never been our way." She sang with the sharpness of the tortured wind that whistles through the high places. "We could not have known, not imagined. Must all die?"

Dusty from her long trek down from the Heights Ridge, she dropped her bag and collapsed, her head bowed on her knees. As the whispering waters sounded in the distance, a gentle hand cupped her chin, forcing her to look up, exposing tears she had hoped to hide.

"You feel their pain, as I do, sister."

"A sea of tears and she could not come back to me, Rjorck. At least *they* will not find her. She is safe in the high fields."

His face twisted. "Only goodness is found in you, my sister. Never will you understand the monsters in the gleaming black deathship overhead. Gods below, may you never understand! I have lived centuries surrounded by Earth-humans, their hopelessness, their petty desires, and their willingness to take, take, *take!* I have shielded Se'Yan't and all my re'aults, protecting you as I could, knowing what humans could do, *would* do when tempted with their darkest dreams."

"But to rain death upon all—" She felt her voice break, and she could say no more.

"I had long hoped otherwise, for my earliest centuries on Earth were as a salvation to me. Oh, but humans have vitality! To live in only one lifetime, in one single *burst* of being. To be young only once, carrying the weary years of existence heavy on old bones with only the snuff of the dry-death to look forward to. I love to partake of their vitality. But it means to learn of their dark sides, too. Now I have failed to protect my people, and they are dying by the thousands. Because of me. Because of my failure."

"Will none survive?" Anger swept through her. "Is there nothing that can be done?" She pictured her sister, then more that had been left to rot in the city. The images were too much, and she felt herself weaken.

"Perhaps a few can yet live." Kneeling before her, he spoke with vigor. "I have a transport. Tell all who will travel with me. We will go offworld, somewhere we can be safe, hide, until the Earth-humans despair of finding that which they cannot share. We will preserve life. We will return when our waters, our lands are ours again, when there is no more *death* hanging over us in our lemon sky. Do you know lemons, Adhor'k? Not all from Earth is wicked. Just this. These madmen. They will tire of our world eventually. Tell all you can find. We have little time."

"Is there time, my brother?"

He brushed the tear-streaks from her face, with tenderness in his touch. Turning, he gazed at the blue waters lapping the shoreline in the distance. Adhor'k could see that his c'habor-reneis't was calling, pulling his hyr'yan't to the sea, rest and renewal in its welcoming waters. The need was in his eyes.

"Curse the gods below, there are too many years on my weary shoulders." Pulling his sister to her feet, he admonished her, "Remember, time is short. Have all you can gather meet me on the yellow plain south of the Ribbon Waterfall. My transport is hidden nearby. Hurry!" Reaching beneath his tunic, he withdrew a slab of nutrient bread and placed it in her hands. "This will give you strength for what is required of you."

"Not all are convinced, my brother. Not all have seen the many who have died the dry-death at the hands of the Earth-humans." She pulled her bag over her shoulder once again, tearing off a chunk of bread before dropping the rest inside. "I will bring all who will come." She broke for a moment, emotion overcoming her need for haste. "Ahhh! Rjorck! So many have died the dry-death! Is it even possible to go on?"

He looked at her tenderly as he grasped her arms. "Do you wish all to go to the dry-death? Many have. Many more will. *You* can help those who would be saved. Go, my sister!" He watched her face.

"I can be strong. My reserves of poi'ntr'in run deep."

He stepped away, his eyes fixed on her. He smiled as she took a deep breath, squared her shoulders, and blinked back her tears. "Yes, my sister, you are a strong one. You will bring others. Some will choose to survive."

They both knew the truth that hung like a fetid cloud between them. Se'Yan't was aflame with death. Only the gods who dwelt below could truly save them now.

Study 3

Compiled by: Ne'rosi El'ganti, SSM.rl.sub.adjunct, UNAS
Subject(s): Willane Bofsky/Ma'jene Holcum
Location: Starstrike Class Battle Cruiser
Earth-Reference Date: 2800 A.D. (O.E. Standard)

COULD THAT ONE NOT SEE? MC. MegaCorp! It was emblazoned across his tunic. That was all the authority he needed to present to these *groundies*. CaptGen'l Willane Bofsky spat on his hand, wiping the residue of blood on a small cloth. How many more would he have to hunt down until he found one who would not just bleed, but bleed *information?*

"Haul that mess out of here! Make sure it is gone before I return."

Slapping the NeuroShok stick down on the table, he spun on his heel, driving his anger through the doorway and into the corridor.

Only when the door slammed behind him did UnderGen'l Ma'jene Holcum let out a stale breath, sucking in much-needed air, only to choke on the stench in the room.

"JE'VARK. REZALTON. Get those exhaust fans going. Thomps'n. Bag this and carry it to recycling. Stat! The gods know how soon Bofsky will have another one in need of this theater. Then the three of you grab a drum of Sterilspray and wash this down. Page me when complete. I'll be in my quarters."

Already lost in her thoughts by the time she reached the door, Holcum strode briskly past glassine clearwalls, oblivious to the stunning view of the planet Rejuvenant hanging just outside the ship. Planets were all the same, places for groundies. Why would she want to look at a place she wouldn't even visit? Her home was shipside, was what she would say to anyone who asked. Most people didn't. Not more than once, anyway. She had little tolerance for taking time out of her life for anything to do with groundies. And that especially included ones who wouldn't ante up.

Only one person aboard the menacing MegaCorp starstrike class battleship felt more strongly about groundies than Holcum. She would begrudge that to him only because of his rank.

CaptGen'l Willane Bofsky.

Study 4

Compiled by: Adel' Eriks'n, SSM.rl.sub.adjunct, UNAS
Subject: WorldPresident Benetin
Location: Earth
Earth-Reference Date: 2799 A.D. (O.E. Standard)

TRANSMISSION 16/000873862-45682 VERIFIED.
SECURITY LEVEL ALPHA.PROXY.DOG.
ORIGIN OF TRANSMISSION: BAR'AKKER'ENT
WORLD.
RECIPIENT: WORLDPRESIDENT BENETIN.
IMMEDIATE REPLY TRANSMISSION URGENTLY
REQUESTED.
-Official government use only. Violators will be prose-
cuted to the fullest extent of the law. Interplanetary
Code 4418.164003.

My Most Humble Greetings to WorldPresident Benetin. In this time of interplanetary peace and prosperity, it is most vital to maintain the open lines of communication that enable our vast multi-global civilization to survive the calamities that history has shown to be most detrimental to single planet cultures. With that in mind, rumors of the utmost concern have reached my ears.

As per our most recent meeting at the Glok'dik Trans-Planet Conference, financial prosperity is agreed to be paramount to the survival of the social ties binding the many planets of our civilization. One of the most stable financial institutions in the entire worlds we know is based upon your homeworld of Earth. This institution is, of course, the corporation known by both name and logo as MegaCorp or MC. While widely noted as the most unprecedented and recognizable name throughout all the known worlds, and while the good that MC does cannot be disputed, a concern has arisen.

As recently as two local planetary years ago, reports were circulating regarding the aggressive nature of MC's advances toward my homeworld, Rejuvenant. Your records will show my previous query regarding this matter as little as one-quarter local planetary year ago (TRANSMISSION 16/000873862-42093.09). Although no punitive action was initiated by your government, I accepted that proof of misdeeds must be the basis of accusations, and without these proofs, action on a matter can be very difficult to initiate.

I believe action must now be commenced. Your office has affirmed by its very charter the sanctity of human life and the due diligence private enterprise must pursue in the respect of that sanctity. That very diligence has now been so severely abused as to be nonexistent.

All communication from my homeworld, Rejuvenant, has ceased. Any and all attempts to contact Rejuvenant have been futile. In the local planetary year preceding this unprecedented collapse of communication with my homeworld, numerous messages of concern were transmitted directly to my domicile via sublight slow-link concerning the aggressive advances of MC. The transmitter was a person of some note on Earth, the Munificent Rjorck of longstanding repute on your planet. Although the fact may well be unknown to you, this Rjorck was, as I am, also a native of Rejuvenant.

His concerns were my concerns. While I encouraged him to absent himself from Rejuvenant until this pending crisis resolved itself, his concern for the homeworld overpowered my entreaties for caution. Since returning to warn our peoples, it is feared this Rjorck has been silenced for his views concerning MC's aggressive stance toward the homeworld.

While caution is always a wise stance when extreme measures are to be considered, I fear that caution in this situation is a measure we cannot afford. I fear great harm may have already befallen my fellow citizens of Rejuvenant. If you can find it in yourself to take great strides toward pursuing the resolution of this difficulty, my greatest gratitude will certainly put me in your debt.

Your honorable and extreme supporter,
GrandSet ComChair Ren'xe t'Le Frieks'n, Rstt.con.
WorldBrittain.ene
WORLD CITIZEN OF REJUVENANT, LOCAL
NAME OF SE'YAN'T
CURRENT POSTING: BAR'AKKER'ENT WORLD
END TRANSMISSION. VERIFICATION CODE
GBER-Y847DI73.

The message faded from the glass, its insinuations still felt throughout the room.

"Shall we tell him?" A male voice.

A dozen breaths exhaled together.

Another voice spoke, feminine. "Let's think through this carefully." Looking around the room, all eyes hers, the flunky continued, "Here we have a clear accusation of malfeasance by MegaCorp. Now, what does that mean to us here on Earth? Of all the inhabited worlds, our planet is the oldest socially and economically. We are long established, and what Earth does carries a great deal of clout with the newer governments found elsewhere."

As she continued, the sense of cohesion on her subject seemed to tighten throughout the room.

"Over the years, our economy has had its ups and downs. It has been very strong for years due to the overwhelming strength and power of one and only one corporation. This corporation has built itself as a power throughout all the known worlds, both economically and militarily." Pausing, she saw the light shine brighter in the others' eyes, enjoining her own enthusiasm to even greater heights. "Do we really think all the successes MegaCorp provides for Earth come with no price? Just as long as the price paid is far, far away, what is that to us? I say to let sleeping dogs lie. Just as the transmission states, there is no proof. What is one person who chooses not to be found? He is of no concern to us."

"You do realize we cannot really hide this direct request. It will make it to Benetin eventually."

"Eventually is not today. Let matters take their course. Let it alone long enough, and it may even fade into the background. I say to let it go. Agreed?" Looking around, the nods of confirmation settling the action, the transmission was relegated to the pending file.

Immediate transmission to the intended recipient would have been the better choice, as they would soon find out.

TO: ALL BENETIN WORLDPRESIDENT STAFF
    FROM: WORLDPRESIDENT BENETIN
    RE: UNDISCLOSED COMM TRANSMISSIONS

HEADS WILL ROLL! WILL ONE OF THEM BE YOURS? IT HAS COME TO MY ATTENTION

THAT NUMEROUS COMMUNIQUÉS FROM FOREIGN OFFICIALS REGARDING A POSSIBLE CONFLICT BETWEEN THE MEGACORP CORPORATION AND THE PLANET REJUVENANT HAVE BEEN SUPPRESSED. I HAVE TAKEN A PERSONAL INTEREST IN THIS MATTER. IF YOU ARE FOUND TO HAVE TAKEN PART IN ANY SUPPRESSION OF THESE COMMUNIQUÉS, NO MATTER HOW MARGINAL OR TRIVIAL YOUR PARTICIPATION, YOUR HEAD WILL ROLL.

AS PREDICTED, many did.

Study 5

Compiled by: Alb't deFralin, SSM.rl, UNAS
Subject: Rjorck
Location: Rejuvenant/Se'Yan't
Earth-Reference Date: 2799 A.D. (O.E. Standard)

RJORCK, OLD NOW, AND WEARY beyond belief, carried with him the news of the human cancer he had sliced away time after time during his many lives. With the information he carried, only dimly could he hope to see Earth and the things he had learned to love once again. The vitality of being *alive* there. *Blue* sky. Lemons. Ahh . . . lemons. The *intensity* of existence on that distant world.

His people. His own jeweled planet. These must be his focus now.

Pushing his heavy thoughts aside, he smiled, turning from the rising sun, and looking back to the clear blue waters of the inlet and the distant ripples just forming on the surface. He squinted, raising his hand to shade his eyes from the setting sun.

Did he see her? He squinted in the glare of the setting sun's fading light as he looked out over the water.

Impatient to reunite with Adhor'k, still, trepidation edged his excitement. Having missed her c'habor-reneis't during his stay on Earth, would she be the Adhor'k he knew? Would her memories of him be fresh? Or would she be *fract*, her partial memories excluding him from her life?

As he waited, watching the disturbance edge closer, he recalled the vitality of Earth. His love for Se'Yan't had brought him back, that and the years he carried. The peace of this planet the humans called Rejuvenant was good for his hyr'yan't, but gods below, the *vitality* of Earth! If he looked down at the blue of the sea, he could pretend the *lemon* sky to disappear, and he could be there again, if only for a moment.

Kneeling, he reached down, holding one hand just over the sea's surface, the water reflecting long fingers back at him. With a flex of his hand, the almost invisible al'las' emerged between each finger. He ran his fingertips over the surface of the water, the movement of the air creating a play of ripples, disturbing its crystal clarity.

With a sudden motion, he thrust his hand into the water's warmth.

Water-weir! As the water rose and ebbed on his arm, he watched the flesh disappear and return with the movement of the inlet's surface. C'habor-reneis't. To go and return.

The years weighed on him. C'habor-reneis't called. And so, now, did his sister.

He stood, shaking the clear liquid from his hand, snapping his al'las' back into its sheaths, watching for signs of Adhor'k's arrival at the shore, knowing he wouldn't see her until she rose from the water's embrace. She would be as invisible as his hand had been. Ripples were all she would tease him with, hints that she was near.

Ahh! There! He glanced at the surface of the water to his right, the disturbance revealing his sister's approach. Their reunion was imminent.

The growing disturbance at the water's edge rose, mounded up, and as the water peeled away, the shimmering form of a young woman appeared. As she stepped from the water, he drew a silken cloak from under his tunic. Holding it out to his sister, he looked into her eyes for a sign of recognition, listening for something, a voice no human would understand, perhaps not even recognize as a voice, the sound of his sister speaking to him.

"Thank you, brother." She sang her whistled reply, the beautiful sounds teetering at the very upper edge of human hearing. Recognition was there. Warmth, too.

Relief flooded his body.

His sister continued, "I had hoped your ship would arrive before it was time for me to return." She slipped the cloak over her shoulders, shielding her body from view. "I have heard many whispers during my sojourn. Others also in c'haborreneis't shared their hyr'yan't with the waters. I feared for my memories of you. C'storr, Berian, and Wolmn were present at my ceremony. Others were not, but it was you I most missed." She reached out and touched his shoulder. "You must swim with me. Your time will be soon. Your years weigh heavily on you. I can see them in your eyes."

With a voice as the sound of a note warbled by a bird on wing, he returned his own musical reply, "You alone lift my burden, Adhor'k. My sister."

She began to walk along the shore. He drew near, cradling his sister's elbow in the palm of his hand, pulling her near as he poured out the reason he had returned early.

"Our people are in danger. An Earth corporation has pointed insidious investigations our direction. I have worked many

37

years to invalidate the reports and deflect their interest, but their suspicions will no longer be ignored." He reached out, pausing, resting his aged hand on a large boulder blackened with eons of rising and falling tides. "I still have time before my c'habor-reneis't."

"And still you do not yet speak your heart. I know you, brother, perhaps better than you know yourself."

"I have grown to love that place they call Earth. But for needing to share my concerns, I would have stayed still longer." After a moment of pensive silence, they moved once again along the stones lining the water.

"We are all aware—and grateful—for your affection for your home-away-from-home, favored brother. How else could you bear spending so many years away?" She stopped, reaching to grasp his arm, pausing his steps, her voice suddenly hard. "But these suspicions. How can there be suspicions? They cannot know, cannot prove what we have never shared. This is our world, our way. They have all they desire and do not need anything from us."

She released him and turned away, her lips pressed tightly together.

He knelt, caressing a smooth stone at the water's edge. Glancing up at her, one gray eyebrow lifted, a cheerless smile at one corner of his mouth, he mused, "You do not know them, sister. They want whatever they do not have. They are a young people. Immature. Short-lived."

"Then they should strive to improve their natures, rather than attempt to satisfy their desires with what they cannot have." Her words were bitter.

Turning his eyes again to the stone, he spoke almost in a whisper, "Humans have one thing they *do* want from us. They think of incredibly long lives as being the greatest of riches in the entire galaxy. Our people will soon find that Earth-humans have grown accustomed to taking what they want, handing out payment in return if possible, violence if necessary."

"Violence!" She spit the word with distaste, the keening of her voice splitting the sky. "We are not a violent people. We know only peace with our world and ourselves. It has been that way since the beginning of all we have known." She knelt, her hand once more touching her brother's arm, speaking in a sequestered confidante's voice. "And they cannot take what we cannot give."

"Sister. Sister. They will try. Our people must prepare. We have a little time, but that is all. A little time."

"Se'Yan't's waters will soothe you, brother. True refreshing will come only in c'habor-reneis't, but just to immerse yourself, the water-weir to refresh yourself. You must miss it with your c'habor-reneis't so near. Come with me. Breathe the waters."

Moving to the water's edge, she slipped her cloak to the stones at her feet. With a pleading look in her eyes, she stepped into the sea, disappearing as he watched.

He trusted her. She had come back to him, her memories true and strong, even though he had not returned for her ceremony. And she spoke the truth. The waters would refresh him. Rising, he slipped his tunic over his head. Laying it aside, he let his breeches fall, stepping to the water's edge. Glancing at the reflection accusing him of many years spent away, he saw the years in his gray hair, thickening middle, and mottled skin.

C'habor-reneis't! To feel youth on his weary frame once again. To go into the sea, to swim for a year-of-months, and to absorb all that was whispered to him. *C'habor-reneis't.* He knew it would be his soon enough. Time for going-and-returning would come when it came. The natural order of things could not be rushed.

He stepped ahead, his body disappearing as he slipped beneath the water's welcoming surface. The sea seemed to rejoice as it wrapped tenuous fingers around his limbs, drawing him ever closer in its much-missed embrace.

Study 6

Compiled by: Adel' Eriks'n, SSM.rl.sub.adjunct, UNAS
Subject: Rjorck
Location: Earth
Earth-Reference Date: 2799 A.D. (O.E. Standard)

Several Months Earlier

"YOU MAY CERTAINLY make such a request. However, Grand Ser, I cannot express an equal desire to accede to your, eh-hem, requests."

Rjorck stood in his most formal robes in the imposingly arranged room, his speech perfectly modulated in the human range of hearing, with a long, heavy table separating him from the highest ranking offic'rs of the largest corporation on Earth. Hanging over their heads was a realtime—and quite believable—representation of a three-dimensional Earth. Clouds moved across the blue sky, miniature ships sailed the green stretches of sea, and in the vast deserts that still blanketed the northern half of Africa, enormous machines tore away the sand, rebuilding old forests that had once existed many eons ago.

It was the man directly under the glowing, pulsing letters M and C superimposed over Earth who spoke next.

"I am MegaCorp! How dare you not turn this information over to us! Humanity demands it! The record crystal you hold in your hand has copies of each and every request made of Rejuvenant. These have been gone over by the very best World-lawyers our company can buy, signed off by WorldPresident Benetin, and encrypted with enough funds to buy your people whole new worlds to inhabit. You do not have the *right* to refuse." Well-tanned jowls shaking as he spoke, the president of MegaCorp slammed his fist on the table, causing men and clear containers of drinking substances to jump.

Rjorck took a moment to peer beyond the men seated at the table, and out the wall of glassine separating the chill of the room and the busy, congested city outside. The equatorial sun punished the many tall buildings thrusting their defiant fists into the sky. Gravships darted between them, teasing the ornate structures, daring to risk their annoyance. Set to mute the vibrant life on the other side, the silent glassine made the room feel even colder.

With a bow, he phrased his reply carefully. "Most Honored Ser, it is my wish at all times to accede to the wishes and mandates imposed upon me by my esteemed betters. If you wish to present a petition for something I am able to provide, I will do the utmost possible to grant your request. However, for those things of which I do not pretend to have knowledge, I am at a loss. All your legal forms, high-ranking initials, and monetary funds cannot purchase what I do not possess." With a slight cough, he stood to again look past the faces of MegaCorp.

The man positioned in line-of-sight of High City Spaceport Control Tower stood, blocking Rjorck's view of the undisputed most beautiful building in the city. "Councilor Rjorck, I have DataRecc records on file going back three hundred twenty years. Your name is signatory to multiple documents throughout this time span. On each of these signatures is your personal DNAuthorize stamp. Each of these is *exactly the same. Throughout the entire three hundred twenty years.*

"Do you mean you wish to tell us there has been more than one Councilor Rjorck with DNA exactly matching your own? Even in our current level of technology, there is one thing that no company, not even MegaCorp, can do, and that is *duplicate human DNA.* Not unless there has been a breakthrough that not even our World-lawyers are aware of. Spare us this farce, Councilor." Slamming his DataRecc on the table, he glared at Rjorck as if he could draw the information out of him with his eyes alone.

"Dear Munificent Ser, my life is as you see it. I am no longer a young man. How can the years be rerun so they can be lived again? Can an old man such as myself extend his reach into the future? Can I live today yet keep my hand on the distant past?

"I am unfamiliar with your files and records, how they are kept and what they record. I am only a humble councilor. My DNAuthorize stamp is mine; I will own that without question. But to have been in use by me for over three centuries? Surely you jest, Worthy Ser. Such a thing could not be reasonable by any practical measure.

"Possibly, if you will search your files, there has been an error in record keeping. Perhaps a glitch in transcribing, a faulty data plate, or a power surge. Surely, surely there must be a reasonable explanation.

"Please, ser, understand that all I have is yours. But this that you demand from my people, this is something I do not have. Your request astounds me."

Inside, he sighed. Perhaps he had retained his true identity too frequently, his aliases allowed to slip into dormancy with too much ease. If he had failed his people in something so simple . . .

"This world of yours is far, Councilor Rjorck. Travel outside the inner systems is slow. But MegaCorp's reach is long. We have the authorization. No one will stop us. You are not the only resident of Rejuvenant. Someone there will tell what we wish to know. If we have to pluck each and every living being from the face of that planet, we will know the truth behind what we've uncovered. Humanity *demands it.*"

The man glared around the room, catching the eyes of the

other MegaCorp minions lined up alongside him. His expression tightening, he turned back to Rjorck, continuing.

"Look around you. Billions of people die each year. How many of those billions will stand up to defend your planet when they know their very *existence* is being snuffed out, and *you could prevent that?*

"You have time, Councilor. Time to tell us what we wish, no, *demand* to know! You have time. For now. But that time will run out. MegaCorp will have its answers. *Humanity* will have its answers! Do you have anything to say?"

Rjorck looked up and down the room at the remaining members sitting behind their impressive table, the men who controlled the most powerful organization in the known systems. With sadness, he realized their faces reflected agreement back at him.

In a hushed voice, he spoke, "Privileged Sers, your power is great, and my ability is poor. I will pray to the gods beneath us that you will find wisdom." With a gracious bow, his formal robes scraping the floor, he backed out of the room, the doors swinging open then shut again as he passed through.

Only now that he was out of the glare of MegaCorp's eyes could he drop his formality, not caring how incongruous it might appear for others to see these elaborate robes draped on someone rushing hurriedly as he was doing at that moment. But speed was now of the essence. His people must be warned.

He pictured the Earth-months he would have to spend in transit. A message transmission would not do, not to convince them of the danger. Only his presence would suffice. At the thought of the news he would bring, his heart sank. He would be arriving on Se'Yan't just to let them know of impending disaster.

However, all the years ... MegaCorp hadn't guessed the half of it. With an inner smile, he let amusement flood his veins. Three hundred twenty years! That was just how long since he'd begun using his DNAuthorize stamp. They could almost double the years and still not measure the period he'd worked tirelessly for his people.

Yet, he knew that all the times he'd successfully deflected curiosity away from Se'Yan't wouldn't stop what had started in that boardroom.

And they were right. They were, oh, so right. Billions of people who weren't prepared to handle either death or unimaginably long lives would climb over MegaCorp if they had to in order to take, by force if necessary, what he and his people could not give them, even if they wanted to.

Entering his suite of apartments, he flicked his eyes past each item, evaluating what to leave behind. Lemons! Reaching out, he wrapped long fingers around a yellow orb and held it. This that grew on no other planet was what he would remember most fondly. This was what he'd miss most.

Summoning his resolve, he put the fruit aside and laid his hand to his DataRecc, requesting the first available flight to Rejuvenant. He guessed he'd get a good view of High City Spaceport Control Tower after all, even if it might be his last.

Study 7

Compiled by: Ne'rosi El'ganti, SSM.rl.sub.adjunct, UNAS
Subject: Ma'jene Holcum
Location: Earth
Earth-Reference Date: 2795 A.D. (O.E. Standard)

THE FLAGS snapped in the breeze as rows of suited cadets, career military persons, and battle scarred veterans, crisp and erect in their dress blacks, faced severely ahead. Atop the slender tower that pierced the sky overhead, surveying the parade grounds, small and barely visible, the moderator's voice rang out from unseen speakers.

"For the protection of all peoples living in systems both near and far, those existing on industrial as well as pastoral worlds, occupants of minor planets and asteroids, thank you for your attendance today."

Those viewing the parade grounds in person stood a little prouder knowing this was being seen live, or as soon as the latest high-speed transmissions could get the signal there, throughout all known space. But to have seen this with their own eyes, the sounds falling directly on their bare ears! What glory! The proxy-holo bands under special invitation from throughout the nearest systems swelled the air with volume, cementing the magnificence of the event, fading in intensity only as the triumphant voice continued.

"For many years humanity has suffered needlessly. Certain groups of people have hoarded the bounty of their worlds rather than sharing for the greater good. That time is finished. Let our peoples raise a shout of triumph, a cry of victory. The mighty arm of our military division has returned to us victorious, the rabble on our latest mining world vanquished. An unlimited resource our corporation has bargained and paid dearly for, the resources for this corporation, for *Earth,* to triumph in its supremacy over all other worlds, has been regained. Raise a shout to our men and women who stand before you, the vanquishers of the rabble, the supreme force of might, our right arm, literally, the MegaCorp Military Arm."

A roar rose from the parade grounds and beyond, reaching out into the surrounding city, traveling across the countryside, joining again as it touched the far corners of Earth before bursting forth to encompass all who were observing the ceremonies.

"But wait," the voice boomed. The crowd quieted, becoming hushed, finally noticing the erect military battalions standing silently on the grounds before the tall tower. "Here," the grand voice paused, waiting for the final sounds to dissipate from the surrounding throng, "in person, is the one who single-handedly led our troops in their successful attack, the career offic'r who selflessly stepped into mortal danger to ensure the continued economic success of our great corporation's endeavors, our very own OverSergeant Ma'jene Holcum!"

Several Months Earlier

THE TIP OF HER WEAPON glowing in the dim light, still hot from recent, repeated use, OverSergeant Holcum crouched on the crumbling pavement. Looking around, sensing movement, attributing it to the wind, she stood and motioned for her troops to follow her. She knew the scum who had sabotaged the mining operation had just been *this* direction. Her team was the best, the reason for receiving a special dispensation to be the final mop-up troops on the planet. With these rabble gone, this unnamed planet on the distant edge of known travel routes would once again send its vast underground resources of metals, minerals, and life-giving fluids back to its rightful owner, MegaCorp, OverSergeant Holcum's employer and legal owner.

Yes, just like this world, they owned her, lock, stock, and barrel.

The dim light filtering through the smoke-shrouded skies ahead of her glinted. Crouching as quickly as the flick of an old-Earth scorpion's tail, one hand at her shoulder bringing her team to an instant freeze, their black invisi-suits seeming to disappear in the dimness, she observed with all her senses.

OverSergeant Ma'jene Holcum's head pivoted left and right. She *knew*. This place. Over that mound of debris. Just *there*. The quarry she sought would be *there*. She shook her head, not sure how she knew. She wasn't a *groundie*, learning her way around *planets*, memorizing *terrain*.

Suddenly she saw a little girl, a frightened little girl who didn't know what to do. A frightened little girl who remem-

46

bered hugs, who remembered color. Warmth. Smiles. Trees. Parents. A little girl who knew only desperation in the dark. Always the hunger. And the men. Chasing her. Doing things to her as she screamed for them to stop.

She knew this place, knew how she could sense just where their hiding place must be. Her anger ruptured in her as she stood, uncaring whether she followed protocol or not, desperately needing to destroy all the tormented memories.

Before she could advance, a primitive shell exploded, taking out the three soldiers to her right, their invisi-suits crackling with twisting electricity before shattering, the explosion lighting up the devastated landscape of the surrounding city. Bright points of exploding primitive firearms ammunition drew her team to their attackers. But the oversergeant didn't need to be shown the way. With an unholy sound from her lips, she leaped in uncontrollable rage, an act that would later be ascribed to selfless bravery, and charged into the remains of the basement of her childhood home, determined, with every ounce of hatred in her black soul, to forever wipe all *groundies* from the face of this planet. Deep in her psyche, somewhere that even the tortured soldier she had become wouldn't have known to look, she hoped to massacre the nightmare that had haunted her for nearly twenty years.

It was the next day before the campaign was complete, and yet another man injured, although not Rezalton, curse the gods. If she'd been able to think clearly, she would have sent him in front of her and shot him herself. Enough action had been going on that no one would have faulted her. It was too late now.

She groaned as she used the hand-grip to hoist her aching body from the transport bench. A clean uniform and a hot shower niche. These two things were worth gold to her. Mountains of gold. It had been a hard campaign, even with the levels of success that had been achieved.

She trudged to her quarters, erect when saluted by underlings, showing her weariness only when they were out of view. Slapping her palm on her door release, she fell inside almost before it opened, knowing she should have stayed in the decommissioning chamber, using the cleaning facilities there instead of returning directly to her quarters. But curse the powers that be, she was tired, too tired to endure those pansies any longer. She sat to begin the process of removing her filthy, battle-stained, *dirt*-encrusted uniform, boots first, her every muscle aching with the attempt.

Standing before the mirror, shower-wet hair in short tendrils all over her head, she looked at herself, dark hair, narrow waist, generous hips, carrying still-firm breasts.

"No damage this time out," she grunted, unaccountably relieved.

However, running her hand over her damp, well-trained body, she knew she could look to a bruise just *there,* would feel pulled muscles in just *that* spot. She slid her palm up and down the skin of her thigh, pressing hard at sore places until they burned deep inside. Running her fingers across her shoulder and down, circling her breast, she winced as pain stabbed deep into her chest. The cool, vented breeze blowing through the room quickly dried the water from her skin as she continued to find new levels of pain all over her body.

"TEAT-SUCKING COWARDS! They want *what?*"

It had been only ten cycles since the end of that last dirt-scrubbing mission. She'd vowed to never set foot on soil again. Now this!

OverSergeant Ma'jene Holcum looked at the orders in disgust, throwing her words as well as the glass in her hand back at the cadet standing just inside her door. The boy jumped aside just in time to see the glass hit the floor, sliding into the corridor to stop just past the door.

Quivering in fear, tears threatening to break from the corners of his eyes, the boy stood as far from her as the cubicle would allow. Moving from one foot to another, panic blinking his eyes to a blur, he waited for permission to be someplace else.

"They think I *want* this? That I *want* the *dirt* of another mother-scrubbing world on my boots? Can't they ever just *promote* without forcing us to *dance* for it?" Turning her growing frustration back to the trembling boy, she burst out, "And you're still here? Gods, get out of my sight!"

As he ran down the corridor, the opening line of Ma'jene's orders were just visible on the top edge of her glass as she reached through the door and slammed her opened palm into it, making it crackle with the force.

"*Congratulations. Proceed with all haste to Earth for your upcoming promotion ceremony . . .*"

Back on Earth

MA'JENE STOOD ERECT, the wind tousling the tendrils of exposed hair showing under her hat. With a snap of her heels and a formal salute, she turned from the flag to face CaptGen'l Willane Bofsky. Feeling her overuniform's lapels being manipulated as her new insignia was attached, she then turned to face the flag again as newly promoted Corp'lMaj'r Ma'jene Holcum.

Finally released from her duties in the ceremony, her new insignia on her lapel, a BraveHeart commendation medal beribboning her shoulder, she dropped into the transport seat, grabbing a disposable towel and wiping dust from her boots with disgust.

"Great gods from the ancient past, I hope I never have to set foot on another planet. Moles. Nothing but slugs. Ground crawlers. That's all planets are good for. My home is up *there*." Glancing through the thick glassine of the clearwall beside her to the darkness of space overhead, she spit out her final word to no one.

"Shipside."

She reached over and tossed the dirt-stained cloth in the disposal chute, the *groundies* and the planet below along with it.

Study 8

Compiled by: Ne'rosi El'ganti, SSM.rl.sub.adjunct, UNAS
Subject: Ma'jene Holcum
Location: FarHoriz'n, MC Military Academy Ship
Earth-Reference Date: 2785 A.D. (O.E. Standard)

THE PSEUDOMETAL DOOR SLAMMED. Undercadet Ma'jene Holcum threw her back against the row of closed lockers, the only person in the vast room. Her head crashed against the plasteel locker, her fist pounding the metallic wall at her waist, the sound echoing through the empty space.

With tears at the corners of her eyes, she felt the disappointment welling up inside her. *A kid! He called me a kid!* She was as good as any of the others. The fighters. The rankers. Why did her upper-cadet leader have to exclude *her?*

"TAKE THIS, REZALTON." Ma'jene handed a detonator to the blond, pale teenage boy crowded into the air duct with her.

"Sure, Ma'jene. What do I do with it?" He reached to touch her leg, her arm out of reach, his skin flushing with the contact.

She glared at him. "Get your arm off my leg, you idiot," she growled. "That pretty face of yours ain't good for *jack* right now. I need *smarts.*"

Just in front of her was the offending uppercadet's vent

screen. She released the catch, flipped it up, and scooted through the tight opening, dropping onto her nemesis' bunk.

"What sort of prank are we playing?" He grinned tentatively, peering after her.

"He's going to regret what he did to me. And you're going to help me make sure he does." Reaching back inside the vent and grabbing his arm, she pulled him roughly into the room. He crashed on the bunk, slipping and falling to the floor. "Hand me the bag."

His eyes jumped back to the dark void from which he had just fallen. "Still in the vent, Ma'jene. I'll get it. Hold on!" Leaping back onto the bunk, he grabbed the bottom of the vent opening, pulling himself up, and reaching back inside to grab the bag. With a yank, he fell back on the bunk as the bag collapsed on top of him.

"Stupid!" She slapped him hard on the leg. "That bag will take you out, and me along with it if you set it off. You idiot! Be careful for a change." With a flick of her arm, she yanked the bag from his chest.

"I'm number two in all my classes, ahead of even you. Quit picking on me." He rolled off the bunk, flexing his arms to show muscles just starting to make him into the man he so wanted to become.

"Pansy. I need brains and a little self-control right now. Not your tos'rone. Keep your shirt on."

"Sorry, Ma'jene." His eyes brightening, he reached over and started to unzip the bag. "What kind did you bring? Light-Crackers? FizzPoppers? Any good ones?" He pulled one of the "toys" from the bag, holding it up to the light. "Whoa! You're kidding! C'mon. A BodyThumper? Hey, not even Overcadet Timons deserves this. Whatever he did to you can't be *that* bad."

The explosive went flying from his hand. With fire in her eyes, she hissed, "You don't know, don't understand. No one can. But pay. Yes, he'll pay. And you, Rezalton, you're in it with me. We're a team now, you and me. So, get with the program. You'll do as I say. Got it?" She prowled the room with her eyes, searching for the ideal hiding place, one where no one would think to look.

Taking the device, sweat trickling down the small of his back, he turned to place the explosive back in the bag, speaking as if to the wall. "Yeah, I got it, Ma'jene." His voice was flat as he answered her. "We're a team. You and me. We're a team."

Subdued, he reached into his pocket and pulled out the detonator she had given him in the vent—back in the vent when this was still just a prank. He rubbed his hands on his pants as he asked in a muted voice, "How can I help you hook this up? What do you need me to do?"

She looked at him, satisfied. He was putty in her hands, even if neither of them realized exactly what putty was.

OVERCADET TIMONS WALKED through his door, closing it behind him. Unsnapping the collar of his jacket, he pulled it off, hanging it according to cadet protocol in the room's stor'lok bin. Removing his shoes and pants, he hung the pants, creases together, beside the waiting jacket.

Stepping into the adjoining cleaning cubicle, he stripped his remaining clothing, dropping the items into a recycle slot. Quickly finished, the fresh smell of soap still clinging to his skin, he reached for a disposa-towel from the wall dispenser, toweling himself dry with the thin, super-absorbent material.

Back in the room, air, cool from the ventilation system, washed over his skin. Yawning, he decided he was too tired to review tomorrow's lessons before bed. After a day of games practice, his bunk simply looked too good right then. After all, as PrimeLeader of an entire squadron, he had to be in better physical shape than all the others. During the exercises, he always had to do more, go further, be the better example that the rest of his team would strive to emulate. Days like today always exhausted him.

Then there were those undercadets always trying to join his team, just because his people were the best. Why, just last sevenday, one had tried to sneak on his team, posing as an uppercadet. What was her name? He couldn't recall. He couldn't even keep his eyes open any more. His bunk was calling his name.

Throwing back the thin covers, he slipped his lean frame between the sheets. A heavier boy might have hit the trigger sooner. But for Overcadet Timons, as his body relaxed into a full, deep sleep, his back depressed the mattress just enough to activate the detonator underneath, the explosion coming straight at his head as the locker next to his bed erupted.

Although they searched thoroughly, his shipmates were never able to locate enough of his head to reconstruct a passable face for his burial ceremony. In fact, they were lucky to find any parts at all.

"CONGRATULATIONS, Undercadets Holcum and Rezalton. Due to your quick thinking and tenacious rescue efforts, what could have escalated into a section-wide disaster affecting the entire uppercadet class portion of the ship was restricted to three deaths, one from the actual, unexplained explosion on Deck 4, and two others from cadets caught in explosive decompression situations when their emergency survival suits couldn't be accessed quickly enough. You, Undercadet Holcum, along with your classmate, Undercadet Rezalton, were most fortunate to have been carrying your ESS's back from maintenance at the precise moment of the explosion.

"MegaCorp Military Training Arm is pleased to award both of you with a two-stage advance, bringing you from undercadet status to uppercadet.

"Congratulations, again, on a job well done."

The MegaCorp Military Training Arm squad overcommander reached out, removing the three-bar undercadet pin from each tunic. He took two fitted uppercadet jackets, handing one to each of the teenagers standing in front of him. Once they donned their new symbols of advancement, the overcommander pinned new five-bar uppercadet pins on each lapel. Each cadet class in attendance, from the most junior to those preparing for graduation, stood, one class at a time, clapping and cheering until all trainees were on their feet.

Holcum's revenge was complete.

Study 9

Compiled by: L'rani Delogosi, SSM.rl.sub.adjunct, UNAS
Subject: Rom'n Rezalton
Location: FarHoriz'n, MC Military Academy Ship
Earth-Reference Date: 2784 A.D. (O.E. Standard)

VOICES WERE LOUD in the corridor at first, telling the news. As word seeped deeper into the ship, hints and whispers reached even the academy, the news finally filtering down to the undercadet wing.

A replacement, joining the program, joining those already a year into classes and training, the voices murmured.

If it were true, it was about more than just a new undercadet. This was about an empty bunk that had to remain empty. Under-cadet Rom'n Rezalton knew there was only one bunk unoccupied in the undercadet group. Just under his, one that needed to remain empty. He'd claimed it, and it belonged to no one else.

"No, it can't be," he cursed. "There's only one spot available, and I know where it is."

He leaped from the shower niche, slid to the bench for his

priv'tshorts, and grabbed them in one hand, bypassing the disposa-towel dispenser. Water dripped from his long limbs as he sprinted from the communal cleansing cubical into the corridor.

Dodging laughing cadets of all ratings, holding his shorts as he ran slipping down the hall, while using his free hand to push people out of the way, he burst into the dormitory, his skin still sparkling with water. Female whistles of appreciation told of the opposite gender present.

As if suddenly aware of his nudity, he bent over to pull his priv'tshorts on, hopping on one foot to get one leg in, then switching feet, not quite stumbling, while using one hand to pull the shorts to cover himself. He stumbled to his bunk. Panting, he grabbed the metal footrail, his free hand still pulling his shorts the last bit of the way into position, his face damp with the *quickness* of coming, breathing hard from the *hurry* of needing to find out.

He stood looking at the strange duffel waiting on the bunk below his, the stor'lok bin open, things already inside.

"It's true, what they said! They've given my bunk away!"

He hit a newly strong fist against the edge of his bunk, his head slumping. With an easy flex of rapidly muscling arms, he angrily flipped his lean body onto the top bunk, *his* bunk. He put his arms behind his head, lying back on his pillow, eyes closed, tuning out the intruder, waiting for the person to *come*. To *see*. See that he didn't need him, didn't want him.

Patiently, the flush of anger and determination coloring his still-damp skin, he waited.

THE HAND STARTLED ROM'N from a dream he couldn't quite remember.

"Hey! Pansy! You gonna greet me or just lay there? You snooze, you lose!"

Before he could get his eyes open, the hand was gone.

55

He grabbed the edge of the bunk, leaned his head over, and looked down at the new recruit sitting below, the legs showing, all he could see, the person doing something on the bunk. He leaned out more, where he could see more.

Those! His eyes were drawn to the chest attached to the person on the bunk underneath him. A *woman.*

He yanked back from the edge of his bunk as the girl, the *woman,* stood. Resting her arms on the edge of his bed, she looked at him, her eyes running over his flushed body, seeing him, landing on his face, resting, looking at *him,* his eyes.

"Welcome to the real world, Jack! What's the name?"

"R-Rom'n," he stuttered, barely able to get the word out of his mouth.

"Yeah, that's right, Jack. Well, you're a pansy. Did anyone ever tell you that? A real pansy. By the way, I'm Ma'jene. All my friends call me that. At least the ones who want to stay my friends. Before you ask, yeah, I'm a year late gettin' here. A year late, and a credit short. Whatever. I'll just have to hustle a little harder, won't I?"

With that, she returned to her bunk and her things.

With anticipation spreading over his skin, he couldn't stop thinking about his good fortune. *A girl. Oh, and what a girl!* He rolled onto his back, put his hands behind his head, and as he lay back on the pillow, he closed his eyes and smiled.

Study 10

Compiled by: L'rani Delogosi, SSM.rl.sub.adjunct, UNAS
Subject: Rom'n Rezalton
Location: FarHoriz'n, MC Military Academy Ship
Earth-Reference Date: 2784 A.D. (O.E. Standard)

"GOT IT? 42A AND 42B. You can decide who's on top. Take

this tag. The bunk numbers are printed on it with your names on the back. Slip it in the slot on the end of the bunk. You're down that green corridor, second door on the left. Mess is down the blue. Three units until mess call. Be ready or be hungry. Questions? No? Next!"

Sil'nov Vasilyev and Rom'n Rezalton threw their duffels over tall shoulders, standing proud, feeling big, older. They were on the *ship!* They were *here!* They were *cadets!* Well, almost undercadets. Not quite cadets. But almost, anyway.

Turning into the door where they would sleep, they looked at rows of bunks, lined up one after another down the long room. Following the numbers marked on each set of bunks, they ran to claim the best bunk, top bunk. Sil'nov pushing Rom'n aside in a last rush, he threw his duffel up, landing it on the winning bunk.

"Mine," he laughed, grabbing the side of the bunk, and jumping up in one great leap.

"Cheater! I had it!" Rom'n laughed, stepping on the lower bunk to punch his friend in the side. Dropping down on his own sleeping pad, he raised his feet, kicking the bottom of the bunk above.

"Hey!" Sil'nov dropped his head over. "I guess I'll have to play nice if I want to get any sleep up here." Rolling off the bunk, hitting the floor on both feet, he pulled the other boy up. "Let's get this tag posted and get our duffels emptied. See, these stor'loks beside the bunks are ours."

Pulling his duffel from his bunk, Rom'n glanced at the other newbie undercadets coming in, locating bunks, some still choosing bunkmates. Whispering, he leaned in to Sil'nov, "There are girls in here. Where are they going to sleep?"

"Sometimes I wonder what rock you crawled out from under. Anywhere they want. Except in my bunk, of course. We're not supposed to sleep in anyone else's bunk, especially if they're in it, if you get what I mean. But when the lights are out, well, I've been told that things do happen. Just not in my bunk, thank you very much." He grinned wickedly. "You can get kicked out of the academy if they catch you."

Turning scarlet, Rom'n turned to his stor'lok, grabbing his duffel to put his things away. Quietly he said, "My brother was here. At the academy. Here at MegaCorp. He never did that, had girls in his bed."

It was important to him that Sil'nov understand that his brother did the *right* thing. Things he wanted to do. Was how he wanted to be. He wouldn't let them take that from him.

THE UPPERCADETS, CADETS, AND ranked undercadets were all in the room. So were the newbies.

"The next test is a strength test," the uppercadet announced to the unranked newbies in the center of the room. He looked tall and sure, his words spoken with assurance, although there was a certain furtive glance in his eyes. He had good reason. If word of hazing these newbies got back to their training commanders, all the dark-sides would come down on them. Hence, it was the middle of the night, the newbies not even allowed to dress.

The uppercadet continued, "Only the strongest cadets can be part of the MegaCorp Military Training Arm. The weak will not be allowed to stay. Every newbie must take down two other newbies, take them down and keep them down until a ranked cadet can come put a mark on your shoulder. Every newbie must earn at least two blue shoulder marks to continue with the tests." He held up a blue marking stick to show them. "You must play to win. Ready! Start!"

The boys and girls in the center of the room were cheered on by those who had already earned the right to watch, those who had been through these tests when they were newbies. Boys would try to take down smaller girls, sometimes successfully. Other times, the girls, desperate, would get the mark on their shoulders.

Rom'n felt himself thrown down by a boy who had knocked him down on the shuttle. As the boy jumped on top of him, sitting on his stomach, he leaned in close, putting his arm on Rom'n's throat, spittle hitting Rom'n's face as he hissed, "I know who you are, Rezalton. *His* brother. You really think no one would know? *My* father told me about what he did. Ran off. Deserted when he was sent to fight. Had his *commission* stripped from him. Died a coward's death."

With anger flooding through Rom'n, his eyes fiery with protection for the honor of his brother, the honor of Jo'n, he felt his muscles tense. Forgotten was the shame of the running, the *showing,* everyone seeing. He *acted.* Grabbing the boy's arm with both hands, he *twisted.* He *twisted* the arm, twisted until it hurt, until the boy winced with pain, tried to move. Then he held on, twisted some more, his breathing fast and angry, his skin moist with the need to *defend* his brother from what the boy *said* about him.

With a grunt of surprise, the boy moved, jerking away from him, yet still held by him. And Rom'n didn't let go. He held tight, *twisting* as the boy moved, making him fall to the floor, putting his knee into his stomach, feeling his skin, his anger-hot skin against the boy's skin, the slickness of the other boy's *hurt,* sliding his knee along the other boy's stomach, then sitting on the boy, still holding his arm.

He kept his legs against the boy, holding the boy with both his legs, squeezing him with his legs, feeling the boy's ribs through his skin, squeezing the boy tighter, twisting the arm, until his attention was drawn by something on his shoulder, something cold. The mark. The blue mark telling others he was on top. He won. He *won!* Breathing hard, he stood, leaving the other boy lying there without a blue mark, breathing quick, shallow breaths, the boy learning what *shame* was like.

Now to do it again.

Study 11

Compiled by: L'rani Delogosi, SSM.rl.sub.adjunct, UNAS
Subject: Rom'n Rezalton
Location: Resort World
Earth-Reference Date: 2784 A.D. (O.E. Standard)

PICKING HIS NEW DUFFEL UP, brushing the dirt off the sturdy new fabric, Rom'n slung it over his burgeoning adolescent shoulder. His parents knew what this meant to the family's survival. Without the credits from MegaCorp, survival on their broken, worn-out world would soon cease for them, as well as for Rom'n's siblings, his sisters.

He had pulled his favorite things from the rafter above his bed, the only things he had left from his brother, Jo'n, that and the glass eye he found in the city the time he snuck out to meet him the last time he'd come home, the time Jo'n wasn't supposed to come, instead had been forced to sneak away from the *war*.

But Jo'n did. Jo'n came back. And Rom'n went without asking, just to see him. It had been just before *that* time his parents wouldn't talk about, remembering Jo'n from *before*, refusing to acknowledge the slo-trak message, already fourteen standard months dated when it arrived, telling what had happened *that time*.

They almost hadn't let Rom'n sign up, afraid they'd lose him, too, not ready to let him be a man. But the need, the poorness, the *hunger*, his sister crying every night, her stomach hurting, another sister too weak to cry. They had to listen, to sign the papers, had to let him go.

His new clothes, the new *duffel* on his shoulder, new things inside. He'd never had new things before, except that once,

Jo'n's things shipped back in the box, the box his parents wouldn't open.

At the bottom of that box, the shirt . . . still in cryowrap. Never opened. New . . . from Jo'n. He wore it even though he had to tie the sleeves up, wore it 'til it got ripped too badly to fix.

He felt his eyes redden and sniffed it away. He was grown up, now. Men didn't cry. Jo'n didn't cry.

He reached inside his new duffel, pulling the glass eye from under his new things, rolling it in his hand, remembering his family, already lonely.

Study 12

Compiled by: L'rani Delogosi, SSM.rl.sub.adjunct, UNAS (Auxiliary Revisions: J. Ret'tsh, SSN.rt, UNAS/UT, 2831)
Subject: Jo'n Rezalton
Location: Ma'jene Holcum's Birth World
Earth-Reference Date: 2780 A.D. (O.E. Standard)

THE DUST COULD BE SEEN covering the horizon. As the mighty transport landers descended to disgorge their contents onto the desolate landscape, troops, dust-caked as soon as they broke through the protection of the repulsor screens, prepared for battle. The distant thump of explosives forced rising tendrils of dust from the ground.

Inside one ground transport, beat down by the dust and heat before even reaching their destination, a team of luckless reinforcements was assembled, the rattle of well-worn machinery assaulting their ears. One of the men, nervous energy built up from the anticipation of his first mêlée, seemed desperate to engage anyone who would open up to his entreaties.

"Hey," he began, calling out into the transport. "This anyone's first time, too? I've never actually been in a battle. Sim'lators, yeah, tons of times. But this is different, ya' know?"

When no one replied, he continued, drumming the tips of his shoes, an unintentional tap dance on the metal floor of the vehicle, "We could die here, ya' know. I mean, like, I knew that. But it was never *real*. Now it's like right out that wall. Just reach your hand out, touch it."

He leaned against the transport's pseudometal wall, his fingers doing a staccato dance on his legs. His eyes were bright, but dark shadows rimmed the surrounding skin.

He tried once again.

"How 'bout it," peering at the soldier next to him, his name posted on the pocket of his shirt, "Jo'n? It is Jo'n, right? I don't always get names right, but yours is right there. On your shirt. They sure did a good job getting it on there nice and clear. I like that name. Jo'n. That was my best friend's name back before I joined up. Not when I was a kid, but from later. Nah, I can't become an offic'r like some of the guys. Not me. Didn't sign up early like some did. I'm just a grunt, out in front for target practice."

"A grunt, huh?" Jo'n gave a sour grin.

"Hey, am I talking too much? The guys back on the ship always tell me I talk too much. That's the *At'micThrust*. Old-fashioned name, I know. Then, it's an old-fashioned ship. At least it was before the refit. Now, it's good as new. The ship is, not the name. They kept the same name, *At'micThrust*. What ship did you come in on? Oh, dog-sheesh, I'm nervous."

The sudden silence between the two men stretched unbroken. Looking over at Jo'n, then away again, the nervousness causing him to spasm from time to time, his eyes suddenly opened wide with realization. Reaching up to brush beading sweat back from his face, he exhaled loudly.

"Oh, wow, I'm sorry, man. You must feel the same way.

Hey, I'll let you be." He made as if to stand.

"Jo'n." The man reached an arm and grabbed him. "My name is Jo'n Rezalton. Stay. It'll be good to have someone to sit with. Thanks, and yeah, you do talk too much. What's your name, soldier?"

"Gabby dePaloma. Well, not really. It's Frankl'n, but growing up, my daddy called me that. Kinda a girl's name, I always thought, but there it is. I'm used to it. I just don't think about it anymore, unless I'm talking to somebody new. Like you. The guys on the ship thought it was pretty funny though. They're okay with it now. I mean, they don't pick on me about it so much now. Not about that, anyway. Uh, oh, I think I'm doing it again, aren't I?"

"Yeah. How are ya' doing, Gabby?" Jo'n turned to face him, reaching out his hand to shake.

As Gabby responded, he glanced down at Jo'n's wrist. "Creepin' lime-burners! What happened to your arm?"

Jo'n traced the bright red, not-quite-healed scar traveling from his wrist to a hiding place under the sleeve of his shirt. "That? That's my kid brother."

"Whoa, what kinda kid brother you got? One with Krueger-hands? I think I'd call up the agency, get him adopted out to another *planet*."

"It ain't like that, man. My kid brother didn't do this to me. This is because he loves me so much. He's nearly eight standards old. My family's had some hard times to deal with. My brother's not got much. Except me. Of course, my parents love him and all. Just . . . when life's hard . . . you know." He watched as his fingers traced the raw scar up and down his arm. "When I got my orders to come here, I had to see him first."

"Hey, man. You did that? And they let you back in? In one piece?" Gabby stopped, understanding spreading across his face. "Not quite in one piece, huh? I'm sorry, man. That's rough."

"I'm academy trained. You know, signed up at thirteen. Graduated. Commissioned, and all. But I had to see him before I left. I'm all he's really got. You should see him. About this tall." He held out his hand flat above the floor, the red scar seeming alive as it moved along his arm. "Eight standards when I last saw him. Probably nine now. With the hospital time and all, I've kinda lost track. Anyway, all that's gone. It was worth the price, though, to see him before I came."

Gabby shook his head. "That must be some kid brother you've got there. You guys must really be close for you to give up your commission and everything, just to see him again."

"Yeah, you could say that," he replied. "Rom'n and me, we're pretty close." He held up one hand, crossing two of his fingers, one over the other. "Just like that."

"SEE, I TOLD YA'," Gabby yelled during one lull, the explosions of the surrounding battle distant for the moment. "Target practice. Captgen'ls in the back, safe. Grunts to the front. We've made it so far, Jo'n. Just like the sim'lators. Nobody dies in the end. Stick with good ol' Gabby. You'll see. That kid brother of yours'll see you again."

Turning to view the overwhelming odds dancing in the distance, the massive fist of military might thrusting skyward through roiling dust, he snapped his visor down, checking the display showing enemy movement despite the black air. He yelled to Jo'n, pointing to the visor, "See? Grunts, like I said. We get the disposable version. These could do with a self-adjusting optical matrix."

They had quickly learned the brilliant streaks of the incoming tracers were the signal to raise the blindingly oversensitive viewscreens and slam themselves under the embankment until the ensuing explosion had passed, knowing yet another massive cloud of dust had been added to the darkness in the air.

"Too much dust. The matrix couldn't cope, even if we were worth it." Jo'n slapped his own visor down, but there was a grin on his face. "That's you and me, Gabby. Disposable grunts wearing disposable visors."

He was right about the dust. It was so heavy that a self-adjusting optical matrix would lock on the incoming tracers and damp out the brilliant trail. Without using manual models, ones adjusted to their most sensitive mode, the tracers would be invisible until it was too late to either return fire or dive for cover. It was ironic in a way that the visors were extremely vital but only functional during the occasional lulls in shelling.

His face streaked with smears from the dirt encrusted around his mouth and in his ears, and his fingernails black with the battlefield, Jo'n flashed a grin visible beneath his visor. "I've got your butt covered, Gabby. Just don't leave mine sticking out when the big one hits. Hey, man, hand me that power cartridge just behind you."

Gabby flipped his visor up as he reached for the cartridge. In that moment Jo'n's visor flashed blindingly bright.

Slinging his visor up, he yelled at Gabby to duck, just as a series of distant explosions shook all sound from the air around them. With more white-hot tracers on their way to greet them, he exploded into action, flinging his body into the only place it could be, over his friend for protection.

As Gabby gave him an uncomprehending look, the world exploded around them. The detonation ripped through the embankment, picking up the dirt, and slinging it away, tearing the very air from around the two men.

As the dust returned, bringing with it the raw noise of the battlefield, Gabby felt the warmth, human warmth, of Jo'n covering his back. Twisting, rolling him off, he reached to catch him, his hand sliding in the wetness of his friend's blood. He leaped to his feet, uncaring whether the war around him went on or not, wrapping his arms around the man he had

65

come to love as a brother.

"I've got ya', man," he cried, holding the bloody figure in his arms. Dragging the limp body through the dust, one hand under an arm, the other forcing the welling blood back, trapping it inside the gaping hole in Jo'n's side, he scrambled for footholds, keeping low, in an attempt to provide protection for his friend.

Seeing the red of blood bubbling from a slack mouth as Jo'n tried to trade the viscous liquid for life-giving air, Gabby pulled his friend close. With a convulsive jerk, the limp form in his arms gasped, clearly on the verge of death.

Crouching at the bottom of a rise, Gabby could only hope the spot was low enough to provide protection. Jo'n's blood-encrusted lips began to move, and Gabby leaned close.

"What, Jo'n? What do you want to say?"

"I knew I wasn't going home." The words were jerky and slurred. "Even before I came. My brother . . . if you make it, Gabby, send my things to him. The place. My home. You'll find what you need in my things." His final words bubbled from his lips, "You've been a friend to me, Gabby. A good friend."

As Jo'n's life seeped from his torn, ragged body, Gabby held him close. His friend. Almost like brothers, he thought. We were almost like brothers.

Tears ran from his face, but nothing could wash the finality of death from his friend's brutally torn body.

Study 13

Compiled by: L'rani Delogosi, SSM.rl.sub.adjunct, UNAS
Subject: Rom'n Rezalton/Jo'n Rezalton
Location: Resort World
Earth-Reference Date: 2780 A.D. (O.E. Standard)

"HOW MANY WERE THERE, JO'N? How many?" Rom'n danced with anticipation.

"You should have seen 'em. Fair-haired beauties as far as my eyes could see. All just waiting for me to walk up and give 'em a kiss."

The small boy grinned, snug under his brother's protective arm, his own arm around his waist as they walked the streets of the city. He wasn't sure he believed all that his brother told him, but he enjoyed listening, anyway. All the things Jo'n had seen, the places he'd been, things he'd done.

"Well, did you?" He looked up at his brother's face, hoping to see his grin, knowing that the grin would mean it was all in fun.

Jo'n returned the look, one eyebrow cocked. "Did I what, little bro?"

"You know what! Did you *kiss* 'em? "

"Kiss 'em? You want to know if I kissed 'em? I'll tell you what I did. I went up to one girl," and he pulled the boy up, wrapping one arm under his legs, the other behind his back, and held him up to his face, blowing on his stomach and twirling him around as he howled with laughter. "I went up to one girl, and I grabbed her just like I've got you."

"Then what, Jo'n? Then what? Tell me!" Rom'n held onto his brother's arms with both hands. "What did you do then, Jo'n? Kiss her?"

"Nah. I didn't kiss her. Nothing like that. I asked her to marry me! And do you know what she did?"

"No, Jo'n. What did she do?" He grinned at his brother, expectant.

"She kissed me! Just like this!" Then he covered his brother's face with the juiciest raspberry kisses he could pucker up, and passersby couldn't tell if their faces were moist from the kisses, or if it might have been tears.

67

"WHAT'S THAT, LITTLE BRO?" Jo'n sat up on the streetside bench and swallowed his bite of p'zzbread, hot with its topping of meat and cheese. "Let me see that."

Rom'n held up the shiny round thing he had found along the edge of the curb. It was a glass ball, a *marble*, they would have said back on Earth. He didn't know Earth, though.

"It was just there by the street. I saw the light shine in it. I don't know what it is."

Jo'n held the object up to the light, his mind already working. He winked at his brother, a ready story jumping into his head, and he licked his lips before beginning.

"Hmm. Shine *in* it? I've heard about this before. It can only mean one thing. I think you've found the Magic All-Seeing Eye." He looked at his brother's face, the small boy's attention instantly rapt, ready to absorb any tale he spun.

With the look of a master storyteller, Jo'n waved the object in front of the streetlight above their heads, the life infused within the glass orb rippling across his thoughts as he spoke, the details coming to him as if they had really happened. "Many years ago there were these two brothers. But they were like one. Two bodies, one soul. One mind." He held the object, the glass ball, the marble, right between his and Rom'n's faces. "One heart. What one brother thought, the other knew. What one brother loved, the other adored. No matter how far apart they traveled, they were always together. One heart. One mind, remember? Don't forget that. It's important." He put his free arm around his brother, drawing him close, and holding the orb in front of them.

Impatient, Rom'n prodded, "Why is it important, Jo'n? Is that all the story?"

"I'm going to tell you why it is so important. And it is very important. So you must remember it always. One heart. One mind. No matter how far they traveled, they were always together.

"One day a great magic man knew something the brothers didn't. He knew a great war was coming. The brothers would be separated for a very long time. This great magic man knew how much they meant to each other. He knew these brothers were one, even though they lived in different bodies. So the magic man decided to help the brothers."

"How did he do that, Jo'n? Did he make the war go away?"

"No, Rom'n." Jo'n winked at him, the motion big and obvious. "He did something much more difficult. He gathered one grain of sand from each of a thousand worlds, all the worlds where the war was going to happen, every world where the one brother would have to go to fight this war, and the magic man cast a spell. Now, this was no easy spell. This was a spell that took many days and many nights. The magic man couldn't sleep or eat until this spell was finished, and he was very tired and hungry by the time the spell was complete. In fact, he was so tired and hungry, he couldn't even take the magic he'd created and share it with the brothers."

"Did he die? I hope he didn't die, Jo'n." Rom'n stared transfixed at his brother's face, the cinnamon skin, chocolate hair, and expressive features, so unlike his own. "You're telling *real* this time, aren't you? I can tell."

"Very real, little bro." Jo'n grinned, continuing, "He didn't die, not then. The brothers, the ones who were the same person, they knew the magic man was tired and hungry."

"How did they know? Did someone tell them?"

Jo'n laughed out loud, squeezing his brother's shoulder with his hand. "Sometimes people just know things. The brothers knew and went to see the magic man, taking him food and a blanket. When they got there, the magic man was very weak, too weak to eat. The brothers were too late. The magic man was going to die. But before he did, he told the brothers the magic he had made for them."

"What magic? Like a magic credit crystal? With lots of credits on it?"

Jo'n laughed again. "No, better. The magic man had used up all his magic making what he made. That's why he was so weak. It wasn't the food or sleep. He didn't need food or sleep to live as much as he needed his magic. And he had used it up in making this special ball." He held the marble up, looking intently into its center as if he could see something far away. At that moment, the reflection inside flared, and the glass orb truly seemed to contain a fire of its own, almost as if the events he told might be more than an imaginative fairy tale. He laughed once more, this time as if caught by surprise.

"It was the only one? How did he know how to make it?" Rom'n reached to touch it with one finger.

"Not the only one, little bro. The only one left. Many years before, the magic man had taken all the sands from the thousand worlds and used his magic to make many Magic Glass Eyes. Over the years of helping others with his Magic Eyes, he had used them up. Now, he had this one left, his most powerful Magic Eye, the very one I'm holding right here in my hand. The magic man held it out to the two brothers. In a voice that was very weak, so weak that the two brothers that were one person had to lean in very close, he spoke to the two brothers who were really one person."

"What did he say, Jo'n?"

"He told the brothers he had put all his mighty magic into this last Magic Eye. No matter how far apart they were, the Magic Eye would help them be together. As long as one brother kept the eye with him, the other brother could look through the eye and see the first brother."

"What else did he say, Jo'n?"

"That was all. As soon as he spoke those words, a glow passed from the magic man's fingertips to the Magic Eye, the last of his magic, and he died."

"He died? How's that a good ending?"

"It's not the ending, little bro. The brothers carried this Magic Eye for many years. The one brother did go off to war. He left the Magic Eye behind, and anytime the war became hard, or the brother saw too many bad things in the war, he could just close his eyes and see his brother through the Magic Eye. And that made the war not so bad. Then, when he came home from the war, the brothers were one again, and the magic man spoke to them one more time."

"Jo'n! The magic man can't speak. He's dead!"

"Yes, Rom'n, the magic man is dead. But remember, all his magic went into the Magic Eye. It was his magic that spoke."

"What did it say?" Rom'n's small voice was breathless.

"It told the brothers, now that they were together again, they didn't need the Magic Eye any more. It told them there were other brothers that were the same person, just in two different bodies, just like we are. Isn't that right, Rom'n?"

"That's right, Jo'n. I'm you, and you're me." He leaned even closer to his brother, as if he could actually make the two of them into one person.

Jo'n held the marble out to him. "The magic told the brothers to put the Magic Eye in a special place where other brothers would be, where these other brothers would find the Magic Eye. So, they did. They came to our world, and to this city. They came to this street, because they knew two brothers would sit on this bench, and the two brothers would be the special kind, the ones who are one person. They left the Magic Eye here for you to find so we can always be together, even when I can't give you hugs, buy you p'zzbread, or run my fingers through your hair." He ruffled Rom'n's hair. "Will you keep this Magic Eye for me so I can always be with you? I'm the brother who has to go away, Rom'n. I am you. We're the

71

same person, you and me. As long as you have this Magic Eye with you, I'll always be with you, no matter how long I'm gone."

Rom'n took the marble, staring inside. "But it looks like a piece of glass. It even has a chip. Right there."

Jo'n grinned. "There's a real word for that piece of glass, you know."

His little brother looked to him, a frown on his face. "What word, Jo'n? Isn't it a Magic Eye?"

"Marble, Rom'n. The word is marble." He reached and touched the marred place in the marble, his adventure up and running once again, the words flowing from somewhere deep inside. "You know that chip? That's what makes it magic, Rom'n. It looks like a marble to everyone except the brothers who use it. It has that chip because every time two brothers no longer need it, they get to keep one tiny chip to always remember the magic man. When we no longer need it, we'll take a chip, then pass the Magic Eye on. Will you keep this with you always, little bro, just for me?"

"I'll always keep the Magic Eye, Jo'n. Always. You can see me anytime you want. We'll always be together." He threw his arms around his big brother's neck, squeezing him as hard as he could.

This time Jo'n didn't care who saw the tears, and they poured down his face.

Study 14

Compiled by: Ne'rosi El'ganti, SSM.rl.sub.adjunct, UNAS
Subject: Ma'jene Holcum
Location: Unnamed Birth World
Earth-Reference Date: 2777 A.D. (O.E. Standard)

FRIGHTENED, THE SMALL GIRL withdrew into the darkened corner, her arms wrapped around her knees. Through tear-burned eyes, she glanced back and forth at the two people she loved most, at least what she could see of them, what hadn't been blasted over the remains of her recently shattered home. With a whimper, she reached one tentative hand out to touch the one arm she could reach, wanting that touch of familiar flesh. With a resounding boom, a nearby explosion yanked the girl's arm back into the dark. Dust drifted from the shattered wall above her head as repeated explosions continued to rattle all around her.

Suddenly, a bright light flashed into her face. "We've got a live one! Quick, before this one gets away!" With a scuffle of sounds, boards being kicked out of the way and household items being thrown aside, black-suited figures appeared out of the dust and darkness.

Her eyes flicking from the menacing figures, to the remains of her parents, to possible openings for escape, she felt her newly feral muscles begin to tense, seeming to focus of their own accord, ready to propel her to safety. Without thought, instinctively, she lunged for an opening. Her feet grabbed purchase where no purchase was available, and the coiled springs of her muscles flung her past the feet of her would-be captors. Their clutching hands provided no more than thrust for her escape, as they vainly grasped for her as she tore away in her swift action of desperation.

Tracing familiar paths known only to her, obscured to her pursuers by the decimation of the damage, she dashed down remembered hallways, dodging objects no longer there, and finding footholds where she and only she could remember them to be, flinging her body through her family's no longer existing back door, straight into the arms of a dark-suited figure.

"Got her!" The arms contained the struggling figure, her bites, kicks, and scratches making no impact on the armor-plated fabric holding her tight.

DARKNESS. ALL WAS DARKNESS. Bumps . . . waiting.
More bumps. Big, jerking bumps. Small bumps. More waiting.
More darkness. Hunger. Always hunger. Trapped. Darkness.
    The girl's thoughts fractured. Flashes of home. Loving
arms wrapped around her. Kisses. Warmth. Bright sun. Happy
sounds. Colors flashing by. Music.
    And interspersed . . . darkness. Bumps. Always the hunger.

RUNNING HER HANDS over the floor of her "room," the
girl felt the ridges, the seams, the *metalness* of it all. Finding
the corners where the walls and floor met, she traced her way
around her "room." Finally, she felt something different. A
crack. A hinge. A *catch.*
    Her feeling of touch overshadowing her other senses, she
reached her slender finger into the cracks and crevices, finding
a bend in the metal just *here,* a joint *there,* something that
moved just next to *that.* Reaching where only her small fingers
could go, she pushed. Hard. Feeling the metal shift, she pushed
harder, and the metal *moved,* just a bit more than before.
    Pulling her finger out, she placed her other hand at the spot
she had found, twisting her shoulder, her *body,* to enable her to
force a finger into the same spot, stretching, finding that spot,
the metal that moved. Forcing her finger, the skin tearing
away, the pain less than the desperation driving her, the metal
had no choice but to relent to the girl's advances, to her determination. With a barely audible sound, it released its grasp,
breaking the barrier that had held the girl in darkness. The box,
the "room," the entrapment, was cracked, broken. The girl's
newly feral brain raced. Possibilities, options. For escape. For
freedom. With a push, the girl felt the metal of the wall, the
door, give way.
    Dim fingers of light pushed through the crack now opened

in her world of captivity, her world of darkness. The tentative, newfound strip of light stretched from floor to ceiling. The scene she viewed through the opening was that of her most dreaded nightmare. No trees. No blue sky. No one she knew. No home. Only smoke, dark-suited figures, fallen buildings. Sadness.

But, better than darkness.

Pushing the metal wall, the *door,* the girl jumped. Jumped for *other,* for escape, for anywhere other than the "room." Crashing to the broken road surface, her tearing skin unnoticed to her desperation-fueled, escape-driven brain, her eyes flashing back and forth, desperate for a path, any *escape,* the girl saw a new darkness. A place. To hide. Where she wouldn't be seen. Taken, yet again.

Her brain, her mind. The little girl she was . . . no longer a little girl. Changing. So fast. Her world was gone. The colors. Arms to hug. Warmth. Gone. Her new world was darkness, panic. Her sadness was used up, dry, gone so quickly, so irrevocably. No more tears. She was becoming who she would be. Changeling, now. She was changing. Becoming.

And as her anger began to grow, the ugliness within harbored a fertile seed that quickly took root.

Study 15

Compiled by: Ne'rosi El'ganti, SSM.rl.sub.adjunct, UNAS
Subject: Willane Bofsky
Location: St'rmBreak'r IV Solar Class Battle Cruiser
Earth-Reference Date: 2775 A.D. (O.E. Standard)

"HEY, BOFSKY. Would you look at this?" Shr'dt, the sector-lieute'nt, tapped the glass, his reflection staring back at him. "Another one of those weird goof-ups. This isn't like the old man. You came aboard at just the wrong time."

"The wrong time? How's that?"

Shr'dt leaned back in his chair, his arms a double-vee behind his head. "You should have served with him during his heyday. That was a captgen'l to be reckoned with. All good times must end, I guess." Turning to the display before him, he continued, "I wonder how much longer he'll be able to hang on. He acts just like it's business as usual, like nothing's wrong. Crazy old bird."

Bofsky felt the veri-sign crystal move in his clothing as he shifted to face the sector-lieute'nt. "I don't know, Shr'dt. The old man's like a father to me. I know I shouldn't, but I've been covering for him whenever I can. What else can I do?" He reached to the screen, sifting the information, seeming the helpful overoffic'r. "Move aside. This might be something I can fix. Let me see what I can do."

Shifting to the seat, he angled the glass to reflect his eyes only. Then, rapidly pinching numbers and pulling information to new locations, he pulled the veri-sign crystal from his clothing. A quick thrust into the approval port, and one more damaging report was docketed, delivery set on the next jumpship to Earth.

Thank you, Jer'son, he thought. That was an innovative trick, seamlessly joining two halves of those passes that time, defeating a foolproof system. Look at what he'd done with that idea.

He snapped the veri-sign crystal from the port and admired it lovingly. Take one temporary crystal with the old man's authorization, and one permanent authorization from a ship's overoffic'r, combine seamlessly, and here it was, his very own veri-sign crystal, making him the essence of the old man, himself. Let him be the perfect ship's capt'n. Bofsky could create all the mistakes he needed in order to destroy him using this little tool alone. Then, each time, he just authorized a report to

Earth. The capt'n would be gone before he knew it.

Bofsky slipped the crystal under his clothing, turning from the glass. "I have it all fixed, Shr'dt. I'm sure the old man's just had a bad string of luck. He'll even out. I know. All this'll soon be behind him."

"Thanks, Bofsky. The old man doesn't know just how lucky he is to have you supporting him. His career couldn't be in better hands." He reached out, placing a hand on Bofsky's shoulder, relief on his face.

A grinning Bofsky glanced up. "I'll take care of him, Shr'dt. You can count on that."

Shr'dt moved aside as the overoffic'r stood to leave. "I know I can. I trust you, Bofsky. Thanks, again."

Bofsky grinned to himself again as he stepped into the corridor, no one to see. *But just what can you trust me to do? Do you know that, Shr'dt? Are you certain you know that?*

THE GREAT VESSEL RUMBLED to a stop, its subtle engine vibrations ceasing, the unknown causes casting a pall darkening the many levels of the battleship. The emergency lighting danced its visual cues as Bofsky's door burst open to the drumming of klaxons, the dim corridor lights shadowing a distraught face.

"Bofsky! All personnel updecks. Stat."

Before he could respond, the face was gone. Turning his eyes to the time image above the door, its numbers glowing the shipboard units he knew it would show, he laid his head back on his bunk. It was perfect. All his plans were coming to a head. This should be the tie-breaker thrusting the old man in front of an inquiry board, his very doom written by his own hand, the veri-sign crystal with Bofsky now. However, he had three units until he needed to set things straight.

Creepin' burners, he wished that friggin' idiot had closed the door. He shut his eyes and slipped off back to sleep, his time for action not yet come.

BOFSKY STRODE PURPOSEFULLY through the great ship, the emergency lighting flashing its hunger for the cure he held in his hand. He couldn't help but smile. Four cycles. It had taken him four friggin' shipboard cycles to set this up. Now look at these idiots. They were panicked over just a few units of not knowing how to fix what was wrong with their friggin' ship!

When this was over, all the blame would come down to the old man. However, the solution would come from Bofsky. Hm, what would they offer to the only one able to fix this terrible, life-threatening dilemma? OverCapt'n Bofsky, will you please accept our congratulations along with the command of one capt'nless battleship?

His mirth missed by those he left in his wake, he laughed inside with the superiority of a planner who has successfully designed, executed, and culminated one of the most ambitious and daring schemes in the history of MegaCorp. Tonight, this ship would be his. He smirked as he arrived at his destination.

A quick rap on the door summoned his entrance. Standing at attention, the visible essence of willing subservience, he waited for recognition. A snap of heels and a sharp salute aimed at him inserted the final key in the lock.

"Bofsky, here. I am aware, as are the entire personnel of this battleship, of the dire nature of our predicament. However," and he turned to pointedly bore his stare at the old man, "time must be made to point blame at the source of the problem. I have here in my hand records showing intentional negligence and willful disruption of the operations of this battleship. Not only have these actions been grossly inflicted on the personnel of this ship, they have been aimed at discrediting the very corporation this ship serves."

The old man sprang to his feet, his hands slamming the table in front of him, anger sputtering from his lips, his words coming in punctuated bursts of cannon fire. "Who . . . would . . . do . . . such . . . a . . . thing?" Flames shot from his eyes as they danced from man to man. "Is he here in this room? Show him to me!" Furor painting his face scarlet, he quivered with rage, fully prepared to personally tear the one revealed limb from limb.

A long pregnancy preceded Bofsky's answer. Taking a deep breath, his reply soon known to all in the room, only the old man left struggling to understand, he slung his response before the others. "The only one with the authority to sign each of these direct orders, the most potent of us, the supreme power with the ability to attempt to hide it all, is *there*." Pointing an accusing hand at the old man, he yelled, "You!"

He strode forward, slamming the record crystal on the table, as if daring the old man to deny all that was inside. Of course he would deny it. He knew nothing of it. However, the veri-sign would clinch his downfall. Then, with the proper pressure on the proper men, this ship would be Bofsky's.

Standing back, once again appearing carefully neutral, he waited. The old man grabbed the crystal, slamming it into a data reader, horror writing itself across his face as the glass spoke its tale to all. The old man knew the veri-sign would not be questioned, and the facts on the glass would stand as indisputable. Shrinking into his chair, he became a rag doll as he was carried from the room, his illustrious career tattered in seconds.

Rapid-fire responses scattered from the walls, finally settling onto one man. All others turned to the messenger still waiting to do their bidding.

"What else do you know, OverCapt'n Bofsky? This information has certainly come to you over everyone else. Can you also tell us the solution we seek?"

"If the good sers will permit, I might have a suggestion for you to try. However, I would very much like one concession from this group should my guess provide the solution to this catastrophe. I note this vessel is now without the services of a capt'n. My offer is for an acceptance of my immediate placement in that position should my information be of service to you . . ."

Two men, both clearly superior to Bofsky, stepped forward in an effort to interrupt the heinous offer, gesticulating wildly, only able to speak in gulps of choking breath, their attempts challenging his precocious affront.

"Wait, wait, my good men. I know your protests, both of you senior to my position and due to move up as the old man moves out. Consider. You have worked to resolve this crisis for some time. How much progress has been made? Any?" He knew better. He had the only cure in his hand. "If the solution I have been working to effect these past units is unsuccessful, bump me back to underpriv't. What can you lose? The alternative is to sit, send out an emergency beacon, and hope we can survive the many sevendays until help arrives. Then we all get bumped back to beneath the military arm's lowest commissioned offic'r. What can my offer hurt?"

He stepped forward, his hand displaying the second crystal, the cure already written, waiting to be plugged into the ship's feed.

Knowing blackmail when it was offered, the crystal was taken from him, the deal sealed with the deed. The lights were back on before Bofsky made it to his quarters, the capt'ncy now his. Looking in the mirror, he tried it on for size. Capt-Gen'l Willane Bard Bofsky, look how far you've come. Then he flashed the grin of the truly evil, knowing nothing could stop him now.

Study 16

Compiled by: Ne'rosi El'ganti, SSM.rl.sub.adjunct, UNAS
Subject: Willane Bofsky
Location: Ev'ntu'lLandfall, MC Military Academy Ship
Earth-Reference Date: 2761 A.D. (O.E. Standard)

GRADUATION DAY! Willane walked along the corridor wall, his proximity waking the glassine. As its molecules shifted, the light of a thousand stars poured through. Dressed in jet black, blending with the blackness of uninterrupted space just outside, he felt invisible to passersby.

Thoughts tumbled in his head, private thoughts, arrogant thoughts. They were the beginnings of plans that would be put into place this night. For many years he had been invisible. Now he had made himself otherwise. Once this day was complete, he would be on the first leg of reaching his goal, starstrike class battleship capt'n. He had now narrowed his choices to three possible commands. By this evening, one of them would be his. The capt'n wouldn't even know he had lost his ship, but that wouldn't change reality. The ship would already be Willane's.

He reached down, straightening the cuff of his overjacket sleeve. Leaning into the glassine, he saw an incoming battleship coloring the edge of the clearwall, one of many arriving for this evening's ceremonies. With narrowed eyes, he evaluated the inky blackness of the vessel as if its command were already his.

"AH, MY GOOD BOY. Do come in, Bofsky. This is a fine day for this academy. MegaCorp will someday entrust the future of a battleship to one such as you, one with the makings of a captgen'l, for sure." The grizzled old man walked up behind Willane, a hand slapping him sharply on the shoulder, nearly flinging Willane's drink from his mouth.

Old fool! Turning from the refreshments, an unctuous smile already writing itself on his face, Willane acknowledged the offending superior offic'r.

"Ser. How good to see you again! There have been many simulated battle maneuvers since you joined us last. May I assume you are here to pick the best of the best?" Ah, he mused, to have reached at least this level of equality, no longer to have to stop and salute, all other concerns forgotten, just because some old fart happens to wander by. Graduation day. He had tasted this for years. "You know better than anyone else that this vessel trains more captgen'ls than any other in the fleet. I happen to know that you, Ser, in fact, trained on this very vessel."

Impressed evaluation fleeting across the weathered face, the old man placed his hand on Willane's shoulder. "Not many people know that, my boy. Not only has this ship been through two retrofits since my day, even the name is no longer the same. We used only number and letter configurations in my day. None of this 'named-for-so-and-so-personage' that you see now. Give me the good old days, anytime. Now take you, Bofsky." The old man walked up to the refreshments, taking a small amount of sweetmeats. "The future belongs to you," the old man continued. "You have proven yourself one who can set a ship on its end, control the rabble serving under you, and make a name for yourself. In fact, I would be surprised if you didn't become the youngest capt'n of a starstrike class in the history of MegaCorp. Come with me, my boy. I'll give you some training, whip you into the man your father Bofsky must have hoped you'd become. What do you say, boy? Care to have a go onboard?"

A glass raised as if in a toast, his words prompting an internal response in Willane the captgen'l would never know of until it was too late, he smiled as he replied, "It will be an honor to serve with one such as yourself, Captgen'l."

Even as the smile painted itself on his face, he fought down bile at the mention of his long-forgotten father and the suddenly intense memory of the man who had taken his place, the man who had created a personal cesspool for the boy he had been, his skin still bearing scars from the since dead man's fists.

Although torn with internal turmoil, he reached out to grasp a proffered hand. The man was an old fool. He had just made Willane's decision for him. Yes, he would join him on his ship. But just wait. He would prove him right. He would become the youngest captgen'l in the fleet, the capt'n of this man's ship. The only problem was, though, the old man might or might not live to see it.

Willane nodded, his acceptance confirmed as he clicked his heels.

More congratulations flowed that night, newly minted lieute'nts soaking up praise, and basking in the perceived assurances that the ships of their choice were theirs for the asking. As the events ground on, many received that assurance. However, only one bore the confident assurance of a capt'ncy, even if that capt'ncy was only within the plans already percolating through his mind. But, there was no doubt. The plans were well in place. The capt'ncy *would* be his.

Willane would make sure of that.

HIS BAGS PACKED, his stor'lok freshly empty, a new over-uniform on his shoulders, Willane looked back at his empty uppercadet quarters. Like it never even happened, all those years. What a punk I was when I first came aboard! I'll be glad to leave that punk and all those years behind.

Clearing the lock memory, freeing the door for whoever would be taking his place, he let it shut behind him. His feet carried him down the corridor, past the events of his life aboardship, his mind quick to discard each memory as nonessential: the freshfaced inductee calculating the easiest way to win; the arrogant youth reveling in his new-found power abusing the undercadets; the boy they had left dead on the utility corridor floor; the friends he had sacrificed. They were no more than the steps he'd had to take to get to the top, useful for the moment, forgotten when their usefulness was gone, leaving the boy he had been behind. As Willane had grown weaker and smaller, the man called Bofsky had taken his place. He was taller, perhaps, his shoulders maybe a bit farther back. However, it was the hard look on his face those around him noticed that day as he showed up at the lift, the look that made them step back a bit, giving the new Bofsky a bit more room than they might have otherwise, understanding just by looking that he had changed, become someone stronger, someone to reckon with, perhaps someone they didn't *want* to reckon with. Bofsky knew where he was going, and although they weren't sure why, that scared them.

They were right to have been scared. Only a fool would serve with Bofsky and not be wary.

Study 17

Compiled by: Ne'rosi El'ganti, SSM.rl.sub.adjunct, UNAS
Subject: Willane Bofsky
Location: Ev'ntu'lLandfall, MC Military Academy Ship
Earth-Reference Date: 2760 A.D. (O.E. Standard)

WILLANE HELD the message crystal and the words it contained, his heart pounding and sweat beading his brow; and the feeling of powerlessness that came when he was not in control assaulted him once again. The message telling what they'd found, intercepted by him, unknown to the others, pushed his thoughts faster than he could think them. He dropped the crystal into the recycle slot, its hated words still fading from the glass in front of him.

Thoughts raced from his brain as his fingers grabbed new images from the glass, drawing them out, the words forming the images into what he wanted them to be. A message log changed *here*. Shunt that order to *there*. Reroute *that* duty assignment record to a different date and time.

His anxiety fading into a new sense of euphoria, the sacrifices he was making giving him a renewed sense of power, he continued his mission of misinformation. After all, the sacrifices weren't going to be *his*. Uncaring who fell into the abyss, he only knew that he, Willane, would no longer be the one to draw the short stick.

WILLANE STOOD and watched from a distance as the message crystals were delivered to his three friends. He shook his head. Friends? No, suckers were what they were. They didn't even know what they were accepting in those crystals. They'd had some good times. He'd admit that. Too bad it was their time to go down. He stepped from the corridor back into the cubicle.

"WILLANE, NO!" Overcadet Steph'ni B'ltn Renhant's eyes were wild, and he grabbed his friend by the front of his overjacket, forcing him to stumble backwards. "You know this isn't the way it went. What did you do? *Why* did you do this? You're the one who convinced the rest of us to go downside. Jer'son and Barn't would've jumped on any idea you threw out. I only went because you three were my friends. Willane, tell them the truth."

A uniformed AP, dressed all in black with the requisite MC emblazoned across his chest, yanked Renhant's upper arm hard, pulling him away. His hand was huge, and it seemed the uppercadet's arm would burst with the force.

"Keep your place, scum! I want to wipe myself on the likes of you." The words were hissed in Renhant's ear, and then he was yanked once more.

Renhant, filled with despair, knew what this meant, that it would have been better to take blame for the girl. Despite his efforts to push the events away, he pictured Zen'ri. He had run from the scene scared, but the blood, and the unseen, final jerking of his body that must have the boy's ultimate, desperate cry for continued life was his deed along with the rest, and it had sucked Zen'ri's life away. That knowledge alone was a torment. The boy had helped them, and someone should have stayed with him. He might have lived, then. None of this had to have happened. But he had run with the others. He had left him to die alone.

All academy trainees knew the ultimate violation. Rule number 832.75: Intentional injury to any legally owned Mega-Corp military personnel with the end result of death will result in permanent posting on prisonplanet Rant.

His eyes wild, he wrested his arm from the AP and leaped for Willane. He grabbed his lapels and shook his friend's overjacket. "Willane, we can all beat this. We *could've* beaten this. We don't understand."

Willane's eyes explored the desperation on his former friend's face. His lips shaping themselves into a response, he gently pushed him away.

"This is the way it's gotta be, Renhant. Someone had to go down. It wasn't going to be me. You were a good friend for a few standards. However, that time has come and gone." He stepped away, his disdain for Renhant's display, the desperation he saw on the other boy's face, written across his own. "I'll be there for the inquiry. Just know this is the way it has to be."

Renhant watched Willane walk away, finality in his footsteps, with no leeway for reminiscing about past times, shared events, or the future of people he'd clearly already written off. He felt his gut twist, and he could only picture Rant as a black hole sucking up the rest of his life.

"LET THE RECORD SHOW that Overcadets Renhant, Barn't, and Jer'son are present for this inquiry regarding the fatal injury and death of Cadet Farbr d'Sen Zen'ri. All rise."

The three uppercadets stood in a line, shoulders touching, as one in the precision of their movements, and also as one in their despair, their faces of stone masking their inner turmoil. The flick of their eyes toward the traitor and back again was all that revealed their overwhelming fear.

"Overcadet Willane Bard Bofsky, please step forward and state the nature of your accusation."

"Yes, Ser." Sharp in his dress blacks, the emblem WC emblazoned on his chest, Willane strode purposefully forward, snapping his heels together as he stopped. He began to tell the story.

It was not the truth, of course.

When the message crystal had opened up its volcanic upheaval, he'd been the first to understand what it meant. He knew they'd all go down, and there was no purpose in not saving himself. So, he rewrote the truth, and that was the truth he told on that day, the truth not as it had really happened, but as he had made it to be, the truth he had created. He told the truth that set him free at the sacrifice of his friends. He did it well. He did it convincingly. By the time he was finished, he had even begun to believe it himself.

WILLANE ONCE AGAIN sat on the bench, his three ex-friends again shoulder to shoulder on the opposite side of the room.

"All rise."

Reassembled, the victorious and the broken, friendships thrown away and friendships renewed, the four stood reunited a final time, events now positioned to vault each life far from its previous path.

"Renhant, Barn't and Jer'son, this board of inquiry has reached a decision in this matter. Your actions have been found despicable. Rather than face consequences for a simple planetside escapade, consequences of which would have been stern but comparatively mild to what you now face, the three of you planned and executed a deed so reprehensible, it brings shame on this training academy. For willfully conspiring to entrap and injure unto death one Fabr d'Sen Zen'ri, this inquiry board sentences you to a permanent posting on Rant. No appeal of this decision will be permitted. Transport to a waiting jumpship has been arranged. You will not return to your quarters. You will be escorted for immediate boarding and transport to your new posting."

A slump of realization was all the acknowledgement the review board received. As the three were escorted down the corridor, Overcadet Je'main Winterd Barn't stole a glance at his fellow victims through red-rimmed eyes. "Posting, my backside. That's MegaCorp cover-speak for sentencing. Our life-posting is a life sentence, and we're not allowed to tell anyone. Shipped direct, prepackaged, with overnight delivery."

"Did you see Bofsky?" asked Overcadet Fal'dera Hult Jer'son bitterly. "We may deserve this, but Bofsky? He's coming out of this with hero all over him. Ancient gods, he set all this up. Why isn't *he* here?"

Under his breath, Renhant whispered, "He'll get his own. Just wait. I'll see to it. Somehow. Someday." He stood facing the landing bay doors, its internal pressure cycling from red to green, as Jer'son and Barn't stepped up behind him. "Just wait," he repeated to no one in particular.

ONCE THE THREE BOYS were escorted from the room, the review board turned its attention to Willane. "Overcadet Bofsky, please step forward. This board has noted your invaluable participation in bringing to light this incredible series of events that culminated in the death of Cadet Zen'ri. Upon completion of your time here at the academy, this board of inquiry has determined that you be offered a position on the starstrike class battleship of your choice. Do you wish to accept this board's offer?"

Starstrike class! His heart slammed excitement through his veins. A direct appointment! Hiding his anticipation behind a steadiness he could barely control, he spoke.

"Sers, I would be honored to accept. Service to the corporation has been my life's goal. Thank you, Sers."

He turned, new plans already churning in his head, the price paid well worth the cost, especially since the ones who had paid were now on their way out of his life forever.

Study 18

Compiled by: Ed'th Ze'pliinth, SSM.rl.sub.adjunct, UNAS
Subject: N'jent City Skyport
Location: Winter's World
Earth-Reference Date: 2760 A.D. (O.E. Standard)

One Week Earlier

THIRD DUTY OFFIC'R ROVEK laid the data crystal on the desk. Beside it she laid a paper report. Why her commanding offic'r preferred archaic hard copy, she would never know. "Ser, there are no matches. All *Ev'ntu'lLandfall* offic'r DNA files are included. None match the four from the sky-walker.

No personnel have been requisitioned for questioning. Case can be considered closed unless new information is uncovered, pending your approval."

"Excellent, Rovek. By the way, it would seem that some additional funds have been located. These funds are due to be rolled back into the general accounts fund if not spent in the next ten days. Have you any special projects in mind?"

Her brain flashed into overdrive, an internal grin lighting her neurons. "Yes, ser! There has been this one project that I feel would certainly benefit the force." She presented her request, knowing this *splurge* was the benefit that made all the grubbing dirt work worthwhile.

Study 19

Compiled by: Ne'rosi El'ganti, SSM.rl.sub.adjunct, UNAS
Subject: Willane Bofsky
Location: Ev'ntu'lLandfall, MC Military Academy Ship
Earth-Reference Date: 2760 A.D. (O.E. Standard)

The Day Before That

"BOFSKY? ARE YOU THERE?"

Lying in the dark, Willane listened to the voice. Just a few more shipboard units of time, and the vessel would depart. Nervous anticipation of what could occur in the intervening units kept his voice frozen.

Again, the inquiry, "Bofsky?"

He brought the lights to a dim glow, peering at the intruder from his bunk, still in the clothes from the escapade, his filched offic'r overjacket crumpled around him.

"Yeah, Jer'son? What's so important? My brain's kinda busy now and all."

"You haven't heard, then. Ship's pulling downship lists, looking for offic'rs that spent time planetside. *Us.* Willane, they're looking for *us.*" His desperation had pulled a more familiar term of address from his lips, one for which Willane didn't especially care. "Ship got a requisition for DNA records over the ship-link before the feed went down. We're running all offic'r DNA records and shipping the info down planetside, stat. Willane, they're looking for *us.*"

Bofsky sat up. "We're not on the offic'r's list. None of us. If they send the profiles of the offic'rs, they won't get a match. It's only a few units 'til departure. That gives us a little time."

"But, Willane." Jer'son looked worried. "Remember that adhesive? When I got it, I had to let someone know what it was for. Zen'ri, in the stores. He knows it was for a pass. What if he puts it all together? We've got to make sure." Nervousness twitching his body, he looked toward the door, as if it might burst open, them both carried away to be sent planetside. "Renhant and Barn't are getting him to meet them in the utility corridor, feeding him a line. He'll go. He'll be scared not to. Dog-sheesh, I'm scared. Let's go, Willane, and make sure the ship's gone before Zen'ri can rat."

Together the boys made their way to their secret place, the long-stolen key code their way in, not knowing that with each step, their hole was being dug ever deeper.

"YOU FOUR. Hey, you shouldn't even have a key code to this corridor." Cadet Farbr d'Sen Zen'ri turned to look at each of them. Realization dawning, remembering the pass, he drew a deep breath, his skin flushing. "*You.* That's what all the flurry has been about. There *were* no offic'rs offship that period. That's why records keep coming up incomplete. They *are* incomplete. That adhesive you wanted." He spat his next words at Jer'son. "You said it was for a damaged pass. You forged a pass. That's supposed to be impossible. They're foolproof. But you found a way. You must have glued half of an expired pass with half of a good one. You did that down there on the planet, what they are looking for DNA about. I have to go and let them know."

He began moving toward the door, only to find his way blocked.

"We can't let you do that, Zen'ri. I'm sorry. What would it look like for four academy uppercadets, just several thirtydays from graduation, to be implicated in some unsavory planetside politics? Just look at it from MegaCorp's viewpoint. That's what they'd think. Now, once the ship is underway, everything will be okay. You'll go back to ship's stores, and we'll graduate, promoted to a battle cruiser. We'll never meet again, and life will be fine and dandy." Willane pushed himself closer to the scared cadet, his presence making his point ominously clear.

Sheer desperation overpowering his fear, Zen'ri suddenly bolted, heading for the door. In a heart-stopping frenzy of motion, his four subjugators also leaped, his escape inconceivable. Arms scrambling and legs flying, it was suddenly over. All four friends showed damage, but Zen'ri couldn't tell. He lay, his head against the corner of a metal flange, his eyes twitching open then slowly closing, rapid-fire electrical charges causing his body's muscles to dance the tired dance of the puppet as it leaps across the stage, no longer firmly attached to its strings.

As the four teenagers watched, a pool of red began to seep from beneath Zen'ri's head. Damage was done that could never be undone. Turning to look at one another, knowing they could never return to this place, they, too, bolted—this time with no one to stop them. Certainly not Zen'ri, although his muscles continued to run their tired dance until his eyes stayed open for good, his life-blood finally exhausted on the utility corridor floor.

Study 20

Compiled by: Ed'th Ze'pliinth, SSM.rl.sub.adjunct, UNAS
Subject: N'jent City Skyport
Location: Winter's World
Earth-Reference Date: 2760 A.D. (O.E. Standard)

Earlier that Same Day

SENIOR DUTY OFFIC'R Boggaletti deTronitti turned the report around on the native ha'aksewood table, his finger on one corner, using the slickness of the wood's finish to spin the papers in a repeating 360-degree loop, his thoughts hard at work mulling over the detailed facts, incomplete though they were, included on the report. A sky-walker dead. Lowlife they might be, they were frowned on by the more conservative of his planet's inhabitants. However, he felt they were absolutely necessary. Working diligently over his term of duty, he had managed to salve the locals' concerns by keeping the sky-walkers centered around the skyport.

Funny, he mused, how a job takes a name. The sky-walkers, so looked down upon, here to service the military stationed in the sky. Walker had to do with their ever-present lack of ground transport, walking to their assignations.

Another realization caused him to hit his head with his hand. Of course! Ship's personnel. That ship, the *Ev'ntu'lLandfall,* was still in orbit, due to depart overnight. That had to be it.

Offic'r deTronitti slammed the comm button with the flat of his hand. "Rovek? That trainer, the *Ev'ntu'lLandfall,* can you get the downship log of offic'rs who've been planetside this maneuver? I need DNA matches for all of them. We can't hold the ship, so that only gives us until tonight. I believe departure is set for 23:00 L.A.T. This is stat. Can do?"

His hand releasing the comm button, he turned to his grid access, barely acknowledging the response he knew would snap from the comm. His mind was already focused on the four sets of DNA recovered from the sky-walker, as he studied the glass, touching it, pulling the information forward, finding just the facts he needed.

The response filtered in, barely heard. "Consider it done, ser. The search is already on the grid. I'm sending a requisition on live ship-link requesting their copy of same. That should be faster as long as they haven't broken the feed. Will be back with list and DNA soon. Rovek out."

THIRD DUTY OFFIC'R ROVEK spoke into her submike, grateful for the senior duty offic'r's willingness to splurge with local enforcement funds from time to time. She *loved* her submike, and being able to communicate with the planet-wide data banks hands-free made her job so much easier. The information grid was *hers* for the taking.

Her grin shining, she stepped into the corridor, off to make sure her superior was thoroughly pleased with her results, knowing his *splurges* seemed to run commensurate with the success she showed.

Study 21

Compiled by: Ne'rosi El'ganti, SSM.rl.sub.adjunct, UNAS
Subject: Willane Bofsky
Location: Ev'ntu'lLandfall, MC Military Academy Ship
Earth-Reference Date: 2760 A.D. (O.E. Standard)

During the Previous Week

94

"HOW LONG HAVE WE been on this ship, here in the academy? The training commanders never let any of the cadets go planetside. Barn't, Jer'son, even you, Renhant. You've been here the longest, too. We're all uppercadets, every one of us. None of us have gone planetside, not even once. We can do this, men."

Willane bore his stare into each pair of eyes sitting in the group, the surrounding lighting dim, all but their faces cloaked in darkness. Overcadet Barn't was the baby of the group, the smallest. He would join in the plan because he was afraid of being left behind. Overcadet Jer'son would jump onboard just for the fun of it. Willane already counted on that. It was Overcadet Renhant who might have second thoughts. However, Willane was determined to get planetside, what with stories filtering in of women just waiting to take MegaCorp offic'rs into their arms, relieving them of some of their hard-earned credits.

"Men, what'll it be? Spend the next several thirtydays wishing to be men, or embark on a wild excursion with a wild woman, turning us into men the way it's supposed to happen?" Willane cast a hard glance to Renhant, daring him to go against this.

"They can strip us of our academy advancements and send us to grunt the front line for something like this, Bofsky. You know that. Shrinking varneys, we all do. This is *crazy*. Just a few thirtydays for most of us, eleven for you, Barn't, and we'll have offic'r status. Planetside is our due, then." His eyes pleaded with the other two of the group for support. Instead of common sense and reasoned thought, he found eager anticipation from boys who considered themselves men, so they thought of themselves, all of seventeen standards old, ready to expend energies they often found unmanageable and overwhelming.

Accepting defeat when it wouldn't quit shaking him by the collar, he dropped his head.

"Good man, Renhant." Willane reached to him, clapping him on the shoulder. "You see how it has to be, how it always had to be."

LOOKING THROUGH THE GLASSINE wall at the ship fading from view, Renhant leaned over to Willane and whispered, "How did you get that pass? There's no way you can dup them. They're foolproof. Give, Bofsky."

"Here," Willane handed the pass to him. "Run your fingernail down the centerline. Tell me what you feel." The pass was their golden key to the world below, one only offic'rs were ever given. Without it, they were stuck on the *Ev'ntu'lLandfall* until graduation. They had, in fact, already been trapped there all their lives, it seemed. This was a taste of freedom.

"Hey," he grinned. "A seam. Two cards put together?"

"All too easy." Willane took the pass back, slipping it down inside his offic'r overjacket. "My only challenge was getting my hands on an adhesive that wouldn't give way while it was being inspected and our escapade approved. Thanks, Jer'son." He slapped his friend's back. "You are a life saver."

Leaning his head back, exposing a neck only recently exposed to shaving utensils, he laughed out loud, glad the transport was nearly empty on this scheduled down-time supply replenishment run.

"HOW MANY CREDITS?" Willane stood listening to the establishment's bouncer, then he made a sour face, turning to his fellow uppercadets. "We've a problem. Between the four of us, there's not enough credits to get even two girls. We need to get together and make a plan."

"Plan? Are you going to steal more credits, Bofsky?" Disgusted at the prospect of his frustrated eagerness going unsatisfied, Willane's friend continued, "Or do they just come out of the sky? Better, let's all reach into the depths of our magic pockets and bring out a magic credit crystal. Great plinkerpups, all that work, these offic'r overjackets, the time we spent planning is all for nothing. Tomorrow night I'll still be on my own in the showers."

"No, no. Wait." He motioned them over to a bench on the street. "Look at this, men. See those doors, all those guys going in and out? We only need one girl. I'll pool our credits and go back."

"Whoa." As a group, the other three stepped back from the bench. "Why you?"

"You don't understand. Once I get the room, I'll let you guys come in, too. I'll make sure the lights are down low. What'll she know? Just that I like it four times."

Sure enough, the open-air establishment stretched along the backside of a low building, and satisfied faces, as well as somewhat rumpled clothing, could be seen exiting various, numbered doors. It seemed Willane's plan might just work.

"Bofsky." Barn't punched his friend's shoulder with a relieved laugh. "Try eight times. I'm going for at least two, myself." Laughter erupting from the others as he spoke, he reached into his pocket, pulling out his share of the necessary funds. When they saw the credits moving to Willane, the other two joined in, wanting to be in on this most special of nights.

THE FIRST THREE TEENAGERS sat on the bench, watching the door, waiting for their final cohort to join them, sated looks of satisfaction settled on their disheveled features. They laughed as Renhant stumbled through the distant door, his overjacket under his arm, shoes in his hand, fastening his pants as he ran to them, clearly frantic.

"Afraid you'll get caught? Or were you unable to, eh-hem, perform satisfactorily, Renhant? Own up, now." Barn't laughed, expecting a rousing rendition, veering from the truth only in the most improbable matters of the event.

"Hey, you! There's a problem back there." Renhant struggled to get the words out. "A big problem." He blanched, and his eyes danced with dismay.

"Don't twit around with us, Renhant. What do you mean, a problem?" Tension laced the words. This night was one for fun, not problems. They certainly didn't need any of those, not with being off the ship without authorization.

"Well, I went in, catching the door just as you were leaving, Jer'son. You looked at me, jerking your head to show me to go on in. Remember? Well, I did. Just like you said. There she was, waiting. I thought she was ready for me, so I got my clothes off quick as I could. Man, was I ready. So ready. Like never before."

"Enough of that. Paint us a picture we want to have in our heads, and you're not in it, trust me."

"Well, there I was, ready, and I climbed on the platform. You know how it was pretty dark. Well, afterwards, I began to wonder. By all the ancients, I think she was dead the entire time."

"C'mon, Renhant. If you were in there with her and didn't go again, *you're* dead." Jer'son laughed at the image, the joke on them well played.

"Guys, I propped the door open. I was with a dead person. Go see. We killed her." Renhant's face growing paler as he talked, he suddenly sat and began to shiver. "She's dead. Maybe I killed her."

Willane turned to Jer'son. "He's spooked. Go run over and see. Come right back." He turned back to Renhant, gently slapping his face. "It's okay, Renhant. Jer'son's going to check. Don't sweat it."

FOUR PANICKED BOYS, barely seventeen, turning into men

in more ways than one, sitting together, although not really, in the dark on a shuttle, returning to the hoped safety of the ship, watching the falling planet through the clearwall. None were speaking, the overwhelming tension separating them into lonely, frightened worlds of their own making.

Below, in a lonely room, in a world of her own, perhaps even of her own making, a dead woman lay, four boys' spent manhood waiting in her patient embrace.

Study 22

Compiled by: Ne'rosi El'ganti, SSM.rl.sub.adjunct, UNAS
Subject: Willane Bofsky
Location: Ev'ntu'lLandfall, MC Military Academy Ship
Earth-Reference Date: 2757 A.D. (O.E. Standard)

"HERE." WILLANE SLAPPED the wad of paper credits on the bunk. "What have you others got?"

The boys, taller in the past year, impatient to be filled out as men, gathered in, dropping their own share. Eyes glued, they eagerly ate up the progress as Willane counted the total amount, dividing it into four.

Handing some to each boy, he grinned up at them. "Just a little organization, boys. Now look at how well we're doing. This is great, taking from the newbies, giving to the needy—us!" Letting a laugh escape from his belly, he quizzed, "Ready for a game? A good bet is the only one in town."

The boys crowded together on the bunk, throwing their *hoar-vlomg* cubes on the sleeping pad stretching between them. Stirring the cubes with the magnetic field inherent in his hand, Willane ran his fingers over them, causing them to rise into the air and dance. He then shook his wrist, triggering them to fall back to the bunk.

The credits made the risks of the game riveting. The newbies made the credits possible. The good thing was, there were always more newbies on the way.

Study 23

Compiled by: Ne'rosi El'ganti, SSM.rl.sub.adjunct, UNAS
Subject: Willane Bofsky
Location: Ev'ntu'lLandfall, MC Military Academy Ship
Earth-Reference Date: 2756 A.D. (O.E. Standard)

WILLANE'S HANDS AND ARMS were lead pipes and bricks, his heart a throbbing recirculating pump. He wore wet rags for clothes. He didn't notice, though, or rather he did, but he blamed it on something else.

He swelled with anger at the Bel'age counselor.

Air rushed in and out, scraping and clawing his lungs as it did. The air wasn't his enemy, though. Someone else was.

He hated Gr'gan, hated that he didn't know the others who had tormented him.

The memory of that night in the showers drove him hard. He pressed himself forward even faster, and his overtaxed body groaned with the effort, moving ahead, maintaining what he hoped was a lead.

"Hey, newbie." A laughing voice assaulted his single-minded determination. "You can stop. The run is over. It sure looks good for you. You passed all the others and came in first. That's some good form, there." A strong hand slapped him on his sweaty shoulder, the skin bare. "You've made a good start, but you haven't proven yourself, yet. If you want to stay, get back with the others."

WILLANE LAY IN HIS BUNK, sleep long ago chased away

by the escapades of the night.

A trick. That was all it had been. He had known it. He had told himself the training commanders would have been there. He had known! He should have told them no. Secretly, though, he was glad he hadn't. He'd won, even at the wrestling, taking down the others and getting the marks on his shoulder.

What he best remembered best were the girls. The priv'tshorts. Wrestling, his skin against the others' skin. The *feel* of it. He did wrestle the big girl, pushed his leg *there*, right on her chest, on *those*. He would always remember that. His last thought before the lights in the dorm came on, the bells shrilling their wakeup song, was how good it was to feel like a man now.

"All out!" A deep, grownup voice intoned. "Ten minutes to roll call. Today we try for our skill levels. Be thankful for a good night's rest. It will be the last one for a good, long time."

The voice faded as Willane's feet touched the cold floor. As he blearily staggered to his stor'lok bin for clothes, his only cheering thought was that everyone else was just this tired, also.

That and the thought of the girl, of course.

WILLANE PEERED AROUND THE CORNER, watching the three bigger boys picking on the newbie. Their target, his eyes welling with tears, stood taking it, the boys much bigger than him. Finally, one of the boys hit and laughed, the newbie falling to the floor, and then they all walked away.

Willane's breath coming fast, he raced from his spot and *kicked* the newbie, running off as quickly as he could. Darting around a corner, stopping and leaning against a wall, and standing very still with his heart throbbing, he exulted in the *rush* of feelings coursing through his body, the feelings of *before* in the utility corridor, the new ache that was a feeling of pleasant pressure growing just where the trunk of his body met his legs.

Again, he thought. The feeling had to happen again. Newly awakening sensations of power weakened his knees, the sudden, overwhelming tingle flooding up into his groin.

He unconsciously held his hand in front of him, kneading the fabric of his trousers with damp fingers as his breathing came faster and faster. In that moment, he knew this *would* happen again. He'd make sure of it. Whether he meant the kicking of the newbie, or the sensations in his knees, he couldn't have said. The two had become so twisted together that they now seemed one and the same.

As he turned, there they were. Laughing, one boy stuck out his hand, grabbing Willane's. "We saw you with that newbie. Good going. Too bad he didn't have any credits. Sometimes they do. By the way, I'm Jer'son, and this is Renhant and Barn't."

Returning the handshake, the pact was complete. What had been three were now four.

Study 24

Compiled by: Ne'rosi El'ganti, SSM.rl.sub.adjunct, UNAS
Subject: Willane Bofsky
Location: Resort World
Earth-Reference Date: 2756 A.D. (O.E. Standard)

Thirty Days Earlier

WILLANE FLICKED the blade of the small knife open, watching it flash in the overhead lights. "Gr'gan, you and your goons had my eyes covered, but I could still hear. You think I didn't know you, couldn't tell from your voice? I haven't found the others, but I bet you'll be glad to tell me. At least

102

you will by the time I finish."

"Whoa, Willane." Jerking away, Gr'gan began pushing himself along the floor, away from the angry knife hanging over him.

"You should feel afraid," Willane sneered with distain. He moved forward menacingly.

"I didn't know that was you. You gotta believe me, Willane. We're friends, you and me."

"Friends! Liar! I could've died. Unlucky for you, I didn't. Nobody came back to help me. Nobody. You're not my friend." Owning too much anger to really care, he raised his arm to vent, to bleed his rage on the boy at his feet. As his coiled muscles tensed to spring, something sudden and tight clamped his wrist.

"So, that's where my lab key went. An old-fashioned security method to have even at this ancient, worn-out school, but easy to track. This little altercation is over."

With a flick of the teacher's hand, the knife was taken from Willane, all the credits from the big man now truly gone, forever wasted.

THE STAMP SLAMMED DOWN on the form. The old-fashioned black ink on the old-fashioned paper document would have been amusing had it not matched the modern one on the attached record crystal. The information was the same. FORCED INDUCTION, MEGACORP MILITARY TRAINING ARM, with a single name underneath. *Willane Bard Bofsky.*

Study 25

Compiled by: Ne'rosi El'ganti, SSM.rl.sub.adjunct, UNAS
Subject: Willane Bofsky

Location: Resort World
Earth-Reference Date: 2755 A.D. (O.E. Standard)

THE COUNSELOR AT PUBLIC ACADEMY, Bel'age, stepped back from the observation window and the glowering boy on the other side. This was going to be a hard one, he knew. He picked up a data crystal, sliding it into the viewer, the glass bringing up details of a life of misery he would not wish on the most despicable student in the school—and gods knew, in a publicly-funded cesspool such as this one, there were plenty to go around.

Sighing, looking at the display scrolling on the glass, he reviewed the details once again with the hope, vain he suspected, that one positive aspect of this boy's life just might have slipped through and attached itself to the file since he last viewed it. That *thread* of hope was better than none.

GENDER: *male*
LEGAL NAME: *Willane Bard Bofsky*
NICKNAMES: *goes by Willy*
PLACE OF BIRTH: *Resort World, System 118B43.6*
DATE OF BIRTH: *8.34.345 local*
PARENTS: *Ten'f Ren Bofsky, d. Usrla Note Bofsky, d. Rod'ln Wldn Wred'rn, step, d.*
NEXT OF KIN: *none on Resort*
GENERAL HEALTH: *minor bone damage from repeated breakage, otherwise good*
EDUCATION: *standard local norm to age twelve with some gaps due to pattern of physical abuse*
HISTORY (BE BRIEF. THIS IS JUST A GENERAL OVERVIEW OF FILES):
-Parents moved to local system on a farming contract before above-named's birth
-Father killed in farming accident, age three

104

-Stepfather, marriage not filed, came on scene shortly thereafter; pattern of physical abuse started to establish itself, confirmed by local school medreports and spotty medcenter records (mostly broken bones)
-Turned in to local police organization by stepfather for theft, later withdrawn, age nine
-Both custodians (stepfather and natural mother) killed and above-named boy found severely beaten, age ten
-Admitted to Public MedCenter #13 for medical treatment and recuperation, age ten
-Assigned to Public Academy, Bel'age, as a charity ward case, age eleven

He laughed sourly. For this one, there was no hope at all.

"CAN YOU TELL where we are? You know this place. You've been here before." The voice was lilting, teasing, as if stringing Willane along. Then it turned sour, its tone rasping and filthy. "We know how to make you scream. Scream for your mommy, little girl."

Willane doubled over as something hit him in the stomach. Then came the *pain* in his back, the hitting making him arch with the *hurt,* and a strange hand twisting his arm, squeezing harder, hurting. Just as he began to gain control of the pain, his feet were kicked out from under him, throwing him on his side, the muscle hurting, causing the searing pain down *there.*

More kicks began, the hurting becoming worse.

"Stop," he begged. He had never cried out when the big man hit him, not after the first time, when the man hit him even harder. This time was different. He couldn't see, couldn't *expect,* couldn't *plan* for the pain.

Soon it was slippery on the cold floor, whether from sweat or blood. With the pain he thought it might be blood, but he couldn't care—there was too much *pain.*

"Enough," a new voice cried. Then it ended, the kicking, the beating.

But not the pain.

Willane, curled on his side, breathing in jerky gasps, the *why* so much of the pain, still hurting *bad*. Then it started up again. Hands grabbed him, jerking him up unevenly and tossing him under running water, landing him roughly, his burning skin making a slapping sound as it hit the slick floor, the blindfold offering his head little protection, still hurting when it hit the wall. The water was *cold*, the controls too far to reach to change. So *cold*. He shivered under the needle-jets, the pain a new pain to add to the others.

Willane lay for a time under the water, waiting, the pain subsiding, becoming manageable. He reached his hand to see, to clear his face. He blinked, the light harsh to long-closed pupils, then clearing with only the water to be blinked from his eyes.

They were gone.

He relaxed his skin against the cold of the floor, looking down at himself, now seeing the red in the water around him, and the red on the floor nearby.

His senses remembering every word, every *sound* of that night, he knew he'd know them. Just give him time. He'd know who they were. Then they had better watch out.

Study 26

Compiled by: Ne'rosi El'ganti, SSM.rl.sub.adjunct, UNAS
Subject: Willane Bofsky
Location: Resort World
Earth-Reference Date: 2754 A.D. (O.E. Standard)

THE CART WOBBLED to the door, its wheels screaming in

torment, and halted, the ensuing silence shrieking its relief. The big man kicked the door open, splintering the rough wood with his anger.

"Woman! Come out here. I've brought you your thief. He couldn't even hang onto any of it. He let it be stolen no sooner than he reached town. Fool!" The man released the cart's tray, and the beaten boy tumbled to the ground, half inside the woman's house and half still outside with the man.

"Willy," his mother wailed, falling to put her hand on his face, touching his bruised skin, his eyes nearly swollen shut with the kicks and the beating. Looking up at the man, pleading in her eyes, she whispered, "It's Willy, my poor little Willane. We have to do something. Please."

With a step forward, blackness covering the man's expression, he growled out a reply, "That's right, woman. Something has to be done." He reached beside the door to the shovel hanging on the wall, calling as he walked away, "Furthermore, I intend to do it."

The ragged boy's mother pulled his head to her. "I'm sorry I wasn't stronger, ashamed I didn't protect you more." She washed his bleeding body with her tears, ignoring the man she had allowed into their lives, wrapped up in her son and his pain.

Sour sweat drenched the big man. The bloodletting anger toward the boy, then the searching and the pointing out by someone who had *seen* the boy, who had seen him drop the credits, grabbing them back up again. Finding him, and then getting the cart to carry him back, still angry, *so* angry with the boy. Now, he was just tired. Tired, and for the first time in many months, sober.

Still holding the shovel in his hand, no longer mindful of it, he walked across the hardened mud, across last month's footprints, across yesterday and back to the now, the broken boy, and the woman at his side.

He had loved her once, even thought he could love the boy. However, there had been no place for him, only for the *father*, dead and gone. The only love he had been allowed was his drink, and his drink had loved him back, making him feel strong and powerful. Making him feel like a man.

Now the drink was gone, and he felt *not* like a man. He knew what it was like to remember, to regret what could have been, *should* have been, and to feel repentant, his anger growing inside at himself. He walked up to the woman, sitting still with the boy, and stood over her, forgetting the shovel still, not knowing what to say, her sobbing finally making him sorry, making him want to hold her like he had wanted to many years ago. He reached down and touched her shoulder.

"No!" she exploded, her arm flinging his hand away from her, her head jerking up from the boy. Seeing the shovel in the man's hand, her eyes hardened, and her mother's protective fire, dormant for so long against the man's stronger fury, exploded with her words, her resolve all the more apparent with the timbre of her voice. "You'll not beat him again. He's my *son*. You've beaten me, and I've taken it. You've forced me, and I've lain under your stink the while, you on top of me, making me ill." Calming for a deceptive moment, she carefully rested Willy's battered head on her wadded apr'n and stood to face the man. Swelling in renewed anger, she lashed out, her hand leaving red streaks across his face. "I'll kill you first before I let you beat him again. You think I don't know what you intend, that shovel in your hand? Look at him. Look! Look what you've done. It's no thanks to you he's not dead on the ground, all for a few credits. I should have kicked you out of my house the first time you touched him. Don't come near us again!"

Not immediately understanding, knowing it was *he* who had pulled the boy from the room, the boy's blood everywhere, and all the credits gone, the man didn't understand. Did she think *he* had beat the boy this time?

Stepping to her to explain, his world exploded.

Like an old-Earth tiger, unknown in flesh or memory to the boy's mother, but one in spirit, the woman, the wild beast, attacking in the fury of her *need* to protect her own, this her death-dance, leaped. Her hands flying, claws raking the man's face, her feet and knees flailing, he fell under her assault.

His breath was knocked from him, and with no drink to fuel his muscles, no anger to fire him on, he struggled, hitting at the woman, trying to breathe, to *see,* to get her to understand. He still held the shovel, and not knowing what his hand was doing, only needing her *off,* to breathe, to tell her he was finally sorry, that it was the *drink,* he hit at her, and again, and again until he could *breathe,* until he could see, until she stopped.

Then he lay there, waiting on the woman to get off, to say she was sorry, for her to let him apologize, too. He wiped the wet from his face, the *sticky* wet, the *warmth* of it finally reaching into his brain, telling him what he'd done, hadn't known he'd done in his desperation, but had done with his own hand, anyway.

His body giving way to grief, his muscles going slack, the shovel, new color adorning its edges, clattered from his hand to the ground, the awfulness of what he'd done becoming real to him. Grabbing her shoulders and rolling her to his side, he caressed her once-beautiful face, his memory of it still beautiful, and began to weep sober tears for this woman he'd once loved, the woman he wanted the chance to love again, and now, never could.

A movement caught his eye, and he turned. The boy! Hoping for understanding, knowing he hadn't meant to hurt her this time, not with him sober, the man rose to step to him. As the mountain of a man draped his shadow over the boy, sorry for the boy's pain, his broken body, sorry for the boy's mother, the woman, her now dead by his own hand, wishing she weren't, and knowing he hadn't meant to, he needed the boy's understanding.

He knelt at the boy's side, looking at his face, one eye shut with the swelling, the other barely open, one eye that had seen, knew, and looked at him, accusing, not forgiving him at all.

The man then knew he would know no forgiveness, not from the boy, and not from himself. Rising and stepping over him, blackness, this time of despair, gripped his soul, a soul eaten away by anger and torment, leaving little left. That little was not enough to sustain him in his darkness. As the man took his only love, his drink, and lay on the bed to drown the horrendous emptiness inside, he did exactly what he set out to do.

That was how the boy was found days later, half in and half out of the doorway, barely alive, covered with blood-encrusted wounds, his tongue swollen with thirst, and still tied to the two people who had torn his world in two, the man lying dead in his mother's world, and her, lying dead in his.

Earlier that Day

WILLY SQUATTED IN THE DIRT, dust swirling around his feet. He was glad the storms had broken early this year. It would have been harder to run in the pounding rain, but he would have. He'd have done it.

Except this was better.

Hunger starting to gnaw at him, he pulled the bag out of his shirt, remembering how he took it, just reached in and *took* it. He grinned, the smile breaking up the bleakness of his dirty face.

The man always kept it on him, in his pocket, even when he crawled into Willy's mother's bed. The man had kept it with him ever since *last time,* the other time Willy had taken it, had found where it was hidden, grabbed it, and run with it. He had used it, too. He bought *things* with the credits—food and a knife, and shoes for his mother. How angry the man had been, throwing the food across the room, yelling about the shoes! He hadn't taken them back, but had thrown them in the fire instead, his mother watching.

Why did he burn them? The credits were gone, wasted. Other than the knife. The man never found that. Willy kept it hidden, had it still. He had it here with him, here now. He needed it now. It was the one thing left from all the credits.

He untied the pouch. He had *more* credits, now. The man would be angry, throw things, hit his mother. She always *took* it, not fighting back. *Why?* he questioned. He wanted his mother to fight back, to tell the man to *leave,* but she never did.

Now Willy was gone. Gone for good. What they did now had nothing to do with him. Not with Willy. He would never be part of them ever again.

Reaching inside the pouch, he pulled out a handful of paper credits, the stink of the man still on them. Stuffing a wad of the credits into his ragged breeches' pockets, he crumpled the pouch and tossed it into a ditch, kicking a cloud of dirt over it, burying his old life with it as he headed into the unknown.

WILLY WAS BUMPED THIS WAY, and then pushed by someone yelling for him to watch where he was going. He had dropped some of the credits when he stopped at a food stall, people looking, staring as he reached for it, grabbing quickly, stuffing it back inside, hoping he got it all, but not sure, not sure at all. The food, though. Hot. Steamy. Bread with rice inside. It had been worth stopping, dropping the credits, with everyone watching.

He was bumped again. Harder. Dodging the bumping, trying to be invisible, he moved to one side, then moved again. He felt the fear start, the sweating, the stink of *afraid* that was his stink. He felt his arm *yanked,* his body pulled toward a dark

111

doorway. Trying to pull away, to not be held, not *go* that way, his feet slipped, the open door growing to meet him.

His eyes, filled with desperation, sought the help of those he had walked among. Those few who did look, quickly looked away. They had seen too many boys, dirty boys who were not quite men, disappear into dark, dark doorways. Some emerged later, eyes downcast, bodies bruised and torn. Many did not. What was one more? Those who did look, looked away, the boy soon forgotten.

WILLY, HIS HEART ON FIRE, his own stink surrounding him, felt rough hands running over his body, under his shirt, and into his pockets.

"Ahh! I told ya' it were 'ere. I saw 'im, out there, 'e was, credits fallin' all over th' ground, 'im yankin' it up like no one'd notice. *I* noticed, did I. And I came for me share. There's plenty for th' two of us."

The hands emptied his pockets, taking what Willy had waited for, watched for, and then *dared* to steal. Then the feet kicked him, the dim light hiding their faces, their meanness.

Willy knew what to do, what he had done so many times before. Wrapping his arms around himself, he curled into a ball on the filthy floor, taking it, enduring the pain, waiting for it to stop, wanting it to end. He waited for a very long time before it finally did.

The Night Before

WILLY FROZE, THE DARKNESS around him all but complete. Afraid to move, horrified of being found out, the remembered beatings making his heart throb in his chest, he listened. Silence, first. Then the quiet breath that was his mother's. With an exhausted sigh of relief, he found the soft snore he needed to hear, the snore that made Willy safe.

In the near-dark room, he slowly withdrew the big man's credit pouch from its hiding place, the blackness of it drawing all his concentration, taking all his care. Slowly, now . . . careful. He imagined he could easily have been a *b'italik* from the old stories his father used to tell, from before the time when the big man came. He was hiding in the dark, luring an unwary victim into his lair, it becoming easy prey. *There!* He grinned.

Looking at the blackness of the man lying there, the stink of his drink still oozing from his pores, seeing him as no more than a vile and hated hole of despair, sucking Willy's life, his very *soul* into a desperate pit with it, he knew he would be glad to be gone. He leaned over his mother, his eyes seeing her once-porcelain skin as still white and unmarred, the darkness hiding the years of abuse. His fingertips brushed a wisp of hair from her cheek, his lips gently brushing her flesh, the smell of her stirring buried memories of life before the *man*, when Willy's father was *alive*, when life had been *safe* and *good*.

But he knew, had known for a very long time, that those memories were no longer his. Those memories of *safe, love,* and *warm* belonged to a small boy who had died long, long ago, who had died when the *man* came. When he rose from his mother's side, he left a gift in exchange for the credit pouch containing all the funds the family owned.

As the boy, not yet a man, slipped with shadowy stealth out of the room and out of the lives of the people he left sleeping, his mother shifted in her sleep, turned as if caressed by an evening breeze, the pale light of the night stars through the open window catching at something on her cheek, sparkling, revealing the boy's gift. It was a tear, the only tear he had shed since having his childhood crushed and bled out of him long ago by the man's hatred of all things living. It was his farewell gift, the last tear he intended his eyes to ever cry.

Study 27

Compiled by: Ne'rosi El'ganti, SSM.rl.sub.adjunct, UNAS
Subject: Willane Bofsky
Location: Resort World
Earth-Reference Date: 2747 A.D. (O.E. Standard)

THE HEAVENS flung their anger at the offending world, lightning from dark clouds streaking across rain-drenched skies. The child's only link to life, to *love,* he held protected by his small arms. The boy crouched for sanctuary under the canopy of a lone tree. The gods, seeking to bleed away their anger, sought him out, flinging bolt after bolt of white-hot energy, destroying everything that might protect the boy. Only the blackness of the day kept the boy safe.

Safe, at least, for the moment.

"CURSE THAT BOY!" The big man strode through the dingy hovel he called a home, his black anger making the dank rooms feel small. "And curse that dog!" Stopping, shaking a balled fist at the peeling ceiling overhead, the man continued to bellow his rant, venting an anger that was eating him from his own dark heart outwards. "That goes for this storm-cursed planet with its black skies and crop-eating storms!"

Across the room, the boy's mother cowered, and she reached one hand to brush loose hair back from her face. She looked as filthy and beat up as the walls around her.

The flames of his rage momentarily subsiding, the big man sank into a chair. He growled to her, "He won't live through the night this time, no matter what you say," Satisfaction painted his features hard. "Once I find that strop, I'll have my way."

"No," the boy's mother moaned, dread washing her pale

114

face. "The strop—" Her eyes were drawn to a chest, one awkwardly askew from the wall, before she glanced away again.

The big man caught her words and exploded. Grabbing her by the breast of her dress, he slammed her against the wall, her head painting its mottled surface red with blood. He breathed the stink of his renewed anger at her. "I will have that strop. And that strop will have that boy. Mind you, that dog will get even worse." He flung the woman aside as he reached for his drink, following her clumsy fall with a snarl. "You try to get in my way again, woman, and that strop will come for you, too."

"Willane . . ." the broken woman sobbed. "Oh, my poor Willane." She huddled in the dimness, one hand holding her matted hair, the other wiping the flood of tears. The drunken man staggered as he rifled her meager possessions, and she scrambled farther into the corner, her eyes on the chest.

"When I get back, I'll have you, woman." He threw his head back and laughed at the fear in her eyes. "Thank you for showing me your hiding place. You'll be just the thing to sate my appetite after I finish with that pup of yours, him and that dog."

Roughly pulling the chest from the wall, he chortled wickedly and grabbed what the woman had tried to conceal. Holding it balled in his fist, he shook it at her. His words rumbled coarse and sodden with a combination of anger and drink, "Hiding it from me, were you? I knew it when it went missing. You, taking sides with that boy. I'll take an extra little morsel of you tonight. Just you wait, woman. Just you wait and see."

Stumbling through the morass of his fury-filled search, the man flung the door open, leaning into the black maelstrom raging just outside, it no match for the black rage in his heart, determined to bleed his anger at that cursed boy and his dog.

LIT BY THE ANGER OF THE GODS, a black shape appeared on the rise. The boy *knew*. Each slap of lightning, and

115

the black shape was closer, coming for him. His eyes bled tears, the drenching rain flooding the salt from his small face even as they fell. He *knew* what the man would do, had taken it before from the man. But the *dog*. Why?

Sensing his distress, the dog whimpered in his arms.

"I promised to keep you safe," he whispered to it, barely heard over the storm. "I can't. Not from *him*." He squeezed the dog, his arms proving at least a temporary refuge from the approaching storm of anger. The expected ferocity of the man's rage becoming stronger than the storm from the gods, stronger than the might whipping around his hiding place, he trembled. Knowing he had no place to run, he huddled around the dog and whimpered his own small noises of fear.

A huge, dark hand reached into the boy's refuge, grasping, touching, *yanking* him back into the storm. The boy could smell the stink of the big man's anger as the hand drew him toward the sneering, drunken face. He could smell his own stink of fear mixed with the odor of urine leaking from the frightened dog.

With terror in his face, he found his voice as the man yanked the dog from his grasp, flinging the boy to the muddy ground. "No! He's mine!" he screamed, scrambling to his feet, slipping in the mud.

Holding the whimpering, struggling dog high above his head, the man looked at the boy, laughing at his feeble attempts to stand. Taking a heavy-booted foot, the man kicked the boy back into the mud. His hand finding the loose skin around the dog's neck, the man glared at the boy as he squeezed the dog tighter and tighter, the whimpering finally subsiding, the furred creature going limp in his hand. "You want the dog, do you? Go get it!" He flung the lifeless bundle into the blinding rain.

The boy scrambled to get to his feet, hoping the dog might still live. That's when he felt the first impact.

Crack!

The pain seared him across his back. Then came another and another. Soon, the dog was forgotten, and the boy was aware only of the repeated crack of the strop and the searing pain.

He curled up in the mud, filled with the pain, just wanting it to be over.

THE DOOR BURST OPEN, puddles of rain soaking the worn floor as the man carried his bundle inside. His anger, temporarily sated by the boy, began to kindle again when he saw the woman still huddled miserably in the corner. He stomped to her, filling the room, dumping the bundle at her feet.

It unrolled into the bloodied arms and legs of a small boy, severely beaten, the rise of his chest yet showing the stubborn resiliency of life. As the woman reached for the torn body, the man roughly grabbed her arm.

"This is my time, not his," he growled. "Come to me, woman. I expect you to at least act as though you enjoy this. I certainly intend to."

With that, his anger-fueled muscles ripped her clothing, tearing it free. Flinging her to the floor next to the bloodied boy, he fell on her roughly, not caring for anyone or anything except for his own desires.

The boy and the raging storm outside were the only witnesses as the man vented his anger on her body, his boots smearing the boy's blood back and forth on the floor in a rising crescendo, their beat finally matching the driving fury of the storm.

Study 28

Compiled by: Alb't deFralin, SSM.rl, UNAS
Subject: Rjorck

Location: Earth and Se'Yan't
Earth-Reference Date: 2683 A.D. (O.E. Standard)

Earth

THE FIRE FLICKERED IN THE OPENING in the wall, heat-flushed fingers of flames pushing dancing shadows into the deepest recesses of the room. Rjorck let the room seep its familiar smells into his pores, enjoying them one last time, knowing there would be no return from this journey, not for the old man he had become. He pressed his hands on the arms of the chair, its ancient tanned hides shifting as his old man's weight overcame the leather's groans. Unsteadily, he pushed himself to a standing position, pausing to regain long-forgotten balance, only remembering *old*. No longer the strong-chinned god of his youth, even the middle-aged businessman of seventy Earth-years gone was barely a memory. He needed *c'habor-reneis't*. He needed the seas of his homeworld. They called him.

Knowing this businessman, this *persona*, must cease just as a man cedes that which he must to the dry-death, he could only return in a different guise, the power and credits he had accumulated transferred, shifted, *hidden* to be at his disposal when he returned after his year-of-months. He could only be Rjorck again after an intervening lifetime spent as someone else.

As his people had prepared him well, so had Rjorck prepared well. A well-phrased letter *here,* mentioning a meeting with that *certain* person. References to legal matters filed in official documents. Forged citizenship papers documented on *that* world. Accounts opened, funds turned into investments, managed by this new individual. Not real. Not yet, anyway. But when he returned, he would be that person, again the youth, wearing strong muscles on enduring bone, his hair thick

118

and long, his face regal and unlined, the Rjorck he barely remembered anymore, didn't really remember, only knew that he *should* remember *something*.

His transport present, he shuffled to the door, exiting, leaving the man he had been back in the chair, the protesting leather whispering its complaints to his tired body, knowing he was no longer that person.

He breathed heavily with the effort of *living* as he made his way to his home.

Se'Yan't

THREE SHIPBOARD WEEKS of travel gone, the mighty gulf of space crossed in sleep. The coughing. Oh, the continued coughing, the many times remembered pouch of nutrients not much help.

Rjorck could have avoided the slow-sleep and this *murderous interstellar hangover* on this much larger vessel, but time was not on his side. He had waited too long to begin his return. To enter into cryo-stasis at this point in his need might be his body's signal to never wake again.

Still . . . more coughing.

He lay in the ship's bunk, discomfort kneading his muscles, sandpaper working his joints when he tried to move. His breath escaping faster than he could draw it in, he felt hands lifting him, laying him gently on soft webbing, the smell of his homeworld surrounding him as he was carried off the ship.

"Who?" He reached a parchment-skinned hand out to touch one of those who carried him. His quivering voice questioned those around him, the effort bringing another round of coughing.

Lips leaned to him, speaking quietly to his aged ears, whispering the words of a friend, a brother, savoring the return of a long-lost treasure, "It's Berian, and Wolmn, too. Adhor'k

119

will be with you soon. Rest, beloved. Rest."

With the peace of a well-deserved sleep, Rjorck closed his weary eyes, his worn, used body no longer important. He was home.

Home.

THE SEA LAPPED the stones on the shore, reaching, knowing. The stones whispered, *We know the joy of the waters. Come be washed with us. Feel the warmth of the sea as it blankets you in life. Come release yourself.*

Rjorck was being drawn to the sea, it working its attraction, calling for its beloved, the one waiting, attended by his own, somehow knowing he was near. Impatient, the sea reached out again, its fingers straining to give blessed relief, to give life.

Adhor'k ran her hand across the weathered skin of her re'anlt's old-man, years-creased face. With the barest movements of her lips, she murmured, "How many of these lines were placed upon your skin in return for working to save our world? How many times have you rescued us, times of which we have been blissfully unaware? You have been good to us, my brother." Running her fingers gently across his skin, she traced his care-worn features, her fingers memorizing each one. "Rjorck," she whispered, leaning close, where only he could hear, "I remember the time . . ." and his memories of his beloved sister were renewed.

At long last, each of Rjorck's loved ones had spoken their love, their memories to him, separately and quietly, renewing the person he would become upon his return from the sea. Then, with his frail form's breath barely swelling his life-scarred chest, each rise and fall growing weaker, his family gathered around, and lifting him with loving hands, his unclothed body ravaged by time, they carried him to the sea. As each stepped into the clear, blue water, lowering their gift into the sea's embrace, answering the entreaties of the pleading waves, his weary body melted into Se'Yan't's warm waters, taken, held, embraced by the waves to be renewed by the sea. His celebrants, knowing he would one day return to them refreshed in youth and vitality, rejoiced in his journey to the sea.

Study 29

Compiled by: Adel' Eriks'n, SSM.rl.sub.adjunct, UNAS
Subject: Rjorck
Location: Earth
Earth-Reference Date: 2395 A.D. (O.E. Standard)

RJORCK SAT DOWN with his record crystal, the accounts, now many years old and flush with credits, flashing across the glass in front of him. The skin on his face was middle-aged, and he carried lines in his forehead.

"Ah, but for the ease-of-use of message-fabric. If only I could teach someone how to manufacture it here on Earth."

Tapping his way through accounts intertwined with business and political entities throughout the twelve systems most frequented by intrepid wayfarers, he located exactly the one he was looking for, a tap of his finger on *this* name, sliding his finger *there,* pulling on the numbers to grow them like *that.*

"Here it is," he said aloud to no one in particular.

To his friends and acquaintances, this Rjorck was no more than a financially fat, savvy businessman. They saw him in the street, appearing prosperous and self-satisfied, content to dabble in the areas of business and commerce where his interests happened to be drawn. To those who might know where to look, if it were possible for them to see past his impenetrable barrier of safeguards, a different man might be seen. There they would view a financial empire dedicated to manipulation of knowledge, to the understanding of the mystery of Se'Yan't. Of course, people knew of his homeworld, calling it by the human name Rejuvenant. But Rjorck had distanced himself from all real connection to Se'Yan't other than as an occasional traveler and tourist to distant worlds.

The real connection, known only deep in his most well defended financial records, was that of manipulator. Withhold a shipment of goods to *this* company verging on discovery of certain knowledge about Se'Yan't, and the company fails, its information absorbed by another company, mysteriously controlled by an unknown source. An anonymous threat to *this* government followed by a large infusion of military supplies and funds, and the neighboring country is enveloped in a war for its survival, its suspicions about a distant planet lost with the key men who happen to be killed in the ensuing conflict.

Yes, Rjorck was more than he seemed to those who thought they knew him. After all, they only thought they knew this man, a man whose life was dedicated to one thing, the protection of the most valuable yet useless secret in the galaxy. Useless, at least, to anyone who had not been born on Se'Yan't.

Study 30

Compiled by: Adel' Eriks'n, SSM.rl.sub.adjunct, UNAS
Subject: Rjorck
Location: Earth
Earth-Reference Date: 2360 A.D. (O.E. Standard)

THE PARTITION OF RJORCK'S slow-sleep bunk slid up, disappearing into the ceiling, the steam of *cold* sliding into the corridor, joining with the cloud gathering from the bunks down the wall. Lights flickered on, his eyes *burning* with the sudden lashing of unexpected photons. His strong, youthful face now heavy with beard, he ran his tongue around the inside of his mouth, his teeth rough to his tongue's touch, the taste of being asleep too long. The stars above, he was hungry, an emptiness that drove upwards from the soles of his feet, piercing his legs, wrapping tight fists around his groin, squeezing, flinging itself through his chest and head. And *thirsty!* The gods help him!

"Here!"

A warm pouch was slapped on his chest by an unseen hand. It was grabbed by another hand, his own, as if in a dream.

"Nourishment. You'll feel better when you get this down. It's always worse the first time. Welcome to interstellar space travel. Not all it's knocked up to be. Drink!" The voice trailed off down the corridor, soon to be heard again as another was encouraged to consume the warm antidote.

He put the pouch to his mouth and was instantly rewarded with a lessening of the discomfort, the nutritious soup of chemicals erasing the interstellar hangover gleefully showered upon all who would dare to drink of the liquor of the heavens in order to travel the domain of the gods.

RJORCK STEPPED ONTO THE PITTED surface of the spaceport, a different *planet* under his feet for the first time in all his many lifetimes. The movement, the vitality, the *noise* of all that he could see was a honey to his senses, and he absorbed it, closing his eyes with a smile, basking under the single sun of a strange world on his face.

He spoke to the sky, his enthusiasm bursting forth, "Ahh! This has been my dream, ever since that day, the day of the blazing third sun that first appeared in our 'little night,' washing the power of Se'Yan't's suns from the sky for a time. Here! Earth!"

A man off to the side laughed, but Rjorck didn't care. He

had traveled to a new world, the first of his race to do so. He now walked under the magic of a single shadow given by the one life-giver above this world.

With enthusiasm, he moved forward across the blackened, scarred surface of the port, diseased with centuries of dreams, the port providing succor for the wounded traveler, offering to others the escape of the desperate. This port, this world, had called him to its surface, giving him renewed life, a fresh reason for his existence.

Making his way into the spaceport, the *crowd* of people, the busy-ness, the *intensity* of all they did buoyed him. *To live so fast, so hard!* He soaked up the vitality, the thing he hadn't even known he was missing, had only known *something* was missing, the energy he sensed in these people, this place called Earth.

He had fulfilled his dream, called to a place where he could feel finally at home.

"THIS WILL DO NICELY." Rjorck looked around the ef'ncy living module with satisfaction, thanking his traveling companion. Registering his presence here on Earth had been as simple as the crew had suggested, and as long as he was satisfied with this single, these living quarters were his at no cost. He placed his few possessions in the ef'ncy's storage locker, and sitting down to the built-in data access unit, known on this world as a glass, he initiated access.

When the images rose from the clear panel's surface, he noted the basic set-up. Those onboard the ship had been much more elaborate. However, this would do nicely. It would enable him to complete all that he needed to achieve.

With his people's preparations, the *knowledge* they had given him, he made unfettered use of his access to Earth's data storage systems. Slowly at first, then with certain information skillfully inserted just *there,* other avenues of exploration bringing new opportunities to be manipulated, he built a history for himself, a story of his own making. Certain financial institutions now had long-standing accounts no one had noticed before. Companies had new records of successful business deals where there had been none before. Transfers of funds and payments for services rendered were noted throughout numerous investment portfolios.

No actual credits changed hands, of course. All accounts registered zero balances. Rjorck, even with the skillful plans from his people, could not create funds out of a few taps on the glass before him. *Although*, he thought, as he built his new history directly in Earth's all-too-accessible data systems, *with the new records in place, all the credits I require will be available just for the asking.*

So, long into the local night, the data storage systems of Earth grew their new histories. When they were complete, and after transferring key elements of his new history to one of the unit's detachable record crystals, he lay down on the ef'ncy unit's sleeping pad, his rest that of one who has done his job well.

"YES, SER, JUST A SMALL LOAN." Armed with the principals and practicalities of Earth's economic systems, Rjorck felt sure of himself. "Eighty thousand credits repayable in ninety of your world's days. Look over my information on my record crystal again. You will see my transaction history is very commendable." How easy it had been to manipulate the data storage systems once he had access to them! Apparently, superior technology and superior intellect did not always go hand-in-hand. Rjorck laughed to himself, the laughter revealing itself on his face as no more than a twinkle in his eye. Handing his newly acquired and very empty credit crystal to the creditor, he knew the sum would be repaid and multiplied many times in the next few Earth-months. His people had prepared him well, and he knew success would be his.

Study 31

Compiled by: Alb't deFralin, SSM.rl, UNAS
Subject: Rjorck
Location: Rejuvenant/Se'Yan't
Earth-Reference Date: 2360 A.D. (O.E. Standard)

Several Months Previously

RJORCK RAN HIS HAND along the surface of the bunk, the place he would spend many handfuls of days on his sojourn to a distant place he'd only recently learned about and never seen. His anticipation as palpable as the fabric his hand was touching, his skin prickled, imagining the *things,* the unknown *events* that might be ahead. His few outward possessions secured in a stor'lok bin adjoining the bunk, his truly valued wealth being the information, the *knowledge,* he carried in his head, his heart pounded with expectancy.

Even during his time spent with Adhor'k, Berian, E'vonn, and the others the past few handfuls of days, his mind had not been with them at all. His thoughts had been constantly swept aside, mere dust from a life already abandoned in his heart, the core being of him needing to *go,* to *see.*

He breathed deeply, his heart afire with looking forward to his exile—an exile to a place of his dreams.

Some Weeks Earlier

"AH, BUT WE DO HAVE CITIES, places where we dwell in groups of many, closely entwined in the myriad activities of each other's lives." The ancient guide spoke with conviction, as he led the way through the low foliage shrouding the densely covered ridge. The sweetmeat had been offered, the invitation presented, the lure cast. "Come and see. Stay. Study. You will be most welcome, if one of you wishes to remain on our world." The learned voice cracked with the age of his many years as he spoke. He motioned for his train of visitors to keep up.

Stepping down the series of low ledges weathered into the face of the escarpment, twisting back, going again the way down, the party descended into the greenness of the rift valley. Long before reaching the floor, a switchback, seemingly unexpected to the visitors, although not to the old man, opened up a beautifully nestled series of lodgings located under the canopy of green trailing down the rugged valley walls. Another turn and the city opened up, the glistening rays of Se'Yan't's minor sun lighting it with a glow of beauty, its stone walkways, aqueducts, and moss-covered walls seemingly out of a faraway fairy tale, shockingly beautiful to the visitors viewing it for the very first time.

RJORCK SAT AT THE ROUND TABLE, handling the many items on its surface, picking up this, turning over *that*. He had never traveled off his home world—nor had any of his race—and these things were from a faraway planet. Anticipation of possibilities to come had his thoughts fractured.

He inspected the strange items, feeling the differences, aware of the touch of space in their manufacture, not knowing if he would be allowed to accompany the strangers to *Earth*. His heart shifted under the woven cloth of his robes, the *not-knowing* excitement making him anxious. He had learned so much. Would his world's leaders allow him to go?

The *landing pod*. How he enjoyed his new words, rolling them around in his head! He knew that word now, *landing pod*. When the *landing pod* had expelled the men, only he, Rjorck,

127

had realized what to do. He had marshaled his resources, his *knowledge,* going to the men, learning their speech, soaking up new information about the men's world. He had realized before anyone else that while the visitors could not form their speech at the melodic pitch his people found most beautiful, he could lower his own voice to a near-growl, communicating with these new men. Although at first it had felt rough and unnatural, he had soon become adept at using this new way of speaking, even finding after many handfuls of days that the words became simple to enunciate.

When the visitors began to tell of their own world, far though it was, with blue skies and bursting with technology, he became a conduit of information. The leaders of his people wisely saw the truth in all he shared. Distant though they were, great power was in this world of interlopers, these new people. Great power, indeed.

Most disturbing of all, they saw something only known to those of Se'Yan't in the small burrowing creatures ever-present across their planet. *The dry-death.* These new creatures did not know c'habor-reneis't, the living of repeated lives. They experienced one life, and one only. The leaders of Se'Yan't reminded their people how the burrowing creatures fought for life, resisted the snuff of the dry-death, would bite, chew, and claw to avoid it, and only accepted it when there was no other way. How could these people, no matter how well educated or civilized, be any different?

It was decided unanimously that no knowledge of c'habor-reneis't could pass to these humans, and one of their own must be recruited to leave Se'Yan't, perhaps for a lifetime, to ensure the safety of their world. It would be hard to leave their planet's soothing waters, the treasure of the *water-weir,* enduring a lifetime on the dry land of another world.

Who would go? A cry spilled across the land, echoing through the rift valleys, and traversing the seas. Devices were called upon to speak across the distances, and not one chose to go, to *leave*. Not one except the one who was there all along, the one who wanted *more*, who was waiting to be asked.

Rjorck.

Plans were made, secret plans kept from the humans. While having no pressing need for technology, and not having spent time or energy developing something neither wanted nor desired, the people of Se'Yan't were by no means uneducated or indolent. Now compelled, needing to know, to learn, they absorbed quickly the knowledge laid at their feet. The mechanics of technology, ideas, even the machines themselves, these things and more came easily to them, as did the newly realized discipline of interplanetary economics.

Se'Yan't's wise leaders understood their emissary would need to be well versed in such matters. So they planned deeper plans, their craftiness thorough, hidden, and sure, and the visitors who might have resisted, had they known of the wisdom and shrewdness moving unseen all around them, were swept along, tidbits of flotsam in the mighty tide of Se'Yan't's plans. After all, a society coming to understand its impending peril, knowing that it can only pile sandbags against the rising tide, must fill those sandbags with whatever they can find.

The door spangles parted, tinkling as the decision was returned to Rjorck and placed on the table. Rjorck, sliding objects aside with a sweep of his hand, excitedly reached for the message-fabric, with anticipation tinging the look on his face. Would the invitation be accepted, the transport made available for him to travel to *Earth?*

Having been made aware of the great distance the exploratory team had traveled after Se'Yan't's twin suns had been discovered, and learning there was space inside for only the original members of the mission, Se'Yan't's leaders had devised a plan—quickly accepted—to dangle the offer to study Se'Yan't, albeit in a limited, controlled way, as a tempting morsel to convince one of the crew members, the team's exobiologist, to remain on the planet, leaving one returning bunk empty on the survey ship.

With sadness in their eyes, Rjorck's people watched him as he felt the message-fabric. Unable to comprehend *anticipation* at leaving their beautiful garden planet, its seas constantly calling them home, they felt they were sending a treasured brother into exile, banishing him in effect, if not in intent, while stripping all life from him. However, unseen to them, surging in his heart, and only hinted at on his flushed face, was the hope, the *need* for the chance to go, to experience that which he'd never lived: *outside*—outside of his safe, welcoming world.

Study 32

Compiled by: Alb't deFralin, SSM.rl, UNAS
Subject: Rjorck
Location: Rejuvenant/Se'Yan't
Earth-Reference Date: 2359 A.D. (O.E. Standard)

RJORCK, FRESH FROM THE SEA, youthful in his rebirth, and full of life, turned to those around him, chagrined at the skepticism in the air. "It was, too, there. I saw the light in the sky, as did others." He turned to look off the escarpment towards the sea in the distance, purposely dismissing those who dared doubt his word.

"You expect belief?" The response chortled with amusement. "Disbelief is more our style. Everyone knows there are no mysterious lights in our sky, and even should it be so, it is so rarely true night that we hardly can be blamed when we forget to look."

Other voices chuckled at the response, for they felt the same.

The response was not entirely inappropriate, for with twin suns circling their home, true darkness rarely wrapped its fist around the light-filled orb. Even when it did, the system's location far past the distant edge of the galactic arm rarely let any other suns show. The twinkle of stars overhead was mostly unknown in this section of the galaxy.

"Come with me during the next 'little night,' and you will see. It was there. I saw it, and so did Adhor'k and Berian. They were there. They saw it, also, with their own eyes. It was brighter than last time, too." He dared the others to doubt what he had seen and knew to be true.

"Rjorck," admonished the one known as E'vonn, back some dozen years from her sojourn in the waters. "You surely left the better part of your hyr'yan't in the sea!" The friends, gathered at the rocky promontory, one celebrated for the magnificent view of the sea below, laughed warmly and with no malice, trusting he would take no real offense.

He turned from the group, this time with a smile, his annoyance dissipating. Facing into the stiff breeze, his hair twisting and dancing with the wind, he knew the unfettered joy felt by those given a fresh lease on a brand-new life; the one pronounced dead only to be snatched back from the grave.

THE LIGHT FROM THE SKY flared brightly, blinding even under the light of the twin suns, creating shadows of black night where none had been moments before. The heat blasted the ground, rolling over the people standing nearby, searing their resolve to stay, to learn what this new thing was, to observe. Even the sounds of the water calming the stones on the shore were stolen from the sky, gathered up and scattered to the heavens, replaced by pain, the sounds wrenching ears and vibrating the very blood of the observers. Cowering in low recesses, and shielding themselves behind large boulders, and some observers simply standing frozen in disbelief, the inhabitants of this newly violated land watched as their world's isolation was shattered, never again to be returned.

Emerging from a dark crevasse of black shadow, one person refused to cower, curiosity and anticipation drawing his eyes to watch, to *see* what this was.

The gloom of the unnatural shadows vanished, the light suddenly extinguishing as if smothered by the planet's touch, and the newly wakened silence screamed its presence. Fascination driving him, the watcher stepped farther from his protected place and approached the object.

Not a thing from the gods.

Rjorck was elated with his conclusion. He would have gloated, if he had known what it was to gloat. This strange bearer of light had been made by tools. Strange and mysterious, yes, but a machine nonetheless.

He wanted to know more.

Like a sea creature's shell torn apart by an eager predator, the strange thing split, cracking open along one side. Screeching in protest, the side of the craft clattered to the rocky ground, forming steps of a sort. The watching men staggered back to life, nervously talking among themselves, moving away from the sudden, explosive sound.

Twelve suited Earth-humans stepped forth, men who, after traveling such a great distance to explore the unknown landscape of a world spinning under twin suns, found themselves to have arrived at a place that could have been home.

Except for the yellow sky, of course.

Rjorck stepped forward, emboldened by a drive unfelt by his fellow re'anlts, drawn as a moth to a flame, curiosity overcoming any misgivings that might have been present. The rush of new knowledge from these creatures, clothed strangely from head to toe, yet still clearly *men*, washed any residual reservations away. While his fellow re'anlts held back, their cautiousness natural to his race, he stepped forward, whistling out a formal greeting of respect.

"Welcome travelers. You must have journeyed far to come speak with us. What manner of vessel is this to have flown through our skies, wrestled courageously with our twin suns, and moved with an intensity more brilliant than our brightest day?"

One of the men reached a suit-enclosed hand to his neck. There was an audible click, and the top of his suit where it covered his head made a whirring sound and gently folded back onto itself to form a wide collar. He took a deep breath. A smile grew on his face, and with a motion, he sent his companions a message to open their own suits.

Opening his mouth to speak, instead of the beautiful, clear words the inhabitants of Se'Yan't were used to, his sounds, low and guttural, assaulted Rjorck's ears. Producing a small instrument, the visitor touched it just *so*, and Rjorck's voice and that of the others sang out at him, the very words they had sung among themselves.

Rjorck turned to his friends, now emerging from their hiding places, and he and his re'anlts smiled at the unexpected revelation of having been overheard during their observations. Their very words had been captured, placed inside the *object*, and returned to them.

How clever, he thought.

Then, the visitor motioned to himself and reached out to touch the instrument again. Rjorck heard yet another series of sounds from the instrument as it skipped from the beautiful whistling words he and his re'anlts had spoken earlier, into the low, abrasive range of sounds the man had made earlier.

He immediately understood. The low, gruff sounds were speech, also. He had never considered that one could speak and not be understood immediately by all within hearing. His world's high-pitched speech and all its words were ubiquitous across Se'Yan't, and had been the same for all living memory.

What courage these creatures, these *men* must have, he considered, realizing they must have used this light-filled *device*, traveling in the blackness from beyond his world's suns. His heart pounded with anticipation. To go places not always familiar, places not lived many times. To see things new and fresh, things known for the very first time. The very possibilities made his hyr'yan't dizzy. He turned his eyes upward to Se'Yan't's yellow skies, the glaring twin suns showering them with warmth, and thought about the "little night," and the darkness with the ever-brighter light falling through the sky.

His newly awaking understanding making many possibilities real, the instrument spoke again, the words once again twisted into the raucous sounds of the strangers. This time Rjorck began to make sense of the low sounds, the tones so different from the way he had spoken them at first. They were his own, for he began to recognize semblances of the sounds, yet containing the baser rumblings of many of Se'Yan't's burrowing creatures . . . slower, deeper.

He could do that, speak those low sounds, this visitor's speech, he thought, and his face twisted in concentration. He could manipulate his voice in that way.

Worlds of understanding and imaginations too grand for his heart to contain opening before him, he stepped forward to greet his future, his manifest destiny.

Section 4

The Rise of Rejuvenant: A Planet Reborn (revised)

A Study to Accompany *The Decimation of Rejuvenant: A Regressive Study of the Motivations that Precipitated the Misuse of Power by MegaCorp Minions*, by El'Tirest'n Ragusin, SSM.rl. adjunct, UNAS

Summary:

This report begins at the precipice of MegaCorp's folly, during which the great organization's evil machinations began to be revealed. Unlike *The Decimation of Rejuvenant,* which was written in a regressive timeframe (at Ssm. deFralin's esteemed suggestion), *The Rise of Rejuvenant: A Planet Reborn* follows a more traditional sequence, although for ease of reading, the format of the earlier work is retained.

Starting at the estimated moment of destruction of the largest (and final) MegaCorp battleship ever built, Ssm. deFralin's extraordinary findings document a daring rescue mission that was both unprecedented and fantastical.

See original report and final comments for additional material. All rights and permissions conjoined with the original study and owned in totality by UNAS/UT. Some of the included studies contain material that is highly circumstantial, and the reliability of the information should be weighed carefully in the reader's mind. Please message Natal La'Sterene, Senior Chancellor, for additional information.

The Rise of Rejuvenant: A Planet Reborn, by El'Tirest'n Ragusin, SSM.rl.adjunct, UNAS

Original Draft, 2819 A.D. (O.E. Standard)

Final Revision, 3299 A.D. (O.E. Standard)

Approved: Natal La'Sterene, Senior Chancellor, University of Terra (formerly UNAS), by the Hand of the Terran Supreme Father on 3301 A.D.

No further revisions planned at this time.

Study 1

Compiled by: Ed'th Ze'pliinth, SSM.rl, UNAS
Subject: Rjorck
Location: Rejuvenant/Se'Yan't
Earth-Reference Date: 2801 A.D. (O.E. Standard)

LYING ON THE STONES of his youth, the emptied shell of his escape vessel at his back, Rjorck's near-empty husk only showed life as the faintest rattling of breath in and out of exhausted lungs. His thoughts were no more than fractured remnants of the brilliance with which he had served his treasured Se'Yan't for so many centuries. That didn't stop the waters from calling him, though.

Gratefully, his broken essence responded, barely, faintly. *So tired,* he felt someone else think. Papery eyelids fluttered with the enormous effort that the *thought* pulled from him. The water was far . . . so far.

The seas of Se'Yan't reached long fingers toward their child, the only one left. They were patient, though. The twin suns overhead would soon wrest the tides from their hiding places, and then the waters would welcome their prodigal son home once again.

My body . . . so empty . . . I feel already gone. I can smell c'habor-reneis't . . . see it. It is so close, so close . . . yet so far . . . so far . . .

Rjorck's eyelids once again relaxed, and only the raspy rustle of air from between his lips told of the life still hiding within.

Study 2

Compiled by: J. Ret'tsh, SSN.rt, UNAS/UT
Subject: A'man Braxtn
Location: MegaCorp Headquarters, Earth
Earth-Reference Date: 2801 A.D. (O.E. Standard)

SECURITY CHIEF BRAXTN glared at the offending glass. Slamming the side of his leathery fist on the desktop, venting his frustration at the only thing within reach, he stretched his fingers to manipulate the images within the glass once again.

"Robn't," he yelled. "Get in here!" Waving his hand over his shoulder at the unseen underling, he called out in a harsh voice, "How did this happen? They were just there. Now they're not. How can a star cruiser just not *be* there? Tell me that, Robn't. How can they just not be there?" He spun around in his chair and glared at his subordinate. Tossing his head at the offending display, he snorted. "My backsides, it had better not be that cursed glitch we had last quarter. Tell me that, Robn't. Tell me it's not that cursed glitch from last quarter." Glaring at the scared rabbit of a man standing in his way, Braxtn was instantly on his feet, his craggy features belying his quickness, his momentum carrying him through the door, the chair spinning in his wake.

"S-s-ser," stammered Robn't. "I d-d-don't think s-s-so,

ser." He reached in a pocket, pulling out an information crystal, nearly losing it to the floor as he darted after his commanding chief offic'r.

The loud clap of receding footsteps leading him on, Robn't hustled to catch up, well aware of the penalty of not being there when Braxtn next called his name. Taking well-rehearsed "shorts" though several connecting cubicles, commiserating looks on glimpsed faces compounding his misery, he slid into place just as his boss slammed the door to his office open.

"Where have you been?" Braxtn saw the same images on the glass in this office, and he slammed his hand against it, the images flickering at the force, his anger seeming to transmit into the circuits themselves. "I've got to have that missing ship up and available. Do you hear me, Robn't? Starstrike class battleships don't just disappear into thin air! This is MegaCorp's newest and most powerful. It can't have simply vanished!"

"Ser," Robn't suggested, offering the information crystal as his buffer. "Ser, this time I think it might have done just that." Dancing away, he moved to a safer distance as the crystal was whisked from his hand.

"What does that mean?" Braxtn thrust the crystal into the terminal slot, slapping his hand against the glass, his anger forcing the images to show him what he wanted. Leathery skin squinting, his eyes absorbed the images as they appeared. Tweaking the information with a flick of a finger, he muttered to himself, "What does this mean? This can't be right. It's there. I saw it just minutes ago. Then, nothing. It was there, I tell you. Now, look at this. What is that signature? An electromagnetic solar flare? I guess it could be with those flamin' twin suns. Who would live on a planet that near two suns, and that big one! My gram's skillet! It could fry a solar kite in a heartbeat. If I owned real estate there, I'd be out in a flash, forget the loss. My lands, I cannot make heads nor tails of this."

Glancing up, seeing Robn't still there, Braxtn barked, "I

want two teams on this. Get to PR to get a group together to contain this mess. My word! How can a ship just disappear along with thousands of people? There'll be bad times for somebody to pay, and I'll be fried if it'll be me!" His glare froze his subordinate in position, the rabbit to the determined predator. Braxtn flung his sentiments across the room once again, yelling them just for emphasis. "I'll be the fool if I'm the one to pay." Chewing his jaw, he continued his riveting gaze, then spat, "Git, you idiot. You think this is going to fix itself?"

"Ser, what about the second team you want?" The sound rasped from Robn't's throat, his nervousness palpable.

"Get it together, man. Don't you have a brain in that body?" The security chief spun around, his hand darting to the glass displaying the unwanted news. With quick motions, his movements yanked forward new, as yet unseen information, as if the chief had known it was there all along. "There! That! Get a military team out there to recover whatever clues are still left. I want MegaCorp's best out there dropping equipment yesterday. Nothing can create an electromagnetic signature that big without some evidence left behind. Go on, man. Get to work."

The chief turned to the display, his confidence in his subordinate dismissing the man from his mind, his only thoughts now how to handle the distress of the events developing around him, surely shredding his career to tatters.

ROBN'T STEPPED BACK inside the control center, color slowly regaining its grip on his face. With the wall supporting him, he leaned his head against its rigidness to give himself time to regain his composure. He felt the rustle of someone turning toward him as a coworker's spoken words cut into his illusory zone of privacy.

"That bad, huh, chief? I'm just glad it was your hide that

got ripped off, and not mine. I've been skewered too many times by the big guy, and I'm glad to let you have it any time." The man gave a grunt of disgust in sympathy for Robn't's predicament, glancing around at the other heads nodding in agreement.

"He's up a creek for sure, this time. I wouldn't want to be him." Ever the faithful team player, Robn't crossed to his desk, his hand waving up the glass as he sat. "Either we find that ship, or he goes down, and you can bet he won't go down alone. Boys, this is a big one. We need to get together two crack teams, one to keep all this under wraps and another to get their backsides out there and find out just what happened to that battleship. There must be something out there, residue, floating ion drive traces, organic materials, or *something*."

Quickly coming up to speed, tapping his glass to bring up the requisition manifests, his mind began doing what it did best, his skills exemplary in pulling together the best in materials and manpower from the vast stores of the MegaCorp empire. Excitement began pouring through his veins, and the scope of what was possible began to grow in his mind.

This was what drove him to endure the tirades of the security chief, this opportunity to mobilize the giant, to garner the vast array of materials and information, to make the mountain finally come to Muhammad, then to have it do his bidding. Drawing his fingers from the glass, watching the commands he had put into motion begin to grow exponentially, he sat back, his arms behind his head.

"My bidding," he said to himself. "MegaCorp, it's time to do *my* bidding."

His new smile was that of one with confidence in his position of authority, that of one who enjoyed being the power broker, even if he was comfortably entrenched behind the scenes.

141

Study 3

Compiled by: Ed'th Ze'pliinth, SSM.rl, UNAS
Subject: Capt'n of the Freighter-tug Capps'nian
Location: Edge of the Spiral Arm
Earth-Reference Date: 2801 A.D. (O.E. Standard)

THE UNEXPECTED RUMBLE could be felt throughout the ship. Something had hit and hit hard.

The accompanying electromagnetic blast sizzled throughout shielding already old and worn, with the sensor array on one side of the freighter slowly accepting an irreversible but well-deserved death. Inside, the internal sensors shorted, failing to pick up the change in the external information feed. Old and unable to self-correct, the lumbering freighter responded by veering onto an alternate course. The ship was now blind on one side, its heading changed just enough to put it on a trip to nowhere.

Throbbing klaxons jarred the grizzled capt'n out of a bleary sleep. One of the benefits of these slow runs on these old freighter barges was that there was nothing to do except just what he wanted, and what he always wanted was to ply himself with drink and have plenty of time to sleep it off. That was why he always picked these runs, and then packed ninety percent of his weight allotment with the strongest old-Earth Scotch he could find. A few days out and there was nothing to do, and no one to see him do it.

Bleary from sleeping off a long binge, he stumbled from his bunk, wheezing, thinking the hooch had never made him feel this bad before, with him not even able to catch his breath. Struggling harder and harder to draw in enough air to satisfy his starving chest, he shook his head, his eyes finally clearing enough to focus on the flashing sensor on the wall.

"Blasters!" The spittle flew from his lips as his brain attempted to grasp the meaning of the red lights. "Exploding meteors! This is empty space. How could I be decompressing? Seals couldn't be gone. I checked 'em back in port."

He hit the panel beside the light, waiting for the status report to pull up. His stomach nauseous, he closed his eyes as his head spun, knowing he should not feel this light-headed. "Dang-slow machine," he mumbled. "Probably it doesn't even know there's a problem, and I'll die here in my own vomit." Peering from one cracked eyelid, he absorbed the report coming up on the monitor. "No, no, no!!! Holed in Bay E? Good heavens!"

His realization of the gravity of his predicament jerked his alcohol-polluted muscles into action, the strain shooting fire through his body. "Arrrrgh," he groaned as he stumbled down the corridor. The decreasing air pressure making it ever harder to focus, the capt'n slapped the control to open the emergency decompression survival pod. The action trigged the emergency air canisters. Their contents exhausting into the pod, he breathed in deeply, bringing urgent clarity to his brain. The detoxicants being filtered in with the gasses quickly flushed his systems of the toxic effects of his self-indulgent binges.

His eyes now clear, the capt'n pulled on training from his youth. A safe-suit from a stor'lok bin, a limited-breather canister, and a foray through the near-airless confines of his ship soon told the story. A starstrike class propulsion actuator arm, or what was left of it, had wrestled with his freighter and forced its way inside, gouging out a section of the hull as it did so. Now it floated weightless in Bay E.

He rubbed his chin inside the lightweight safe-suit, more a giant bag rather than anything resembling an actual spacesuit, as he pondered how this unusual part could have gotten way out here.

"Sensors could possibly have picked something up. They

should have." Ideas now starting to rattle around in his head, a tinge of the old excitement precluding the drive to sedate himself with his alcohol, the capt'n grabbed a metal panel and a Patch-o-Torch, sealing the offending tear airtight.

Making his way back to the control room, with the air slowly coming up to standard pressure, he spread long-unused charts over the windowless space. Thinking, his own sour smell redolent in the small room, he retraced his course. Pulling out a small reader, he ran it across the hard copies and then plugged it into a feed line, initiating sensor input. Seeing the wallscreen as it displayed the realtime coordinates of the ships' travel itinerary, he was perplexed until half of the display suddenly went black.

"Not good," he spat into the room. "Solar-suns-take-the-hindquarters not good." Flipping old-fashioned switches and toggles to bring up live feeds for the ship's external sensors, he groaned. Half the mother-scrubbing sensors were shot to tarnation. There would be no self-triangulation with only half the sensor array up. This was going to be a long trip, maybe even long enough for him to find out where he was and just what had happened.

The capt'n rubbed his weathered hand across the stubble sprouting from the hillocks of his face. The wadded skin of his eyes creased into squints, his concentration on the scanty facts from his sensors making his head spin. He knew that something had blasted his sensors, yet the computers hadn't registered an alarm. That meant it had to have slipped inside the sensors' shielding, and that also meant it had to have been electromagnetic. Then, there was the debris still in the hold. That actuator arm was definitely starstrike class, but which model he couldn't identify. This old clunker had received its last info-update so long ago he sometimes thought it was doing good to recognize MegaCorp as a military force.

Pulling his reader out, he flashed the image on the wall,

running it back to the collapse of the sensor arrays. There. That was where his ship had gone off course. He decided to time it back to that point. He might yet tweak this machine into telling him how to get home, even with using just half the stars showing in the sky.

His mind exhausted, but his course reprogramming finally complete, the capt'n smiled contentedly to himself for the first time in many old-Earth months. He hadn't been sure he could still do it, but it was there. He could still pull it from the old noggin when he needed to.

The ancient ship once again on automatic, the capt'n's need for self-medication temporarily adverted, he began to compose a message to MegaCorp, informing them of what he was carrying in his hold. Who knew, there might even be some credits in it for an old capt'n run upon a piece of debris way out in deep space. Wouldn't that be nice, to nearly die and earn an extra credit or two out of it?

Concluding his message and palming the transmit panel, he lay back on his bunk, the adventures of the day enabling him to sleep for the first time in many standard years without the aid of his beloved alcohol.

Study 4

Compiled by: J. Ret'tsh, SSN.rt, UNAS/UT
Subject: MegaCorp StarGen'l Grix'm Janet'
Location: Earth
Earth-Reference Date: 2801 A.D. (O.E. Standard)

"THAT'S WHAT NO ONE can understand, ser. This *is* star-strike class, and not an earlier model, either. This is the top secret one. No, no one knew about the mission, ser. It was certainly kept under the tightest of wraps. Yes, ser, I know what this could mean to the corporation if word leaked out that one of our ships was in the vicinity of Rejuvenant when we lost contact with it. Thank you, ser. I will, ser." The blurring of the privacy field faded from around him as he broke the connection.

MegaCorp StarGen'l Grix'm Janet"s eyes devoured the attention of each of the faces in the room, both those in flesh as well as those in proxy-holo. He growled, "Who's seen this report from that freighter out in the arm?" A hand or realistic facsimile from every attendee begrudged acknowledgement. "Ben'frn, have we contacted the capt'n, yet? Do we know anything more than just what he sent us in that slo-trak?"

"No, ser." The man shook his head negatively. He was calm and collected. His job was to assemble the information already received, not go into the field and actually fondle it. The onus was on those standing in the room with him.

Seeing the nervous eyes of each person or holo flicking back and forth at each other, Janet"s mouth tightened, and he slammed his fist on the real-wood table, lashing out, "Then find something!" With a crash of his hand onto a sensor, the proxy-holos winked out, and the flesh copies jerked from their seats, hoping for escape.

Growling, Janet' pulled them back with the steel in his voice. "Our military arm is known for supporting the policies of WorldPresident Benetin. Our other activities are entirely secretive. Each of you knows that. To update you on this mission, CaptGen'l Willane Bofsky was given unprecedented liberty to achieve the required objective no matter the cost. As of the last received transmission, he had been rather permissive in allowing his crew to attempt to persuade the inhabitants of Rejuvenant to accommodate our requests for certain information they possessed. It would seem this information was unable to be acquired even at the cost of the entire indigenous population living on the planet.

"Here is one of our major concerns in this situation. Rejuvenant was known to be an unarmed planet. Yet, our most advanced starstrike battleship simply winked out within one AU of the suns of the Rejuvenant system. My best analysts say it was even closer, perhaps within a hundredth light year. There was no warning that we have been made aware of. There have been no reports received from any nearby quarters indicating any unusual activity in the area, and at this point, sers, we are, without question, clueless. Does anyone have any input or suggestions in this matter?"

"Um, ser, could this possibly be something new?" The voice was tentative, the speaker's forehead damp with nervousness.

Janet' exploded, "Be specific, man! Something new? Like what?"

"Ser, a new class of technology or even a new race of sentient beings?" The face had gone white.

Feeling the distaste seeping down his face, Janet' threw back his head. "Am I always to be surrounded by idiots? A new race of sentient beings? May God save us from the idiots at our sides! Out! Out! All of you, out!" His eyes closed, and with the heels of his hands pressed to his face, he shook his head back and forth at the stupidity that daily sat in his conference chambers with him.

When the room was again silent, he reached to the table and touched a sensor. The voice exploded into the room, its background chatter of static unable to adequately disguise the alcoholic tremor in the voice as well as the extreme distance of the slo-trak transmission.

"This is the capt'n of the freighter-tug Capps'nian out of Wendy's World. I have a piece of one of your ships you might be interested in, a starstrike class propulsion actuator arm. It might go credits to the highest bidder. Any of you in there interested?"

147

"My word, what a note to end on, and him still years away." Janet′ stood and walked to the glassine clearwall, the city spread out before him. He knew they would pay, and no price would be too much. He just hoped the capt'n of that freighter-tug didn't get too greedy, or else he might be the one who would pay his all.

MEGACORP STARGEN'L GRIX′M JANET′ drew his civilian ceremonial robes snugly around his waist. He hated these blasted civilian accoutrements! Give him a good old military overjacket any day. Straightening his head, he strode into the corporation headquarters of the largest commercial and military enterprise in the known planets. The huge MC emblazoned over the real-time Earth dominated the enormous room.

His data crystal in his hand, his verbal summary weighing on his mind, he stood tall, hoping for the best but realistic in expecting the worst. These corporation overlords wanted profits, profits, and more profits. How they got them was unimportant, but the profits had better keep rolling in. Just don't embarrass them with a foul-up, and by heavens, this was a ball-crusher of a foul-up.

StarGen'l Janet′ bowed and began to speak, his strong voice belying the tremor in his belly. They would hear what he had to say, even though they might not like it. Let them deal with the consequences.

"Gentle Sers, let me acquaint you with some matters that in the past have not been deemed worthy of your concern. One of these matters is the true nature of the so-called defensive capabilities of our corporation battle cruisers. Recently, one of our most state-of-the-art starstrike class cruisers was sent to an isolated system of two tidally locked stars. You may have heard of the inhabited planet that revolves around one of these stars. It is called Rejuvenant, although it is a planet you might be more familiar with as the Garden Planet.

"Over the years, information has been collected to very strongly suggest the indigenous peoples had developed a process for the indefinite extension of life. In an effort to obtain this process, our cruiser was sent out to negotiate with the inhabitants of this world. It would seem the negotiations became a little one-sided, and as of the last registered report received, the local populace had succumbed to the capt'n's interrogation methods.

"It is unknown just how, but we have lost contact with the cruiser. It would seem to have simply vanished except for one isolated message received from an old freighter-tug plying the area at sub-light speed. It claims to have been damaged by a fragment of the aforementioned cruiser, retaining the fragment in a smashed hold.

"As you might imagine, plans to contain the financial and political fallout have been initiated . . ."

Uproar ensued from the men underneath MegaCorp's symbolic Earth, effectively ending Janet''s discourse. It was as well, he thought. The news only got worse, and he bowed his head to await their pleasure, knowing they would have their way in this room, and he could only bide his time.

Study 5

Compiled by: Ed'th Ze'pliinth, SSM.rl, UNAS
Subject: Dr.Sci. Refren Ascott
Location: Alpha Station, System 1509.87b
Earth-Reference Date: 2801 A.D. (O.E. Standard)

THE GREAT WHEELS PRESSED against their foundations, their tremulous quakings stirring age-old dust into renewed life. With mighty groans of protest, the weary giant rose from its slumber, pressing its massive shoulders into service once again. A great crack opened, the slumbering giant awakening from its sleep, the daylight its time of slumber, the darkness its call to life.

Alert now, the mighty eye turned, its gaze piercing the blackness of the heavens, the offerings the universe laid at its feet soon absorbed into its long memory, its great hall of machines recording the eons-dead images sent its way so very long ago. The giant moved slowly in its familiar world, the changes it observed minute, the occasional quicksilver recording of movement taking days or even weeks of local realtime to reach its peak.

This night something new was seen. The giant observed, its recording instruments absorbing this new information, the ponderous discovery of this event just one more detail dutifully recorded in the halls of its memory.

"RUN THAT REPORT ONE MORE TIME. This can't be right." Dr.Sci. Refren Ascott pulled at the display glass. His forehead was furrowed as he puzzled over the discrepancies in the previous evening's observatory report.

For years he'd dreamed of being here, on Alpha Station, with its original McRam'n-Foser telescope at his disposal, its ancient well-oiled metal heavens-only-knew how old, but of the highest quality. The lenses, the most finely ever ground, had never needed attention other than occasional polishing and buffing. In other areas, the university had wisely spent credits on maintenance of the telescope's mechanical infrastructure. State of the art when new, given countless upgrades over the centuries, the old girl was Dr.Sci. Ascott's first love. Gingerly, he ran his hand over the gleaming colossus. Then, taking a deep breath, he turned back to the necessities of the moment.

"Do you have it, yet?" His attention smoothly transitioning to the needs at hand, he strode purposefully down the steps to the main interface bank. "I need that information up now so I

150

can balance the patterns in the memory log of this week's reports." His fingers already probing the data flashing at him on the glass, he knew the answer was in there. He just had to ferret it out.

NIGHTLY REPORT: Alpha Station, System 1509.87b. Optical McRam'n-Foser Virtual Scoping Interferometer.

A FIR high-resolution survey of massive star formation has been effectively concluded. Twenty-three regions showed warm dust emission. The FIR emission distributions and radio free-free emission tended to be coincident, with the masers not usually coincident with the FIR peaks. Several examples of emerging massive protostars with no radio continuum counterparts may be the precursors to UC HII regions.

Referring to archival HST NICMOS images of Class 1 stars combined with 4-D image-synthesis codes, the disk/envelope structure of several observed young stars show observed scattered-light morphologies produced by jet-evacuated "cavities" in large circumstellar envelopes, and in several examples, the absence of circumstellar envelopes by jet-remnant material. At a distance of 142 pc, the observed masses are 1.7 and 0.9M. The semi-major axis is determined to be 0.0987". At these locations, methyl cyanide (CH_3CN) is strongly enhanced.

Unusual for the H-201.15n quadrant, an observed electromagnetic burst disrupted the study of high excitation Planetaries (Fe5-1, OHE 4450, and NGC 99-4b). Exact cause of this burst is unknown at this time. Total energy output will not be known for some time, but measured in joule/m^2, the total output is estimated to exceed the minimal planetary disruptive capability. Ranging near 2000 Hz, the burst was easily detectable. The megawatt output is still undetermined. The event seems to have dissipated completely. Further study at close range may indicate the cause of this incident.

Dr.Sci. Refren Ascott looked at his desk, irritated at the third paragraph's distraction. Electromagnetic burst. Total output estimated to exceed the minimal planetary disruptive capability. The event seemed to have dissipated completely. The information was not consistent with what should be out there. It was an anomaly.

Then there was this red light blinking on his glass, determined to remind him of another piece of unfinished business. Both things worried under his skin. He knew the report's anomaly would be criticized if left unresolved. It was the second thing that gnawed at him, though. Sighing his acquiescence, he reached a bone-weary hand to the glass and pulled the red light to sub-display status, ready for opening as soon as he worked up the nerve. First he would know what this anomaly was. If left unresolved, it could leave a mark on his tenure that would be unacceptable.

He stepped to his assistant. "Have any other sectors reported this anomaly? The EMP output is certainly a cause for alarm. I see no way this could be a natural occurrence." When his assistant shook his head, Ascott sighed, admitting he had no choice but to access the dreaded message behind the red light. Pushing the offending nightly report into the background, a finger twitch brought up the cause of the even more ominous assault to his ulcer. Running fingers though his tired hair, he reread the hated lines displayed on the glass.

"Please resolve this electromagnetic discrepancy with all

haste. Sector funding reports are imminent. University funding cutbacks, including those for the Loritmar Observatory, have been initiated. Our continued success has helped us escape the ax up to this point. No allowances will be made for poor performance."

Ascott's stomach forced an unwelcome sourness into the back of his throat, its sudden, encapsulated pain one to match the mood of the day.

As he tapped the reports back into their hiding places, his eyes disinterestedly skimmed the background display showing the internal university news feed. In spite of his distraction, one phrase clearly jumped from the glass. "Starstrike class battleship goes missing in the vicinity of a distant binary star system." That, he knew, was not information for the general public. It was only available on his glass because of his university priority access. Only MegaCorp had starstrike class ships, and they must be really sitting on this one.

Then the details lined themselves up nicely for him. Electromagnetic burst. Starstrike class battleship. One dual star system.

Dual star system! The situation began to gel in his mind. It was obvious! The dual star system limited the location, and that cinched it for him. These were inextricably connected. However, there was still the matter of the immense power recorded in that electromagnetic burst. He knew the propulsion systems of starstrike class vessels were enormously powerful, but able to produce EMP waves in the intensity observed by the telescope, even in a severe destruction scenario? Still, it might be a good lead. Now if he just knew where that dual star system was in relation to his anomaly.

He tapped up a star reference chart, pulling the news reference over it to interface the two. The similarities were too great to be coincidence. This just might save the funding after all.

His confidence in his intuition growing, his skin was soon

flushed with anticipation. Only a fool could not see that the destruction of a starstrike military vessel might surely have caused that burst. Now if he could just determine what else might have been involved to get the power levels up to the amounts registered on the report. Just what could take out a starstrike class battle cruiser? Just what could do that?

Fingers tapping out queries, his movements pulling up additional information to verify his hunches, he soon had messages sent to his colleagues. Before long, the entire department at the university was moving toward the answer MegaCorp was trying so hard to hide.

Study 6

Compiled by: Ed'th Ze'pliinth, SSM.rl, UNAS
Subject: NewsVids
Location: Throughout the Twelve Systems
Earth-Reference Date: 2801-2802 A.D. (O.E. Standard)

JUNE 1. Newstribune. New York, Earth. UNPRECE-DENTED DISCOVERY BY LOCAL ASTRONOMER. Last month, local university phenomenon Dr.Sci. Re-fren Ascott (University of New American States) made an amazing discovery during a routine survey funded by the Loritmar Observatory. Currently on university loan to Alpha Station, System 1509.87b, Ascott was us-ing an outdated Optical McRam'n-Foser Virtual Scop-ing telescope when a spike in EMP (electromagnetic pulse wave) emissions hit his location. Thankfully, due to the extreme distance from the EMP, no damage to the station was reported.

Dr.Sci. Ascott reports the chances of inadvertently

154

pointing the telescope in just the right direction at just the right time were astronomical. He attributes credit to the Optical McRam'n-Foser Virtual Scoping telescope he had at his disposal. Although this telescope was put into service over 200 standard years ago, the precision with which it was built as well as the high level of maintenance it has received have enabled it to perform flawlessly in this unique situation.

Dr.Sci. Ascott also reports that the cause of the EMP is under investigation by the university and should be revealed soon. –by D. Wymen Ragnost'en.

OCTOBER 3. IntergalacticNews.news. Ares City, Mars. MEGACORP STUMBLES. During a routine investigation, a glaring discrepancy in MegaCorp's accountability has been brought to light. Citing a growing need for advanced military capability, the controlling faction in this enormous corporation has cajoled the voting shareholders into approving vastly enormous expenditures on new and extreme weaponry. It now seems that MegaCorp has lost one of these new weapons. This latest in technological advances in military hardware, an entirely new class of battle cruiser, is the newest and most expensive military armament ever produced. Although technically still designated as starstrike class due to its basic propulsion design, it in reality far surpasses the much-heralded starstrike class. It is larger, has a more powerful propulsion system, more firepower, and deploys a crew of more than twenty-one thousand men. According to the published minutes of MegaCorp board meetings, the cost to build this behemoth was originally estimated at $470T. Before final completion, the actual cost to the corporation shareholders exceeded $1.78Q.

Where has this vastly extravagant game piece gone? According to unnamed sources embedded deep within the MegaCorp corporate hierarchy, all communication was lost with the battle cruiser while it was on a "routine" mission to the distant world of Rejuvenant. Official MegaCorp sources are mute on the validity of this report, leading this reporter to believe there is an overwhelming degree of truth in this obvious connection, a fresh revelation that simply can't be denied or swept under the rug.

MegaCorp, own up to your failings. You've pushed and bullied your way to profits long enough. Now is the time to come clean. –Staff Reporter Ch'onksi Welhem.

OCTOBER 3. Internal Memo. MegaCorp Corporation. Earth. THERE HAS BEEN SOME DISSENTION ABOUT QUESTIONS THAT HAVE ARISEN CONCERNING DISREGARD FOR ESTABLISHED MEGACORP POLICY AS WELL AS THE STABILITY OF CERTAIN ASSETS AND COMPANY INFRASTRUCTURE. BE IT KNOWN THAT THIS CORPORATION IS STABLE AND SOUND, AND IT IS EXPECTED THAT ALL MEGACORP EMPLOYEES AND ASSOCIATES WILL SUPPORT THE POLICIES OF THIS ORGANIZATION, WHETHER THEY BE FINANCIAL OR MILITARY-BASED.

THERE HAS BEEN AN OCCURRENCE IN WHICH A MILITARY-BASED TRANSPORT HAS BEEN

OUT OF CONTACT WITH MEGACORP'S MILITARY COMMUNICATIONS CENTER FOR SOME TIME. THE REASON FOR THIS BREAK IN COMMUNICATIONS IS UNKNOWN AT THIS TIME. ALL EMPLOYEES AND ASSOCIATES OF THIS CORPORATION ARE HEREBY INSTRUCTED TO CEASE AND DESIST IN ANY AND ALL COMMUNICATIONS WITH THE MEDIA OR OTHER OUTSIDE ORGANIZATIONS WHICH MIGHT IMPACT NEGATIVELY ON MEGA-CORP'S PUBLIC IMAGE OR FINANCIAL STABILITY.

WHEN ADDITIONAL INFORMATION IS AVAILABLE CONCERNING THE WHEREABOUTS OF THE MISSING TRANSPORT, ALL EMPLOYEES WILL BE NOTIFIED. MEGACORP SENIOR STAFF ARE CONFIDENT THAT THIS TRANSPORT WILL BE FOUND AND THE REASON FOR ITS DISAPPEARANCE EASILY EXPLAINED. –Official Mega-Corp document. Private use is prohibited.

OCTOBER 11. San Francisco Examiner. New San Francisco, Earth. IS NO NEWS REALLY GOOD NEWS? According to sources deep within MegaCorp, a certain missing company battleship may not be found soon. Although official sources deny any wrongdoing, saying that the missing ship is simply on "secret" maneuvers, family members of ship personnel claim to have been unable to contact shipboard children or siblings, giving rise to rumors the ship has met an untimely end. While MegaCorp vehemently denies this, claiming shipboard personnel are rarely given leave to contact planetside family, it is well known that this communication does occur from time to time. There have also been reports of off-world citizens of the planet Rejuvenant who have tried in vain to establish contact with their homeworld. With the last known location of MegaCorp's battleship placed well within striking distance of Rejuvenant's binary star system, these two events seem to coincide too conveniently to be unconnected. There has been no news, not from MegaCorp, and certainly not from Rejuvenant. The question we must all ask is whether this is good news. That is something this news source cannot decide for you. Make up your own mind. Is no news really good news? –Staff Reporter

JANUARY 9. InterWorld Geographic. Earth. CRACK SEEN IN MEGACORP'S FACADE. Standing firmly unified until now, a junior vice-president of MegaCorp has broken rank. Meeting secretly with an unidentified reporter, the rogue employee now makes claims that fly in the face of MegaCorp's official stand. He has produced official internal memos from as far back as October 3 showing that the upper echelon of Mega-Corp knew and hid from the public and its own shareholders the disappearance of certain cutting edge military hardware near the vicinity of a planet that has been incommunicado since this series of events became known.

This employee states that he was put under pressure to willfully aid and abet this charade at the dire cost of his livelihood. He is now coming forth to salve a conscience torn by the reports of distraught family members unable to get word from the now confirmed missing battleship.

"I am so very sorry that each of these families has had to suffer this uncertainty during these past weeks. I can only pretend to imagine the sleepless nights and tearful days of these good people when they were unable to find anyone in this corporation honest enough to come clean on the matter of this missing battleship. People across the known worlds must be able to trust Mega-Corp, or the economic ties fostered by MegaCorp's dominance in the financial and economic sectors will collapse, and world economies across space will be shattered."

Thank you to one honest MegaCorp employee. I know more will come forth once they see that honesty before others is rewarded, even by MegaCorp. –Rev. Ran-jacket Boos'tle

Study 7

Compiled by: Ed'th Ze'pliinth, SSM.rl, UNAS
Subject: CityGvn'r Reenson
Location: City Offices, Aregas 4
Earth-Reference Date: 2802 A.D. (O.E. Standard)

CITYGVN'R REENSON walked the long distance from the door to her desk, the plushness of the carpets making the calves of her legs ache with the strain. Looking for the message stick she expected to find, she was puzzled to see only something flat and brown. Picking it up, she held it in her hands, the *unusualness* of it meaning little to her, only to find it was in layers, all the same size and weight.

How curious! She ran her hand over indentations filled in by a black substance—ink, she thought it was called. She knew this. With her brow furrowed, she reached to the recesses of her memory, knowing this should be an easy word to recall. How foolish she would feel when it came to her!

Throwing her head back with laughter, she knew. *Paper!* Immediately, the well-known putdown came to her, *Texting for the poor.*

Embarrassed to have let the thought run through her head, she studied the script on the unfamiliar paper. Squinting, she turned it to catch the light. It wasn't so hard to read if she could get the light directly on it. Not being glass-based was so different, though. Walking around the room, she slowly began to absorb the text, its impart becoming clear to her as she found herself able to read the unusual medium more and more rapidly.

Dear CityGvn'r,
We don't got much here down in the city, not much that ain't been thrown away by one of you. One thing we got is our pride, though. We are born and die, just like you, and when things go good, life is happy for us. Sometimes things ain't so good, though. Lots of us just barely get by. Getting food is hard, and getting sick is likely a death sentence. But we do what we can, and sometimes life is good.
Now, MegaCorp, there. They been good to us. Wherever we go, they sell us stuff. We can get it at fair prices. My wife, she worked in a MegaSales Center for a long time. She didn't make much, but they was good to her, and she liked her work. She got real sick there for a while, and we all understood she had to be let go. You can't keep paying someone and have to hire someone else to do their job. But it was tough when she was let go. They did throw her a nice little party when she left, and gave her a little cake and all. She

did enjoy that. She kept the little decorations until the day she died, kept 'em by her bedside and all. She always thought of MegaCorp as a guarding angel.

But now, we're all together. We don't think Mega-Corp's on our side anymore. Sure, when times got really tough, the credits from sending our boys and girls to the academy was a godsend. Lots of us used those credits for feeding our families, otherwise we wouldn't have had anything to eat. We appreciated it. We really did. But now things seem different.

That ship they say went down out there in space. All those kids were on board. MegaCorp won't tell us nothing. Myself, I got a nephew on board. Never had kids of my own, the wife getting sick and all. But that boy I thought of as my own. He's only twenty standards old. He should be fighting for us, for our betterment, for the good of MegaCorp and all us down here in the city. Now he's just dead, from what they say. Gone. And they don't tell us nothing.

Me and all the people I know feel the need to do something. Well, they won't listen to us talk, so we feel there might be more than one way to talk. We've got some stuff stored up, all of us do. A couple of us have little pieces of ground we can grow things in. Our clothes will last us a few more years. We think we don't need to buy from MegaCorp anymore. A few of us still have jobs there. We can sure take their credits, but that don't mean they'll get any more of ours.

This might not make much of a difference. But if enough of us got together, maybe they'd have to listen. That's why we're writing you. We don't have much skills at these kinds of things. We just figured if enough of us signed this petition, you might be willing to get something going, talk to some other high-placed folk,

get the ball rolling, just do what you got to do.
Please help us. We can't do this on our own. We don't
know how.
Yours,
Johnie L. Bean

"My word," the citygvn'r said aloud to the room around her. "They treat his sick wife like dirt, and she grovels for them. They take their children for a few dollars, and they worship them. Now MegaCorp is playing god. These poor people. How can I not give them all the help I can?"

She shifted the pages, looking at the list of names filling the lines behind the simple, handwritten sheet. "All these names. No telling how long it took to go from person to person gathering all these names. This is the story that'll get the ball going against that monstrosity. I couldn't have put together anything better if I'd assembled a team of PR people to work on this for two weeks. I won't even need to rewrite this."

She sat down in a richly appointed chair by the flames of a real-wood fire. Reaching beside her chair for a portable glass, she stroked its surface, awakening the transmitting circuits inside. With the spare movements born of much practice, she gently pushed and tugged the information within, her highest-level contacts soon receiving copies of the heart-wrenching letter she held in her hand.

Standing, pausing by the fireside to soak up the heat from the flames, the full impact of what she held in her hand drew a slow tide of sadness from her deepest being, its building sorrow wrenching its payment in wracking sobs of grief for these people she didn't even know. When, in exhaustion, they finally subsided, she turned and opened the personal safe in her desk, placing the letter inside, its presence comforted by her most treasured possessions. This she knew she must keep safe always to remind her of what her life, under other circumstances, might have been.

Study 8

Compiled by: Ed'th Ze'pliinth, SSM.rl, UNAS
Subject: CityGvn'r Reenson
Location: Legislative Chambers, Aregas 4
Earth-Reference Date: 2802 A.D. (O.E. Standard)

CHIMES SOUNDED THROUGHOUT the room, the red lights blinking off, green taking their place, the visual acknowledgment of opinions imparted. Scattered throughout the vastness, numerous amber lights indicated abeyances, assurances that participation was indeed voluntary.

This was no mere vote summed up in the electrical movements of data in a machine. This labor intensive process went back centuries, old fashioned and outdated, a long-established, human-driven mechanical ritual that no one was willing to change, update, or improve. Possibly, the lag between the final votes and the count being displayed above the speaker's podium gave the participants time for an internal discourse over whether they had made the wise decision their constituents entreated them to court, or perhaps at least it gave them the time to justify their selfish decisions before the final tally was shown.

A somber mood spread its great shroud over the attendees, the richly adorned buttresses overhead held in place by the scores of carved cherubim that watched over their charges. Today's actions were no small matter, for they were being repeated in similar chambers all across the known worlds. The members gathered here knew they themselves might very well suffer the consequences of the decision they made in this room. Each one drawing into his or her own private shell of safety, eyes were kept averted as the tallies were clicked into the machine.

With a crash of wood, the speaker's mallet awakened the giant display overhead. Initiating an uproar, each person who had voted stood and cheered, claiming the decision of the group as his or her own, no matter which toggle he or she had flipped. Today, all was glory and excitement, and a sense of victory infused the air. Today, the giant was defeated, its wings clipped, its arrogance brought down to size. Today, the price for that arrogance would be deemed high, and the monolithic monster would be called upon to pay.

What happened on the morning might be something else, indeed. Tomorrow's secret scurryings of the power brokers gathered all together cheering in this one room might belie the votes they had just cast. Their greed might create new alliances for the purposes of profit or divide the closest of bonded brothers along lines of principle. But today, everyone was in agreement. Lies had been told, a cover up attempted, and the abuse of power against the little person wielded shamelessly by a giant corporation. That would be permitted no longer. Mega-Corp would be brought to its knees.

Observing from the worldgvn'r's suite overlooking the voting floor, the mood was subdued. "I wouldn't count on this making any real difference, you know." The worldgvn'r swirled a frothy liquid in his glass. "Sure, they've voted to slap MegaCorp's wrist, but that's all it will be. A slap. They've phrased their vote to appeal to the little guy, but the little guy wouldn't know the difference between a $40K fine and a $40B fine. All the numbers are just that, big numbers." He paused to sip from his glass, his tongue holding the froth at bay while the bitter liquid burned down his throat.

"I should know that," sighed the citygvn'r. "I wish I could say that the people who started all this would see something from it, but the types of changes they need are beyond anything

164

I can do." She looked out over the floor, the tinted real-glass hiding her observations. "There they are, putting on a show for the people they claim to represent. At least we got this, however small a victory it might be. God knows the corporation will simply sic some World-lawyers on this, dumbing down the effects until they mean nothing at all. If MegaCorp weren't the glue holding our world's economy together, I'd sure like to stick it to them. For the little guy."

"We'll see that your little guys get something. At least the ones who signed that petition. We'll show them taking a chance like that has its rewards. And remember," he paused, walking over to the window to stand beside the citygvn'r, "those guys down there still get to vote on the sentencing. This might still get really good after all." Thrusting one hand deep into a pocket, he threw his head back, taking the last of the bitter liquor and its sickeningly sweet foam into his mouth, adversaries fighting each other for dominance as they slid down his throat.

Study 9

Compiled by: Ed'th Ze'pliinth, SSM.rl, UNAS
Subject: Legislative Voting Member in Good Standing
Location: Aregas 4
Earth-Reference Date: 2802 A.D. (O.E. Standard)

NOT EVEN THE HEAT of the shower and repeated scrubbings with the strongest soap he could find had managed to scrub the stink of what he'd done from his body. He could feel it on himself as he slipped beneath the sheets, sliding up to his bonded woman's warmth for the comfort of her body.

"Hmm . . ." She placed a sleep-warmed palm against his face, her touch relaxing the brittle edges of his racing thoughts.

That vote, how pathetic he had been! He had wanted to vote with them, but all that stock, the income he and his bonded woman depended on for this lifestyle they led, all of it depended on Mega-Corp. Voting against MegaCorp was voting against their lifestyle, no matter whether he agreed with them or not. Then he had cheered with all the others, a fraud on the outside, a traitor on the inside, silently cursing what he saw on that board. My word! He must own hundreds of thousands of shares of stock. What would happen if the corporation were hit the way the wording in those bills would allow? Bankruptcy! He had to think. What could he do?

Wakefulness his enemy tonight, he wrapped his arms around his sleeping lover, wondering how it had come to this, and his mind began to tick along, his brilliant legal-bent brain clicking off paths he could take, flicking away those that would turn into dead ends, letting the brightest of his imagined possibilities lead him through the night. By the time his bonded woman awoke to the brilliance of the morning sun, he was far along in his plans to moderate the damage that he had cheered on just the day before.

It seemed so simple, finally. He didn't know what had been with him last night. Just a few guiding nudges with just the right people, and he would ensure the continued success of his financial stability. He was certainly brilliant and deserved every credit he could earn.

His beautiful spouse awoke, and he wrapped his arms around her, certain he must lead the most charmed of lives.

Study 10

Compiled by: J. Ret'tsh, SSN.rt, UNAS/UT
Subject: MegaCorp Headquarters
Location: Earth

DARKNESS PERMEATED THE BUILDING. The verification team walked down long halls, the vast banks of overhead lights dimmed, the glassine clearwalls muted and opaqued. Conference rooms had been cleared of furniture. Mechanical systems no longer moved their breath of life throughout the building. Death and darkness held the huge behemoth in its grip, squeezing it tightly, pressing the joy of existence from even those who came to verify its demise.

"Hey. Look at this."

The words reverberated harshly as the other members of the team stopped and glared. The sound of the speaker's voice seemed almost disrespectful in this empty cathedral to greed. The others followed him, moving as one, silent and respectful of the death around them, into the once great boardroom of the MegaCorp Corporation.

"I saw this on the Vid once. I never thought I'd see it in person, though." The voice was hushed this time.

Looking up at the great iconic symbol of the MegaCorp Corporation recognized throughout the known galaxy, the team stood in awe. The brilliance gone, and with the live feed no longer powering the representative Earth, death shrouded the iconic symbol. Its life had been taken, and the visible heart of the building was dead. That was what brought home the truth to the team. MegaCorp was truly banished from this great city. Control had been stripped from the ruling echelon of the corporation, the military arm spun off as a separate entity; Mega-Corp had been effectively dismembered, its universal power sheared down the middle, the whole now broken in two.

True to the intent of the bills enacted into law, MegaCorp's malfeasance had spelled doom for many of its ruling elite. But the individual parts would go on. Too big to be allowed to fail, too strong to be allowed to continue, legal minds and legal entities had pushed, prodded, and leaned in just the right places to shackle the beast, yet to let it live on.

However, those who had truly brought about the many cruelties crushing the corporation to its knees were often the very ones who were not prominent, enabling them to wriggle even deeper into the living entity that MegaCorp had become, unseen, scattered maggots in the writhing masses that made up the behemoth. Hidden, their secret jobs and subversive agendas unknown except to the few, even the people they worked alongside of had no clue who they were.

Keeping in contact with those who had been their cohorts, even those who had been banished from employment in the corporation, the scheming continued. The power built by so many over the centuries would not be allowed to slip away so easily. With the votes counted and sentencing pronounced, the courts would have their way. After that, so would the infestation within the broken corporation.

The rot of centuries would not be cleansed so easily.

Study 11

Compiled by: Ed'th Ze'pliinth, SSM.rl, UNAS
Subject: WorldPresident Benetin
Location: Earth
Earth-Reference Date: 2804 A.D. (O.E. Standard)

"REVENGE IS SUCH AN UGLY word." WorldPresident Benetin glared at the assembled ex-offic'rs of the diminished MegaCorp Corporation. "What you have done with your company in the name of profit has been heinous. Entire worlds have suffered for your gain. If you couldn't buy people out at fire-sale prices, your military arm cleared them out with weapons and firepower. I am ashamed to think my stamp of approval ever went on any MegaCorp documents."

Benetin walked across the chamber in front of the convicted offic'rs, his gaze riveting each one in turn. "Not only did you take what you wanted in the way of resources, you took from people who had no choice but to depend on you for their very substance, your employees. You drove them into the ground, paid them a pauper's wage, and washed your hands of them as soon as they were no longer of use to you."

His face betraying his anger only in the bright spots of color gracing his cheeks, the WorldPresident went on. "But the most heinous act of all was the buying of children in order to indoctrinate them into your military arm, owning them life, limb, and soul, the property of MegaCorp. They were nothing more than slaves to your corporation.

"Each of you disgusts me. Several of you have claimed plausible deniability. Let that fly in an appellate court of law. You may feel the harshness of this sentence is more than enough, but rest assured, you should feel very lucky that your only penalties have been to be banned from ownership in any MegaCorp-owned or -controlled company and banishment from Earth for a minimum of ten standard years.

"Be grateful. If my input had been heeded, you would not have gotten off so lightly." WorldPresident Benetin dismissed the scum without another look, his quick steps carrying him out of the hall.

"Sers, you have heard from the highest political power on this planet. I must concur with each point he has made. Consider yourselves fortunate. At this time you will be escorted to a waiting transport for immediate deportation. A limited line of credit has been established for you, good for one local year on the planet of your destination. At the end of that time period, you must have made arrangements to provide for yourself as no additional funds will be made available, and any funds still unaccessed will be rescinded from your control. Use these

169

funds well, sers." The magistrate turned and began addressing the team overseeing the transition of MegaCorp into two separate entities, military and economic. "Sers, it is imperative that teams be sent immediately at MegaCorp's expense to explore the area of the reported anomaly that started this entire affair. I understand there was an altercation leaving Rejuvenant's population decimated. I expect to see ongoing reports transmitted directly to me summarizing the results of the teams, and that is plural with an ess, sers, because I mean *teams* sent to survey the damage on Rejuvenant.

"I hope to hear that there were survivors on that world. If not, I expect to see that the resources and infrastructure are thoroughly surveyed with the intent of allocating these items to the remaining off-world populace. Of course, there may be those who wish to return to their homeworld. That desire must be accommodated, whatever that entails. This mission is entrusted to make sure any necessary repairs, restoration, or construction is immediately initiated to ensure no one with a legal claim to that planet is denied his or her wishes in returning as soon as humanly possible.

"This court will pursue answers and retribution if it even suspects this directive is not being given one hundred percent compliance, no matter the cost to MegaCorp Corporation. Both the economic and military arms, although now divided, may be called upon to effectively wrap up this directive in a timely manner. Am I clearly understood?"

Without even a chance for the transition team to formulate a reply, the magistrate was also gone from the hall, his anger still resounding from the walls. Relieved to be out of his presence, the transition team looked for the quickest way to the exit, hoping to avoid a repeat performance, showing their true colors, jackals out for an easy meal.

Study 12

Compiled by: Ed'th Ze'pliinth, SSM.rl, UNAS
Subject: A'man Braxtn
Location: Badlands, New American States, Earth
Earth-Reference Date: 2804 A.D. (O.E. Standard)

"GET OUT OF MY FACE, BOY," growled the gnarled visage.

Spitting fire, an angry bobcat of a man, A'man Braxtn, one time MegaCorp security chief, kicked a booted foot in the dusty soil, showering his unwelcome visitor with debris. The MegaCorp glass he'd been handed was an unwelcome weight in his hand, and he cursed its very touch, feeling the hook it had already set into his soul.

Giving the intruding man a cold shoulder, Braxtn turned back to the river, its lifeforce sucking his thoughts through the desiccated terrain, pulling him back into the morass his life had become. His leathery skin twisting into a scowl, he squinted into the noonday sun, its heat charring the moisture from his eyes. Why couldn't they just leave him alone? He had given his life for that company. Sixty-two years and he had been kicked out the door on his backside. Good lands, six months of peace on his river, and the maggots were crawling over him again.

Flinging the glass he'd been handed to his feet, the sharp crack of the device against a stone echoed across the flat-bottomed canyon, reverberating in the dryness of the air. He whipped around, pouncing on the man standing patiently behind him. "Curse you and your corporation! You knew I couldn't turn this down. How dare you bait me back into MegaCorp! You dirt bag. I'll do this for you. I'll be there to lead your team. But a black hole take you if this doesn't give me back my good name. MegaCorp *stole* that from me." The old man reached to the dusty glass he had thrown at his feet, one corner cracked from its violent impact against the stone.

"We can get you a new one of those, ser."

"Blast it, boy. Does it still work?" Brushing the dusty surface with gnarled fingertips, the glass shimmered, the occasional flicker reminding the man of his anger. Tapping one piece of information, separating it from another, pushing each aside when his steel-trap brain had absorbed it, his cold eyes flickered back and forth. Lost in concentration, back in the element he had so missed the last half-year, his keen gaze was unaware of the smile on the other man's face.

IT WAS IN THE RECORDS. The corporation minion had fought for Braxtn's return, arguing that A'man Braxtn was a keeper. He had assured the courts this would pull the old man back into the fold. He hadn't understood how the security chief could have been let go in all that mess. Braxtn was the jewel in the crown. With this prize on board, the security teams could rest easy. Braxtn would cull the best from the list flickering across the glass in his hands. He had that knack, that innate ability, that *proclivity*.

The MegaCorp minion stood silently, his patience equal to Braxtn's immersion in his new project. As he'd told his superiors before coming on this trip, he would wait, if only he knew Braxtn was interested. Yes, he would wait on Braxtn until the end of time itself came to take him. Even that wouldn't be too long.

Study 13

Compiled by: El Tir'd O'doon, Consultant to UNAS
Subject: Ex-MegaCorp Employees

Location: Earth
Earth-Reference Date: 2804 A.D. (O.E. Standard)

HER BREATH FROSTED the surrounding air. She pulled her furred collar closer, its warmth wrapping her snugly in its embrace. *Hard copy!* Did someone really think she was that poor? Her hand crumpled the unopened sheaf of paper in her pocket. *Hard copy!* Disgust poured its bile into her throat. Tears at what she had lost when MegaCorp brought her down came near to overwhelming her self-control. With one glove she brushed the moisture from her face and turned from the cold, her dingy quarters at least warm.

Spreading the crumpled *paper* on an empty surface, she looked at it, wishing it away. *Poor! Paper!* The tears surged forth again, the sobs returning. She was poor . . . nothing. She had nothing. She was left over, and nothing mattered anymore. They were right to send her paper. She didn't even own a glass any longer.

Resignation providing at least the comfort of numbness, she reached for the paper, flattening its myriad creases on her leg. She looked closely at it, the words in ink. *Ink!* How quaint! Well, at least the ink spelled her name. Someone sure enough had managed to find her way up here in her frozen, forsaken hole.

She held the paper up, unsure how to get at its contents without damaging what was inside. Finding an overlapping seam, she tugged until it separated, and two smaller papers fell to the floor. Laying the packaging—the envelope, if she'd known what it was called—aside, she knelt to retrieve the smaller items, her heart catching at the symbol emblazoned across the top. MegaCorp! Hadn't they abused her enough?

Dragging in a ragged breath, her knees suddenly weak, she knelt to read the dreaded news.

173

"BABY," ENS'T DOLPH SLEEPILY pushed on Sunsett Starr's shoulder, "your turn." He could barely make himself understood, but he had no interest in waking further. Once she heard the glass chiming, she'd catch on.

"What is it?" Groggily she turned to the man at her side, her eyes equally bleary with sleep. She pushed at his shoulder. "Ens't, wake up. You've got a message. It's your glass calling." She sank back into her pillow, throwing his arm from around her waist. "And don't lie all over me. You're sweaty."

"Baby, you could get that and let me sleep," he slurred, his tongue still thick from repeated nightcaps over enjoyed. At the moment he was unemployed, and he didn't have to get up in the morning. He was grateful Sunsett earned enough for two.

The glass still chimed, though, and he knew she wasn't going to give in.

Crikes, he felt his head was going to explode. He sat up, his feet jerking back from the cold of the floor. *Oh, why me?* Stumbling into the next room, he hit the send icon and barked, "Ens't, here. Can't you check the time?" He paused, grabbing his glass, tapping the time to the front, spitting out his irritation to his unknown caller. "It's two in the morning."

With an audible groan, he threw himself onto a padded bench, his head crushing a decorative pillow as he closed his eyes, wishing the message and the night away.

"Trust me, buddy. You don't want to miss this call." A voice crackled into the room, the static of a live outsystem call making it clear this was special. With a peal of static-laced laughter, the caller's voice danced. "You really do want to take this call, Ens't. You know that bombshell that nearly took out MegaCorp? I've got us on the gravy train to help clean up the mess. Get your lazy tail out of Sunsett's bed and get on a transport out here. I've got a message stick on the way to you encoded with all the details, that and a nice chunk of change. This is the opportunity we've been looking for. By the way, it's five-thirty in the evening out here in the real world, you pile of rotted meat. See you in two weeks."

Ens't groaned again as the line went dead.

SHE WAS FINALLY WARM. Even without her fur-lined coat, she felt renewed. She could leave this dingy, frostbitten hovel and *live* again. Tears, this time of joy, caressed her face as she crushed the paper to her breast. Paper. *Paper.* No longer poor, she was glad now to have this paper. This *paper* didn't make her poor. This *paper* was her ticket out of this frozen hellhole.

Standing in the snow, the cold no longer her enemy, she hugged herself, joy wiping away the months of misery she had endured. The ink on the paper had breathed new life into her with its words.

MEGACORP CORPORATION IS FULLY FUNDING AN EXPLORATORY TEAM TO INVESTIGATE THE ANOMALY RECENTLY DISCOVERED BY DR.SCI. REFREN ASCOTT OF THE LORITMAR OBSERVATORY, WITH A SPECIFIC EMPHASIS ON THE ANOMALY'S EFFECTS ON THE PLANET REJUVENANT. YOU ARE HEREBY INVITED TO JOIN OUR TEAM AS AN HONORED PARTICIPANT. YOUR EXPERTISE WILL BE FULLY REMUNERATED IN APPRECIATION FOR YOUR SERVICE AND COOPERATION. PLEASE SEND ONLY REGRETS. YOUR ACCEPTANCE MAY BE ACKNOWLEDGED BY YOUR ATTENDANCE AT THE ORGANIZATIONAL MEETING SCHEDULED AS STATED ON THE FOLLOWING PAGE. WE HOPE TO SEE YOU THERE. ALL TRAVEL EXPENSES WILL BE ADVANCED DIRECTLY TO YOU. USE TRAVEL CODE 34.LK

Study 14

Compiled by: Ed'th Ze'pliinth, SSM.rl, UNAS
Subject: Preparations to Leave
Location(s): All Across Earth
Earth-Reference Date: 2807 A.D. (O.E. Standard)

STARING OUT OVER the shipping yard filled with supplies accumulated for the upcoming juggernaut to investigate the events that had occurred on and around Rejuvenant, anyone could see that no expense had been spared.

Not everyone was happy with the way things were going, however.

"This cannot be loaded into the cargo hold."

A mighty crane weighted down with massive tonnage whirred to a stop. Kel'eena Sutura was the nighttime loading-supervisor, and it was her voice that rang out over the commlink. She didn't consider that the change of plans wasn't her decision to make. Still, new instructions were given, even though the authority to do so was woefully absent.

"It must be shipped separately. The hold on this ship will be filled with personal effects and the most sensitive monitoring equipment. This other will be fine on a military transport."

A flick of her wrist and the crane reversed its tortuous path, its goods bound for another yard where more friendly eyes wouldn't see its load as a nuisance to be sent off to become someone else's responsibility.

It wasn't long before her glass chimed, though, and it sang the ominous tone of a warning from the central office. With a snort of contempt, Kel'eena pulled out the glass and thumbed

176

the message up.

REGISTRY OF INTERNAL DOCKING AND LOADING PRIORITIES. PREMIER IMPORTANCE. It has been noted that certain shipments for the survey and reconstruction teams to Rejuvenant have been re-routed to military transport. This is not to be continued. Only authorized personnel will receive permissions to modify cargo manifests and loading procedures. Anyone receiving a request to do so should immediately request verification of authorization. Full documentation of the change and the individual initiating the change must be duly noted on the manifest. Thank you. –OFFICIAL PORT DOCUMENT. NOT FOR PRIVATE COMMUNICATION.

"Well, they think they can just have their own way. Well!" Indignation puffed Kel'eena with anger. And they didn't think people played favorites, anymore. She could let them have an earful, she could. Well, she had her own ways to get that cargo loaded when and where she wanted. There might just be a few surprises when some of those yellow-livered suckers started opening up their cargo holds. Yep, they'd know they shouldn't have toyed with her.

A HUNDRED HEADS DUCKED, hands grabbing ear-mounted commlinks in pain.

"Has anyone seen that lazy idiot, Ollen Wychert?" Ens't Dolph's voice boomed over the internal comm system. Two hundred eyes turned and glared at him. He shrugged his shoulders and thought, Well, it didn't hurt to ask.

His hands in his pockets, he whistled a tune as he jauntily strode off through the jumble of supplies being assembled for transport. He knew where he could probably find Ollen. He

177

would just look for the most beautiful women and the darkest, most remote corners. Ollen would be found just where Ens't would be if he had the chance. In fact, if he couldn't find Ollen, he would just have to see about making his own plans. That might even be the better choice, anyway.

After that thought came to him, somehow finding Ollen didn't seem quite so important anymore.

BRAXTN LOOKED AT THE REPORT pulled up on the glass. Reaching out, pulling the names into groups, verifying those who had accepted his summons, he manipulated the information in the glass, watching each name he indicated light up as confirmed.

"There." He spoke aloud. Doing so helped him focus his thoughts. "That one takes care of our biologist. Fourteen engineers and their crews. Hm . . . this one, that woman hiding in the northern Polar Regions. Never did get her name; thought she wouldn't make it, but she sure has the qualifications. Then there's the medical team all in place. Seventeen ships fully crewed. It seems we have a full complement of support personnel."

Whole banks of personnel shifted within the glass, the names going from tentative amber to confirmed green.

"Wait!" He had to look twice to make sure his eyes weren't deceiving him. "Those two. What are they doing on this list? They were banned from MegaCorp by me personally before any of this ever became public. Somebody'll pay for this."

Tapping them, the two names began to glow red.

The security chief slapped the comm button beside the glass. "Offic'r, get in here." Turning to his newly appointed underling, Braxtn barked, "Two of these men. I need to know who hired them on. Ollen Wychert and Ens't Dolph. I know these men personally. They might be good at their jobs, if they

178

would choose to do them. They're good at the women, too, and that'll be the real rub. We don't need silly dalliances fracturing this team's cohesion. Better yet, get them both in here today. I want this cleared up before we get any further along this path of action. Thank you. That's all." The offic'r nodded his understanding, doing double-time back out the door.

Braxtn's eyes followed the man. That would be an efficient one. He'd bet his wages on that. He'd be glad to have him around come a tight spot, unlike those two fools who'd managed to get their names on his team.

He turned his leathery face back to his reports, noting his approval for additional names on the list.

"LIPSTICK? THAT'S LIPSTICK on your face? Curse you, that's why you were kicked out of MegaCorp's services in the first place. Tell me this. Was the girl a member of either the survey or reconstruction teams? And the answer had better be no, because we can't afford to start selections all over again." Braxtn paused for the men to respond and got nothing. "I'm taking that for a no. Men, you'd better toe the line while you're on my watch, or you just might not have any line to play with. Is that clearly understood?" He slapped his open hand on his desktop, the sharp sound a clear emphasis for his harsh words. "Men?" he barked again.

Ollen and Ens't finally jumped, startled at last by the harshness of the chief's final word. Rapidly nodding their heads in unison, the pair escaped for the safety of the hall outside the chief's office.

This team just might pull this off, Braxtn mused to himself. Just get 'em packed up and on those transports, and this might pull even his tail out of the fire.

For the first time in many months, he felt himself relax. Yes, he considered. This just might work.

"I DON'T CARE WHAT this ridiculous paperwork says. When I'm on duty, I run this loading facility, and those containers go where I say they go. Now get your backsides on the ball before I crush you like the weaklings you are."

Kel'eena Sutura's anger throbbed in her temples, and the loading supervisor glared at the night crew, daring them to defy her words. Just let one person say just one word. Do it, she mentally dared them. She might regret the consequences, but she would love to take one of them down just to show them who really was the boss here.

Study 15

Compiled by: Ed'th Ze'pliinth, SSM.rl, UNAS
Subject: In Transit to Rejuvenant
Location: MegaCorp Interstellar Transport
Earth-Reference Date: 2808 A.D. (O.E. Standard)

THE GOLDEN LIQUID SWIRLED in the slender container. Warmed by carefully manicured fingers, it burned as she tilted it past her sensuous lips. The lights sparkled in her eyes as she swung around the room, her partner for the night new to her. Who knew interstellar transports like this even existed? She could get to like this life.

Holding the container in one hand, she wrapped her free arm around the man with her. He smelled so good. Three weeks on this can with nothing to do could get the thoughts to thinking, and she was thinking of how enticing this man smelled.

Lost in her reverie, she danced through the evening, the next morning not remembering just how the rest of the night had played itself out.

BRAXTN STRODE THROUGH the slow-sleep bays, the bunks sealed for the trip, the lights glowing green to indicate the condition of each occupant. The underlings, the grunts, were traveling here. They would wake at the end of the journey. Not even during MegaCorp's heyday could this many people travel in the high style afforded to those above.

At each bunk, he stopped and peered inside, considering every member of the team his personal responsibility. One foul-up and he would be sunk, just like last time. He was determined to be thorough. He refused to let that happen again.

Clearing the concealing condensation from the occasional bunk, he was struck by the *youthfulness* of so many of the team. "My lands, was I ever that young?" he whispered. Their eyes were closed, with scraggly beards forming on the smooth faces of the males, and the females so *beautiful*, all in the standard slow-sleep slipsuits, revealing their well-toned bodies underneath. Peering in at one especially beautiful girl, he leaned his forehead against the glassine, his eyes refusing to continue without rest.

"I have been old too long," he said aloud to no one. His mind drifting, he was suddenly back in the smooth skin of his youth.

"Tianne!" She was alive again! He ran to her, his heart racing from the fire of her skin, her hair a golden halo, the sweetness of her smile an ointment as she turned to greet him. "Tianne, you are alive again!"

She brushed a freshly scented hand alongside his face, her shockingly clear eyes searching his. "Of course I am, dear Brax. Why do you say 'again'? You old silly, you. I never know what will come out of your mouth each time I see you. I do love you so."

Her hand cupping itself around his neck, he was drawn into the tender pillows of her lips, his body giving itself to her embrace. How he had missed his beautiful bride all these years!

Now he had her back again; he could tell her all she hadn't been there to share during the lonely times.

"I'm an old man now, Tianne. You should see me. Mega-Corp has been shattered, and I've been given a second chance. You would be proud of what I'm doing now." He rambled in his excitement, her presence overriding his well-ordered mind. After a time his voice slowed, and he stood. Just to look at her filled him with joy. Suddenly he realized she was laughing, and at him! Shaking his head to gather his thoughts, he realized his puzzled looks must have caught her attention.

"Why, you're not hearing a single word I'm saying, you mean beast. Look at you, that hound-dog expression on your face. What is all this about a second chance? And you an old man? What does that make me? Twenty-four standards? Why, you mean man, I don't want to be twenty-four for another three standard years. Let's go somewhere, Brax. I have missed you so."

Her arm his guide, he could only follow, his heart having been made alive again. His mind raced to devise a plan, to think of how he could hold her in his arms and never let her go, and he leaned close to her, the smell of her just as he always remembered. Closing his eyes, he drew in a deep breath. Remember. This smell, the smell of Tianne. Remember, he told himself.

His forehead grown cold, his eyes opened to the girl inside the bunk, her body young and firm, not looking so very much like his Tianne, his love gone so many years ago. Stepping back from his reflection, his gnarled image in sharp contrast to the memory from which he had just emerged, he stood very still for a moment, gathering the self-control he knew he would need in order to simply get through the rest of this day.

"FOR CRYING OUT LOUD, will you look in this crate?" Sweat staining his 'tigues, the handler climbed down from yet another disaster. Slapping the manifest in his glass, he rolled his eyes. "This is the third crate in just this hold. What idiot loaded this bird?"

Holding the steps as his workmate climbed up for verification, he knew the next few sevendays would be busy ones. He would have to log each errant package, tag the contents with their eventual destination, and repack them for redistribution when the destination was reached.

He called to his partner, "Zi'nene, do you have any inkling how hard your next few sevendays are going to be? You might as well cancel all those sky-walkers you have lined up. They won't be getting any. Not from you at any rate. Let's pack it up for this workday. We'll tear these crates apart tomorrow and see just what else is inside."

Pulling the lowest rung of the steps to collapse them, he quickly stored them on his drivcart. He would use them tomorrow, but this night was his. He wanted at least *something* to take home as a memory from this stinking journey. Brown hair and hazel eyes sounded about right to him tonight. Yep, that just might do the trick after all.

Study 16

Compiled by: Alb't deFralin, SSM.rl, UNAS
Subject: Arrival at Rejuvenant
Location: MegaCorp Interstellar Transport
Earth-Reference Date: 2808 A.D. (O.E. Standard)

TRANSPORTS WERE readied while crates of cargo were sealed for their final destination. Relabeled with corrected manifests, planetside dock handlers cursed for ineptitude, and tired bodies stoked with stimulants, Rejuvenant would be a welcome relief. It had been three shipboard sevendays of travel for these teams, three weeks by their old-Earth calendar, but many feared they might be eight years too late to save a world.

ABOVEBOARD, TEAMS pulled themselves back into form, three weeks of leisure activities put behind them. In the slow-sleep holds, nutrient-packs were slapped on groggy grunts as they stumbled out of frosty bunks. The ship was coming to life again, just one link in the juggernaut traveling across the vast reaches of space to undo what might be undone, repairing the slash of greed that had been so ruthlessly struck upon the approaching planet. Not certain the extent of destruction they would find, the lack of knowledge a type of security in itself, the teams moved forward as one.

Study 17

Compiled by: Alb't deFralin, SSM.rl, UNAS
Subject: A'man Braxtn
Location: Rejuvenant
Earth-Reference Date: 2808-2809 A.D. (O.E. Standard)

"FIRST APPROACH TEAM on the ground, Braxtn speaking. All seems clear. Will check back in five. Out."

"Acknowledged. Will wait for check. Out."

The clearing seeming secure, the team stationed themselves around the lander. With armaments ready and tensions high, each man claimed a range of degrees, standing at first posture and monitoring possible movement. Braxtn held up a scanner, its signal looking for heat signatures. None found, he signaled the team to secondary posture and started forward.

"Gods in the heavens above, this is beautiful!" He could hardly hold his sentiments in. "The colors, so saturated, intense. I've never seen green fields this brilliant before." That

184

was God's truth, too. Since the collapse of Earth's ecological systems centuries ago, much of the planet had been left a wasteland shadow of its former glory. Only the reconstructed parts carried the feel of old-Earth's lushness, and not everyone could live there.

Pausing to look up, the twin suns now low on their opposing horizons, he just shook his head. Who would have expected that, a stunning yellow sky? He was convinced this must be the old-Earth Eden his old great-grandmother used to tell him stories about. Its exquisiteness was a breath of fresh air. He could almost feel his youth again. What was MegaCorp fighting for here on this beautiful planet?

Raising a hand, his mind clicking back into security mode, he motioned his team to pace him. Touching the comm at his throat, he spoke, "First approach team clear. Moving forward. In five. Out."

"Acknowledged. Waiting. Out."

Relaxing, he knew the other teams would be landing soon. What a treat they had in store for them! He smiled to himself as he walked through the waist-high grasses. He was going to like it here.

AT A'MAN BRAXTN'S direction, his word final, the great landers began settling themselves around the planet. Construction crews unloaded massive quantities of equipment to put previously known infrastructure back into prime condition. Transport landers ferried workers to their various locales across the planet. Most importantly, survey teams began cataloguing the resources of the world, both for redistribution of the planet's wealth to those who had been off-world during the MegaCorp incident and in the hope that life would be found, the hope that some of Rejuvenant's inhabitants had survived.

SQUATTING AT THE shoreline, looking out over the brilliance of the blue sea, the team grunt, a young man by the name of Nalt'n Barrick, rested. He was here at Ssm. deFralin's largesse, his true qualifications near nonexistent. The young man's approval to accompany the more learned members of the team had come courtesy of a strong back, a clean record, and a willingness to do whatever deFralin and the team needed. Carrying the packs was debilitating, but that's what he had been qualified for when he had pleaded his case with deFralin back on Earth. Someone had to provide the brute force, he'd entreated. Never mind that he didn't have a scientific bone in his body.

The sense of eyes on him running a shiver down his back, he took a deep breath. It was a feeling he'd experienced numerous times since landing. Now, even accompanying this group of scholars, the eerie feeling haunted him still.

Resting his hand on a boulder, he happened to glance down just in time to see the remains of a damp, very small footprint fade from the surface of a nearby flat stone. Startled, his mind suddenly tight with the possibilities, he held his breath, afraid to let it out. Letting nothing more than his eyes betray his movements, he tried to dutifully survey his surroundings.

In a tight voice, hardly audible even to himself, he squeaked, "Hey, guys." When there was no response, he cleared his throat, attempting a louder call. "Guys, you need to see this." Overcome by the fear welling up inside, his vision went black, and he collapsed on the ground, his training leaving him unprepared, his body betraying him in what might well be the contact they were all hoping to find.

Coming to at the hands of his teammates, Nalt'n shook his head at their questions. "I'm fine. I really am. What you need to see was right there." He pointed to the stone. "A footprint. Wet. It just faded away as I watched."

"Like this?" A teammate wet his boot, placing it on the dry stone, leaving the imprint of its treads, the marks fading as they dried.

Suddenly, Nalt'n knew what had been so startling to him. Grabbing his own boot, he pulled it off, stripped his undersock from his foot, and stumbled to the water's edge. Slapping his bare foot into the water, he hopped back to the team, placing his wet foot solidly on the selected stone. Lifting it, watching the water begin to fade, taking his footprint with it, he grinned.

"No, like that!"

Pockets and carrying cases all over the planet chimed in one voice. Hundreds of hands pulled comms and portable glass units out, the message on each the same. With the discovery unverified, life had not been confirmed. However, hope had been.

A renewed sense of purpose spread across Rejuvenant.

BRAXTN SPUN HIS GLASS in his hand. He needed time to think, and keeping his hands occupied gave him just that.

Before departing for this planet, he had researched all he could find about Rejuvenant. The native name, Se'Yan't, had come out early. However, buried deeper, he had uncovered rumors about the inhabitants going through some kind of reincarnation, some sort of life renewal.

Through a *rebirth*.

The very idea was farfetched to him, but he also knew that all rumors carried a kernel of fact buried somewhere deep within. Reincarnation, if the reports were true, might be no more than a family name repeated over and over, or a physical likeness that ran across generations. Medical miracles? Not so likely. That was the thing with rumors. Sometimes the facts inside never revealed themselves. Then, sometimes the rumors proved themselves, indeed, to be fact.

There was one thing for sure. He wasn't ready to believe in reincarnation as a fact. Not without further proof, anyway.

He spun the glass again, the report still on top. A watery

footprint on a stone. A bare footprint, at that. How very bizarre! The next step might be to check up on the trustworthiness of this grunt, this Nalt'n who had been the only one to see it.

Grasping the glass, waving the report away, he sent a query. He'd get that grunt here to speak with him, but before he did, he'd have all the records available upship downloaded to him. His ducks would be in order. Finding someone alive mattered to too many people. This was simply too big to allow people's hopes to be unnecessarily buoyed. He could not pull back the initial, enthusiastic gossip that had spread across this world's surface, but before confirming it, he must be sure.

The reports on the grunt already appearing on his glass, he began sorting them, pulling the pertinent ones to the side, throwing away any that didn't seem to matter, and telling his glass to sort the rest by relevance. Within minutes he knew he'd better talk with the man. And from what he was seeing in the reports he'd just received, chances were, he'd better be prepared to believe him.

"I DON'T KNOW, SER. The reports just keep coming in. Who would have put any real credence into that footprint sighting? The guy was just a grunt with no credentials. There was no verification by anyone else on his team. Just his word. And he was passed out when the team found him. Bizarre. Now," and the exasperated scientist shook her head, flipping the glass through the reports, hundreds of them. Catching one, she pulled it back to the front. "Like this one, ser. The prints seem to come right out of the water. See?"

"Send it to my glass." Braxtn reached to his side, the unit the same one he had cracked beside the river.

She flicked the image, one edge of it jumping out at them. "You can see it right here. There's the water, then there's the first print. And another thing, ser. None of these prints, not *one* of them found at *any* of the sites are adult size. My best guess as to the age? Eight to maybe ten local years. And that's been verified by our sociological survey division. There's a Ser Alb't deFralin who heads the team. He's a full SSM.rl, so you can't fault his credentials. He assures me these prints cannot come from one of our teams. He pulled up the stats on this entire mission, and not even the smallest of our females has feet this size. I just don't know, ser. Like I said earlier, bizarre." She turned to her glass, the reports sliding under her fingers as she shook her head. As if to herself she repeated, "I just don't know."

Braxtn studied his glass as she walked out the door. It was clear from the expression on his face that he was equally stumped.

Study 18

Personal Journal, UNAS Archives, Unpublished
Subject: Alb't deFralin, SSM.rl
Location: Rejuvenant/Se'Yan't
Earth-Reference Date: 2809 A.D. (O.E. Standard)

"JUST BEHIND that large rock. Yes, right there. Good. Aim it to pan this entire beach area. If anything passes here, we'll get to see it on the glass. Good work, team." deFralin turned, the incessant tugging at his sleeve finally getting his attention. "Great solar suns, what is *wrong* with you, dancing there like your feet are on fire?"

"You won't believe this, ser. You might as well take all this back with you. You don't need it anymore. All these sightings? Well, there's more. So much more. The latest reports flooding in aren't on the coasts, anymore. They're coming in from *everywhere*. Just check the glass, ser."

His heart racing, deFralin reached for the proffered tool. His thumb twitching, the images flashed past his eyes, his laser-precise mind absorbing what he saw. Excitement building, he reached deep inside the glass's interactive matrix, pulling to the very front one old message he had saved.

From: Security Chief A'man Braxtn.
To: Sociological Team Leader Ser Alb't deFralin, SSM.rl.
Please view the following attachments offering insights as to the possible meanings of the alleged sightings being reported across Se'Yan't. I have culled this information from many hours of research involving sources spanning centuries. I firmly believe that all rumors are based on kernels of fact. Please look for the facts inside, and they may help you make progress toward the answers you seek.

By now, deFralin knew the attachments by heart. He no longer needed to look at them to see their words. They were Braxtn's references to reincarnation.

"What if it could be true?" he muttered to himself.

"What, ser? Is everything all right?"

"It's nothing. Just the wishful fantasy of an old scholar who's already chased too many empty dreams in his career. I'll be fine. Just keep up the good job you're doing for us, son," and he turned back to the glass, his sureness of reality tempering his desires. He closed his eyes for a moment, not really willing to let the dream go. What if it really could be true?

Taking a deep breath, he climbed out of his fantasy and back into the reality around him. Slipping the glass into his tunic, he pointed, "Okay, team. Let's pull it all down. The real excitement has moved on. Let's head inland."

190

A DOZEN PAIRS OF eyes watched them from under the gently moving surface of the water, waiting. They had waited eight years. They could wait one more day.

"NOW, SER, I WAS IN this building yesterday. This simply wasn't here. You know it never gets really dark on this world, at least it hasn't in the time we've been involved in this survey, what with the nearest major eclipse still being several months away. Well," the man threw in, rolling his eyes, "it would be several months if this world had any moons with which to count lunar months. But we do plan a night in our schedules. You know, there are only so many people on each team, and we really can't work around the clock, even if it is always daylight.

"Well, we are in the process of refurbishing this series of buildings. With the city vacated for so many years, things have been let go, you know. This is the building my team was working in just yesterday. I tell you, none of this was here."

deFralin's excitement began to build at the sight of the debris scattered about the place. It was what children would leave when unsupervised. He walked over, picking up discarded plant materials. Foodstuffs. They had scavenged for the planet's natural foods, brought them here to consume them, then when they were satisfied, left, the debris forgotten. How like children!

He walked to the door, taking a deep breath in the clear, bright sunshine, the building creating one set of shadows, but his body forming another. They were here, somewhere. He was convinced of that. He just had to find them.

The biggest mystery, he knew, was going to be just how they'd gotten here. Reports just like this one were coming in from all over the planet. Would he ever find out if there was any substance to Braxtn's rumors? He didn't know. But it was going to be stimulating trying to find out.

191

AN UPROAR FILTERED in through the closed door. Portable buildings had been set up for offices and sleeping quarters wherever people had been assigned, but they were temporary, and that meant lightweight. They weren't designed to keep out every sound.

Irritated, deFralin turned to his youthful aide. "What is that infernal noise out there, anyway? Don't they realize some of us are trying to get some work done?"

As he stood to stomp outside, intent on silencing the disruption, his glass chimed. Touching the corner, Braxtn's face swept across its surface, his attention clearly in two places at once.

Breathless, the security chief's voice barked, "Get out here, deFralin. This is your moment to shine. They're *here*." A distant sound grabbed at his face in the glass, shifting the image's attention elsewhere. Without warning, he was gone.

deFralin was taken aback to be cut off without so much as a by-your-leave. Opening the door, his aide peering over his shoulder, he was astounded. Even with all the reports that had been rolling in, this he never expected to see. Standing throughout the compound were hundreds of children, all appearing to be about the same age. They were beautiful, golden-skinned godlets, both boys and girls.

And every last one was totally naked.

Study 19

Compiled by: Alb't deFralin, SSM.rl, UNAS
Subject: Rjorck
Location: Se'Yan't, Eight Years Earlier
Earth-Reference Date: 2809 A.D. (O.E. Standard)

(Note by Natal La'Sterene: This section references an event occurring in 2801 and was not included in the original 2819 draft, as it was considered outlandish conjecture that pushed the bounds of incredulity. Now, however, events brought to light since the original draft was published lend new credence to deFralin's fantastical claims.)

THE JEWELED WORLD TURNED, its twin parents keeping it bathed in life-giving rays. Unseen gravities from both suns reached out, caressing the jewel they cared for, tugging the seas on the surface of the planet, gently shifting the waters, as a withered, exhausted form lay, eyes closed, the slightest of movements registering life in the rise and fall of a hollow chest.

Slowly, ever so gently, the waters of the sea were given leave by the twin suns to reach for him, their slender fingers wrapping tentatively around the limbs of the dying form, then falling back to rejoin anxious brothers and sisters, quivering with anticipation at the job they needed to do. One at a time, the watery fingers grew stronger, touching, stroking the tired limbs, teasing them with the water-weir, hinting at the deeper gift they wanted to offer, returning time and again to caress Rjorck, cradling him in their grasp, covering him at long last with the sea's protective warmth.

As he slipped fully beneath the blanket of life-giving waters, his eyes fluttered open to peer through the clear blue sea, viewing for the last time his yellow sky. No, he corrected himself, the slightest of smiles cracking the corners of his broken lips, his *lemon* sky.

As the waters of his homeworld did what they had done for those of his race over countless millennia, he felt the release of his burden of years; his suffering at the hands of the humans; and his worn-out shell. His body returned to the sea, dissembling, becoming ten thousand individual parts, spreading throughout the seas that had been calling him home. Life had already begun its age-old cycle, bringing a new crop of children to a world that had been decimated in the name of greed.

Life on Se'Yan't had not been defeated at all. It was really the first moments of a brand new birth. Rjorck's sacrifice was giving his people a second chance. One day soon people would again walk the surface of this world, enjoying the magnificence of her beautiful shores.

Time would heal the wounds that had been so cruelly slashed across Se'Yan't's beauty, and until it did, she had all the patience in the universe.

Study 20

Re'Jenni Fra'gammasi, Se'Yan't Recovery Team
Subject: The Children of Se'Yan't
Location: Se'Yan't
Earth-Reference Date: 2809 A.D. (O.E. Standard)

THE GOLDEN-SKINNED BOY stepped from the sea and blinked, water dripping from his naked limbs. Turning back to the water he had just left behind, he squinted through the glare of his planet's twin suns, making out ripples, surges . . . *others,* their teasing evidence on the water's surface, on their way to join him.

His mind was blank as he took in all around him. There was something he should know. He arched his neck to one side as he tried to bring the thing in his head, the *thought,* to sharpness. *Ahhh . . . there!* The boy stood for a moment. *And there!* He continued to stand motionless as others joined him on the beach. *Others.* He felt as much as heard them stepping from the water, standing still with him under the jewel-colored sky.

There. He had it. *Se'Yan't.* The young boy let that word

194

settle in his head, turning it over, looking at it from one side, then the other. *Se'Yan't.* With a frown, he pondered this new word. *Se'Yan't.* The word's meaning slowly became clear to him. *This planet. Our place-of-being.*

He turned his head to look up and down the stone-strewn beach, knowing each rock, each boulder, as if he had lived this place before. As he waited patiently, hundreds, then thousands of others soon stood with him on the stones that seemed so familiar.

This was their world, he knew. Their time. A time for beginnings. A time for childhood.

This was a time for life.

Study 21

Personal Journal, UNAS Archives, Unpublished
Subject: Alb't deFralin, SSM.rl.
Location: Rejuvenant/Se'Yan't
Earth-Reference Date: 2810 A.D. (O.E. Standard)

"ARE THERE MORE?" deFralin flipped through his glass. "Look at this one. It's exactly the same as the one I was sent from the southern continent. Here," he called out to his sociological team. He held out the glass, two examples displayed. "Check this out. The one on the left was sent in two weeks ago. It came from the south. Now look at this one that just came in from a local group. There is no difference. These are *children.*"
He looked at his team, their expressions as mystified as his. "Racial memory? This is your field, people. Give me some answers." He waved them away, his expectations on them, now.

"Ssm. deFralin?" He turned, not recognizing the voice. A man bearing a very smug expression walked brazenly up to the exasperated sociologist. His mannerisms were both arrogant

195

and condescending. Without waiting for an answer, he lifted his nose and threw out an unexpected statement. "I'm sure you have been apprised of the situation here."

"I'm sorry. I don't understand what you mean."

"Ser, these children are obviously indigenous. Do you understand what that means? This world is theirs." The interloper snorted a rough laugh, as if that told everything he needed to say.

"And that means . . ."

"We must document them. Children! Have you totaled the reported number seen so far? It's in the thousands."

"I plan to do just that. What is your point, and who are you?"

The man smiled, his intent quickly revealed with his answer. "We are all here on MegaCorp's meal ticket. You see, everyone thought this planet's population was decimated. Yet, here we have thousands of live Rejuvies roaming the planet. With proper documentation, surely it can be proven that Mega-Corp was not the aggressor in this situation. Damages can then be limited to basic restoration of the planetary infrastructure, teams can be pulled to return home, and the punitive damages can be dismissed. If you can help me, I'm sure Mega-Corp will find a way to reward you in the future."

Instantly understanding the man's intent, and unable to contain his building fury, deFralin lashed out, "Away from me! How dare you try to coerce me into twisting this situation to MegaCorp's benefit!" Livid, he stepped toward the odious man, pulling his glass from his pocket. "I am contacting the security chief at this very moment. How dare you claim to be here as part of this effort to restore the damages inflicted on this civilization!"

BRAXTN, HAVING RESPONDED to deFralin's call with a haste fueled by personal fury, glared at the intrusive man's back as he was taken away.

"My most sincere apologies, Ssm. deFralin. I've had my eye on both this man and a partner of his for the entire mission. This is the first opportunity they've given me to haul their backsides off for deportation back to the main transport. They'll be in slow-sleep bunks quicker than they can blink, I'll tell you that."

deFralin bowed his upper body in a quick dip, the redness in his cheeks telling of his undiluted anger.

As Braxtn headed after the security team, he cursed under his breath. "The hottest of the suns' fires take that Ollen and his partner, Ens't. I knew something like this would happen to me when I saw their names on the list."

"THESE ARE REALLY GOOD, Alb't. How many of these do you have?" Jordiń Hogaramusta, one of deFralin's most treasured team members, looked over one of the latest poems collated on the glass in his hands.

"At last count, more than eight hundred, and there are more still coming in. Not as rapidly as at first, but I still see several new ones a week."

"They're all documented? Every one?"

"I only officially track those coming in from multiple locations. Every example is documented with the location, the time, and the person who recorded it. Look at this one here. It came in from seventeen locations, nearly all simultaneously. Listen:

When the fire above
Falls from space,
Water below
Is the safest place.
Land in between
Is where death is sure,

197

Se'Yan't's seas
Will make us pure.
Let us live in peace again.

"Cryptic, wouldn't you say? What do you make of it?"

"I've puzzled over that. Somehow the children must be collaborating, but I can't seem to make the connection." He shook his head and chuckled. "Two children can't have communicated across the planet with no communication infrastructure in place, can they? If two can't, then how have seventeen managed it?"

"Are they all like this?"

"Cryptic? Pretty much." deFralin scrolled through several more. "See? Look at this one." He handed the glass over for the other to see. "Read it."

Old age, old age,
You wait for me.
When life is through,
I'll see the sea.
Return, return,
Life lives again,
My youth renewed,
I'll walk on land.

Retrieving his glass, he paused. "Almost like a chant. Fascinating, though. I've inquired as to the possibility of publishing the collection with any proceeds coming directly back to the children. Once MegaCorp steps back from this salvage mission, these kids are going to need some help."

"That's good of you." Jordiń tapped the table three times, then murmured, "That's very good of you."

"There's one other thing I can't seem to get past. Why have there been no adults?"

"Why not, Alb't? Is it possible the populace knew what was coming and hid their children away for safety?"

"Possible, perhaps. Yes, it's certainly possible, but *thousands?* It's just hard to explain away."

The two men going silent for a time, deFralin ran his finger across the surface of his glass, the information inside flickering as it tried to guess what he wanted. His mind was on something else, a memo Braxtn had sent him some time ago about reincarnation. He couldn't prove it, wouldn't even try. It would be career death for sure. But he could come up with only one scenario that came even close to offering a plausible explanation, and Braxtn had given him that.

Thanks, Braxtn, he thought, *but for just what?* He stared at the shifting images on the glass in his hand, none of them clear, all of them simply possibilities. He swiped his hand across the surface, wiping its display clean, always one to bend to reality. With a toss of the instrument to the counter at his side, he stood and faced his companion.

"Well, come on, then. Things won't get done without us, will they?"

With an accompanying grin, Jordiń's answer followed him out the door. "No, ser. Things sure won't."

Whatever the reasons or causes, there were ten thousand children to care for, and deFralin strode forward purposefully, determined not to let them down.

Study 22

Compiled by: J. Ret'tsh, SSN.rt, UNAS/UT
Subject: JumpShip Commander Bethany D'Arc
Location: Deepest Space
Earth-Reference Date: 2895 A.D. (O.E. Standard)

A RAGGED SIGH etched the darkened cabin. Jumpship Commander Bethany D'Arc gave a reluctant glance upward, her eyes fighting for escape, not wanting to see. Heaviness engulfed her just as it had each time before, the memories bearing down on her, reminding her of her choices on Se'Yan't as MegaCorp's decimation of the populace had become clear.

Another quick glance.

A shift sideways in her seat.

The knowledge that this was something she must do; she had no choice; the time was near.

A deep intake of breath and later its release.

Click.

With a choking sob, she removed the clasp holding her glove to her suit. What she needed to do could not be done inside her private world, within the protection of her suit. She felt the near-silent hiss of the pressure readjusting, listened to the tired air dispersing, and knew her free will, her choice, was slipping away.

One part of her fighting the need of this, a tear gathering at the corner of her eye, she felt the bare skin of her fingers grasp the cool, lifeless handle recessed in the gray plasteel.

If only she could let go, return to her bunk, and close her eyes. Let the pain of distant Earth and the terror it had danced across Rejuvenant fade away. Oh, the sweetness of the dark, to no longer endure the torment, just to navigate by the songs of the stars.

Her hand on the plasteel, she could feel her muscles quivering, resisting, refusing to release what her eyes, her *self* couldn't bear to know. Not again. Not after last time. All the times before.

Then, with determination, lightning fast, her jaw clenched, and her body jerked in a spasm of searing effort. Her hand had no choice. With a condescending chime, the handle danced its quarter circle, withdrawing into its recess.

THE FADING LIGHT of decades earlier settled in pools among the boulders, Bethany's mind seeing the moment as if it were happening once again, and feeling the inky blackness as a welcome respite from the warmth of the day. The brilliance of a yellow sky washed by two suns had faded against the unyielding fist of a total eclipse. Nearby, the water whispered to the stones as its fingers tenderly traced their outlines one final time before the tide ran from the shore, only the moist caresses of their kisses to mark their passage. With the barest of sounds, it made its eternal promises.

Tomorrow, my love. Tomorrow. Until tomorrow . . .

Rob't ran his hand through her hair, his love for her in his tender touch. His soldier's protectiveness provided reassurance against the night, even as it wedged a strained note between them.

Half obscured by the gathering shadows, his hair throwing the last gleam of the occluded sun her way, she retreated into the gloom of the encroaching darkness. Hiding from what the future promised to bring, she turned a cruel glance to the retreating tide. Once her trusted friend, she had known its beauty, had parted its waters, and had been buoyed by its loving touch . . . before, knowing it would always return, *she* could always return. Now, to leave, with the tide running from her, she felt reproach in its abandonment.

There would be no tomorrow, she knew. Not for her. Not for Rob't.

Nor for Rob't's love for her.

SE'YAN'T'S REASSURING GRAVITY gripped her still; in her heart, *Rob't* gripped her still, the memory of his voice washing desolation over her emotions. In her grasp of what she had lost, she could only run, taking herself far away.

She felt that day as if the decades had never happened. Her

201

ship had been waiting.

Click.

Each closing connection of her suit had brought pain. Separation.

Click.

Further gone.

Click.

The tendrils of her life had rushed from her as she had reached to her wrist, yet another connection to be closed.

Click.

Without Rob't, his love for her, there was no existence. Flexing her soon-to-be-dead fingers, only the shock of the suit's chilled air making her aware that life still resided within her flesh, she had slipped into her artificial world.

Red flashes.

The first light, telling her to wait. The time had not yet come. Rob't had been still there, still within her reach.

Then the light had turned green, the signal to countdown.

She remembered the sunset as Rob't had kissed her neck, whispering, *"Return, my love."* That moment was long gone, though. They had just arrived on Se'Yan't. The tears had blurred her eyes as she swallowed her answer. Her response had bared its spiteful teeth.

Just not then. Later. Much later.

The end of her life had come on that disastrous day, had only been final when death had reached out—and it had become a living death. She had been the one to force it into being. With one finger, *her finger*, the decision had been made, and she had swallowed death, lived it still.

Why did Rob't not keep her on that beach? He could have hidden her in their cave. They could have been the shadows no one ever sees. She would have traded all this for Rob't, even if it had meant the end of her life.

Click.

All the lights that day had finally shone green, hovering nervously over the switch, burning steadily. She had reached her suited hand out, her finger reaching.

In her memory, he was waiting still . . .

No! Rob't was here, his love wanting her to stay. He must still love her. She had to believe that.

Her eyes burning, blurring her world, her finger had jabbed the final deathblow. As the boosters flared their defiance at the gravity well that had held them since their arrival, she had died inside.

Flames of death had licked the pad as she reached for the sky.

Study 23

Compiled by: J. Ret'tsh, SSN.rt, UNAS/UT
Subject: JumpShip Commander Bethany D'Arc
Location: Deepest Space
Earth-Reference Date: 3045 A.D. (O.E. Standard)

HER SHIP HAD JUMPED so many times, the engines screaming their defiance to the stars, skipping the minutes and hours, leaving uncounted decades of unlived years in Bethany's wake.

The dream had awakened her again. The words in her dreams. The pain. Sometimes the hope. They returned to her again and again.

She had to clear the words out of her brain. Only writing them would give her release. The children she dreamed of . . . always underneath Rob't's precious, lemon-skied Sc'Yan't. Could the words really be from them? All she knew was she had to write, and write she did . . .

Study 24

Compiled by: J. Ret'tsh, SSN.rt, UNAS/UT
Subject: JumpShip Commander Bethany D'Arc
Location: Deepest Space
Earth-Reference Date: 3195 A.D. (O.E. Standard)

WITH A CRASH, THE BIN once again dumped her life into her lap. A piece of bark. A flower long faded and dead. Memories of possibilities . . . choices. Roads not chosen. Hiding under it all . . . Rob't . . . smiling, his wind-blown hair dancing life's song. His song . . . *their* song . . . what should've been.

Rob't, your picture. A ragged breath clawed out of Bethany's throat. She had flung herself away, the ship's jump engines thrusting her through time as well as space.

A glint yanked her eye to the console. The smashed glass display. All the years gone. Rejuvenant, Rob't's precious *Se'Yan't,* devastated. Earth, no longer hers. Rob't, gone . . . dead. How many years? The ship could never tell her now.

As the painfully familiar thrumming of the ship's jump-drive once again wrote its symphony of unimaginable energies, she reached to her wrist, pulling herself back into her suit once more.

Click.

Her world was again enclosed and complete. It was time again, the song decreed.

Looking up through the glassine blister . . . only blackness. The sweet, sweet blackness.

"Sing to me, stars. Sing my way to you. Oh, sweet stars . . ."

Study 25

Compiled by: J. Ret'tsh, SSN.rt, UNAS/UT
Subject: JumpShip Commander Bethany D'Arc
Location: Deepest Space
Earth-Reference Date: 3280 A.D. (O.E. Standard)

THE WORLD OUTSIDE THE PLASTEEL and glassine ship shifted, the spectrum flashing through multicolored rainbows, and the jump was over. Bethany jerked her head, her hand automatically reaching to touch the overhead bin. She couldn't feel it, not really, not enclosed in her suit. The touching alone, even through the gloves, brought her comfort, as if her Rob't had not sent her away. However, the pattern of the stars through the glassine told the real story. Even this galaxy was no longer hers. She had pushed her vessel unmercifully, the jumps taking her farther than anyone else had ever gone.

She felt the familiar tingle at the base of her skull. She cringed, knowing what it was that she felt, something endured so many times before. She keyed the ship's internal data store, dictating as she had done so often already.

"Eyes following me. Pulling inside, I hide. I see them, still. They are in me."

She paused, watching the words scroll across her glass. Only by this act had she been able to relieve herself of the poems' haunting poignancy.

She understood, now, some of what Rob't had done. That didn't mean she would have left, but his protection, the pain he must have gone through to see her safely off the great MegaCorp battle cruiser, was some consolation.

She waited. She knew what would happen next, and she held her hand over the console, ready to make the next jump. It was only a symbol of her desire to run, though. She couldn't jump the ship again so soon, even if she wished to do so.

More poems would come, and she would record them. They would enter the world of the glass, and she would broadcast them off into the depths of the heavens.

Again, she wondered where the poems were from. She had come so far from Rob't's children, those precious ones he had loved. He had realized what MegaCorp had come to do on Se'Yan't, his love for that world drawing him to the local name used by the natives. Her love for Rob't had caused her to do the same.

The children were gone now, as were the adults. Perhaps the poems were coming from the stars. They were singing their sorrow for all the deaths MegaCorp had slashed across that one beautiful world.

Bethany's eyes teared up as she instinctively looked to the smashed display. She could never again know how many years Rob't had been gone as her ship jumped blindly through the decades, life somewhere going on without her.

She could write, though, and that she would. Later, the jumpdrives would thrum with their energies, and more years would be gone. The stars would always be there, though, and they would continue to sing to her.

Stars above, she thought. *My dearest Rob't. Must I listen to the stars forever? I begged them to sing to me once, and now I beg them to stop.*

Why did you send me away? I loved only you, my Rob't. I loved only you.

Study 26

Compiled by: J. Ret'tsh, SSN.rt, UNAS/UT
Subject: Exploratory Team
Location: Edge of the Galactic Arm

Earth-Reference Date: 3280 A.D. (O.E. Standard)

"I KNOW, SER. IT IS ODD, but you see it there. It's just come in, and it's not from in this galaxy." Removing his earpiece, Carlos Calderón, the communications offic'r, swiveled his seat around to look at his superior, frowning. Something else bothered him, if he could just put his finger on it. It was odd that his dermal reader hadn't picked the signal up. That meant the transmission must be very old.

Tuan Phan, the acting capt'n, narrowed his eyes at the communication offic'r's remark. "A joke, right? That's what this is. A joke. That was my great-gran's favorite poem from that book she kept in her glass. I have it still. Four hundred standard years old, that glass is, and it still works perfectly."

The crew all knew the story. Old MegaCorp technology, the best there ever was, was the stuff of myths and legends. However, four-hundred-year-old MegaCorp technology did often still work, and that made it real.

Carlos closed his eyes and located the correct relay on the inside of his eyelids. With a twitch of his facial muscles, the poem they had received jumped onto the viewwall in front of them.

Eyes following me.
Pulling inside, I hide.
I see them still.
They are in me.

The capt'n leaned forward as if the words were too blurred to read. In a small voice, he whispered, "It is the same. I've loved that poem. I've had it said to me over and over since I was a child. How could this have happened? Can you verify the signal?"

"Ser, sort of. The source is using jumpdrive technology,

and the ion traces say it's of out-of-date manufacture. Very old. Ser, maybe even old MegaCorp."

That made sense since the signal hadn't shown up on the communication offic'r's dermal reader. Old-MegaCorp signals wouldn't.

One of the other offic'rs chuckled and called out, "Someone out there must be thinking of you, Capt'n. They probably sent this to you to cheer you up."

Tuan was, for a moment, uncharacteristically pensive, thinking of the time they still had ahead of them on this mission and all he had left behind. *Not likely,* he thought. *Not likely at all.* What he said was, "An old girlfriend, maybe, or maybe my great-gran is trying to come back from the dead. Wouldn't that be a starstrike explosion?"

Everyone laughed at the capt'n's joke, even if none of them knew just what a starstrike explosion might be. It was funny to them just the same. It was also the acting capt'n's joke, so it would be funny to them no matter what. He was the capt'n, after all.

In Conclusion:

We hope you have enjoyed this study of the Garden Planet.

The Research Team at UNAS/UT would like to make some final comments over *The Rise of Rejuvenant: A Planet Reborn.*

While this study has relied heavily on currently known facts as well as established historical data, it must be stated that UNAS/UT recognizes the implicit impossibility of many of the concepts centered on Rejuvenant, hereafter called the Garden Planet. For that reason, it must be stressed that UNAS/UT in no way accepts responsibility for any inaccuracies in differentiation between facts and ideas that some may consider no more than fiction.

Our appreciation to Section Advisor Ssm. Rect'l Aggalonta Cotal for securing funding for this project.

Also, special commendations go to MegaCorp Special Projects Director Ger St. Regis for opening the MegaCorp historical vaults for our general perusal.

NL'S, UNAS/UT, 3301 A.D.

Additional sources for further study on the Rejuvenant/MegaCorp debacle:

Chasing Credits, Rstt.con ComChair Framen LeTosi (2540 A.D.)

Collected Verses for Children, edited by Alb't deFralin, SSM.rl (2810 A.D.)

Dark of Space, Nerl't reGalin (3026 A.D.)

Inside the Mind of MegaCorp; An Insider's Guide, Ssm. Eldrin Agassi'rel (2788 A.D.)

So You Want to Be a Rejuvie, Shirl Rainey (2843 A.D.)

Wading the Waters: A Time of Spiritual Renewal, Rev. Ranjacket Boos'tle (2813 A.D.)

Note:

The Following Addendums Are Individual in Nature and Do Not Reflect the Opinions or Policies of UNAS/UT.

(Added by permission of: NL'S, UNAS/UT, 3303 A.D.)

—Addendum 1—

The Magic Man
A Long-Forgotten World
The Dawn of Time

THE WIND AND THE RAIN beat the trees, twisting at their roots, pulling the branches as if to eradicate them from the land. In the dark, snaking streaks of lightning made the old Magic Man's headdress of fur and horns glisten in the blistering rain. His back hurt. The frown on his face reflected the pain in his heart. He glanced up, his words hissing from his lips, "This weather! It makes my old bones hurt so! Curse the gods in the skies, if ever there were any."

Slowly, he made his way up the hill, the lone tree at the top his destination. His staff pointing an accusing finger toward the gods in the sky with each step he took, the old man knew they were not happy with what he'd done. Saved a life was what he'd done. Not just one, either. More than one.

Even in his anger at the gods—or the lack of them—he knew his weariness was more than just of his flesh. The horrors he had witnessed. Admit it, he winced. Carried out was a better word. No matter how he had tried to spare the village, their simple ways would not be wiped away.

Reaching within the tree, he felt the dark object hanging from a frayed grass rope. The shape, two arms, two legs, with a head that only resembled a man. The old man knew what he'd done; would do it again. Pulling the effigy from the tree's swaying bough, he tossed it over the cliff. Sheep's legs and dog's fur. They wanted the real thing. Scared. That's all they were. Poor J'seryn. The old man trudged back down the hill, the blowing, blinding rain a suitable accompaniment to the miserable thoughts he carried in his head.

The wind whipping his ragged tunic, he knocked at the hut's roughly cut door. A wail of anguish answered him. Sounds of calming, barely heard over the whistling wind, tore at the old man's heart. He would spare the boy this if only the people would let him, for his memories of young J'seryn were strong on this wicked night. Curse the gods!

He shook his hand at the dark skies laced with lightning, not caring when they drove the rain down his nostrils, making him cough and shake. "What do you care about this little one? He is all his parents have left from the eight I've whelped for them. And I am supposed to serve you. Bah!"

He pushed the door, swinging it open to reveal the waiting youth in the dimness of the firelight.

"Come, J'seryn. The time is nigh. The lodge fire of the gods awaits." Not able to look the boy in his frightened eyes, the old man hid behind his headdress and took the youth's arm, leading him down the path to the village, the stink of the boy's nervousness made worse by the rain in the air. The fire blazed in the distance. The old man could feel the youth's shaking through his thin tunic.

"Will it hurt? Much?" The boy's voice shook, his attempt at bravado slipping as he spoke.

Putting an arm around his shoulders, pulling him close for

what comfort he could give, the darkness hiding the truth in the old man's eyes, he slipped a leather cord attached to a glass bead over the boy's head. Then he reassured the youth that the gods would be with him, and he would feel no pain. Feeling the boy relax with relief, the old man took his arm from his shoulder, afraid he would feel his lie as they walked.

Entering the village, wind and rain beat down, and all was darkness except one hut especially built for this night directly in front of the lodge fire. Cursed backward people, to do this to the boy, to his family! But he knew their fear would have this with or without his help. Perhaps he could ease the way for the boy. Just perhaps.

At the door of the hut, he relinquished the youth, eager hands pulling the boy into the interior, the hands those of the fervent village maidens. He knew what would happen inside. The youth, given his manhood by the gods just the previous twelve-month, would be stripped of his simple clothing. Zealous hands would run fingers through his hair, applying scented oil as an ointment to the gods. His body would be coated with thick grease to ease his way into the afterlife, and eager hands would offer him small fruits soaked in fermented milk so the boy would not disgrace the village when his moment of glory came.

Humph, the old man thought, when he considered the number of maidens that had volunteered—and several quite fervently. It seemed to him they were a bit too anxious to placate the gods. However, at least poor J'seryn would have this one small pleasure before this deed was done, him only sixteen winters and all.

Throughout the lodge fire watch, well into the small hours of the morning, the storm shook the village, attempting to peel the very substance of its foundations from the earth below. Inside the hut where the boy was experiencing the attentions of the village maidens for the first and last time in his young life, a different type of storm raged, one stirred and controlled by anxious hands dipped in oil, creating a whirling maelstrom of sensation to challenge the raging tempest the gods were flinging at the village just outside the hut's quivering walls.

The village men keeping watch over the lodge fire were subdued with the wrath of the gods raging all around them. In their fear, they cowered, crawling from their hiding holes just long enough to throw new timbers on the fire.

After many hours of preparation, the rough skin covering the door of the hut was drawn aside. The youth stepped out, clothed only in his loincloth, his hair combed with the scented oil, and his body slick with the lubricated ministrations of the maidens' hands. His only ornament was the glass bead around his neck. The fire glistened on his greased body, the spark of the flames seemingly one with him already, drawing him to the gods, his way made easy by his preparations.

The youth waited, his brain numbed with the fermented fruit, reassured in the moment of his impending death that his life would bring an end to the wrath of the gods, a wrath aroused from being cheated by the old man's deceptive tricks.

The village men stepped forward, reaching out for the youth's hands, this the part they were forced to play, offering another man's son to the gods. The youth looked them in the eyes and stepped forward to take their hands, the Magic Man's glass bead glowing with the light of the waiting flames.

THE OLD MAGIC MAN stood in his headdress of fur and horns, wondering how many more centuries he could endure this backwardness before the people truly would want to be helped by what he could offer. Looking up at the hill in the distance, he could see the lone tree silhouetted against a cerulean sky. Just visible hanging from one bough, swinging in the sweet breeze from the sea, was a charred shape with two legs, two arms, and a face that was little more than a leather-bound skull. The old man shook his head. The storm would have passed without this, he knew. It was their fear that had driven them.

Poor J'seryn.

In that moment of despair, the old man felt himself for what he really was, just a tired old man. He reached above his shoulders, pulled the headdress down, and then he turned, planting his staff ahead of him, and walked away, a certain bag of glass beads always at his side, now safely tucked away inside the lining of his tunic. There would be another time and another place for his magic, just not here.

In the distance, the shape in the tree turned in the wind, a mute testimony to either the limits or the strength of the power in the beads.

Just which, the Magic Man didn't know.

—Addendum 2—

Compiled from *The Garden Planet, An Overview*
of Rejuvenant,
Courtesy of Prof. Rud'n Haxmyr, MLS.dn

SPARSELY POPULATED, saved from trampling hoards only by its distance from the heavily populated inner systems, Rejuvenant with its twin suns is a stunning jewel of brilliant colors, languid days, and few nights. Because of its suns, seasons are virtually nonexistent, and its expansive ocean waters are perpetually warm. Known as a garden planet, food-producing shrub-like growths thrive mostly in interior rift valleys with lush grasses covering coastal plains. Shorelines are rocky or have wide beaches covered with smooth stones. A few large woody shrubs provide some shade, but trees as they are known on Earth are nonexistent. Wildlife tends to be small in stature, most being burrowing animals.

While not genetically related to humans, Rejuvies (as humans know them) look superficially similar, enough to mingle with humans undistinguished. However, there are a number of less noticeable differences. Rejuvies have nearly invisible gill slits along the lower edge of the shoulder blades and a tendency among females to have slight webbing between the toes. Both sexes have retractable webbing between the four fingers on each hand as well as the most carefully guarded of all, the gift to all Rejuvies, the water-weir.

Rejuvies rarely reproduce, living unimaginably long lives. However, they do age on a human scale of 120-150 Earth-standard years. At the end of a Rejuvie's life, friends and family gather for the *c'habor-reneis't* (literally "go-and-return"), sharing in a ceremony in which old memories are relived, friendships are cemented, and dreams are shared. Then the aged Rejuvie is helped into the waters of the sea and fades into the depths, averting the "dry-death" that haunts all the other known worlds. Without the *c'habor-reneis't* ceremony, he or she might return new in body but with the *hyr'yan't* (literally "essence-of-soul") fractured or possibly even unformed. The body might live, but the person, the memories, the hopes, the dreams, would be gone.

The language of the Rejuvies is found at the extreme upper limits of human hearing. Visitors to Rejuvenant have remarked on the locals' speech resembling whistling[1]. With practice in their lower vocal ranges, human-speech is easily acquired by the Rejuvies.

Their name for their home world, *Se'Yan't*, is loosely translated as Place-of-Being.

—R. Haxmyr

[1]Domesticated animals are kept by Earth-humans as companions; a common pet, the canine, has hearing that is extremely

sensitive at pitches too high for human ears to hear; canines are often communicated with using *dog whistles*. Rejuvies are able to communicate effectively with canines without using *dog whistles*. Rejuvies consider canines to be much smarter than even dolphins or whales.

—Addendum 3—

The Tale of the Peoples of the Waters of Se'Yan't

MANY WERE LOST before the warmth gave back hope.

For eons there had been nothing but the cold blackness crowding in, winnowing the weak, and sapping the strong. At first, the new warmth-giving light was very dim. The Old Ones encouraged those who had come after to hold fast to each other, to protect the young. Yet, the way was hard to travel, and the young were not strong.

Thoughts of the Ancient Home demoralized even many of the elders. Those who had not really believed in the reality of the End Time Harmonics let their memories of the time before draw them from the journey; their life-forces grew weak, and their strength bled into the blackness. Those who had drawn upon the nonbelievers' strength to supplement their own were whipped about in the turbulence, the spinning vortex of the nonbelievers' dissolution wreaking havoc on those too weak to pull themselves back into the core. The Peoples were sorely tried. The darkness pressed in, and for many the Ancient Home became nothing but a myth to comfort the weak.

Even the strongest of the Old Ones had begun to privately voice their doubts amongst themselves by the time the outermost vanguards sent the news. A spark of light had been sensed on the edge of the dark at the most distant reaches of the blackness. Risking those whose essences were most tenuous, the Old Ones pulled on fading reserves, jettisoned mass, and drove the pods on even more strongly toward the hope of the newly discovered light.

The lights were soon bright enough to be seen true. Their warmth was a promised hope held in reserve for the future, and preparations began. Secretions were dissolved and redistributed. The weakest of the Peoples were secured deep within the core. Long-stored gasses were expelled, shifting the course of the Peoples, ensuring their final destination. Each action cost the Peoples dearly, but not to perform them would have cost even more.

When the light grew bright enough to warm those at the forefront, the initial preparations were already in place. Measurements of the new discoveries were made. Gravities were compared to those of the Ancient Home. The heat signature from the approaching light was recorded, and the temperatures revealed a strong solar output.

Not all the Peoples were assured. Would there be food sources and breeding abscesses? Would the suns, for it was noted early that there were two, rend the Peoples' molecular structures, making them unstable? Would this new land provide the Peoples' descendants the sweetness of life they had enjoyed for so long in the Ancient Home?

The Old Ones knew the truth they had long kept from the others. The Peoples had no choice anymore. Supplies had been depleted, for the Peoples had journeyed long. Before leaving the Ancient Home, it had been stripped of all its resources, providing the Peoples with the riches of a thousand eons to begin their epic journey. To sustain themselves in the long darkness, much had been used up, with even the emptied store-houses converted back into useable secretions.

For good or ill, this new warmth-giving light would be their home. If the Peoples perished, they could rest in the knowledge that their intent had been true. If the suns were circled by worlds, the Peoples could adapt; they *would* adapt. Adaptability was the key that had stood them in triumph after triumph for the many lifetimes of their existence.

But the Old Ones knew there must be worlds. Not even the Peoples' ancient skills at adaptation could suffice against the shearing forces of a solar furnace. If there were no worlds revolving around the approaching suns, this would be the last crossing for a truly ancient race of Peoples, and the tears they would shed for their own deaths would be consumed with them.

As they fell into their new home, it was as the doubters had predicted, and they discovered the *burning*. The heaviness of the air tore at the fabric of the Peoples. Those farthest from the center were ripped away, flashing to nothingness in the super-heated passage to their destination. The eons of cold forgotten, the Peoples cried for relief from the heat. When the mighty furnace of their atmospheric passage created hereto unknown levels of intensity, their core was shattered, many smaller groups flying off in different directions. Cries of dismay reverberated throughout the Peoples, friends and family lost from their loved ones' very grasps.

Unknown to them, this event was what would ensure the Peoples' survival, even if it did not play out in exactly the way they had planned.

Meteorite after meteorite slammed into the ground of the planet, burying deep within the dry crust. To the edge of the horizon, there was no end to the destruction wrought by the impacts. For many turns of the planet, the devastation continued. Then, the end finally coming, the dust of those that had been incinerated in their first frantic flight through the atmosphere settled out of the air, an insulating blanket for those that had survived the final stages of their long, long journey.

Deep within the soil of the planet, one of the Peoples stirred. An unnamed acolyte, simply referred to by its birth number, 607.5, crawled to the surface and turned its eye sensors around its surroundings. *It is so dry,* it said to itself. Even this young acolyte had residual memories about the Ancient Home; it had been a world of moisture, waters, and streams.

Its throat dry and cracking, 607.5 knew this place of desolation and heat was not a safe location to remain. It would have to move. Traveling over the jumps and turns of the craggy landscape, it looked everywhere for the thing it craved most, water.

Exposed to the searing blast of the twin furnaces overhead, its skin began to dry, and as it did, it cracked, the very surface of its body peeling slowly away. 607.5 looked up at the suns and cried out in desperation. *Too bright! The sun is too intense. What can be done?*

607.5 called and called for its pod mates, its silent voice ringing out through the air. When no answer came, it knew its siblings must be long dead. Many had made it through the rain of fire. It had heard their voices. Now they were gone.

607.5 lay wearily, its skin mostly burned away, its eyes blistered into pockets of ashen pus. Feeling the blood start to boil in its veins, it knew its brain would soon follow suit. With the last of its resources, it sent its strongest cry into the thickness of the surrounding heat, its overwhelming need for communication with its kind its final deed.

As its brain began to bubble, 607.5 lapsed into the Final Death from which none returned.

However, unknown to 607.5, its cry had been heard.

STRINGER6 HUDDLED IN THE SHADOWS, the keening of

the sunlight rasping a dirge of torment across his very being. A discordant blade cutting him to the quick, he longed for it to stop. His place of safety dwindling as he watched, the knife edge of sun and shadow stalking his shrinking redoubt from death, he closed his eye sensors, reaching deep inside for the peace of the Ancient Home. He searched desperately, and it would not be found.

He and his pod. They had trusted the Old Ones implicitly. During the eons spent battling the turmoil of the darkness, none of his pod had questioned the vision. Even when rumors had begun to circulate telling of doubts among those who led, Stringer6 had kept his faith.

Huddled in the shadows, hunting for relief from the fingers of light reaching out to steal his essence away, he was now unsure. The terror of the Great Falling. The rain of fire. The blistering and the tearing as all he knew was shattered in the *heat.* The weight of this unending gravity.

Unknown to Stringer6, this new place was already becoming his home. Forces deep inside of him were sensing the stresses on his body. This chromosome was released from his DNA, an adaptation no longer needed to survive. Another was moved to *there.* Yet another chromosome was tweaked just *so.* Deep within the nuclei of his cells, unfelt changes were already at work. He sensed none of this. He only knew the pain of *alone.*

The Old Ones had been with him and his pod during the Great Falling when the rain of fire had blasted their world apart. He had felt them calling for strength. Their voices had been the comfort that kept him from giving up, from letting himself succumb to the terrible heat of the passage. But he could not feel them now. The silence of his aloneness assailed him, causing his eye sensors to bleed precious moisture.

I am alone, he wailed, his words echoing in the blankness. Not even those of his pod whom he hoped would survive the breaking away during the Great Falling sent him back reassurances. He felt more alone than ever.

He also knew the painful need of *moisture*. The great light from the suns, and he knew there were two, for the Old Ones had proclaimed it loudly to all as a call for hope during the final leg of the burning cold in the great darkness, was pulling his life from him. He must have moisture.

Flattening himself ever deeper into the crescent of his hiding place, he reached out with his most sensitive receptacles, fighting past the pain of the blinding light, past even the loneliness of *all alone* to find the moisture he must have if his existence was to extend past this last moment of painful awareness. His receptacles sifting through the molecules in the thick air, the planet's life-gases excreting the remains of this world's creation-essence as they tumbled and swirled past him, he reached out and snatched a molecule *there*.

Moisture.

The discovery filled him with hope; he might yet find the life-giving substance he so needed just now. His senses now heightened, renewed hope for his survival buoying his spirits, he searched anew. And as he searched, the twin suns turned; the shadows of his sanctuary were given respite; and the searching fingers of the suns were forbidden for a time to take this one's moisture, and in the process, his life.

Finally, in the waxing of his shadow of safety, Stringer6 found two things he was searching for: a trail in the air, the molecules teasing him to follow their path to the moisture he would find just *there;* and a cry from one of his own kind, the cry that told him he was not alone.

He knew he must hurry. Exhaustion nearly overcoming him, he struggled to follow the meandering leadings of the water molecules tormenting his dust-cracked skin with the hope of relief. Drawing on the strength he *must* pull from within, he knew he could not fail those who had sacrificed their lives in the journey to this world.

His footpads soon blistered and painful, it was not long before the travails of his search, his incredible loneliness broken only by the solitary cry he had heard just as the sun's fingers had turned, their punishing touch banished from his hiding place, wore sorely on him. He could feel the pain, the moisture-starved cells inside his body collapsing one by one. Giving his final, greatest effort, he topped a rise.

There, reaching to greet him, was moisture as far as his eye sensors could see. His receptacles had not failed him in their quest for the life-giving substance his body craved. The molecules in the air had led him on the true path. The cry that had told him he was not alone had given him the hope he needed to pull from his inner being the strength he did not think he possessed. He was grateful for these things that had led him here.

Stringer6 knelt on his moisture-starved pads, the setting suns in the distance only another's danger now, and thanked the Old Ones for leading him truly home.

AS STRINGER6 SLIPPED his moisture-starved body into the water, he breathed in the glorious liquid, the soothing of its touch satisfying his very cells. Even the suns' fingers reaching to him through the softness of the waters were now the tender caresses of a lover's touch, their silken strokes enveloping him in the ecstasy of warmth.

Awareness of others around him slowly penetrated his consciousness. Stringer6 flicked his eye sensors across the multitudes and called to the many that stood before him. All were silent, filled with the soul-rending dismay of the dispossessed. No cries were heard from the many that turned their eye sensors his way.

Stringer6 called to them. *Brothers! Fellow travelers! I was alone and afraid. Long did I travel the dust above, searching for the moisture my body so craved. Our Peoples' journey through the cold, empty blackness has been met with success. Many were lost, but I now see many survived. The Old Ones' vision was true. The End Time Harmonics have been thwarted, and our Peoples will triumph. Rejoice with me!*

For a time, silence assaulted Stringer6. Then, almost unfelt, a mere vibration in his body more than words, growing in intensity as the masses joined in, the impart became clear to him. It was the combined voices of the Peoples, and they called to him.

Great One from the Dry! Lead our Peoples. The Old Ones are gone, and our direction is without purpose. Many acolytes have perished, and we are afraid. Lead us, Great One.

Stringer6 voiced, *There was another. I heard the cry, the call that gave me hope and strength. Where is he? He is stronger than even I am.*

He rested his eye sensors on one after another, and no answer came.

Finally, one stepped forward.

There was one other. Some of us felt the words you speak of. The calling was very faint, and none other came to lead us. You are the only one.

Unsure at first what to do, then coming to believe in his own heart that his tortuous passage through the Dry Above must have been guided by an unseen purpose, Stinger6 vowed within himself to take the reins of leadership the Peoples had offered to him. He knew his people would be strong. He would see that they would live to reproduce, and many new acolytes would fill the breeding abscesses. He reached his mind out and drew his people to him, his strength becoming theirs.

THE GROUNDS SHOOK with the joy of their passing. Footpads raised (although not quite footpads anymore), thrown forward, and raised again, the walls of the cave writhed with the tumultuous celebrations of all who were gathered within, the crashing of steps in unison followed by the cheers of many unseen voices. Stringer6 stood, his happiness in the Peoples' joy being broadcast to those around him.

Even in the midst of the happiness, there was an ache in his side. He called, *Have still more yet been located? I must know if another from the Dry has been found.* He would never be able to rest until the source of the great cry that had given him strength was found. He felt pride in his leadership, but always there was the nagging sensation that one out there was stronger and more capable than him.

Great One! A small pod has been contacted in the southern seas. The distance is far, but their voices are strong. The speaker paused, fully aware his message failed to fulfill the desires of the Great One. *My leader, they have heard no messages from the Dry. They are few but report their life essences are prevailing. Many of their pod were lost in the Great Falling. There has been sorrow, but they rejoice in our success.*

Waving his not-quite-footpads in the thick liquid surrounding him, he moved away from Stringer6, his reverence in the Great One's presence complete.

Stringer6 turned to look out over the crowded cavern. His thoughts strong, he called out, sharing his news, *More survivors have rejoined our numbers. Their voices are strong! Rejoice for them!*

And the walls reverberated with renewed vigor.

THE PEOPLES GATHERED under the sun-dappled water. Few remembered any longer the cold time spent in the darkness traveling to this home. Fewer still had any recollection of the Ancient Home itself. This was now their home, their bodies changed, adapted to suit their new lives.

Gathered around Stringer6, the Peoples kept a respectful distance, waiting, their fins gently brushing the water aside, keeping themselves stable amidst the scores of currents stirring in the water. Stringer6, his fins nearly motionless, the currents undisturbed in his empty space, hovered silently, waiting for all to be prepared. Farther out, the most powerful of the Peoples' senders waited to spread the message. It was time to celebrate the completion of the change.

No longer did the Peoples resemble the legged creatures that had traveled across the emptiness of space. Their bodies had read their new environment, adjusting each element of their DNA to be perfectly suited for this new world. The names of the Peoples had been many over their long existence, always left behind when circumstance or desire necessitated a change in where they lived. Now the Peoples would cement this new world and themselves, bonding their existence here, making both one. To always be a reminder of their new union, a new name for the Peoples would be chosen. All the Peoples spread throughout the seas of this planet would spend a time of rejoicing, their new name a mark of pride.

Stringer6 stirred, knowing the time was right, and his fins carried him high above the plane of the surrounding Peoples. He drew in a deep breath, focusing on sending strongly.

My glorious people! Now we are a new race, new in place and new in body. No longer are we of the Ancient Home. We will celebrate our success with a remembrance we will carry with us each and every day. We are on a world of two suns. I have walked the Dry above the water. There, the suns wrest the moisture from our bodies, taking us to the dry-death from which none can return. Only here in our gentle seas are the suns our compassionate lovers. Here, our suns warm us and give us life. We are the Peoples of the waters. I hereby give us the name, Peoples of the Water. Let us call ourselves by the inner, true name, C'reneis't. My people, spread the word throughout the seas to the ends of the world. C'reneis't. We are C'reneis't.

Stilling his fins, Stringer6 let himself drift down to join his people. Pride residing in every part of his being, he basked in the glow of his people's exultation, their new name bonding them ever tighter, their true name spreading from sender to sender, this world now truly their home.

STRINGER6 TURNED, the intrusion unexpected but not undesired. A puzzled look grew across his face as he waited quietly, his only motion the gentle brush of his fins. The newcomer was in the advanced stages of breakdown, its body barely able to maneuver the currents in the chamber. Alongside swam several other C'reneis't, giving the visitor support when needed. The new, unknown C'reneis't moved in front of Stringer6, nodding its respect for the One Who Had Walked in the Dry.

Great One. I bring you the news of which you have searched for many turns of this world. I fear it is not happy news, and for that, I also bring the tears of my people.

Stringer6 fluttered his fins, drawing closer to his visitor, hoping against hope what this news must be. His queries of long ago still brought the occasional response from his worshipful people.

Speak, Old One. You must have seen much in this life. I face you with the utmost of respect. I listen for your sharing of that which you bring. Stringer6 bowed his body, the gentle brush of his fins gently pulling him upwards once again to face his messenger.

I am the one known as Farfind14. I traveled the Great Dark. When the Great Falling took place, I was cast from my pod. The rain of fire burned my body. Because of that, I have adapted poorly to this new world. My body will work for only a short time more. Forgive me, Great One. Even though my only solace will be a quicker death, I have long wished to bring you this news while I yet live.

As the stories tell, when you Walked the Dry, the journey was very hard, but you were given strength to go on by the cry

233

of one of our people. It is also well known that you have searched far and wide for news of the one who gave you this strength. The battered old C'reneis't paused. Its body shook with a series of spasms before continuing. *I apologize for my long wait in coming to you, Great One. As I have shared, my body has been poor, and I have only now been able to travel to bring you the news. However, I would share before I die, if you would hear.*

Patiently waiting, Stringer6 dipped his head in encouragement, his fins gently stirring the water.

When my pod was cast apart, I was flung wide over the seas. Much of my pod was burned to ash in the great heat. One of my pod mates, just an unnamed acolyte, called to us from the dry. I was injured and could not reassure him. Oh, Great One, his was the cry you heard. He was strong in the sending way, and the time of his sending is the equal of the time of your hearing. I am a poor messenger to bring such sorrowful news, One Who Walked the Dry, but my life will end soon. I would have you know this before my time is consumed in the waters of this world.

With the ending of the tale, all was still. Stringer6 drew to Farfind14. Brushing Farfind14's bloated skin with a gentle fin, Stringer6 shared that which no longer had meaning to the Peoples except as an expression of tenderness. He wept the tears of thankfulness, his moisture blending with the seas, grateful that his long search was over.

SWIMMING AT A RESPECTFUL distance, the great masses of C'reneis't watched as Stringer6 drew near the recently sealed cave. In the full view of his people, he hovered, his fins rocking him back and forth, as he shared his moisture once again, the passing of Farfind14 bringing him an even greater sorrow than when he had lost his pod many world turns ago.

Unseen to Stringer6, all C'reneis't wept with him.

STRINGER6 LET THE CURRENTS flow past his fins. He was old, and he could barely move his fins anymore. His people could wait for him for another span of time. Once he rose from his slumber, there would be no rest for his weary body.

All this time. I do still remember that which others have chosen to forget. The Ancient Home. It has been so very long, but the memories of the Ancient Home are still mine. The long, cold Dark is one of my less desirable memories. My memories of the Walk in the Dusty Dry remind me both of how I came to be the leader of my people as well as of the voice that led me home.

Here, he paused in his internal reminisces. Almost choosing not to go on, he pulled one more memory from his long experiences. *I also remember the Great Falling and all who died. My life has been full of many experiences. However . . .* and here moisture floated from his eyes as he paused. *However, I do not remember one thing. The abscesses we so need for new life. We have yet to find the life-giving breeding abscesses. We cannot reproduce without the nurturing chemical soup from which to draw our reproductive enzymes.*

His tiredness, the weariness in his fins that intruded down to his bones, was sometimes more than he thought he could bear.

Oh, Great One, another's voice rang out.

Yes, acolyte. Stringer6 shook his head to clear his thoughts, the currents swirling from him, their motions causing the waters to return with the new fragrances of *others.* He had found this latest adaptation so late in his existence to be one of the most pleasurable changes his body had made. The waters, he was assured, as with the loss of the footpads, had been the cause. He glanced at the attendant waiting patiently, his fins still, his eye sensors pointed to the floor of the chamber.

I'm sorry, Stringer6 apologized. *I was reminiscing about memories of things past and others not yet experienced. You are*—he paused in thought, his memory suddenly supplying the name—*Randon3.*

The C'reneis't before him beamed. *Very good, Walked in the Dry. You remembered.* His fins fluttering with joy, he drew closer to Stringer6. *There are those here who wish to bring their voices to your attention. Their concern is an old one, but they are insistent.*

Randon3 danced around Stringer6. The legend of the Great Dry was known among all the people. Just to be *near* the one who had walked it and lived was to be celebrated.

Of course, Randon3 had no clue what walking pads were— or walking, for that matter. He had been one of the few very young acolytes to survive the Great Falling and had no real memory of the tearing and burning. The adaptation that took the pads happened to him as to the others, but this body was all he remembered.

Shall I invite them in or tell them you are weary from the great length of your long life? Gathering his self-control, Randon3 danced back to his formal position of reverence, shifting his eyes once again to the floor.

Ah, Randon3. Stringer6 fluttered his fins, bringing his body to an erect position. *I will smell their smells this day. If I always claim tiredness from my long life, however true it may be, I will never see another C'reneis't. Send them in to me. Have them speak gently, though. My head cannot absorb the explosive abuses of my youth.*

His receptive membranes were no longer those of a mere acolyte, and strong sendings caused him unwanted levels of pain. For that reason alone, this new change was appreciated. Fragrances did not hurt at all.

He floated forward on a current, gathering morsels of food for sustenance as he passed into his receiving chamber. Slowly chewing, he thought of what he knew these supplicants would

236

request of him, and it was the thing he also knew he could not supply. Breeding abscesses. He had challenged his people to search to the ends of the seas to no success. Now the Peoples were growing too mature, and there had been found no hope for release.

He stilled himself as he felt his visitors approach.

Ah, there you are. He sent his thoughts gently into the currents. *Come close to me. My old eye sensors no longer give me the long sight I so remember from my youth.* His visitors drawing near, he tested the currents, their fragrances bringing him their news before he heard their words. *My good people, may I know who speaks with me?*

This smelling, this *knowing* what they had to say even before they started to speak gave Stringer6 a pleasurable sensation. It was wonderful, and yet, taken aback by a sudden thought, he entertained the disquieting notion that they might equally be able to smell the same from him. Naught could be done about that, he knew.

I am Gather9 from the undersea range at the end of the southern lands, Oh Great One. These are my companions, Hindre7 from the cold north, and Farve19 from your own pod lands. Gather9 nervously fluttered his fins, his anxiety filling the water with the fragrance of the ill-at-ease.

Yes. Go on. Stringer6 wafted his words gently in the direction of the visitors, suspecting they smelled them as well as heard them.

Tilting his eye sensors hesitantly down, then quickly back to look straight at Stringer6, Gather9 inhaled a great breath of the sea and let his thoughts loose in a great torrent of pain. *There are no acolytes, Great One! Many turns of this world ago, those of us who reached this new home included both named ones as well as many acolytes. Thank the Old Ones they ensured the survival of all acolytes possible by securing them deeply in the pod. Those of us who were the named ones have now become the Old Ones. I know that name is less well known to many C'reneis't on this world, but surely you know it, Great One Who Walked the Dry. Turns from now, we will pass to the death from which none returns, and the now-named acolytes will become the Old Ones. Did our people come this far, traveling the eons through the Great Dark, just to meet our end here? What can we do, Great One? Our people cry out, and there is no answer.*

With his final words, the thickened moisture of his tears began puddling in the stillness of the water around his eye sensors. Hindre7 and Farve19 gathered near to comfort him.

Farve19 turned to Stringer6. *These have traveled far to touch your knowledge. Your strength and goodness are legend, Great One. We know if this malodorous situation has any gleaning of joy in it, you will ferret it out. Praise be to the One Who Walked the Dry.*

The three turned, their awe overwhelming their politeness, sending the three scurrying from Stringer6's presence.

Left behind in their currents, he could still catch the multi-faceted whiffs of their sorrow and desperation. No matter how well phrased their words, their need was clear.

This calamity must be averted.

THE DREAMS CAME YET AGAIN. The dreams were those of the Ancient Home, pulled from the racial memories all C'reneis't carried.

A great creature, one native to the Ancient Home, yet so huge as to be incomprehensible to the diminutive C'reneis't (still known only as the Peoples), had reached the end of its mortal life. Old age had stripped the life-affirming enzymes from within the cores of the creature's cells and then deposited them on the swelling abscess walls, as the creature faced an imminent death. These were the walls of the very abscesses that were so important to the renewing of the Peoples.

Only the oldest of these massive creatures could provide the proper breeding nutrients for the weaving of the enzyme strings and the Peoples' successful reproduction. As the enzyme strings were woven, they absorbed the fragmenting substances of the dying Old Ones, releasing the memories, loves, and desires of their lives to mingle in the nesting cocoon, and providing the soup that would breed the renewal, the birth of many new acolytes.

There was a secondary benefit from the Peoples' reproductive cycle. As they drew the needed nutrients from the walls, the enormous living creature that lived and grew around the abscesses was released to disseminate into a hundred million parts, until each cell was built afresh over the course of time, then drawn together again, soon renewed to a long-forgotten youth.

Within one precious abscess, darkened, and with the walls full of breeding material, two Old Ones held each other, limbs entwined, their long memories overlapping, their experiences now no more than pleasant dreams of their time spent together during many turns of their world. Weary with age, new life from their essences would now begin as they gave of themselves. They began to weave the nutrients from the walls into strands of enzymes with which to build a nesting cocoon.

As the weaving started, the Old Ones finally felt the joy of release as long-forgotten memories teased themselves from their minds.

The dreams continued, those of lives lived long ago . . .

Barlay1 jumped, the water barely wetting his walking pads. *Ha!* He laughed. *You always were the slow one.*

Turning from his companion, the beautiful Apson51, he looked ahead, his breath taken from him. The glow of the land ahead was the glory of the Peoples. It was what they lived for. Reaching out, he pulled his companion near.

She put her face next to his and rubbed it gently. *And you rush too quickly.*

He responded to her movement, speaking his heart. *This is what drives our people. The beauty of the glow is the greatest thing we know. But that is not my greatest love.*

The glow, my favored companion. Apson51 pressed against her companion, her pleasure in him complete. *How can there be a greater love?*

Barlay1 turned his eye sensors to the female next to him. Speaking intimately as if to a lover, he gave her the greatest of gifts he could offer as he shared his deepest feelings. *You are the love I cannot live without. You are a treasure to my life. When I am the oldest of the old, I will carry you to the most nutrient-rich abscess and weave enzyme strings with you. Then, after many turns, our life's experiences will come forth as newly-alive acolytes who will be so very lucky to live lives as richly blessed as those we are experiencing at this very moment.*

Turning their faces back to the deepening glow, they relished each other's touch, their lives bonded for eternity.

And yet another dream resonated . . .

Get me! Get me! I'm too quick for you to get me!

Acolyte 214! Get your pads over here just now. Do it, or I will send you back to the enzyme strings from which you were created!

Frustration causing her to vent angrily, Apson51 knew the rigors of many siblings. However, this was a pod to be driven back to the abscess from which they'd come! What were their Old Ones thinking when they wove their strings? Sticking a quick walking pad in 214's way, she felt vindicated when the young acolyte went sprawling.

Got you, you pain in the seating area. Now you'll know what my manipulator pad feels like. For once Apson51 didn't tell the acolyte it would hurt her more than the acolyte. She made sure it didn't, either.

240

As soon as 214 was released from Apson51's manipulator pads, it was instructed to go directly to its assigned resting spot. Its whimpers of pain were no match for Apson51's unfazed frustration. Apson51 was gratified to see 214 soon lying down, drawn into the exhausted rest of the very young.

Now, if she could just get those other acolytes from this pod into the resting chamber, then she could get some chores done. Greatness above, with this many siblings, there was a great deal of it to do, also.

Then, as dreams will sometimes do, they turned dark . . .

The illness had spread to many. The Peoples struggled to ensure the task endured. Rumors had arisen that the glow across the land suffered from the pulling away.

So be it, thought Apson51. *When the people suffer, the duty they've given of themselves to complete is no longer a love. A burden will be cast aside when a greater duty arises.* She looked at the pallid face lying under her ministering manipulator. *Oh, my Barlay1. Do not go from me. Our enzymes have not yet been woven. Our acolytes will not know our song. Do not go from me, Barlay1.*

With that, she pulled a container of the most nutritious moisture from beside her and began to sprinkle it over her male, the glistening drops inviting her to rub them into his dry skin. Gratefully, she did just that.

After a great many turns, when the illness had faded, numerous Peoples did not return. The glory of the land had suffered. The glow was faint. Many Old Ones then tried to weave the enzymes, but the illness had damaged their bodies. When the enzymes could not be woven, it affected the carriers of the abscesses, also. Many of the enormous living creatures in which they were found suffered, growing ever older instead of being renewed to youth once again. The illness continued to bring destruction on the land for many, many turns of the world.

Without ceasing, the dreams continued, skipping many seasons of time . . .

The rarest of the rare, a long-desired cocoon, writhed with energy. The people gathered around. A cocoon had not burst forth with life for many turns. With trepidation in their eye sensors, and depletion in their numbers, for the first time in the memory of many, hope at the sight of the promising envelope of life bloomed again.

My own pod had 318 acolytes. I hope this one has half as many, one voice whispered.

I hear this cocoon is Apson51 and Barlay1's. They were so devoted to each other. If this births, their enzyme strings should bring forth the most precious of acolytes. The response carried the tension of excitement.

Then, the waited-for cry was given. *Look! There is the opening! The birthing has begun.*

As with all young, this most fecund of pods soon wearied even the most ardent caregivers, and the most trying of all was the final acolyte birthed, the runt, 607.5.

FINS STIRRED THE SMELL of excitement throughout Stringer6's watery chambers. Even the very old and weary were drawn from their seclusion. C'reneis't could hardly contain themselves, their senses adapted to read the emanations given off by their pod mates.

Stringer6, ensconced within his watery domicile, roused himself from his slumber, although his tired fins were unable to carry him into the currents stirred with the exhilaration of the news on its way.

Acolytes! He called harshly as he waited, the intensity of his anxiety searing the thoughts of the attendants who came to aid him. *Show me now, C'reneis't. This is your duty to the One Who Walked the Dusty Dry. Quickly!*

In his advanced age, Stringer6's patience sometimes wore

thin, and it was very thin just now.

Quivering at the unexpected rebuke, the two C'reneis't—truly no longer young and hardly acolytes—cautiously drew near, fanning the water to ease Stringer6's passage. Reaching the chamber opening, he drew in a deep draught of the waters, absorbing the odors as they wafted through him.

It's true! Stringer6's long-dreamed desires crystallized into his thoughts, but it was his odors that carried the news to his companions' sensing organs. *The reports carry the hope we had all but forfeited in our exhausted searching. How? This question must be answered! How?*

He released the scents into the waters, his tension eased, quickly snapping to face the two C'reneis't. With sharp pains shooting through his fins at the sudden motions of his ancient body, he slowed his movements, grateful when help came from the two waiting on him, their respect for He Who Survived the Dry overpowering any sense of offense he had earlier given.

Stringer6 knew remorse at his earlier harsh sending, and he spoke of such in regret. *My apologies, my helpers. The excitement of the news . . . the frustrations of this old body. I must not allow these shortcomings to justify inconsiderate behavior. Will you forgive me my offense toward you?* And he stilled his front fins, his tired, old body slipping into his best semblance of a bow.

The two looked at each other, confusion in their eye sensors. *How can the Great One offer us apologies?* Sudden smells of their confusion filling the waters, their fins spun, stirring the water greatly, although not yet carrying them away. *Gr-gr-great One! We are but the lowliest of the Peoples. We were at fault. Pardon us for our slowness, Great One.*

In a cascade of eddies and artificial currents, the two were off and gone before Stringer6 could call them back.

Tired in his mind, and disappointed for snapping at those who had come to give him aid, Stringer6 was just as disappointed in the C'reneis'ts' reaction to his apology. He was no great power to be worshipped. All he had ever been was one lucky traveler who happened to be at the right place at the right time.

A very long time ago, he had ceased believing in his special guidance during the time his people had arrived on this world. His extreme age, a sorely worn body, and the inability to save his people had taught him otherwise. *Just one abscess,* he had long ago breathed to whatever gods that might answer. *Let my people reproduce.* And the answer was always the same. There had been no answer at all, at least not for him.

He hardly dared believe, anymore. Even this time, it seemed too good to be true.

THE ACOLYTES—mere suggestions of C'reneis't, with their diminutive size—were hushed just as soon as they drew near, their caretakers retrieving errant strays from wherever they happened to slip out of sight.

Let them come close to me, Stringer6 breathed, his mind barely able to concentrate. Just the strain of staying alert was taking a toll on his weary body. So many days were sleeping days, now. He refused for this to be a wasted day like so many others. Holding a fin out, he reached to brush the newness of the acolytes' smooth skin.

How? he questioned. *Our teams have searched the seas.* What did this pod know that had not been shared with him? He touched one of the young ones. They were real.

In his mounting excitement, his question was pushed aside. *Acolytes,* he marveled to all those around him. *Hope has returned. Rejoice!*

His people did so enthusiastically.

TRULY, THIS WAS the way it happened. Who would have thought?

The story seemed almost implausible, it was so simple.

Shall we tell him? Old One is very fragile, his mind not prepared for strong thoughts.

The two C'reneis't brushed the waters very carefully with their smells, their minds adding the details that the fragrances of their words could not convey. Such was their communication.

Both of the C'reneis't were startled at the sudden brilliance of unspoken words that echoed in their heads, the sending that of long ago, decimating their very attempts at subtlety.

Out with it! What do you not wish to tell the fragile old one?

Although Stringer6's fins were weak, he could still glare, and he did so unabashedly. He rarely hesitated these days to express himself fully, knowing his people were indulgent with him. Even those who worked to aid him in his goings in the waters just smiled when he sent them his strongest smells. Only his still-powerful *sendings* could convince them to jump at his commands anymore.

The two turned, truly indulgent smiles gracing their faces just as Stinger6 knew they would.

The breeding abscesses have been here all along, Great One. Seeing the harsh look appearing on Stringer6's face, they jumped to reassure him this was no silly acolyte's tale. *The floating mountains that move so quickly among us. The ones that move all about the seas of our existence. We all know that sometimes these mountains fall to the floor of the sea. Those that have graced the waters well are lifted by the holy bubbles of the Final Death, rising to sing their praises to the twin suns above. We have explored these holy mountains as they have rested on the floor of the seas. However, we have never approached one as it has moved among us.*

The C'reneis't turned to his companion, the excitement evident on his face as well as in the waters surrounding him.

And? Stringer6 sent. *I am now very old. I have little time for your suggestions and obscure observations.*

The C'reneis't continued, *One we thought had fallen to await its chance to sing to the suns above was not as the others. It was still in motion, its life not gone. Our Peoples went inside to explore, not knowing life was not gone from the mountain. The abscesses were there, just inside, as they must have always been!* The C'reneis't now danced the chamber in his excitement. *The abscesses! Oh, Great One Who Walked the Dry, your enzymes will be woven. The moving mountains bring our breeding abscesses to us! We know now their breeding abscesses must be ready for our Old Ones only just before they fall to the floor of the seas.*

So, the news is true. Stringer6 wafted odors of gratitude at the revelation.

But there is more, He Who Walked the Dry. The C'reneis't's odors carrying the exhilaration not even its dancing could convey, it told the last of his news. *Great One, listen to this. As the old stories tell, after our Old Ones weave their enzymes in the mountains, they move again as young mountains to carry the cocoons until the acolytes are birthed. Old One, we give them back their time in the seas just as they give the life of renewal, our acolytes, to us.*

His fins stilled, his odors controlled, Stringer6 could find the peace his leadership had never completely suffered him to know. His heartfelt words bled themselves to his companions.

The Peoples will live. Our existences will not fail with this generation. Let all C'reneis't know.

And the two C'reneis't darted from the chamber to do as their leader bade them to do.

THE CHAMBER WAS OLD, its surface worn smooth with the passage of many currents of visiting C'reneis't. Although his enzymes had been woven long ago, the Peoples had never

246

forgotten The One Who Had Walked the Dusty Dry. His deeds were now only myth, told to the youngest of acolytes as rest-time stories, and most C'reneis't could no longer imagine the stories to have ever really taken place.

BUT SOMEDAY I BET I COULD.

The acolyte with the birth number 34 had that look on its face, the one its caregiver knew wouldn't go away until she could distract it. This one was determined to have its way, refusing to take its required rest, and it must be coerced with all haste.

Gaya4 carefully composed her odors, wanting the acolyte to smell her instructions clearly. Releasing the compounds in the currents, she moved her fins just *so,* the gentle currents she created pushing the odorants toward the sensors of the acolyte. Its attention diverted, the odors commanding its acquiescence, the young acolyte sullenly left its determined dreams at the doorway of the cavern and followed Gaya4 inside to the resting spots, its sleep soon underway.

DO YOU KNOW, 34 really believes it could? It is so ridiculous. Walk in the Dry. How could our fins carry our bodies without the seas' support? Even the smallest of acolytes would not think to do something so foolish except in pretend. But I think 34 actually believes the myths of The One.

Gaya4's fragrances wafted her story to all in the chamber. She was pleased to breathe in the disapproving agreement the others sent out. She knew 34 must be restrained before it did itself harm or convinced others to do something stupid. She continued, *Why, the last time I served as caregiver to its pod, it swam into the shallows. Then, and you will never believe this,* her smells now streaming from her, pungent and clear, *it actually leaped into the Above, touching the gasses with its own skin!* She led the others in a shiver of terror, the very thought making their fins quiver.

Another of the C'reneis't nearby ventured, his odors tentative, *How would we communicate in this, what did you say, gasses? How would we share our thoughts? As it is, the bubbles of air that rise from the deepest depths disrupt our fragrances when we swim through them. How would the same not happen if the seas no longer surrounded us?*

The unpleasantness of the concept creating upset digestive systems and sending shivers down the fins of those in the chambers, the topic was quickly changed and forgotten, but one was listening who was not so easily dissuaded.

Having crept back to the doorway from its resting spot, Acolyte 34 had overhead. Determination once again coagulated in its inner being as its odorants bled from its speaking pores.

He did, too. The Great One really did walk the Dry above the waters. The dust of the Dry covered him, his skin dried from the heat of our twin suns, and he found his way by the sound of a great voice. Then, its eye sensors puddling body moisture in the water around its head, Acolyte 34 shimmered back to a recess in the rock wall. *I'll show them one day. Just wait. I might not be able to go into the Dry on these fins, but someday . . . someday.*

Acolyte 34 drifted sleepily to the floor and was later moved back to its proper resting spot, Gaya4 unsure just how it had wound up there.

THE OLD C'RENEIS'T HUDDLED in the waters, their unspoken concerns palpable. The mountains were no longer moving nearby. The breeding abscesses that the Peoples so depended on had grown few in number. In deep discussion over the state of the seas, many explanations were offered, but the reality still remained.

It was said that in times long past, it had been possible to call to others in the seas even though they were on the far side of the world. Even the oldest of the C'reneis't could not recall a time when that had actually been so. What was nearby was what could be smelled. How could the smell of words travel the seas without dissipating?

In fact, the many turns of the planet it took just to travel a short distance had caused a breakdown in communication between C'reneis't pods. The fish the C'reneis't had learned to use as their breeding abscesses had become thinned by poor feeding grounds in this part of the world. Having moved on to richer waters, these C'reneis't unknowingly had been left behind. Not able to comprehend the renewed life the microscopic creatures gave when weaving their enzymes, death had once again become a facet of the fishes' existence, the difference to them one of a matter of the quantity of days, their time and their simple minds filled with the effortless pleasures of feeding and mating, one day very much like the rest.

While other C'reneis't pods were glad to see the new mountains moving in their waters, the Old Ones here still huddled, unaware why their breeding abscesses had gone from them.

I USED TO BE AN ACOLYTE just like you. The C'reneis't known as Zente16 sent his words in odors to the young ones in his care. *Guess what I liked most to do?* He looked around the group of acolytes, their eye sensors trained on him as one. *Has anyone here ever heard of the One Who Walked the Dry?* Fins fluttered in excited anticipation, the stories ones they had all heard time and again. *Do you really think he walked the gasses above our seas?*

Nothing could live in the gasses above the waters. All the other caregivers tell us so, piped one acolyte, the scent of his words bright and sharp with youthful arrogance.

I bet the other caregivers do, projected Zente16's ardent odors. The fragrances of his words grew faint as he whispered his next sentence. *I've seen the creatures there.*

A tittering of odors suddenly permeated the chamber. Quickly, in order to quiet the rising laughter, the caregiver C'reneis't quizzed, *Guess what my acolyte number used to be before I got my name?*

The acolytes looked back and forth at each other, their fins fanning rapidly, and they turned back to him, waiting for him to give them the answer.

I was known as Acolyte 34.

At that name, the attention of the acolytes was lost as they burst into rounds of pungent laughter. Zente16 sighed, long ago resigned to the cutting comments he had once been called, as the acolytes began ribbing each other with names like *Dreamer, Off His Rocker,* and *Silly C'reneis't.* The most hurtful of all had been *Believer of Stupid Myths,* because he knew the myths weren't stupid. He had jumped into the gasses of the Dry and seen the creatures there. They had no fins.

He knew the myths were real.

AS IS THE WAY of oceans on worlds across the wide expanses of the galaxy, where life has fled, it once again returns. The mighty moving mountains once more came to the pods of the waiting Old Ones.

However, it was too late for many. Having waited with only their aromatic words drifting through the seas' currents for communication, they could not know that other C'reneis't not so very many turns of travel from them were rejoicing in their bounty of breeding abscesses. Those who did survive until the mountains returned, waiting patiently in their distress, found time to dredge the old memories, the knowledge of sharing over the ocean-wide distances of the past not really forgotten, just buried so deep as to seem forgotten. As the enzymes began to weave afresh, these memories were released, and in response to desperate circumstances that had nearly wiped out a whole generation of C'reneis't, the resourceful race did what it always did when faced with calamity.

It adapted once more.

The old gift of *sending* turned out to be a necessity after all, and the new generations of C'reneis't received the forgotten ability to *send*, the one that would enable them to bring their mountains to them.

One C'reneis't who had lived a long, although at times frustrating life, soon found a new purpose for this fresh-again skill. This was the C'reneis't known by many names. Some called him *Dreamer, Off His Rocker,* and *Silly C'reneis't.* The name he had slowly begun to claim with pride was *Believer of Stupid Myths.* As an acolyte he had been called 34. He had once been given an adult name, Zente16, but not even he remembered that anymore.

WHAT ARE THEY SAYING to each other?

The currents swirled with the question as one caregiver wafted her scents to another resting at her side.

It is so hard to tell. These acolytes don't seem to communicate as we do. Although they can certainly understand our scents, they seem to have a secret language. If only I could find out just what it is.

The second caregiver shook her head, her fins flashing back and forth, the currents swirling in response to her frustration. *I feel they are laughing at me when following in my most deliciously scented currents. I turn to find them watching me innocently as if they have no clue why I should be suspicious. These will be the death of me, yet.*

The one once known as Zente16 sniffed the odors drifting through the waters, the conversation faint, just pungent enough to underscore the speaker's acrid anger underlying her words. He had heard the tales of the newest of acolytes, and he knew this skill was the same as he had heard about in the old stories,

251

ones he recalled from his days as an acolyte, although no one told the newly-birthed ones the ancient tales anymore. The old chambers with their walls worn smooth no longer entertained supplicants anxious to feel the waters that might have surrounded the One Who Walked the Dusty Dry.

Though old in his body, he still remembered the time when his skin had touched the gasses of the Above. His memory of the legged things walking in the Above were as clear to him as the acolytes and their caregivers across the chambers.

Now this, the young ones speaking without odor. Already there was evidence some of the older acolytes could entice the mountains to shift their positions, the great behemoths not just wandering where mountains seemed to wander, but often seeming to be instructed not to disturb the acolytes' play-spaces.

The one once known as Zente16 let his thoughts ramble, his ideas not constrained in the way things might become, as many of his C'reneis't were prone to do. And as he thought, the glow of how to know more of the ones who walked the Dry began to enlighten his brain.

THE C'RENEIS'T ONCE KNOWN as Zente16 called to the acolytes frolicking in the open waters in the midst of the moving mountains. He sent his odors pungently, his words to be clearly understood. Fanning the fragrances with his fins, he waited patiently for a response. He needed to know if the new gifts he suspected they had been given precluded the old speech of scent, or whether they could speak well in both languages.

After a time, faces turned toward him, a few at first, then more and more. Excitement making the old C'reneis't's blood pound, he watched them turn and dart to pause in front of Stupid Believer of Myths.

It was time to play.

EXHAUSTED, BELIEVER OF MYTHS watched the acolytes. His old body was unused to the strain of working with so many energized young ones but very satisfied with what they had been able to do; he was mentally recharged. Involving himself in old dreams he had many turns ago abandoned, much was returning to him. *Zente16.* He turned the old name over in his mind.

How strange it seems in my thoughts, that old name. He turned, his fins carrying him back to his cavern, many plans in his thoughts. *They did it. They controlled the mountains. Their minds can speak the speech afar. The old stories of our bodies changing*—and the word "adaptation" came to him—*must be real. These acolytes have changed. Perhaps they can be taught even more.*

His plans formulating a series of actions he knew would be harshly frowned upon, the old C'reneis't set his mind to secrecy, his intents that of a renegade determined to follow through with secret plans without regard to the consequences.

WITH HIS INQUISITIVE acolytes at his side, he moved to the water's edge. Waiting where he used to hide so many turns of this world ago, the memories flooded back. This was a spot where the creatures in the Dry Above, enormous beyond imagination, had often come, falling flat to the surface of the Dry. They would stay motionless, at times moving not at all until others would walk up to them and drag them away. Would they come again this day?

After much waiting, and with the acolytes exploring the crooks and crannies of the shoreline until they felt they knew them well, many of them soon began to show the restlessness of the young, bored if not constantly entertained. Then a few noticed a motion through the ceiling of the waters. One was moving there in the Dry!

Quickly, Zente16 called. *Send a strong word. Tell the one in the Dry to come greet us. Tell it as you told the moving mountains. Make it* know *what you want it to do.*

His expectations high, the old C'reneis't waited, remembering all he had once done at this place, his practice at patience coming back to him as well.

Then, without warning, the world exploded around them. Zente16 was carried far, and the acolytes were scattered in a mighty blast of water droplets along with him. Flung through the gasses, safely encased in fragments of the protective sea, the world was visible as through the eyes of the ones in the Above. The C'reneis'ts' watery blue home stretched as far as could be seen . . . the Dusty Dry . . . it was real, and the things there! There were no words to describe the World Above, so different it was from their own. What a story there would be to tell!

The end finally did come, the airborne travelers crashing back, rejoining their watery world. Enthusiasm bubbling up from their journey, they quickly located Zente16, anxious to share this new adventure.

We called to each other through the gasses, enjoying the unexpected adventure, but the moment was not enough.

Did you fear your demise was at hand? Zente16 trembled, for it was possible the acolytes would not want to continue with his plan.

They only laughed. *There was no time to concern ourselves with the end of our journey. The world above was too big, too grand!*

Tell me of it, called the old C'reneis't. *I sent my odors, but you could not scent them. Tell me, what did you see in the gasses above?*

It was all as you said, the acolytes exuded. *The Above goes on and on.*

Another joined in, *What was the great explosion that sent*

us on our journey? We called as you said, then the world sent us up into the Dry.

Zente16 became aware of the massive shape in the water near him. Indicating its presence, he sent his odors to the acolytes to draw their attention. Their amazement was obvious. Their excitement was equally clear. Even their puzzlement came through in no small regard. What sort of thing was this that had come into the waters? Was it like the moving mountains, able to be controlled but having a mind of its own?

He sent his best explanation. *Through the ceiling of the seas, there are many things. There can be found the gasses of the Above, other creatures that move in the distance, as well as the suns in our skies. But this thing that has come to us is too huge to imagine. We must know more.*

He led his charges forward, exploring the unimaginably massive thing. Soon he found it had similarities to the moving mountains. He took the acolytes inside the thing where the seas were now filling its internal cavities. There were those areas that showed remarkable similarities to breeding abscesses, although they were dank and dead, for the thing was now still and not alive.

It came when we called, he spoke to the acolytes. *Like the moving mountains you direct in your play, it knew when you called.*

Still filled with amazement, Zente16 felt he had finally fulfilled his dream. He had made the connection he had been told he could never experience.

Contact with the Dry was finally his.

THE GATHERED PODS of C'reneis't had come, and they moved closer to see the phenomenon. The size, the immensity of it was more than they could fathom. Even Zente16 wasn't able to explain the colossus that had fallen in the water. From under the water's ceiling, while still in the Above, it had appeared far away and of a large size. However, once the water had been breached, it became very clear that the size was far beyond how it had appeared before.

Definitely not alive, spoke the Old Ones. *We have toured the object from the inside and out, and there are no signs of life. Teams have reported back with their findings, and it does not meet the criteria. This appears to be a natural phenomenon that has simply fallen into the seas. This is certainly another good reason to avoid the shallows of our world's waters.*

They turned disapproving glares toward Zente16, their censure that of long-remembered animosity.

It moved when the acolytes called it, Dreamer of Dreams insisted, his frustration at the Old Ones' narrow-mindedness almost too much to withstand. *Ask them. Have you seen them tell the moving mountains to shift positions?* His words strong and acrid, he washed them forward with vigorous swipes of his fins.

True laughter rang from the Old Ones, its fragrance permeating the waters. *The mountains go where they will. There is no telling them where to go or what to do. They move, fall to the floor of the sea, and rise again to worship the suns. Only when we have Old Ones who need the breeding niches do the moving mountains serve a purpose.*

Zente16 rebuffed the old fools harshly.

Watch the acolytes. Watch the moving mountains. You will see. These do not need the odors we use to communicate. They have adapted. Have you forgotten the word? It is the word that describes what we do best. Pull your oldest memories from the crevices of your minds, and you will know. I am proud of the name given to me long ago by the acolytes. Believer of Stupid Myths. I claim it. You should be named Too Stupid to Believe the Myths. He fluttered his fins, a lifetime of ridicule triggering his bold venting at the Old Ones. *The acolytes called, and the colossus came. It no longer moved only after it came into the* seas. *The acolytes have the speech that enables them to call these creatures of the Dry even through the gasses of the Above. After a time, perhaps these creatures of the Dry can provide the breeding abscesses we need in abundance. Is it not worth a try?*

The thing is not alive. It will dissolve into the sea. It has abscesses, but none are breedable. The Old Ones refused to cede Zente16's reasoning.

He tried again. *Remember the moving mountains. In the distant past, they were not known to provide breeding abscesses.* He looked at each of the Old Ones, his eye sensors locking with them one by one, his commanding look giving him the presence over them he desired. *We thought they fell to the floor of the sea then rose to the ceiling to worship the two suns, that they had no other purpose. We know now if we inhabit the breeding abscesses they carry just before they fall, we can weave the enzymes and the moving mountains do not fall. They go about as new mountains.* He indicated the outsized monstrosity at their side. *We must learn, and possibly, they also must learn.*

The long-ago acolytes who had now become the Old Ones relented, for they saw the truth in his words. They remembered the time the moving mountains hadn't come, and they remembered the stories of learning of the mountains' uses for breeding. They could not deny much of what Zente16 said.

Then they did what their race of Peoples did best. They began to adapt. They called the Peoples together and began to plan. Perhaps there might be something to this. It would take much discussion and much trial and error. The acolytes would have to participate in exercises to show that the adaptations Zente16 claimed for them were for real. If this proved as they were being told . . . but as for that, they would just have to wait and see.

THE TEAM SWAM GENTLY around the shape floating in the seas, the enormity of it enough to unnerve the most stalwart of hearts. Another from the Dry had been commanded, and the sea had been broached once again. It was as before, though.

Yes, we admit it is true. The acolytes have adapted, their voices able to call the moving mountains that swim in our seas, directing them to do their bidding. We don't understand how they can call without using their scents, but there can be no denying what we have seen. Their fins stirring the currents of the waters, the team backed from the massive shape.

The moving mountains from our seas are not able to listen well. Simple commands are all they can hear. The eldest of the team, a C'reneis't of much wisdom, spoke with the softest of fragrances. He did not like the calling of these creatures from the Dry. *Why should we expect more from these creatures from the Above? How can anything so large have the ability for intelligence? Let us leave these great creatures to their doings.* His scents now tinged with heaviness, he continued, *We cannot be responsible for more of their endings.*

Responsible? A just-named C'reneis't known as Quikn8 jetted out an intense odor of superiority. *What is there not to be responsible with? Eldest says the moving mountains within our seas are not good listeners. No one here would disagree. The mountains move where they will as the currents carry them. They show no motive or desire to control their destiny. We barely acknowledge them as living, and then only in some bizarre fashion we can only surmise. But these things we've learned to call from the dry gasses above, do they appear to think at all? We call them, and crashing into our world, they expire. Can they not breathe the seas' wetness? If that is so, do they not know it? How can their endings matter if they are creatures without thought?*

Yet another of the team stated his stand, expressing the feelings of others with his comments.

In our oldest of memories, those of us who have searched them out have seen the changes of which we are capable. Could we not do for these in the dry gasses of our world as we have done for the moving mountains, and then do perhaps more? Is it possible to find a way to help them adapt as well? Our people are now limited in our reproduction. When our Old Ones feel that the time to weave their enzymes is upon them, they at least have the choice to go on for a time. If there are no moving mountains at the stage of full readiness, the Old Ones must wait for the opportunity to avail itself. There are times the Old Ones face the Death that Cannot Be Undone because the breeding abscesses are unavailable. Now truly engrossed in his argument, the fragrances he sent grew more potent. *We have seen the many abscesses within this massive creature. True, none are prepared for the weaving of the enzymes, but these creatures are being called to the seas, perhaps when they are unprepared. What if our ability to adapt could somehow be used to remake these creatures? More of our people than we could ever count could breed in just one of these massive forms. Is it even possible?* He looked around at the team members giving him their undivided attention.

The eldest turned from one to another. *This is truly a most monumental concept. There would be benefits to what you say. The breeding abscesses on this world do exist in creatures that seem to receive benefit from our weavings. But this you speak of has never been done. Is it possible? I do not know. Perhaps if the enzymes could be woven in a new way, or if these poor creatures could share our adaptability . . .* Regret tinged his odors, and in his moment of pondering, he seemed willing to let the matter die.

However, not all felt as he did.

When do we access our most hidden memories? Quikn8 pressed his agenda forward, the excitement in his scents obvious. *It is when we weave the enzymes. That is when we pull from our most inner thoughts the very things we thought for-gotten. Can the Old Ones not help us? Have them search their thoughts deeply when weaving their enzymes. The memories will enter the soup of creation, and their acolytes will do what all acolytes do. They will absorb a portion of these memories, and perhaps the solution will be ours one day.*

Acceptance from the eldest seemed to sway the remaining doubters.

This will be a project for the generations, he announced. *Few of us, if any, will live to see its culmination. Even the youngest of us,* and he glanced at Quikn8, *will likely weave our enzymes before the fruition of this knowledge we speak of. Are we in agreement to search whether this is possible before pull-ing another of these creatures into the seas?*

Fins stirring, bodies bobbing in the gentle movements of the waters, an agreement was reached among the C'reneis't. No others would be called from the Dry for many generations of the C'reneis't. But one day, they hoped, the knowledge would be found enabling this treasure, adaptability, their most valuable ability, to be gifted on the ones from the dusty, dry world above theirs.

THE TWO OLD ONES had waited far longer than they wished, the moving mountains few for many turns of their world. Their fins weary, their hearts wearier still, even com-munication with other C'reneis't was now difficult. Of the last of their kind to know the language spoken through the water in the pleasant way of the fragrances, they did not know the send-ing of the mind that adaptation had restored to the C'reneis't. To the newest acolytes, the two Old Ones were both deaf and dumb. Able to converse fully only with each other, the strain of their existence cried for release.

I remember an old goal I helped set as a young male, the ancient one known as Quikn8 wafted to his mate.

She sent back the sweet fragrance of laughter. *Ah, I see you are growing younger these turns. Your memory of old times is better than your memories of the last meal we shared. Revisiting the past! Soon, will you become an unnamed acolyte, your improving memory helping you forget your aging mate?*

Amusement clouding the waters, Quikn8 waited a time before replying. *This was an important goal, or so we all thought. We wanted to pull an old memory from the distant past, thinking the weaving time would be when the memory might most likely be revealed.*

What good would that do? We will not return from the weaving of the enzymes. Our bodies will be woven into the chemical soup that starts the new lives we produce.

Ah, and Quikn8 gently rubbed one fin against his mate's side. *That was the crux of the thing. The acolytes must be the ones to remember. I guess it never happened, and I am the last.*

Your chance, then, is now, with me. Let's weave your memories from the distant past into our memories of each other. If you are there, I will be glad to share any of the memories you wish to search out.

His love for his mate filling him to the top of his being, he brushed her fin, and they swam into the breeding abscess, their enzymes soon woven with memories as far back as the beginnings of the Peoples.

When this cocoon matured, the acolytes remembered, and the memory of how to bring the adaptations of the C'reneis't to those in the Dry Above was soon shared with the other C'reneis't.

The plan had finally come to fruition.

THEY DON'T ALWAYS LISTEN.

The descendant of Quikn8 spoke with the assurance of one who had been involved in this project for a quite long time. An expert, truly, in these matters, he did in actuality have the authority he exuded.

Pushing ahead, he continued, *The young, and we know now how to recognize the young even as they move to and fro in the Great Dry, have minds that race too fast for them to hear us. We can see it in the way they tear about. The ones in their middle spans of years hear us well but do not respond. It is those whose lives have been long, and whose existences are at the very end that we can call out. Remember, we must call them as they still live, not as we have in the past, filled with the waters of the ocean.*

Another queried, *You feel confident this is the way?* Uncertainty rang in the question.

It has been done before. The memories of a long-ago Ancient Home had been dredged from the deepest of ancestral reservoirs. In that distant time, C'reneis't, as a different Peoples, had adapted—and adapted other creatures around them. Now, the memories of those events, reawakened, were known by all of Quikn8's descendants. *We have the knowledge of how it was possible when our Peoples were a previously named people. By weaving our enzymes with other creatures', we were able to share the gift of adaptations in ways to benefit the Peoples. We have seen our own bodies adapt.* The one descended from Quikn8 stressed his words, his very manner filled with reassurance. *This will work. We have all seen it, in our memories, if not in fact. However, we must have many, many C'reneis't to do this.* He laughed, now poking fun to pull the others into his plans. *If these creatures from the Dry are as mindless as the old memories suggest, perhaps we can even remake them in our image, weaving our enzymes, and in the process, improve their thinking organs. Then, at least, they won't fall into the waters and die before they are of use to us.*

Those around him shook with laughter, imagining the great creatures that walked the Dry as one of them. It was more than reason could fathom.

THE OLD WOMAN, little more than an insensate ape, her thoughts unable to comprehend deeper than the barest glimpses of the world around her, knew not that she was old. All her life she had known little more than youth and procreation, and dimly, she had been aware of the best trees for fruits. It was true of all her race. They had progressed into racial maturity only the slightest amount. Hunters and gatherers only, they ate, copulated, aged, and died. Life on their world was easy, and if it was also short, no one knew what short was. Each day stood alone, apart from all others, and when life was done, it was let go with little regret.

This day, the old woman just knew it hurt to arise under the suns' brightness, that her body leaked strange smells, making her food place feel bad, and she had to get to the water. Hardly understanding more than just this one day and that she was now always hungry, this pull she felt toward the waters, she knew without question.

She had always known her entire life the call of the waters. The calling sometimes frightened her, and all of her days she had kept far from the sea when she could. But now, to climb to the steep place of safety, then to return to slake the thirst she always felt, was more than she could do. The water's edge had become her world, her aging body penning her there.

The C'reneis't swimming in the seas of the old woman's world sensed her presence. Constantly sending for those from the Above to come to them, the C'reneis't waited patiently. For generations, and the C'reneis't generations were very long indeed, they had waited. A short time more was of no consequence.

The old woman's body finally failing, her breath coming in tortured gasps, she knew the pull of the waters stronger than she had ever felt it before. There was only hunger and pain and over all else, the calling of the waters.

Barely alive, she let herself be drawn to the shore, the lapping waves of the sea, the water she needed to visit daily for drinking, yet was always afraid to be near.

Entering the waves, her body giving way to its final exhaustion, the waters' embrace was no more than a pleasurable touch on her weathered skin. Unseen and unfelt to her, untold billions of C'reneis't swarmed over her body, the Old Ones searching for the breeding abscesses desperately hoped for, with many, many others gathering to intermingle their enzymes with hers in order to change the old woman into something her world had never seen before.

The C'reneis't soon swamped the enormous creature that had crowded into their waters. With the most ancient of the C'reneis't flooding the precious abscesses, their time for reproduction at hand, their weaving of the enzymes would both pull the residue of a lifetime from the barely surviving carcass as well as build a cocoon of safety for the birthing of a new generation of acolytes.

With the trading of enzymes started, the C'reneis't began to transform the woman.

The process did more than renew the old woman. It also gave her the al'las' with which to swim, and the gill slits with which to breathe. In addition, the mingling of the enzymes forever bonded the sea-bound C'reneis't's genome to that of the land-bound creature they changed.

The woman would arise after a year in the seas, having harbored and released immense numbers of new acolytes, each built from the residue of the individual cells in her body. Her flesh would be transformed in the process, the residue of a lifetime's ageing scoured clean. She would arise from the water to walk once again upon land, youthful, and with new levels of intelligence in her brain, given her through the adaptive gifts of the C'reneis't.

Alas, she would not bring any memories with her; instead,

her mind would be fresh with the newness of the first time alive.

Future generations of her race would come to the seas when called, and in the process, they would continue to develop in intelligence, thanks to the hard-working C'reneis't, just as the C'reneis't would continue to increase in numbers due to the bonding the woman would pass on to her progeny.

When the C'reneis't finally grew great enough in numbers, their voices would be so strong that no native born on the world that would eventually call itself Se'Yan't would be able to resist. The C'reneis't, now irrevocably bonded to their land-dwelling counterparts, would find the pleasure of the strange race's touch so alluring that even the simplest brush of skin in the waters of the seas would renew the love affair between the two races. Billions of C'reneis't would swarm over each person's skin, and with each C'reneis't being the color of Se'Yan't's blue seas, they would create a gel-like coating so like the seas themselves, that the very skin held underneath the water's surface would seem to disappear, the C'reneis't slipping away with the waters as the skin returned to the air above, torn from the lover they had created.

Now fused irrevocably together for all time, it was ironic that neither the C'reneis't nor the race they had forever bonded themselves to had any real idea just what the other actually was. Their existences were too many layers removed from each other. But, to proclaim that they had once again become a new Peoples, the C'reneis't took a new name, C'habor-reneis't. They would no longer be the Peoples of the Waters. Now, they would forever be known as the Protectors of the Peoples of the Waters.

All C'habor-reneis't rejoiced, for they had adapted one more time.

—Addendum 4—

Adhor'k and the Miracle of C'habor-reneis't Se'Yan't
2799 A.D. (O.E. Standard)

ADHOR'K FLOATED, UNFETTERED by the bonds of her body, the sparkle of the suns creating stars even on this, the brightest of days. This was a time of rebuilding, of remaking, of returning to a youth she had not known for decades upon decades.

Pausing in her journey, thinking only of *nothing,* she existed, not quite under her twin suns, yet with her twin suns giving her life. The swell of the seas gently tugged her one way, then another, never quite managing to break her bond with life and not able to do so even if it tried.

Not quite memories brushed her thoughts.

Adhor'k.

A voice called, one not her own.

She remembered her name, who she was, or at least a fragment of who she was. The rest, the voice, the desire to answer, would come later, slowly, although it would certainly come.

A sparkle in the seas caught her attention. Her identity forgotten once again, she felt herself slip once more into the sensations of the water around her, her world, its touch all the existence she could yearn for.

Her body shifting with the wash of the waves, tenuous, she felt herself pulled to the shallows, the rocky sea floor undulating against her, the familiar stones ones walked lifetime after lifetime. With each stone, memories were stirred. This one refreshed a time spent with a loved one, the experiences warm and deep. Brushing another stone, a renewed feeling of separation, a beloved brother resting his hand on her arm, telling her unwanted goodbyes.

The tendrils of past events touched her thoughts, stirred her memories, sometimes with feelings of joy, and at other times bringing an involuntary recoil to every fiber of her being. Fleeting, sharp, sweet, and sour, and then forgotten as quickly as they arrived, she continued to float, the seas her home, her being, all her lives a dream, no longer real, and quickly released into the void of *other*, always awakening back to the *now,* the softness of the water, with her life-giving twin suns sparkling above her.

One dream returned again and again, and she remembered. It was an old pain, a part of her for the duration of a very long life. She drew back within herself, hiding from the memory, the pain, as it became her present once again . . .

She felt as a child, running free. Fresh from c'haborreneis't, she always felt the giddy freshness of the first-alive she once was many lifetimes ago. The excitement she knew in her rebirth was fleeting, though, for she was always reborn as an adult, and she ran to catch the youthful moment, the sensation there and gone within a day.

Flying through fields, dancing the dance of the child-at-heart, she soared, her feet touching only air, thrilling in the newness of life. Turning her head, blinking in the sudden brightness of her twin suns brilliant against their yellow sky, she did not see the edge of the escarpment, the falling away below, the sharpness of the stones at the bottom. The ground vanished from under her feet, leaving her arms pinwheeling. Shadows of desperation flashed past her eyes. With a suddenness she could have never expected, the stones met her. The sharpness of the pain surprised her, the intensity ravaging even in memory.

She lay still, unable to comprehend the strongness of the feeling, how the pain could be so big. Her heart surging, she was afraid to disturb the pain, to draw it to her attention. Tears tickled her eyes, bringing a realization that renewal could not come to her here. Her seas were far, for she was just returned from her year-of-months, and there was no one to carry her back. In any case, the waters were unable to cure these wounds, even if she could be covered again.

She allowed the easing of sleep to take her in its arms, its relief welcome at last, only awakening to the arms of a re'anlt, a brother who had searched and was come to carry her to safety.

She felt the waters easing the old, remembered pain. Releasing those memories, her discomfort was finally alleviated. The pain shifted, becoming *other,* no longer the lifelong companion to be dreaded. Only the memory of the *how,* of the event, the happening of it remained. The pain itself was no longer a part of the memory of how the injury had come, and she could see it and not run. The event was now hers to possess, to remember, to keep as part of who she was. Covered by and within the waters, she turned again, and she rested. Her seas, her suns were again her only companions, their soothing touch her only desire.

Her memory embraced, she garnered it as a treasured gem, collecting and storing it in the deeply guarded vaults of the

269

person she would eventually become. Fading from her awareness were the sharp edges of existence, those thorns driven
deep into every life.

She turned, another dream calling to her . . .

"Rond'nt. Come to me." Adhor'k laughed as the small boy
scrambled over the rocks. Her hand reached for him, his laughter snuggled into her embrace. She stroked the boy's fine hair,
its silky strands soft against her fingers. Her heart swelled with
the uniqueness of this small creature within her embrace.

So seldom and so special, she mused.

This was the rarest of all that happened on this beautiful
world of theirs. For this one, life just now had begun.

He was a first-alive, born fresh from Se'Yan't's seas. He
had never walked Se'Yan't's shores before, and the world was
new to him. No old memories would come to him as he matured.

For this one, life was unique, the specialness of that which
would never come for him again.

She ran her fingertips up and down the boy's side, his ribs
rippling a mirthful tune, laughter bubbling up from within her
small companion. Sharing the freshness of his childlike enthusiasm, she felt the tune well up in her also, bursting forth in a
duet, singing among the stones along the beach.

"Can I do it again? Addie? Can I?" His eyes pleaded with
her, his thrill in the water-weir pulling him back again and
again.

She thought of her favorite brother, Rjorck, so far away on
Earth, for whom every lifetime was special. For him the water-
weir had always been especially so.

She tousled Rond'nt's hair, laughter in her voice. "Of
course, little one. As often as you want. My favorite brother
has this same love, and I do so enjoy that about you." She
pushed his nakedness away from her, watching the joy of discovery in his movements as he splashed into the waters of the

seas, laughter his forever friend, following alongside him into the rippling tide.

"Where do I go, Addie? My legs are gone, Addie. Will they always come back?"

Laughter erupted from her. "Always, dear one. Your legs will always be yours. Just walk out of the water and see."

And in her watery year of renewal, Adhor'k turned once again, yet another gem collected and carefully preserved for the future when she would once more arise from her seas to walk under her twin suns.

Her memories now at peace, her dreams wrestled and conquered, Adhor'k could release herself to rest in her seas, the warmth flooding her body with renewal as she enjoyed the relaxation of knowing nothing at all. Her senses served the most basic needs of her awareness. Calmness. Peace. The touch of a seastone. A ray of warmth from the life-giving suns overhead. Light. Floating. Periods of darkness in the rare eclipses covering the seas. Connections sometimes felt. Life's fingers reaching out to her, her fingers reaching back.

Always the calmness. Always the peace.

For her year-of-months, Adhor'k floated, and she was renewed.

One Year Earlier

ADHOR'K DREW A DRY BREATH, the pain tearing her chest.

"The years," she gasped, the sounds barely slipping from dry lips, no one around to hear anyway. "I am so tired of each day, the chore of this life."

She placed her withered hands on the mat at her side, pushing her pain-wracked body erect, forcing herself to greet the morning's new torments. It had been so long that she could barely remember not feeling pain, only that she once might have been young. Oh, but no longer.

Her face wincing at a newly discovered discomfort, one more on top of all the others that no longer seemed to go away, she dropped onto a small stool.

Even to walk across this small room was almost more than she could do. Yet, she knew that now was not her time. Life was hers to endure for another of her torturous mornings.

Tears growing in the corners of her eyes, frustration heavy on her heart, she released herself to the self-pity she so despised, sobs sending shockwaves of pain throughout her frail form. Her tortured lungs, unable to draw in sufficient air, screamed in a protest of pain, their final affront the spasm of coughing tearing her from her stool and throwing her to the floor, releasing a pool of blood, the life-liquid running from her cracked lips to the floor.

From her huddled position on the chilling stones, she watched the light stream in from around the opening door. Suddenly, words called for her attention.

"Honey? Adhor'k, sweet, are you in here?"

Her friend, a familiar voice, here at last.

"Come this way, Bree'an," she ground out painfully with her broken voice. "Please rescue me from this ridiculous position. This floor no longer tastes quite so delicious."

With a dry, humorless laugh, she offered one frail hand to her rescuer.

Bree'an dropped her basket of supplies onto a nearby shelf, rushing to kneel by the old woman's side. "My dear, how did you get yourself into such a position?"

She gave a wry grin. "Self-pity, my friend. Never give in to it. It always wins in the end." Her short speech sending another wave of coughing, racking her in her frailness, her hand squeezed her friend's arm, finding life there, her fingers painting her own pain on Bree'an's skin. "Sorry, my friend," she gasped in apology.

"It's what I'm here for. Do you feel today might be your day? Your re'anlts are prepared to come at anytime. Just a word, Adhor'k. You just say the word."

Adhor'k pulled herself to her feet, pain etching her features. "Just help me sit. Today is not my day. I will know no relief while these suns are in today's skies."

She gritted her teeth, waiting for the agony of this new torture to ease, melding itself into the dull roar that for Adhor'k had become the price of enduring yet another of life's excruciating days.

FROM THEIR PERCH ON ARCHING walkways or while walking across broad, balustrade-lined aqueducts, the city's inhabitants admired the beauty they had constructed with their own hands during their many lifetimes.

The suns reached deep into the fairy tale towers, its fingers of warmth searching out open windows, doors left ready for visiting laughter or the resting traveler freshly arrived from the sea. The dueling suns took turns, one reaching down the walls of the lush rift valley to warm the inhabitants during morning, the other reaching the opposite side just before weary eyes drifted off to sleep. Moss on stone walls teased the suns' fingers, glistening with the tempting moisture of morning, and crying tears of farewell at evening.

Deep within one recess, the window still shuttered, the protection it provided giving relief to eyes too weary to face the suns' brightness, an old woman waited, neither aware of the beauty of the city which she called home nor of the other inhabitants that dwelt there by her side. Her eyes were closed, every thought focused on just drawing one more breath. She only found strength to endure her body by lying motionless, even the breathing almost too much to bear.

Today.

This was the day she felt her seas calling her home. She

273

waited, Bree'an soon to come, waited for the end to all her pain.

Adhor'k drew still another breath.

And she waited.

HANDS HELD ADHOR'K'S WORN-OUT limbs, their very touch like fire and ice. This familiar act providing at least the warmth of closeness, she was held by hands just *there*, her weary limbs allowed to relax and let others support her. Then, steps, her body jarred by the shifting of her weight as her re'anlts and friends, gathered by Bree'an's call, carried her gently toward the sea. Each jostle brought fire to her inflamed joints. At each indrawn breath, needles of pain tore additional insults through her belabored chest.

Each moment only bearable due to the nearness of c'habor-reneis't, knowing she would soon find relief, she smoothed her face and waited, the pain a small price to pay for the comfort of her loved ones gathered around her, carrying her to her sea. She smiled at the suns overhead, their round orbs huddled closely today, the yellow sky above giving them special mean-ing, bonding them as in the old tales of the Dance of the Skies.

It was so strange that at this late hour of life she could still find joy in the tales of her world's past. Things could still be meaningful to her, even through all this pain. Glancing at the faces carrying her to her rebirth, seeing them smiling back at her, she was grateful for this life, the ending of this stage, knowing her readiness for the beginning of another.

Tender hands laid her carefully, the prepared mat welcom-ing her to its embrace. The gentle sounds of the water brushed warm, dark colors on the stones as it kissed each one, running embarrassed back to the sea, the song of a siren, calling, call-ing, calling. She felt a warm cloth brush the day from her brow, her eyes claiming exhaustion, refusing to open. A voice whispered in her ear, the words stirring her memories, bringing back a time far away. She listened. She remembered. The words told her of her youth, fresh and strong, a memory of a time shared with another . . .

The loom rocked under Adhor'k's sure hands, the shuttle speeding along its journey, her fingers touching just *there,* a color of thread worked in, creating an image, a pattern to express just what she wanted others to see.

"You are the best at this, you know. All across this world, people treasure your creations." Bree'an, little more than a child, handed her friend a small spindle of the finest thread, the brilliance of its color potent against her skin. "I do so love to hear your stories when you let me assist you. Tell me one about this weaving." She wrapped her hands around her knees, expectancy giving her face an engaging glow.

Never slowing, the steady *chock, chock* a comforting background melody, fingers twisting this color around *that* thread, Adhor'k felt a warmth of pleasure as the story burbled from her lips, laughter at the telling part of the joy. "He was tall, you know. Even as a child, and not many people alive today remember Rjorck as a child, not truly as a child. We were birthed together, he and I.

"It is so sad when we don't know the why someone's poi'ntr'in is lost. We can only rejoice in the rebirth that arises from their sacrifice. We were of many hundreds born from that sacrifice, Rjorck and I.

"They say, I've heard, that the number reborn is determined by the seas themselves. It would be possible for one to return as ten thousand should the seas be empty of all others. Such a sight would be amazing to see, ten thousand walking from the seas, all with the newness of first-alive, seeing all things for the very first time.

"Rjorck was there with me. I have kept these memories each time of my rebirth. These hundreds of siblings, my re'anlts, some of which did not make it to their c'habor-

275

reneis't, are the closest to me of all those on our world, even among those who have chosen not to remember.

"I also remember those who are gone, unable to return." Her eyes turned moist. "My brother has taken many risks, he one needing to always find *more,* never satisfied with just *being.*"

"Will you weave their stories into your creation?"

"Whose, my dear Bree'an?"

"Those no longer with us, the ones who didn't make it to c'habor-reneis't. Will you weave them, telling me the stories so I can know and remember?"

Bree'an was the storyteller, Adhor'k knew, and these stories would be absorbed by her compassionate soul, stored for the need of being told to comfort others. She did not mind. Rather, her friend's interest spurred her words.

"Well, there was this one. This was the first time, our time of first-alive, the newness of our world rippling across our senses, playing the tune, the *symphony* of life across the instruments of our bodies. Oh, it was a glorious time!" Adhor'k laughed with the memory of the sights and sounds, the *sensations,* all of which became real to her again, with just the subtle tickle of the memory. "We ran across the fields, our small bodies *alive!* I especially remember the swimming, the water-weir." Her eyes misting with the fondness of the memories, she continued, "Rjorck so loved to dive in, only a ghostly disturbance if you knew just where to look, and then he would spring out of the water, surprising us all. As a boy, he loved to do so at formal, seaside gatherings, his nakedness an affront to some of our more staid people. How he would laugh! He could stay under for hours, he having the most developed gill slits of any I have ever seen. Once, while underwater, he let me run my fingers along their unseen edges," and here she lowered her voice as if not wanting to be overheard, "even letting me touch them inside." She shivered with the memory of it, the intimacy of

276

having touched such a thing in another. Unseen, functional, and nearly invisible when not swimming in the seas, most never thought of these gill slits on themselves or others. She remembered this as almost an adolescent foray into a forbidden realm of behavior. "But poor Rjorck is very much still alive. I must choose another to tell about."

"Yes, dear. Poor Rjorck is still alive, if you wish to call it that. Many of our people seem not to think so, him on Earth, and all. But, do go on, sweet Adhor'k." Bree'an laughed the laugh of the truly tolerant friend, allowing her companion the freedom to diverge with her story onto her favorite topic, trusting her to return again, remembering the stories she wanted to hear.

"Bree'an, you are the one able to pull my stories from me, engaging vamp that you are. You shall hear my stories, even if I do vacillate a bit, my favorite topics wedging themselves in despite my best efforts. I will go on." Adhor'k winked one playful eye at her friend, her hand never slowing, pointing out the colors to be given her, the creation in the loom continuing to build. "My poor brother. Not Rjorck, dear Bree'an," seeing the warning look sent her way, "but one other. You did not know him. He was one of three. Me, that one I'm no longer allowed to speak about, and he, the third. We *lived* that first free year. We reveled in the seas, not a stitch of clothing touching our bodies, just soaking up the warmth of the suns."

Her hands sure, not slowing, Adhor'k closed her eyes, the deepest of breaths reliving the memories of standing under her twin suns, her young body absorbing the warming rays, her brothers beside her. Turning again to her weaving, both the material and the telling, she continued. "The fields, all the way from the shores to the lushness of the rift valley, we would run. His name was Ten'di. Not many people remember. He also was the prankster. One time he was in the city, and he sneaked an armload of flowers, you know those yellow and white ones that make your head spin if you lick the inside? A whole arm-load he dropped into the highest aqueduct. For days, all the people were doing the most unusual things."

"Such as?" Bree'an's eyes glowed with anticipation.

"Remember the place in the city paving where the pattern goes all wrong? They were building that paving when Ten'di did the thing with the flowers. Once the waters were clear again," here Adhor'k let out another of her laughs, "Ten'di really heard from the elders about that one. However, a few of our wiser leaders were indulgent, and the pattern was kept. Then, when Ten'di was gone, no one would think of correcting the errant paving stones."

Quiet now, Adhor'k continued to weave, her color choices darker, the pattern becoming Ten'di, becoming the life he no longer lived. Moisture salving her eyes, an ointment for the remembered sadness, she reached again to her loom.

"When the rest of us began to cover ourselves, Ten'di could not bring himself to do so. He loved the freedom. All the people indulged him. He would slip into unfamiliar houses at night, sliding under covers to warm himself with the body heat of whoever he could find. He would be the warmly welcomed surprise at unsuspecting meals, his tanned nakedness his well-known signature. He charmed everyone, that Ten'di could.

"Reaching his maturing, although still a boy, indulged as all first-alives are, Ten'di's pranks got bolder. One day, he found a stone that struck his imagination, one that formed the archway support of one of the walkways. He decided he would construct a new dwelling for himself with the stone as its centerpiece, one that would be set apart from the others in the city." Adhor'k did notice Bree'an's raised eyebrows, taking a moment to clarify her words. "No, he did not want to build elsewhere, out of the city. Ten'di loved to be around people. He wanted it to stand out as different. He started, and many others helped him. However, there was still that stone. In spite

278

of others' well-intentioned protests, he had to have that stone in his new dwelling.

"He went out one day, alone, a cutting tool in his hand. Chipping, not learned of the geometries of stone archway dynamics, he just wanted this one stone. When the great noise happened, all the people rushed to see."

Now the colors entering her weaving took on the reds and blacks that told the end of Ten'di's story.

"Poor Ten'di. He only wanted to be *alive*. I did not see him then. I have only been told. I'm glad I did not see him until he was removed and his broken body cleansed. Poor Ten'di. Not once in his short life did clothing ever cover his sun-soaked skin. As he lay on the finalstone, I ran my hand over my brother's skin, its surface no longer filled with our suns' warmth. It broke my heart seeing him there, his body just beginning to enter manhood, now broken, never to experience life again."

The blues of the waters of the seas beginning to mix with the colors of her tears, Ten'di's story weaving itself to its end as the shuttle finally began to slow, Bree'an's request was fulfilled, the memory collected to comfort others.

Laying the colored threads aside, Bree'an reached for her friend, wrapping arms of compassion around her, soothing the renewed intensity of memories lived many lifetimes ago. In the comfort, Adhor'k weaved a new tapestry of designs on her comforter's shoulder, the dark colors of her tears on the fabric a pattern of memories, ones that both knew would fade, just as the pain of the one called Ten'di would again fade from life's memories.

Then, to Adhor'k, another voice brought a different memory, that of a time of travel far away, and with the memory, Adhor'k stirred, drawn with the voice into other memories almost forgotten . . .

"But, you chose, Addie. It won't be that much farther, anyway." A hand took hers, tempting and encouraging, the difficult goal tantalizingly close. "The Ribbon Waterfall is something you *must* see. Come on. You can't turn back, now."

She sat, her pack resting on its built-in legs, her muscles sighing in relief. "Rond'nt, my dear. I *have* seen the Ribbon Waterfall. It was just many lifetimes ago." She looked at the excitement on the young man's face. Although no longer a child just birthed from Se'Yan't's perennially warm seas, his fascination with life was still true and strong.

Pulling strength from within, hoping to match that seen in the young man's eyes, she regained her feet, her pack bearing down on her tired shoulders. Soon he would make himself another life, no longer needing or wanting the old woman she had become. However, for this one day, she could do this for him.

"Come over here, Rond'nt, and help Addie adjust the straps on this pack. They do cut into my shoulders so."

Enjoying the strength in his fingers as his hands released tight straps, adjusting them for her comfort, she patted his hand as he tightened the final one.

"Ready, Addie?"

At her nod, he led down the rocky trail, offering his hand for reassurance over the roughest of steps.

Tired from the day's exertions, the glare of the twin suns finally too much for even her heat-thirsty skin, she stepped to the top of the ridge only wanting to rest, the need of her muscles crying for her attention. Hearing, finally, the tumbling cacophony of the falls reaching out to her, capturing her attention, she looked, her spirit suddenly filled with the splendor.

Great gods below, but she had forgotten. Poor Rond'nt. To think she had tried to discourage him from this, claiming to have seen it all before. How glorious this, their planet was!

Tears ensnaring her eyes, the weight of the pack forgotten, even the man at her side no longer in her thoughts, she joined in the hundred others who had walked the long trail, bringing them to one of the eleven highlights of Se'Yan't.

Finally noticing the hand holding hers, she turned to watch Rond'nt, the thrill of his seeing this for the first time surpassing even hers.

What a beauty this young man had become, she allowed, admiring the curve of his cheek, his hair glistening from the airborne mist showered upon them by the gods thundering nearby. How lucky she had been to befriend this one, to have raised him as her own. Unlike her brother, Ten'di, an indulged treasure to all, this one had been bonded to only her. She would miss him when she sent him on his way for the final time. Maybe someday their emergence from c'habor-reneis't would coincide, and they could both be young together. Someday, she would wish for that.

And the whisperer continued, "Don't forget, dear Addie. Keep me with you always. Return to me, and we will visit our waterfall once again."

Adhor'k's eyelids fluttered with the intensity of the moment, the memory strong, her attachment to the boy/man still stronger. The exhaustion of her extended years was once again pushed aside as a new voice whispered of an event attended, its memory refreshed in the telling . . .

"It's the celebration. Come dance. No one is allowed to be sour on this day."

Re'leli'n swung the cloth high above her head, laughter tinkling from the bells on her feet. She ran to her sister, grabbing her by the hand, tugging her from her low stool.

"You must come, Adhor'k. Forget that boy, Rond'nt. He has his own friends, now. He was your toy for all of his years of newness, but now you're mine again. Let your spirit fly, dear sister."

Re'leli'n pulled her sister into the brightness of the day, wrapping her cloth around her sister's neck, the ends still in her hands, her sister snared for the duration. Pleased with herself, she twirled, flipping the ends of the cloth over and over, going back again as the cloth tightened, not daring to draw it too tightly to her sister's gloomy mood.

"You will have your way," grudgingly smiled her captive. Knowing the choice was no longer hers, Adhor'k could begin to remember the celebrations of years past. Friends would be there. Food. Ah, the choices of the food, brought by those from far and wide. Just the thinking had her mouth watering already.

More broadly, her smile admitting defeat, she called, "All right, sister. Enough of this leash. I will go willingly. Yes, you are right, and I am wrong." Seeing her sister's grin of vindication made her laugh. "You wicked girl! You knew I would give in. Oh! I will so try to have a time at the celebration even as I think of evil things to come your way." Running to wrap a firm arm around her sister, she gave her a kiss on the cheek, with pleasure in her voice. "I do love you, you know. Thank you for getting me out. This will be a joy to be able to spend this time with my friends."

Colorful cloth fluttering in the warm winds, the yellow sky setting off the blue of the distant seas, laughter followed the two as the celebration drew them near.

"E'vonn, Wolmn, and there's H'bladt." Adhor'k laughed with her first sight of her favored friends. "And Berian. Re'leli'n, this will be wonderful."

Adhor'k took her hand from her sister's and ran into the crowd. Her most beloved friends and family greeted her, knowing of the grieving that had almost pulled her away. A container of drink and a morsel of food, and the dancing was begun.

Laying her food aside, Adhor'k laughed as Wolmn grabbed her waist, lifting her high, swinging her over his head, admonishing him, "Silly Wolmn! This old woman needs to keep her feet on the ground."

"This old woman isn't so old. You do yourself an injustice, Adhor'k." Setting her on two feet, he drew close. "Your beauty is still legendary. I remember your last c'habor-reneis't ceremony, you on the mat, memories being whispered in your ear. You were beautiful even then. Even if you should meet the finalstone, I would still find you the most beautiful of women, forever mine in many lifetimes of memories." He swung her out, the music starting a dance fast and sharp. As he drew her back in, a wink sparkled from his eye. "Or should I get your Rond'nt to tell you that?"

"Finally I can laugh at you, Wolmn. You have made me feel alive again. No, Rond'nt has another he has befriended." She brushed her hand along his face, her lips pursed as she spoke. "He was only a child, but I was attached to him so. All first-alives are like that. You will find out someday."

"Ah, Adhor'k. I see the honesty in your voice even as you speak. You do treasure the first-alives more than all others. I think it is the thirst for the new you miss in that brother of yours, he who is never around for you. You find release in the first-alives, so like Rjorck they are. See, I do know you, beautiful woman." The dance over, he led her back to her refreshments. As he released her hand, he drew her to him one last time. "I do know you, Adhor'k, and like many others, I do love you for all you are."

The scene shifted, new memories now whispered to her, her thoughts turning to a memory of a difficult deed done for another . . .

"I could not bear to see him that way. I had to run. It was truly an accident, my sister. Even so, I could not stay. Poor Dre'en. I did not mean to leave her with the pain, her so tender and all. I just know I cannot go back."

"What have you done, Mno't, leaving her like that? Can you expect her to deal with this pain on her own? Can you even know what this betrayal will mean to her?"

It was a betrayal, too, to abandon one so dear in the time of need. Admonishment in her eyes, Adhor'k turned to the window, time to think given her in the movement. What could this brother have been thinking? She shook her head, unable to turn to face the bringer of the news.

She spoke sternly to him, "You must go to her, take a gift, one that shows your contrition, one that is truly a meaningful gift to assuage her pain. She will know pain over this, Mno't. You know she will. Go. Now."

Hearing the door at last, the silent air telling her she was alone, she turned, the room truly empty.

She also would go to her, far though it was. Dre'en would have need of her.

Taking a basket from a high shelf, she began preparing for her journey, and in a matter of moments, stepped through the door.

"Going, Adhor'k?"

She turned at the question, the way nearly empty of people, not surprised the reason for her trip was known to all.

"Can I be of assistance?" The questioner placed a concerned hand on her arm.

Appreciating the kindness of the offer, wishing she were able to gift her burden to another, she instead bowed her head in appreciation. "Not today, friend. This duty must be mine. On this journey, I travel alone. Thank you for your offer." Turning before tears could strip her of her dignity, she pulled her tunic tight, moving forward, her destination far.

Weary, well doing this time an exhausting journey, Adhor'k spied her friend. Alone. Broken. Calling to no response, she set her basket down and ran the final few steps, knowing the comfort needed, the pain that must be endured. Putting her arms around broken shoulders, hugging through her friend's pain, her own tears were given to wash away the hurt. The two cried together, their sobs bonding them closer, the immediacy of the pain less in the sharing.

"Gel're was just here, Adhor'k. Then he was gone, the tree

fallen, his life snuffed from his grasp. It was not his time. Then Mno't ran from us, left me to carry him from the valley alone. Where did this come from, two of my own to cause me this pain?" Dre'en brushed tears, old and new, from her face. "Can this much sadness be borne alone?"

"I am here, Dre'en. Mno't will return. He has assured me of that. He was only frightened, fearing he had been the cause. Give him time." *Or else, he will return,* she growled to herself. "Where is poor Gel're? I will wash him for you. Then we will go prepare the finalstone."

Dre'en's hand motioning the way, Adhor'k moved to one of the adjacent buildings, the path leading the way.

This was the saddest of what was endured on this beautiful world, to die the dry-death, no hope of rebirth given, all the memories left to rot with the body. Only the strongest could ever hope to deal with this alone. What could Mno't have been thinking to run like that? At least he had come to her. At least he had done that.

Entering the door, she found her friend's brother, the blood still staining his limbs. With the tenderness of one who knows the pain that must have been endured, she reached for a container of water and gently began washing the lifeblood away, the red stains on the floor a testament to her strength, the torn body to the harshness that life can mete out. With the motions of her hands, tears began to fall from her eyes.

"Remember, dear Adhor'k. Remember what you did for me," the whisperer said. Adhor'k reached one weary hand to touch the speaker, her memory renewed. And the whispers continued . . .

As the stories were told, the events glittering like old-Earth diamonds in Adhor'k's memory, her beloved family and friends eased her way into her long-awaited c'habor-reneis't.

Then, just before she was carried into the waters, new words floated into the old woman's ears, drawing her from her remembered dreams, whispering as one, "It's time, dear loved one. You are in our thoughts always, and your memories are now strong, one with ours. Go, find peace. Find comfort as our arms carry you to your rest, your year-of-months a deserved respite from a long life well lived. Find comfort, dear one. We care for you and will await your return."

Gently, those who had shared their memories began to unwrap the layers of cloth surrounding her body, removing the coverings given by the living, readying the aged form underneath for its journey to the seas.

Lines showing the journey of life etched the now-uncovered body. The scars of life's events were exposed for all to see. This journey through life had been hard for Adhor'k. Her body had suffered much. Tender hands caressed her flesh as they reached under her, lifting, supporting, and finally carrying their treasured burden. Careful to not jar the whispers so recently given to refresh long-ago memories, her consorts carried her frail limbs to the shore's edge. Stepping in, each companion's feet and legs responding to the water-weir so familiar to all, melding with the liquid, greeting it in kind, disappearing in the welcome embrace of the microscopic creatures that lived within Se'Yan't's seas, the convoy seemed to float on the clear blueness of the sea's surface. At Adhor'k's first contact with the waters, recognition flooded through her, the brush of old, well-rehearsed memories, those of an old friend, and they elicited a gasp of deeply indrawn breath, expressing both joy and relief.

"My friends," came the cracked whisper, her once-sensuous lips moving painfully. Her hands, knobby with time, brushed those arms nearest, a caress of appreciation for this day. "You have come for me, helping me to this moment. None can be as true and faithful. I will return to you and be there for you in your time." For a moment her face clouded. "Rjorck. I do not recall his whispers. Did he come?"

"Addie," a near voice quietly nudged. "Earth."

The voice changed to another. "He has been gone half a lifetime and could not return so quickly. Try to carry him with you as you enter your year, dear Adhor'k. He will be with you in your memories. Don't forget, sister. Rjorck would not want you to forget."

Adhor'k's eyes closed in concentration, fluttering underneath her lids as though reliving a lifetime of love for her favorite companion, her treasured brother, Rjorck. She knew she would not, *could not* forget.

Desirous of their promised reunion, the waters wrapped themselves around their welcomed guest, rippling in anticipation, anxious to give of their life-renewing energies to this one, a long-remembered love, to whom youth had been renewed time and again. As if in joy, captured bits of Adhor'k's beloved twin suns, wrapped in fragments of Se'Yan't's blue seas, leaped from the waters around her body, traveling up to land against her age-wracked skin in a dance of life, exploding in joy as they contacted her skin.

Adhor'k felt the voice of the sea now, its presence excited at her touch. *Come renew yourself. Relax in our warm embrace. Find our peace.* During all her lives, in all her walkings on the land, the call of Se'Yan't's seas had been there, omnipresent in every cell of her being, as it was for all her re'anlts, her siblings. All the people of this world felt the call. But only when the body was ready, finally meeting the seas for life's final reunion, did the voices truly become real. Cell by pain-etched cell, Adhor'k's body responded, the tearful embrace of the dispossessed, finally returning to a treasured home, one always remembered, daily desired, now regiven after a lifetime denied.

Not knowing the old-Earth story despite having lived it herself, the tale found in the forgotten annals of a religion long out of favor on a distant world, a son demands the riches of his father and wastes them on a lifetime of sensuousness, only to be relegated to the lowest level of existence, life demeaned, even sharing the food of another's livestock. His life's resources used up and wasted, the son wearily returns home, hope barely alive for an end to the misery his existence has become, and instead he is given the keys to his father's home; in a great feast, the riches of life are returned to him.

The old story unknown, the series of events the same, Adhor'k took the proffered keys, the feast of renewed youth that was her reward for her return to the waters of her world. The unknown gods inhabiting the watery lands below the yellow skies of Se'Yan't would shower her with the riches of their watery heavens.

Finally, Adhor'k felt herself think.

Then all was the peace of the waters.

AS HER RE'ANLTS eased Adhor'k into Se'Yan't's waters, each cell in her body welcomed the water's embrace, and her renewal began. The miracle of the waters flowed between and through each fragment of her being, the very bonds of her cells relinquishing their hold, giving permission for the year-of-months to begin. C'habor-reneis't. Life anew. Life renewed. The miracle of rebirth.

Long-ago injuries began to change, the damages pulled apart, reworked, renewed cell by cell. The changes finally complete, with only the intrinsic bonds of her molecular structure keeping her very being from being scattered across her world's seas into a million individual parts, Adhor'k faded into the beginnings of a new and refreshed life, unlike those who had released their poi'ntr'in, giving of their life-essence to help another. Those bodies would be scattered, the bonds of their molecular structure dissolved, never to rejoin again. Each of the different parts would carry the necessary DNA for replication of a complete person, allowing the first-alives to rise from the seas after eight turns of Se'Yan't's great globe.

That was not to be Adhor'k's fate. Her re'anlts had stirred her to renewal with their memories shared. She would return whole and new.

As she floated, she felt the pull of others in their own year-of-months, their unseen presence an integral part of c'habor-reneis't. These were the source of fresh memories that would bond her to new, as yet unknown friends, creating ties that would last for a lifetime. She would experience them and remember.

MUCH OF HER YEAR GONE, Adhor'k felt the first intrusion as a spot on her glorious suns. Irritated, she brushed the offending fleck from her world. She withdrew into herself.

There! Again! She twisted, willing the blackness away.

Go away, she demanded. *This time is mine. I will not share my year-of-months.* Turning her back on the goading thorn, she refused to acknowledge that which she would not permit to join her in her world.

The speck waited. Finally, after much inward loneliness, Adhor'k grew tired, and turning, was ready to listen.

Sweet, the words called to her. *Here I am, favored one. I have waited for your hyr'yan't to be renewed. It is soon time for my return, also, my youthfulness restored. I will return to celebrate the banquet that is life, spending it wantonly, only the coming of time to slow me down. How blessed we are to know that chances are not once in a lifetime, but rather, many in many lifetimes.* The words slowed, became still, changing in tone. *How sad must be the lives of those who exist within one lifetime only. To know that chances missed are never given again. Sweet, are you there?*

The words, the voice so familiar, sparked Adhor'k's interest. Tendrils of her mind reaching out to *connect,* a bond with another also in c'habor-reneis't was reforged, and knowledge began to seep along the threads of shared interest.

Adhor'k's connection with her old life was refreshed, and reaching out again, yet more memories touched her mind, ones that belonged to others she did not know . . .

The wind stroked Ti'get's brow, its tender touch drawing her attention from her pain. Glancing down at her ragged wounds, she knew the healing would take long.

Re'anon!

There was no answer, and yet the wind sighed its warm caresses, reaching to her again, its touch wrapping her in a measure of comfort. She reached up as to embrace her comforter, the tenuous flesh of the wind as diaphanous as the substance of one already in c'habor-reneis't. In that touch, its presence seemed that of her long-dead Re'anon.

Realizing she must move, her shredded muscles screamed as she drew them into service, the vitality of her continued existence validated by their very protest.

She whispered to the wind, *You have come to me again after all these years. You see, I have not forgotten what you did for me, your touch. You became my Re'anon, wrapping me in your arms, warming my flesh with your fingers.* Tears came to her eyes, the long-treasured memories dancing through the fire tearing her body, the pain made bearable only by the sweetness. Raising one hand into the air, she called to the wind once more, for to her, the wind had become her lost love. *I will always return to this, my Re'anon, this that we enjoyed so together, even though it took you from me, lashing upon you the curse of the dry-death. Oh, that we had been nearer the seas. The renewing powers of the water-weir might have been enough to allow you to survive. I tried, dear Re'anon. I really tried. You were carried on my back for the long journey down from your height of glory. The wind you so loved, the joy it brought you, I could see in the laughter in your eyes. The last time you rode the wind, your wings of cloth carrying you into our yellow skies, its song burst from you, resounding from the corners of our beautiful world. You were so glorious up there, the suns' brightness obscured by your own pleasure in the life you had been given.*

She bowed her head, tears running down her face.

Oh, Re'anon. The suns and the winds could not bear your happiness to be so great. They blinded you, flinging you back to the soils, the dry-death their payment required in return for the pleasure they had gifted you. For all my lives I will reach for you in the winds. Each time I am crumpled back to our world, I am only closer to you. I can still feel your touch, although it has been many lifetimes since I held you close to me.

Those together with Ti'get in her year-of-months, Adhor'k among them, listened, giving her what comfort they could, as the pain of her memories tore through her until her strength was exhausted.

As the intensity of the sharing faded, Adhor'k felt the touch of a special story, that of a first-alive that had yet to walk upon the sundrenched surface of Se'Yan't. Turning her attention its way, allowing it in, this life shared its tale . . .

Two eyes observed their watery home. All that was around within the sea was new and unfamiliar. The freshness, the *aliveness* was the electric charge of *first*. Not even knowing *first*, this one carrying none of the memories of a previous life, the eyes observed, all things deserving of the closest of looks.

Fleeting thoughts, whispers barely, briefly here then forgotten, carried the shadowy sense of having remembered something, only the vagueness of the *knowing* lingering. With the remnants of the memory, the eyes burned. Not understanding tears, unable to cry them in any event, knowing only the remembered sensation, then forgetting the burning as the whispers passed, a shaping was happening. This new life, this *first-alive*, was *becoming*, and would soon walk the soils of the planet above.

This first growth from another, a renewed life brought forth from the traumatic loss of poi'ntr'in, the gift of its power available only during the most dire need, was c'habor-reneis't in its purest of forms. The seas, truly alive, knowing all who swam within, enveloping all who came, calling to those whose bodies were ready for renewal, then reaching inside to find the person's poi'ntr'in, allowing the renewal of the body to begin, were aware.

Should the wellspring not be found, the body could not be renewed. The seas would then allow the bonds holding the body during c'habor-reneis't to fade, cradling each cell of the body as a template for renewed life. Many new lives would be brought forth during an extended c'habor-reneis't, the new lives arriving on the shores of the seas as children, as *first-alives*, their newness and joy in life treasured by all on the planet.

This new life would remember. Not the experiences of another. No, only the *idea* of those experiences would be there to shadow the start of this new life.

As the first-alive floated, the shadows of the memories returned, and the first-alive knew how it came to be . . .

Breathing hard, Dan't turned, the crush of the pain behind him unbearable. His re'anlts, his unwary siblings, were in danger. The spark of the sudden storm, so rare under the yellow skies of this, his treasured planet, and then the fire was everywhere, eating everything.

They don't know to run.

Tears bled down his face as he stumbled once again, the heat of the flames licking at his bare feet. A sudden blast of hot air blazed a trail as the flames exploded around him, and his skin crisped, sending searing pain shooting deep into his innermost being. With a vengeful cry, desperate that his re'anlts must be made safe, he wrapped his grasp around the sustenance he found at his innermost core, and in desperation, *re-*

leased!

Later that day, the fleeting firestorm finally dissipated, his re'anlts found him, burned beyond recognition, with only the barest spark of life remaining. Tenderly they carried him, knowing his poi'ntr'in had been released to give them warning. In a sudden shift of their surrounding environment, they had strangely found themselves far from the approaching conflagration. Upon finding him barely alive, they knew he had given them his all, even that which could not be renewed, yet still, if they could transport him to the sea in time, his body would give new life to many. They could look forward to his return from Se'Yan't's seas. He would not return to know them, but they would know the children he would become.

Gently, they released him into the sea, the renewal ceremony unneeded. Se'Yan't's waters accepted him, cradling his ravaged body, bringing peace to the sacrifice he had become. Then, the seas began to work their magic, bringing the newness of life once again.

As the whisper faded, the first-alive *shifted*, forgetfulness its due. The memory would not return, not in its truest form, but the shadow of the sacrifice would always be there.

Adhor'k let the inrush of memories fade, the waters that held her bringing her the solace of release. She had been reborn in her seas time and again. However, some c'habor-reneis'ts, some years-of-months, were more memorable than others.

One thing was always the same, and she gave herself to it. Her twin suns. Always there were her twin suns and the sparkles they created in the ripples of the waters. Always there for her, the twin suns of her world's yellow skies washed her with life. She watched their movements as they raced across her world. This measure of peace was all she coveted, all she had desired for the final ending to a life that had been long and harsh.

She waited, floating, letting the warmth of the waters and

her suns touch her, caring for her, the troubles of her body gone, soon to rise anew from Se'Yan't's comforting seas.

2799 A.D. (O.E. Standard)

ADHOR'K. RJORCK. Her re'anlts.

The woman who'd entered the seas of her world almost one full year ago now remembered, the knowledge exposing itself to her, staying more often than fleeing back to the recesses of the sea. She knew she was drawing to the close of her year-of-months.

She began to turn the memories, making them hers once again, their very presence drawing her from her sojourn. Slowly she felt the tenuous sensations that told of the bonds of her body growing stronger. Swept by the currents, the brush of the seafloor no longer a dismissed annoyance, it became a remembered caress of sensation, the touch alive in her mind. The warmth of the sun reaching through the shallow waters became as real as the memories from long ago.

Turning once again in the waters, she felt her strength renewing. She began to anticipate her return, her thoughts dwelling on her beloved, hoping Rjorck would be there.

The warm currents rippled down her arm. She could *feel*. She turned her eyes toward the sun, blinking. She could *see*. She moved her shoulders, feeling the gill-slits along her shoulder blades expelling water for her to *breathe*.

This was to be her day.

Swimming now, she drew to the surface, the ever-shallower water showing her the way to land. Finally breaking the surface of the sea, the warmth of the suns touching her skin for the first time in a year, Adhor'k gloried. Standing, she stretched, relishing in the newness of her body.

Ah! To be renewed again. Life was fresh and good.

Feeling each droplet of water as it found its way down her

body and back to the sea, the sensations renewing her feelings of life, she stood, enjoying the caress of the breeze on her naked skin, her youth a gift to be spent well. Hearing steps rustling the stones on the beach, she opened her newly sharp eyes, looking for the disturbance. Laughter lit her face as she stepped forward.

"I had so hoped you would come, favorite of mine." Accepting the proffered wrap, she covered herself, placing her hand on her brother's arm. "Thank you, Rjorck. I kept your memories strong. I kept you with me always during my c'habor-reneis't, my year-of-months, as I swam in the seas."

Life had been renewed, the gift given by Se'Yan't to her treasured children.

—Addendum 5—

The Tale of Se'Yan't's Twin Suns

TWIN SUNS BURNED in the lonely blackness of space, tongues of fire leaping a dance of life, sending hope, warmth, and spirit to the worlds in their care. For the many eons since the two suns had felt that first sensation of *other,* that gentle wooing as of a lover and her consort, the planets had danced the Dance, the Dance of Life. It was indeed the Dance of all the Ages.

MORTAL BEINGS CANNOT SENSE the dance. In the unimaginable blackness between the stars, time seems to grind to a standstill, mortal beings living out the passions of entire generations in a single, solitary note as the Great Conductor directs his orchestra to accompany the Dance of Life, tuning the mighty galaxies as each spins on its axis. For the bright flashes of passionate existence mortal beings experience, time freezes the Dance, keeping the stars and the planets ever in balance with each other. For mortals, the heavens crawl through clockwork motions so slow as to seem inviolate.

On a galactic scale, the story is told very differently, indeed. Civilizations are pinpricks of light, flashes in the darkness that are extinguished in no more than a single beat of the Conductor's wand.

The Conductor choreographs the celestial bodies as he pleases, spinning them through the Dance across the vast reaches of space.

IT WAS BILLIONS OF YEARS earlier, and the twin suns did not yet know each other. One of the suns, blazing, played its private, tuneless melody, isolated and alone. The Maestro looked for the discordant note and began to gently pull it into harmony. Still, the sun strummed its song unconcerned.

The initial tug of distant gravities from beyond the outermost reaches of the sun's solar winds was at first easily dismissed. The loss of a few million solar particles seemed insignificant when more were constantly being released by its internal furnaces, only to be quickly absorbed into the blackness of the star's solitary surroundings.

By the time the encroaching gravities had become strong, their siren call finally resisted, the course of the star had changed. The shift was only minutely measurable to begin with, but micron added upon micron soon created an unstoppable alteration in the sun's path. In the slow passage of the movements of the stars, this sun was joining the Dance.

The great tuning mechanism of the universe, the Maestro's choreography of the Dance of Life, eventually became punishing for the sun to learn. Its molecular dynamics shifting just *so*, the pull of the distant gravities causing a difference just *there*, the sun became a reluctant changeling. No longer did its surface show the smoothness and evenness of its youth. New swirls appeared on its face. Eddies of fuel spewed their new frustrations into the sky. Dark spots appeared, giving a mottled appearance where once the surface had been pure. Roiling releases of ejecta edged the temperature of the burning gasses down those few degrees that someday just might make the difference between an intolerant furnace and a life-affirming parent.

Many discordant macerations of the Dance would be heard before the sun's part would be perfectly played. In time, the Great Conductor would move on, another found to be in need of instruction. For now, however, this sun must be tuned, no matter the cost.

ANOTHER STAR, ISOLATED in the darkness of the vast distances between galaxies, thrust its energies into the blackness. This sun was a gentle life-giver, caring for many children in its own private dance. It shepherded its children, those planets making up its local system, through the steps of its dance as it caressed their surfaces. Atmospheres and liquid seas were gently massaged with the twisting and the turning of the sun's dance. This sun knew of no other and was content to dance through the eons to its own private melody.

Then a gentleness brushed the sun's outermost solar winds. The stroking fingers of this touch, the caressing wisps of newness, barely felt, intertwined gently with the sun's gravity. At first simply feeling the difference, only much later recognizing its distant source, the sun had been invited into the Dance.

The children were bound to their parent sun. The Dance would also be gifted to them, whatever the cost.

The first notes of the orchestra's new melody were felt, no more than gently fleeting snatches of song, as the planets dutifully accompanied their life-giving parent. Then, the notes began to grow bolder, and the discordant gravities grew stronger. The planets' childhood, in which they had been both doted on and protected, their parent's dance having been that of a lullaby, soon began to change.

The Great Conductor raised his wand as the symphony

prepared to play.

AT FIRST THE DANCE WAS KIND. The children's parent was tenderly and lovingly wooed, caressed, and given gentle entreaties. The children continued to play, albeit following new, unknown rules. As the Dance grew faster, the rules changed further, and the children began to suffer. Seasons were altered, long-stable crusts began to split in two, and the children cried out, spewing debris into space, their cries the pleadings of desperation to stop the Dance. However, once begun, they learned, the Dance could not be returned to the void.

Millennia passed, and the Dance became harsher, more violent. The children's parent, no longer knowing the children, only her approaching escort, her lover, danced the Dance without regard to anything except the Dance. Faster, more violent, the dance was one of lovers circling, each other's slightest contact electric, blinding them to all else, the passion all-consuming, the violence sweeping formerly loved things aside, uncaring of anything except the Maestro's orchestrated steps.

The children learned to survive within the Dance. No longer innocent, no longer content to amuse themselves with the games of childhood, the children now played roughly. They twisted, screamed, and spit. They became violent, throwing things at each other, slinging unwanted parts of themselves at the dancers forcing them to parade along.

Anger drove the brittle chords of the Dance, and there was no way to stop the maelstrom forced upon them. The very pit of despair, indeed, had come to make itself known in the song.

THE FIRST WORLD CAUGHT ON FIRE, and the maelstrom coursed across the surface of the planet with the vehemence of a thousand nightmares.

Bolts of lightning leaped from angry clouds, the wrath of the gods flashing through the black sky, striking out with vaporizing fury. Beneath the onslaught, the planet cowered, its screams of pain echoing across its surface. Twisting tendrils of flame scoured the roof of the world, the sun's mighty arms violently tearing through the layers of its upper atmosphere. Soon, the protective clouds were eaten away, and the waters on the surface began to boil.

Its exhaustion complete, life slowly surrendered to the cruelty being slashed across the land. Relentless change was being forced on this world, the closest to its mothering sun. Soon, the world's siblings would also know the increasing decimation of this new violence, the old rules of their well-loved dance now abandoned.

The orchestra had struck up its first resounding chord, and a new movement in the great Dance of Life had been stirred into motion.

DEEP WITHIN THE GATHERING ELEMENTS of the orchestral arrangement, discordant overtones attracted the attention of the Maestro. He turned his attention and began once again to tune.

The second planet's crust was fragile, its interior filled with the rumblings of molten rock and metal. It had long ago adapted to the tidal forces of its solitary sun, the balance between its crust and core stable, its Dance well known. For a very long time after that first touch of those distant gravities, all within the planet seemed the same. The steps of the Dance went on as rehearsed.

Then, the first misstep appeared. Used to the pull of long-accustomed gravities, this new choreography was unexpected and disastrous. A cavernous crack ripped through the planet's crust, the super-heated interior finding its way through the insulating shell. Steam from long-submerged groundwater was driven ahead of the advancing furnace. It erupted, scouring the atmosphere's placid skies. Wildlife, long adapted to peace and stability, cried for relief from this new torment.

Now freed, the planet's core exulted in its wanton destruction. As the opposing gravities of the two suns pulled at the fragile crust, more and more openings were gouged into its bedrock. Even from the blackness of space, the raw wounds of the planet's torments could be seen. Deep under the oceans, currents once running cold and deep were boiled to the surface, with great swaths of steam coalescing into moisture-laden clouds.

During the occasional lucid moments when it realized the damage being done, the parenting sun tried to reach in, to tenderly caress the world back to its former glory, but the crushing gravitational forces, the world's new overlord, simply laughed, its conquest complete. Wildlife lay rotting, carcasses cooked from the heat of the soil. Leafless trees reached into the sunless skies, roots smoldering, the superheated soil initiating combustion that forced the unseen flames upward, exploding each lifeless trunk into a thousand burning fragments.

The last to succumb to the torment of the new master were the mountaintop snowfields. When they at last gave in to the superheating of even their lofty altitudes, for a time, respite was given in the form of the icy snowmelt gifted to the plains below. However, the relief was short lived. The snowfields were soon gone, even their glacial substrate finally eaten away, and yet, the atmosphere continued to boil.

Nothing mattered to the tortured world any longer; only the terror and pain of the changes taking place within held its attention. Ejecta unable to achieve escape velocity fell back to the planet's surface, creating towering volcanoes reaching to the skies. The planet, shifting on its tectonic plates, eventually pulled these titans to their knees, only to have others rise to take their place, their fight for supremacy soon challenged by yet others.

Even that wasn't the worst. In due course the coilings and

wrenchings of the crust became so violent that more and more often, matter thrown into the atmosphere managed to escape, lost from the world forever.

Eventually, the planet's core was diminished, and the stabilizing gravities that had once endured for so many eons readjusted. The battle-wounded crust settled into deep valleys surrounding far-flung escarpments. Weakened too far to fight further, the planet resigned itself to the terrors that continued to be slashed across its face, its continuing groans of tortured rock echoing down the millennia.

Far overhead in the inky blackness of a starless void, the far-reaching fingers of the Dance tugged the competing suns ever closer.

AT LAST, ALMOST TOO DIM TO BE SEEN, the companions became visible to each other. The unbroken darkness that had surrounded the suns since the beginning of all time was shattered, never to be regained. Over the next several thousand millennia, the great plan orchestrated for the Dance visited additional unheard of atrocities on the planets as the two suns pulled at each other. Entire worlds were twisted and torn, the remains sometimes being drawn into the very core of their parent sun. Twisted new moons, remnants of planets captured by the strongest of the worlds remaining, still carried the long-dead ashes of whatever life had once existed on their tattered soils.

Renewed life would be a long time in returning. The millennia would come and go, the planets reshaped time and again, the very violence of their existence becoming the norm, peace no longer remembered even in the age-old histories of the most enduring rocks found in the deepest recesses of their scarred crusts.

Moving ever closer, drawn by the constantly tightening grasp of each other's massive gravities, the suns themselves convulsed in their parody of a dance. No longer were their solar winds gently drawn away. The wrenching forces whipping through their coronas ripped massive quantities of solar matter from their surfaces, flinging it through space, carelessly washing over any object in its path. Already overheated planetary atmospheres were stripped of protecting layers, further exposing the planets to the destruction being wrought upon them by the movements orchestrated in the heavens above.

The Maestro of the Dance had crushed the worlds to remake them into instruments better suited to his plan. As the Dance of the suns continued, they would suffer still. The suns, oblivious to all except each other, drew ever closer, learning their assigned steps in this great orchestral Dance.

AS THE AGES GROUND ALONG, the worlds tired of the violence. The roughshod rules of the Dance had remained the same for a very long time, and the children had learned to dance within those rules, to eventually use the rules to their own advantage. Older, wiser, they now wanted children of their own. They were ready to become parents.

The matriarchal sun locked arms with her consort and began to dance the children's Dance, the Dance of Life.

Within the Dance of Life playing out among this slice of the galaxy, smaller melodies were being written. The intricacies of the great galactic orchestra sounding out ever-finer music, light blazed across the planet's surface. Jagged outcrops of stone, twisted into bizarre forms by the repeated heating and cooling of tortured rock, threw shadows from the twin suns, one caressing the world with the brilliance of the daytime sky, the other banished to become a secondary light to brighten the darkness.

The nights of long ago had been washed into nonexistence by the light of two suns. The twin furnaces poured their energies unabated onto the surface of the world, leaving only a shadowy twilight on the dark side of the planet as a poor imitation of night. The Dance had finally evolved into choreographed beauty, and the new energies showered upon the worlds by the second sun began to bring forth new life.

The stirrings were not yet sentient, but the building blocks had been aroused. Deep within the recesses of the world, molecules of life-enabling gasses violently fought to break free. Scrabbling to the surface through minute fissures in the oft-reheated rock, the glow of an atmosphere could be seen cradling the lower recesses of the planet in a thin layer of air. Deep down where this new air was thickest, single-celled organisms began to form from the amino acids needed to bring forth new life.

Life would return to this world. Not that which had been before, certainly, but something that was different and new, perhaps even improved.

THE DANCE HAD BECOME a thing of beauty. Relegated to the status of step-parent, the massive new sun arced high above the plane of the original system, the path of the interloper dipping lower and lower during its year, until it dropped thorough the system's plane to continue its path below. In a much longer year than its consort's, the mighty sun repeated its maneuver as it reached the opposite side.

The planets danced around their mother to a much shorter, more familiar year, one long ago established in the tumultuous tuning of the Dance.

The massive consort continued to pull both mother and children through the steps written eons before by the Great Conductor. As the massive new sun approached the system's orbital plane, the planets aligned, dancing the Dance of the solar eclipse. Only in the solar eclipses did true night grace the second planet. The total blackness of the double eclipse was even more rarely written into the Dance, the suns lining up with each other to be further eclipsed by a sister world.

In their acceptance of the Dance, the children had adapted. New rhythms had been forged. Interactions of life-building chemicals had once again been pulled into play, and life had begun anew. Under newly colored skies, bright with the refractions of two suns, the chemical makeup of their new atmospheres forming from the molecules escaping from their soils, life breathed once more.

THE PLANET'S YELLOW SKY reached arms toward its twin suns, basking in the life that washed its lands and seas. Ever warm, the world of Se'Yan't treasured the life it had brought forth. Its renewing seas, fertile rift valleys, and gentle climate had become a part of the Dance of the Ages, the everlasting Dance of Life.

First Glossary

Note: Terms in First Glossary are specific to Se'Yan't.

Adhor'k – n. sister to Rjorck; returned from *c'habor-reneis't* as Rjorck brought news of the aggression of MegaCorp.

al'las' – n. webbed membrane between the fingers; can be sheathed when not needed.

c'habor-reneis't – n. the renewing of the body during a year at sea; only occurs when the person is near death; literally "go-and-return." During this time, the body dissolves into a multitude of independent parts, absorbing nutrients from the sea and discharging residues built up from a lifetime spent on land. At the end of one year, also known as a "year-of-months," the independent parts come back together again, youthful and renewed. This process has been observed, but the mechanics have never been explained or understood. Only the native-born seem to be able to achieve this "renewal." It is generally thought that death before reaching the sea locks the body's cells into a cellular "rigor mortis," preventing c'habor reneis't.

c'habor-reneis't **ceremony** – n. a ceremony in which old memories are relived, friendships are cemented, and dreams are shared in order to prepare the *hyr'yan't* for its year-long journey into the sea.

Collected Verses for Children – n. These verses were discovered being used in oral tradition during a sociological survey mission to the planet Rejuvenant by Ser Alb't deFralin, SSM.rl. Amazingly, thousands of young children of the same approximate age were living all across the planet when the mission team arrived. The verses were virtually identical throughout all the groups surveyed. It should be noted that no adults were present on the planet when the team arrived. Curiously, the survey mission was initiated after the reported disappearance of a MegaCorp starstrike class battleship while it was involved in outspace maneuvers near the planet Rejuvenant. The connection is unknown.

dry-death – n. 1. a death away from the seas of *Se'Yan't*. 2. the death of any human not native to the planet *Se'Yan't*.

fract – n. short for *fracture*; a person emerging from *c'habor-reneis't* with incomplete memories.

Holy Writ of Poi'ntr'in – n. religious writings thought to have been lost in the sea at some point in the distant past; occasionally reported to have been experienced by persons returning from *c'habor-reneis't*. (Author's note: Perhaps a better choice of words would be read, or, studied. However, all sources are explicit in the use of the word experienced.)

hyr'yan't – n. literally "essence-of-soul"; the ongoing set of memories, hopes, and dreams that a person keeps as the body is renewed during *c'habor-reneis't*.

poi'ntr'in – n. literally "wellspring of goodwill"; often thought to be a gift of the gods; in times of extreme stress, the *poi'ntr'in* becomes a primal, driving force attributed with mystical powers.

re'anlts – n. plural form; siblings.

Rejuvenant – n. human name given to the planet *Se'Yan't*.

Rejuvies – n. human-like residents of the planet Rejuvenant/

Se'Yan't with incredibly long lives; they age in a similar fashion to humans but are able to regenerate to a youthful state through *c'habor-reneis't.*

Rjorck – n. brother to Adhor'k; also known as *The Bringer of News* and *The Renewer of Lives.*

Se'Yan't – n. the local name for the planet humans know as Rejuvenant.

water-weir – n. 1. the action of melding with the surrounding waters on the planet *Se'Yan't*; mild, incomplete form of *c'habor-reneis't.* – v. 2. to become invisible to others.

Second (General) Glossary

12 known systems – n. the most accessible and heavily populated colonized solar systems.

832.75 – n. inviolate internal MegaCorp policy stating: Intentional injury to any legally owned MegaCorp military personnel with the end result of death will be permanent posting on prisonplanet Rant.

A'man Braxtn – n. security offic'r for MegaCorp.

academy – n. MegaCorp Military Training Unit.

Adel' Eriks'n, SSM.rl.sub.adjunct – n. participant in UNAS study; concentrated on Rjorck and Adhor'k, especially when activities were centered on Earth.

Alb't deFralin, SSM.rl – n. assembled the verses discovered on Rejuvenant; participant in UNAS study; concentrated on Rjorck, especially when activities were centered on Se'Yan't.

Alpha Station – n. scientific observatory.

Alpha.Proxy.Dog – n. security verification code.

AP – n. MegaCorp Military Academy Police.

apr'n – n. apron.

At'micThrust – n. Gabby's Ship.

AU – n. astronomical unit.

b'italik – n. predator; hunts by luring prey.

Barn't – n. Je'main Winterd Barn't, Bofsky's friend aboard ship at the MegaCorp training academy.

Bel'age – n. public academy planetside on Resort World.

Ben'frn – n. subordinate to StarGen'l Grix'm Janet'.

Berian – n. "Rejuvie" friend/sibling of Rjorck and Adhor'k.

Bethany D'Arc – n. jumpship commander; left Rejuvenant just before the debacle that destroyed the ship.

Body Thumper – n. illegal explosive device; deadly when ignited in close proximity to people; falls in the category of old-Earth fireworks.

BraveHeart commendation medal – n. given for bravery beyond the call of duty; often awarded posthumously.

Bree'an – n. helps Adhor'k in the infirmity of her old age.

bunk – n. shipside sleeping berth.

C'storr – n. "Rejuvie" friend/sibling of Rjorck and Adhor'k.

cadet – n. second lowest level of trainee at MegaCorp training academy; just under overcadet.

Capps'nian – n. freighter-tug which found the actuator arm.

CaptGen'l Willane Bard Bofsky – n. MegaCorp military over-offic'r; born on Resort World, System 118B43.6, year 8.34.345 local to Resort; parents Ten'f Ren Bofsky (d), Usrla Note Bofsky (d), Rod'ln Wldn Wred'rn, step (d).

Ch'onksi Welhem – n. staff reporter for Intergalactic-News.news.

citygvn'r – n. mayor.

civilian ceremonial robes – n. high-ranking dress for formal occasions.

clearwall – n. wall made of glassine, an impervious substance that can become opaque or transparent when a sensor is triggered.

comm – n. communication device.

construction landers – n. massive orbit-to-ground transports.

corporation overlords – n. top corporation executives.

corridor – n. ship's hallway.

Counselor Renan – n. 13-14 counselor at Public Academy, Bel'age.

credit – n. an amount of money.

credit stick – n. similar to a credit card in function and a memory crystal in appearance.

creepin' lime-burners – interj. term used to show amazement.

cruiser – n. starstrike class battle cruiser.

cryowrap – n. clear packaging that preserves its contents almost indefinitely.

cubicle – n. workspace aboard ship.

cycles – n. equivalent to planetary days; term introduced by the MegaCorp military academy; used inconsistently as most academy inductees came from onworld at age thirteen; in some contexts, a period of shipboard time approximately equivalent to a month.

D. Wymen Ragnost'en – n. contributor to the NewsTribune.

dark-sides – interj. term used to show strong disapproval.

data access unit – n. used to access planet- or ship-wide data banks (a.k.a. glass).

data crystal – n. another form of a record crystal; less permanent, smaller, a more personal size.

DataRecc – n. handheld information storage and retrieval unit; used for personal legal and financial purposes.

dirt-work – n. leg work as performed by a go-fer.

disposa-towel – n. one-time-use shower towels.

DNAuthorize Stamp – n. used to verify an individual's identity.

dog-sheesh – n. often used as an interjection; invective showing strong emotion.

downside – n. planetside term for people visiting a planet as in *a list of downside offic'rs visiting from Ev'ntu'll.andfall.*

down-time supply replenishment run – n. ship supply replenishment.

Dr.Sci. – n. combined degree title of Doctor of Science.

Dr.Sci. Refren Ascott – n. discovered the anomaly around Rejuvenant.

Dre'en – n. friend of Adhor'k; her brother was accidentally killed.

drivcart – n. portable, drivable, self-powered vehicle for onboard transport.

dup – n. short for duplicate; sometimes used as a verb, as in *to dup the chart to my glass.*

duty offic'r – n. policeman.

duty-assistant – n. see duty offic'r.

Ed'th Ze'pliinth, SSM.rl – n. participant in both UNAS studies of the decimation of Rejuvenant and the resulting implosion of MegaCorp; was a major contributor to the second study carried out in 2819 A.D. (O.E. Standard).

El Tir'd O'doon, Consultant to UNAS – n. participant in 2819 UNAS study; concentrated on ex-MegaCorp employees.

E'vonn – n. "Rejuvie" friend/sibling of Rjorck and Adhor'k.

ef'ncy – n. short for efficiency; one-person living unit provided to singles free of charge.

Ens't Dolph – n. tried to sabotage the mission to salvage Rejuvenant.

ESS – n. emergency survival suit.

Ev'ntu'lLandfall – n. MegaCorp training ship from which Willane Bard Bofsky graduated.

feed – n. ship-link information flow, often to a ground-based connection.

feed line – n. hard line information transfer.

first posture – n. military stance requiring a high level of preparedness.

FizzPoppers – n. safe, non-lethal explosive device; falls in the category of old-Earth fireworks.

freighter-tug – n. slow moving hauler; usually sublight speed only.

friggin' – adj. invective designed to denigrate; often used to express dismay, as in *a friggin' crock of dog-sheesh.*

Gabby dePaloma – n. a soldier who fought alongside Jo'n Rezalton; a.k.a. Frankl'n.

Gel're – n. brother of Adhor'k's friend; accidentally killed.

glassine – n. interactive, transparent material; often used in military installations due to its extreme tensile strength.

Glok'dik conference – n. financial conference bringing multiple world leaders together once every ten standard Earth-years.

Gr'gan Rhnst – n. boy, 15, at Public Academy, Bel'age; led the group that beat up Bofsky.

GrandSet ComChair – n. honorary diplomatic title; high planetary office.

gravships – n. ships with gravity repulsion drives; the technology is derived from the magnetic resonance core in the interstellar ion drive.

great plinkerpups – interj. used either to express dismay or anger; originates from the artificial lifeforms created by Dr.Sci. Gre'lowski Plinker in 2514 that ravaged a commercial star cruiser, leaving only a handful of survivors to tell the story.

grid – n. information grid; analogous to old-Earth Internet.

ground transport – n. land-based troop carrier.

groundie – n. derogatory; anyone living on a planet.

grubbing – adj. invective.

H'bladt – n. "Rejuvie" friend to E'vonn, Wolmn, and Berian.

High City – n. location of MegaCorp's central headquarters.

High City Spaceport Control Tower – n. centered in High City.

hoar-vlomg cubes – n. used in a game of chance; cubes are naturally magnetic, floating easily in a strong magnetic field, and able to be manipulated by the weaker magnetic field in a human body.

housing block – n. ground-based dorms.

info-update – n. information download; usually done each time

315

a starship is docked insystem.

interstellar hangover – n. extreme hunger and thirst after the interstellar slow-sleep required for passage between worlds.

IntergalacticNews.news – n. Mars news source.

Interplanetary Code 4418-164003 – n. code permitting payment and transmission of intersystem communication.

invisi-suits – n. military camouflage suits.

J. Ret'tsh, SSN.rt, UNAS/UT – n. participant in UNAS study; completed auxiliary revisions for the first study in 2815 and worked on compilations for the second in 2819.

J'seryn – n. boy sacrificed to the storm gods.

jack – n. slang for a male; in some instances a non-gender term referencing males and females, although usually in a larger group.

Je'Vark – n. worked alongside Rom'n Rezalton aboardship.

jeenky sticks – interj. invective indicating derision.

Jer'son – n. Fal'dera Hult Jer'son, Bofsky's friend aboard ship at the MegaCorp training academy.

Jo'n Rezalton – n. Rom'n's brother; member of the MegaCorp military arm; graduated from the academy but was demoted for desertion.

Jordiń Hogaramusta – n. survey team member sent to Rejuvenant to assess the damage done by MegaCorp.

jumpship – n. small, light-drive ships; fastest known transport; secretive, military-controlled; no known public use.

kro-ball – n. game played with a ball and sticks.

Krueger-hands – n. deadly hands; derived from an old-Earth action figure.

L.A.T. – n. local access time; gives time in local terms; often used when a ship docks at a planet.

Le'rane – n. undercadet at MegaCorp training academy.

L'rani Delogosi, SSM.rl.sub.adjunct – n. participant in 2815 UNAS study; concentrated on Rom'n and Jo'n Rezalton.

Lem Report NAS.Univ.gov – n. preliminary report sent to the

University of New American States during the efforts to rehabilitate Rejuvenant/Se'Yan't consisting of a general observation by the esteemed Alb't deFralin, SSM.rl. with regards to the necessity of research into the past in order to understand the present.

lieute'nt – n. lowest rank of offic'r in the MegaCorp military arm.

LightCrackers – n. safe, non-lethal explosive device; falls in the category of old-Earth fireworks.

limited-breather canister – n. emergency use oxygen container found aboard ship.

little night – n. eclipse of one of Se'Yan't's two suns, providing a brief twilight.

Loritmar Observatory – n. university observatory located on Alpha Station, System 1509.867.

Ma'jene Holcum – n. MegaCorp military overoffic'r.

Magic All-Seeing Eye – n. the marble Rom'n found; used by his brother Jo'n to weave a story about a magic man who could link them together even when they were apart.

medcenter – n. hospital.

medreport – n. medical reports.

MegaCorp – n. largest corporation in the galaxy; works to gain control of the life-extending process behind *c'habor-reneis't*, resulting in the corporation's eventual dismemberment.

MegaCorp Military Training Arm – n. official name of the division of MegaCorp corporation that provides recruitment and training for its military.

MegaSales center – n. big box store; sells low to middle quality goods at reasonable prices.

message stick – n. long-term mobile information storage unit.

message-fabric – n. on Se'Yan't, special fabric with woven fibers that retain impregnated information; with proper training, can be read using the natural magnetism in a person's body.

Mno't – n. left Dre'en when her brother was killed, running to Adhor'k.

mother-scrubbing – adj. invective not acceptable in polite company.

N'jent City – n. a news report was received from this location; location of sky-walkers.

Ne'rosi El'ganti, SSM.rl.sub.adjunct – n. participant in 2815 UNAS study; concentrated on Willane Bofsky and Ma'jene Holcum.

NeuroShok – n. instrument that interacts with the central nervous system.

newbie – n. slang; first-year recruit to the academy.

NewsTribune – n. Earth news source.

nutrient-packs – n. used to raise the body's energy level after slow-sleep.

O.E. Standard – n. Old-Earth Standard, a universal method of measuring years.

offship – n. any place not onboard ship.

Ollen Wychert – n. tried to sabotage the mission to salvage Rejuvenant; Ens't's cohort.

Optical McRam'n-Foser Virtual Scoping Telescope – n. outdated telescope used to discover the anomaly around Rejuvenant.

outsystem call – n. realtime personal communication between systems; uses microburst technology and is too expensive except for the very wealthy; one identifying characteristic of an outsystem call is the electrical buildup that is heard as static during the conversation.

overcadet – n. third level of trainee at MegaCorp training academy.

overcapt'n – n. overoffic'r rank just below undergen'l.

p'zzbread – n. flat bread with various toppings.

Patch-O-Torch – n. emergency device for sealing metal to metal in a vacuum.

planetside – n. synonym for downside; shipboard term for planet's surface.

planetside dock handlers – n. grunts who load ships for transport offworld.

planet-wide data banks – n. publicly accessible information grid; used in a similar fashion to old-Earth Internet.

portable glass – n. portable information terminal; especially lightweight with limited functions.

PR – n. image consultant.

PrimeLeader – n. main man; political leader.

prisonplanet – n. planet maintained as penal colony; an example is the planet Rant.

priv'tshorts – n. loose-fitting military issue underwear worn by both genders.

privacy field – n. temporary light and sound barrier.

proxy-holo – n. holographic image used to simulate someone's presence; often animated by the person in realtime.

Q – n. very large number; quadrillion.

ranked (cadet) – adj. officially a MegaCorp cadet; no longer a newbie.

Rant – n. prisonplanet where Jer'son, Barn't, and Renhant are posted.

Re'anon – n. the memory of his death is shared with Adhor'k during her c'habor-reneis't.

Re'Jenni Fra'gammasi – n. on the Recovery Team that arrived in 2810; participant in 2015 UNAS study; concentrated on the Children of Se'Yan't.

Re'leli'n – n. Adhor'k's sister; convinced Adhor'k to attend a celebration.

reader – n. small device to transfer information from hard copy to an interactive format.

realtime – adj. events monitored as they occur; replay of those events.

real-wood – adj. anything made from the fibrous part of a

woody plant.

record crystal – n. type of old-Earth flash memory.

recycle slot – n. shipboard disposal chute.

Registry of Internal Docking and Loading Priorities – n. handles cargo loading rules and regulations for interstellar flights.

remote – v. to initiate by a remote link.

Ren'x – n. long dead language from the planet Agraren.

Ren'xe t'Le Frieks'n, Rstt.con – n. off-world worldCitizen of Se'Yan't originally from Rejuvenant.

Renhant – n. Steph'ni B'ltn Renhant, Bofsky's friend aboard ship at the MegaCorp training academy.

repulsor screen – n. environment containment barrier.

Resort World – n. Bofsky's homeworld; System 118B46.6; also home of Jo'n and Rom'n Rezalton.

Rev. Ranjacket Boos'tle – n. contributor to InterWorld Geographic.

Ribbon Waterfall – n. one of the eleven wonders of Se'Yan't.

Robn't – n. aide to A'man Braxtn.

Rob't Thangorsen – n. logistics overoffic'r; sent Cmdr. Bethany D'Arc on a jumpship mission just before the MegaCorp cruiser stationed around Rejuvenant was destroyed.

Rom'n Rezalton – n. member of the MegaCorp military arm; academy graduate betrayed by Ma'jene Holcum for which he was stripped of all rank; was onboard a MegaCorp starstrike class battle cruiser when it was lost near Rejuvenant; one of the few crewmembers who managed to access a survival pod.

Rond'nt – n. first-alive; favorite of Adhor'k.

safe-suit – n. shipboard suit designed for temporary service in a vacuum.

San Francisco Examiner – n. Earth news source.

scanner – n. detects heat signatures.

secondary posture – n. military stance used when a military situation is secured.

sector-lieute'nt – n. offic'r over one sector of a ship; superior to lieute'nt.

self-triangulation – n. using known points to locate a position.

sensor array – n. external set of sensing instruments.

Ser – n. formal; military term of address; informally used as ser.

service – n. casual term for MegaCorp military arm.

shaving stick – n. consumable razor.

shiking – adj. invective.

ship-link – n. ship-to-planet communication.

shipside – n. onboard a ship; sometimes used as a descriptive term as in *outgoing shipside transport*.

shorts – n. shortened form of shortcuts.

Shrd't – n. sector-lieute'nt under Bofsky.

shrinking varneys – interj. term showing dismay.

Sil'nov Vasilyev – n. Rom'n's first friend when he arrives at the academy.

sim'lators – n. short for battle simulation training device.

sky-walker – n. also skywalker; a woman of the night.

sleeping pad – n. mattress.

slo-trak – n. message sent by sub-light intersystem message transport; something done slowly or incompletely.

slow-sleep bays – n. inexpensive interstellar transport option.

slow-sleep slipsuit – n. used to keep the body protected during slow-sleep.

solar kite – n. device used by asteroid dwellers to collect the sun's energy.

StarGen'l Grix'm Janet' – n. given directive to search for MegaCorp's missing battle cruiser.

starstrike class battleships – n. largest, newest level of military weaponry; specially developed for the MegaCorp military arm.

starstrike class propulsion actuator arm – n. only recovered part from MegaCorp's missing battle cruiser.

starstrike propulsion technology – n. cutting edge ship drive.

Sterilspray – n. biological cleaning agent.

stor'lok – n. storage locker usually found aboard ship.

stores – n. ship's supplies.

submike – n. subvocal link for data access used for subvocalization; often implanted under the skin.

Sunsett – n. Ens't's mistress; works as an exotic dancer.

System 1509.87b – n. coordinates of Alpha Station.

T – adj. trillion.

T404Trainer Pocket Ship – n. small ship used for training exercises, especially in ship-to-planet maneuvers.

teat-sucking cowards – interj. often used as an invective; in context can also be a noun.

Ten'di – n. Adhor'k's sibling; killed at an early age.

terminal slot – n. glass input slot for a data/message crystal.

texting for the poor – n. something printed on paper rather than being sent by glass; derogatory.

The Angoni'st Conflict of 4315, F.E. – n. war confined to the Angoni'st quadrant.

Thomps'n – n. friend of Bofsky's at the academy.

'tigues – n. fatigues; work clothes.

Zi'nene – n. one of the ship's crew.

tos'rone – n. testosterone.

training commanders – n. instructors at the academy.

Transmission 16/000873862-45682.09 – n. transmission from Bar'akker'ent World suggesting Rejuvenant might be in trouble.

transport landers – n. orbit-to-ground transport for light objects or people.

turn – n. roughly equivalent to one year; alternate meaning of one day planetside.

undercadet – n. lowest level of trainee at MegaCorp training academy; lower rank than cadet.

UnderGen'l V'jork – n. MegaCorp military overoffic'r.

underjacket – n. light jacket for casual, private attire; usually worn under a more formal overjacket.

underoffic'r – n. any rank under the level of capt'n; has minimal authority.

underpriv't – n. lowest rank in the MegaCorp military arm.

undersock – n. worn next to the skin.

units – n. shipside unit of time; approximates an hour; hours.

utility corridor – n. maintenance section of a ship.

uppercadet – n. general term for anyone ranking higher than an undercadet.

vee – n. anything shaped into an angle; adj. resembling the letter v.

veri-sign crystal – n. embedded with authority to act on behalf of another; carries the full weight of one's available authority without any legal restrictions or waivers.

vid-ghosts – n. poor recording leaving washed out images; anything pale or colorless; frightening images.

VidPlay – n. realtime recording; includes visual and sound.

Wendy's World – n. a fringe world where a ship's registration cannot be easily checked or verified.

Winter's World – n. planet where a war broke out; the conflict was precipitated by Rjorck as a diversionary tactic to protect discovery of Se'Yan't's secrets.

Wolmn – n. "Rejuvie" friend/sibling of Rjorck and Adhor'k.

World Geographic – n. successor to old-Earth National Geographic organization (now defunct). A.K.A. InterWorld Geographic.

worldgvn'r – n. government posting just under that of World-President.

WorldPresident Benetin – n. president of Earth during the Rejuvenant Crisis.

year-of-months – n. time at sea in c'habor-reneis't during which an aged Rejuvie is returned to youth and vitality.

Zen'ri – n. Cadet Fabr d'Scn Zen'ri; assigned to ship's stores; gave adhesive to Jer'son; died in an accident.

ziptites – n. retractable straps; often used as handcuffs.

Read all the books in this vibrant new series!

The Se'Yan't Chronicles

Get Yours At:

www.ThreeSkilletPublishing.com